MY SCANDALOUS BRIDE

CHRISTINA DODD

STEPHANIE LAURENS

CELESTE BRADLEY

LESLIE LaFOY

St. Martin's Press

CONTENTS

THE LADY
AND THE TIGER

CHRISTINA DODD

CHAPTER 1

Kent, England, 1813

Miss Laura Haver groped her way toward the ocean cliff, guided only by the sound of the waves and scent of salt water on the breeze. Clouds streamed across the stars, blocking the feeble light, and her foot skidded down the first few inches of cliff before she realized she'd reached her goal.

Sitting down hard, she pulled herself to safety, then scooted back and huddled in the rough sea grass. Pebbles scattered down the steep slope to the beach on the Hamilton estate, and she listened for the shouts that meant she'd been discovered.

There was nothing. Just the endless rocking of the waves on the sandy beach below.

It had been three months. Three months of lonely torment as she pored over her brother's diary and tried to decipher his cryptic scrawls. Three months of futile visits to the London townhouse where Keefe Leighton, the Earl of Hamilton, resided and kept an office. Three months of listening while Leighton assured her the government would avenge Ronald's death.

Three months of knowing that he lied.

A boat crunched on the sand below as it drove onto the beach. Shivering with chill and fear, she pulled the dark hood over her brown hair and scooted back to the edge of the cliff. Although it was a moonless night and so dark she could scarcely see her hand in front of her face, she nevertheless observed as covered lanterns flashed like fireflies. They showed bits of light only as the men deemed necessary, and in their movement she counted at least twenty smugglers—eight unloading the boat, eight receiving on the beach, and three men just standing, apparently supervising the operation.

One tall figure moved back and forth, and from the consideration all the men paid him, it was obvious he was the leader. Ronald's diary mentioned him only as Jean, but Laura feared she knew his identity. She strained her eyes wide and prayed for just one moment of light—and when it came, she stood in indignation.

"He *is* the smuggler."

As if her words caught on the wind and blew to his ears alone, Leighton turned and looked up toward the top of the cliff. She saw the glint of his eyes, and with the instinct of a hunted creature, she crouched behind a rock and froze. She didn't want Leighton to see her here. She couldn't let him find her here. All her ugly suspicions had been proved true, and if he had killed her brother to silence him, she doubted he would hesitate to murder her, too.

Her heart pounded and she wanted to flee with unrestrained panic, but she'd come too far and too much was at stake for her to lose her composure now. Straining to listen, she could hear men's voices above the lap of the waves, but no shout of discovery gave her reason to run. She had to keep her head, get back to the inn, and write her report to give to the authorities. It would be difficult to convince them that a member of the House of Lords was nothing but a common criminal, but with Ronald's diary as corroboration, she'd do it.

She had to, for Ronald's sake.

She crept backwards. Her skirt caught on her heels, rocks ground into the palms of her hands. She stood finally, and leaned to dust off her skirt. When she straightened and squinted toward the horizon, she realized a tall figure blocked out the stars. She stared, pinned by fear, then with a yelp and a start, she whirled and ran.

She could hear the sound of thudding boots behind her. The gorse grabbed at her skirts and the ruts of the mostly untraveled road moved and twisted in snakelike guile. The wind gusted at her back and carried a man's warm breath to touch the nape of her neck. Gooseflesh ran over her skin and she moaned softly, clutching the stitch that started in her side. When she could run no longer, she dared a look behind her.

All she could see was black night. The stars had disappeared completely and the upcoming storm splattered the first raindrops in her face. She'd imagined Leighton when he wasn't there.

With a ragged sigh of relief, she slowed to a walk and trudged toward the inn. How stupid and cowardly she'd been in her precipitous flight! But for weeks she had dreamed about Leighton chasing her. She'd seen his face on every dark-haired man who walked the streets. Something about Leighton convinced her she should flee and never stop.

It hadn't always been that way. When Ronald had been killed, she'd gone to meet Leighton for the first time, confident he would help her. After all, Ronald had been Leighton's first secretary, and he spoke of Leighton in dazzling terms.

Instead, Leighton had actively and personally repelled her inquiries. According to him, she should remain at home like a proper lady, and the smugglers would be brought to justice when the time arrived. But she couldn't bear to be patronized, especially not by Leighton. She just clenched her teeth and faced up to him, ignoring the breadth of his shoulders, the sculptured perfection of his features, and her own untutored desire to hurl herself into his arms and let him care for her. Early in their relationship, she might have done just that, but from the very beginning some instinct told her that his placid exterior hid something deep, potent and deceptive.

Still apprehensive, she glanced behind her again. Ronald had always said she was too straightforward to sneak around and too blunt for diplomacy, but now that she'd read his diary she'd learned that her brother had led a secret life. He had her convinced he was nothing more than Leighton's secretary, when actually he had worked to uncover this ring of smugglers. A frown puckered her forehead. He hadn't told her because he didn't want her to know and worry. He'd been protecting her, and now she was alone with no one to avenge his death but her.

She'd do it, too. She'd make sure those responsible suffered as she had suffered with his loss.

The rain began to fling itself to the ground with increasing conviction, and she wrapped her redingote, that coat which she'd sewn with her own fingers, tighter around her shoulders.

When she saw the lights of the Bull and Eagle, she fixed on them as if they were her salvation. She knew, of course, that Leighton might seek her, but not tonight. He had brandy to unload and reckless men to pay, and he would never imagine that she'd be on her way at first light, even if she had to walk.

Carefully she crept through the now-muddy inn yard and pushed the outside door open. In the two days she'd stayed here, she'd ascertained that it squeaked if not handled properly, and that brought Ernest bustling out of his quarters to smile and bow and greet her as if she were the salvation of Leighton Village.

And all because of one little lie she'd been driven to tell.

God would forgive her, she was sure, for she'd told it in pursuit of truth and justice, but she didn't know if hearty, bald-headed Ernest ever would.

The hinges didn't make a sound. The taproom was empty, as it had been when she left, and she didn't understand how her luck had held. She didn't want anyone to know she'd been out, yet at the same time during the other evenings she had been here the townsfolk had congregated in the taproom for ale and conversation. Briefly she wondered what kept them away, why the fire burned low and place looked abandoned. Then a burst of angry shouting from the kitchen sent her fleeing up the stairs. At the top she paused and listened.

Ernest's voice she could recognize, and he sounded both agitated and afraid. The other voice was a man's, lower, less distinct, but with a tone that raised the hair on the back of her head.

Who was it? Gripping the rail in both hands, she crept down two steps and listened intently. Why did he sound so menacing? Heedlessly, she stepped on the edge of the third step and it creaked beneath her shoe. The conversation in the kitchen stopped and she froze. Footsteps sounded on the floorboards and Ernest stepped into the common room. She tried to melt into the shadows, and he stared up at her. He saw her; she would have sworn he saw her, but he shrugged and walked back into the kitchen without any indication that he'd noted her presence.

The conversation began again, lower this time, and she sneaked to her room. Silently, she took the key from her reticule and unlocked the door. Slipping inside, she shut the dark oak panels behind her and turned the key again, protecting herself from all comers.

It was just as she'd left it. This was, as Ernest had told her the night she arrived, the best bedchamber in the inn and the one which had served Henry the Eighth when he'd been stranded in a storm. Laura didn't know if she believed that, but certainly a gigantic old-fashioned bed dominated the room. It rested on a dais in the corner, and the canopy was hung with velvet curtains which could be drawn to keep in the warmth. Gargoyles decorated every bedpost and each rail between had been sanded and polished until it shone. Ernest had proudly told her that over two thousand geese had been plucked to stuff that feather mattress. She only knew she'd been lost in it when she slept.

The fire in her fireplace burned, piled high with sweet-smelling logs. On one side was a settle, a bench whose high back protected her from drafts when she sat there. On the other stood a desk and a chair. As she always did, she went to the desk first. The candles had burned down while she was gone, but they still illuminated the papers that were strewn in artful disarray. Beneath them rested a diary. Ronald's diary. His diary was the one reason she knew to be in Leighton Village now, tonight. It was the reason she'd scouted the area earlier in the day and had deduced that the cove would be the landing place.

She reassured herself the diary remained safe, then thoroughly covered it with the papers again. Ronald had taught her that. Always hide things in plain sight, he said. He'd learned that while in service to Leighton, and she'd found it good advice.

Flushed with guilt, she opened the desk drawer and pushed her hand all the way to the back. Her fingertips touched the cold metal, and she drew out a small silver pistol. On this matter, she ignored Ronald and his advice. She couldn't bear to leave the deadly thing out. She'd stressed her need for privacy to Ernest and been careful to lock the door whenever she left, but possession of such a firearm made her nervous. It was Ronald's, and until he'd been killed she'd never imagined she would want to carry one. She knew how to use it, of course. Her father had insisted on her learning self-defense while they lived in India. But back in England, she'd believed herself inviolate. Now, with Ronald's death, her veil of security had been ripped and she trusted no fellow being.

Strange, but her sense of being threatened by Leighton had started long before her suspicions that he was the smuggler congealed into a certainty. Once when she turned suddenly, she caught him contemplating her with a look she'd seen only one other time. When her parents were alive and the whole family lived in India, she'd seen a tiger concealing itself in high grass, waiting for his prey. Leighton's mien betrayed a tiger-like confidence in himself. He was sure he could have her if he wanted, but the time wasn't yet right. His expression had given her a shiver, but when she tried to verify her impression, all expression had smoothed from his face.

But as the months had worn on, she sometimes thought she could sense the impatient twitch of his tail and the way he crouched, waiting to pounce.

Shivering, she replaced the pistol. Stripping off her wet redingote, she flung it over the back of the settle, then laid her gloves by the feeble flames. She slipped out of her practical boots, now covered with mud, and placed them neatly by the gloves. Her dark blue walking dress, so suitable for the city and for the occupation of seamstress, was bedraggled from the night's ill-use, and she touched the hem with trembling fingers. She hadn't the money to replace it; every cent she had had gone into this trip to Kent. Still—she firmed her chin—it was worth the loss of a mere gown to bring Ronald's murderer to justice, and she was close to that now. Kneeling, she repaired the fire so it burned brightly again, warming her hands all the while. As her hair dried, the short strands sprang away from her head and curled in wild abandon, but she didn't care tonight, for who would see it?

"She's at the Bull and Eagle." Keefe Leighton, the Earl of Hamilton, gave the boy a push. "Go back and tell the others, then return and wait in the stable. I'll be out when I've got the information."

In the dark and the rain, he couldn't see Franklin leave, but he knew he would be obeyed. Every one of his men was loyal to him, and only to him, but tonight something had gone wrong. As he kicked the door of the Bull and Eagle, he cursed the woman he'd seen silhouetted against the stars.

Laura. His instincts told him it was Laura Haver, and his instincts were very active where she was concerned. What was she doing here on this precise night? What did she know, and how did she know it? What had her brother told her that he hadn't been able to communicate to Leighton? Leighton needed to get the answers, so he'd abandoned his men as they unloaded casks of brandy and hid them in the caves on the cliffs above the beach. Leighton had to follow the woman.

The taproom was empty. Not even Ernest stood before the fire that sputtered on the hearth, and Leighton's gaze probed every corner as he scraped mud off his boots. Then the innkeeper bustled out of the kitchen, wiping his hands on his apron. "Hey, what are ye doing out tonight?" he demanded roughly. "Ye know—"

Leighton swept his hat off and Ernest stopped in his tracks. Something that looked like horror flashed briefly across his rotund face, then he wiped his expression clear and allowed a slow grin to build. Hurrying forward, he took Leighton's cloak. "M'lord. How delightful! M'lady assured me ye'd arrive."

"M'lady?"

"M'lady arrived yesterday, but she didn't expect ye for several days."

What was the man babbling about? Leighton kept his face carefully blank. His mother was dead, his grandmother seldom left the manor, and they were the only noblewomen Ernest called "m'lady." In a neutral tone, Leighton asked, "Didn't she?"

Chuckling, Ernest slipped behind the bar and opened the tap on a cask of Leighton's favorite ale. Brown liquid splashed into the mug while Ernest said, "Aye, 'twill be a surprise sure to please her. Almost as pleasant as the surprise ye've given us." He winked and passed Leighton the glass. "Marrying the young lady, and at Gretna Green, too! We'd never have thought it of ye, m'lord, but when love strikes as sudden as all that, a man's got to leg-shackle the heifer before she's had a chance to think."

"My opinion exactly." Leighton clutched the handle of the mug and wished he could clutch someone by the throat with equal fervor. He'd come in, furious and determined, and been knocked completely awry by Ernest's babblings. Now he found he was supposed to have married—and at Gretna Green. "Who knows about this?"

"Ah . . ." Ernest swabbed the length of the bar with a rag. "Well, to tell ye the truth, m'lord, word seems to have got out in the village."

"Now, how did that happen?"

Ernest scrubbed harder.

Taking a chance, Leighton used her name. "Did . . . Laura . . . mention this to many people?"

"Nay! She was as discreet as ye instructed, and told only me."

So it was Laura who awaited him in the bedchamber above. Of course, she didn't realize her lord would ever truly arrive, but perhaps these events could be turned to his favor.

Leaning on his elbows, Ernest smiled at Leighton feebly. "But of course the women wondered, and I gave 'em just one hint, and before I knew it—" He flung up his hands in a helpless display. "Ye know women, m'lord. They're terrible gossips."

"Damn!" Leighton paced away from the bar. The whole village knew that their lord had supposedly married? Laura Haver had a lot to answer for, and the list grew with each passing minute. "Gossip can be the cause of a lot of trouble. Did m'lady happen to tell you why I wasn't with her or why she didn't go on to Hamilton Court when it is so close?"

"Aye, m'lord, she told me everything."

Ernest beamed with pride at being trusted with so many

secrets, yet at the same time lines of worry marred the baby softness of his skin and his dark gaze darted toward the kitchen as if he perceived danger within. Leighton had never seen him look so beleaguered, and it stopped him in his tracks. In his business, he recognized the signs of a traitor, and he softly paced back to the bar and leaned on it. "Ernest, have you got a problem you'd like to discuss?"

Leighton well knew the power of his gaze, and Ernest cowered, then dropped his rag to the floor and bent down behind the bar to pick it up. "I'll take ye up there now, m'lord." He bustled out from behind the bar, his shoulders hunched. "I know ye're anxious for a reunion."

Wanting to see how badly Ernest wanted him gone, Leighton said, "I ought to eat first."

"No!" Ernest turned on him, then tried to smile. "Not here. In yer room. I'll bring up a meal to yer room."

"Ernest . . ." Leighton drew out his name in warning.

"Where's yer valet? Is yer horse in the stable?"

Leighton watched Ernest sweat and contemplated the situation. Ernest would have to be dealt with, but Ernest and his family had been the innkeepers at the Bull and Eagle for two hundred years. Ernest would be waiting when Leighton walked down the stairs once more.

Laura Haver was his first priority. She didn't know it yet, but she was going to tell him every bit of information she knew. He would work on her. Hell, he looked forward to working on her. Decision made, Leighton answered Ernest. "I walked over."

"From the manor?" Ernest's eyebrows lifted so high they would have touched his hairline, if he'd had one. "Didn't ye know to look for m'lady here first?"

"We haven't been speaking." It wasn't a lie. He could scarcely talk to m'lady when no m'lady existed.

"A tiff already?" Ernest clucked his tongue and bent down and rummaged under the bar. "But an evening visit such as this will cure that honeymonth uncertainty. Here."

He handed Leighton a dusty bottle of wine. " 'Tis one of my best. Share it with her tonight."

Leighton took the bottle, looked up the stairs, and for the first time allowed himself to wonder what Laura would do when he knocked on the door. She didn't plan on him arriving to claim his "bride," but . . . his vision blurred in a sudden flush of heat. He'd caught her at last. He'd have to question her about her presence here, and he knew from experience she was stubborn, bad-tempered, and determined.

He might have to question her all night.

He looked at the bottle in his hand. She might need to have her tongue loosened with an application of truth medication, and if that didn't work, he might have to seduce her—for the good of his operation, of course.

He grinned. The little fool had played right into his hands.

CHAPTER 2

Laura listened as the two men spoke in the taproom below. It was probably nothing, probably the first of the villagers arriving for an ale, but the events of the night had made her wary, and she slipped over to the door and laid her head against the boards while straining to hear.

The knock on the door made her jump backward, stumbling on the thin carpet that covered part of the floor.

"M'lady?"

Only Ernest called her by that title. "What?" she called, and her voice quavered.

" 'Tis Ernest, m'lady, with a surprise for ye."

"What kind of surprise?" She feared suspicion colored her tone, but Ernest sounded as cheerful as ever.

" 'Tis something to warm yer bones." Metal rattled against metal. "Shall I just unlock the door and pass it through to ye?"

She stared in horror at the metal lock. She'd thought herself inviolate in here, and now Ernest announced he had another key. Should she fling her weight against the door and block it? She looked down at herself and at another time, she would have laughed. "Bird-bones," Ronald had called her, and "Shorty."

Should she start pushing furniture against the door? Her gaze swept the room. No, she wouldn't be able to move big enough things fast enough. And why was she worried, really? As far as she could tell, Ernest had been totally trustworthy, keeping the secret she'd entrusted to him with perfect consideration. Only the events on the cliff colored her suspicions of him.

"I'll open it," she called. She wanted to retain control of access to her room, and not have Ernest thinking he could enter any time. She produced the key and turned it in the lock, then opened the door a crack and peeked through.

Leighton.

She tried to ram the door closed but obviously he anticipated her action, for he shoved and the door sprang open under his weight.

She stumbled back and when he boomed, "Darling!" she almost fell. But he rescued her, swept her into his arms, lifting her until her feet dangled, and kissed her.

For the watching innkeeper, it must have looked like romance personified. For Laura, it was the most frightening experience of her life. Leighton clearly intended to impress her with his size and her lack of it, and he succeeded quite impressively. She jerked her head back, wanting to free her mouth to scream, and found his hand cupping her neck. Where was his other hand? Her mind scrambled to adjust, to discover, and found he held her close with one arm under her posterior. Her posterior! She, who maintained dignity at all costs, had Leighton holding her up by her posterior! Then his mouth invaded hers, and she forgot about dignity and struck at his shoulders. He didn't seem to notice. His smooth lips followed hers with a sure instinct, blocking every little evasive maneuver and countering with some maneuvers of his own. She'd never had a man nibble at her lips and when she opened them, slip his tongue inside. And when she kicked his legs, he chuckled as if he were amused!

So she bit him.

He dropped her to her feet and grabbed at his mouth, and she backed up as fast as she could until the edge of the desk struck her thighs and stopped her. A glance at the door proved it to be shut, and she stammered, "He's gone."

"Quite a while ago."

While Leighton dabbed at his tongue and looked at the blood on his finger, she filled her lungs to scream. He reached her with one giant step, but made no attempt to smother her. He just watched her with a wicked amusement, and her cry for help disintegrated into a whimper.

"Go ahead," he said. "Yell all you want. No one dares interfere between a married couple." He cupped her chin and leaned down to whisper, "And you're my little wife."

Dear God. He knew. She could scarcely speak with dismay. "We're not really married!"

"You told Ernest we were." Leighton straightened and with a swirl of movement swept off his black wool greatcoat. Beneath he wore loose, rough clothes, more fitting to a fisherman—or a smuggler—than to a lord. "Imagine my surprise when I arrived at the inn to be informed my bride awaited me upstairs."

He swung his fist and she ducked, but he did nothing but thrust the papers off the desk and deposit the bottle of wine he held in one fist. Ronald's diary landed on the floor with a thud, but with an effort of will she kept her gaze fixed on Leighton's face.

He didn't seem to notice the precious leather-bound volume, but she could see it out of the corner of her eye, lying with its ruby cover glowing on the otherwise scattered sheets. Leighton seemed to consider her wide-eyed terror nothing but just trepidation of his reprisal, and he said, "I'm not a man to let opportunity slide, especially when I'm long overdue for a wedding night."

She didn't know what to do. Her fingers trembled with the desire to pick up the diary and hide it behind her back, but she didn't want to call it to his attention. At the same time, he was making threats. His voice, always deep and mild, had slipped into a husky whisper, and his eyes gleamed like blue coals from the hottest part of the fire. His black cravat was nothing more than a scarf to warm his neck, tied with true carelessness into a twisted knot. His dark shirt laid open to the middle of his chest and drops of water clung to the curls that poked forth. The cotton stuck to his shoulders in wet patches, and she could almost see steam rising because of his heat. Her personal fright warred with her fear he would discover what she knew, and it irritated her that she could worry about her own safety when she had a chance to avenge herself on Ronald's murderer.

Moving her hands along the desk top behind her, she crept sideways away from the spilled papers. She had to concentrate on removing his attention away from the betraying diary, and she seemed successful, for Leighton watched her, only her. When she'd reached the edge of the desk, he turned and strode to the settle. Fingering her redingote, he said, "It would seem you've been out tonight."

"Why do you say that?"

"It's damp." He tossed his own heavy wool greatcoat over the top of hers in what Laura thought a most suggestive manner. "And it didn't start raining until a few moments ago."

"I went for a walk."

He nudged at her encrusted boots with his foot. "Through the mud?"

Cocking her head, she replied, "Much like yourself."

"You're a clever minx. Saucy, too." For such a large man, he moved gracefully, and he eased himself down on the settle as if he planned to remain there a long time.

The high back of the seat protected most of him from her sight, but she could see his hands as they came forward to grasp each one of his work boots, and jerk it off.

She stared. What was he doing?

"I'm removing my boots," he answered, although she wasn't aware of asking the question aloud. "I'm wet and I'm cold, and I'd like to spend an evening alone with my new bride—and so I informed Ernest."

She couldn't believe that Leighton spoke to her so frankly and with such provocative intent. Then she remembered the image of the Indian tiger. The lying in wait, the stalking of the victim who, unaware, walked into the trap, the brief race, the tiger's final success. Gulping, she tried to wet her suddenly dry throat. She tried to speak, but knew no words that would sway him. He'd waited, he'd stalked her, now her escape depended on her own speed and dexterity. She paused only long enough to scoop up the diary and thrust it in the pocket of her skirt, then allowed her panic to move her toward the door. Grasping the knob between her sweaty palms, she tried to twist it open, but her grip slipped on the cool metal.

The door was locked from the outside.

Was that part of Leighton's trap? No, more likely Ernest wished to give his lord and new lady privacy. She plunged her hand into her reticule, wanting the key, wanting desperately to escape, but Leighton's next words brought her to a halt.

"Smugglers were plying their trade on the coast tonight. Would you know anything about that?"

The key slithered away from her shaking fingers and fell to the floor with a clink. She dropped to her knees and groped for it, grasped it, stood and tried to insert it into the lock.

"Miss Haver, I asked you a question." Leighton leaned around the high edge of the settle and fixed her in his gaze. "Or should I call you 'my lady'?"

She tried to appear innocent, as if sneaking away from this room was no more than should be expected, and indeed, he didn't seem surprised.

"Are you leaving?"

Show no fear, she told herself. *Stare the tiger down.* "Yes." Her voice squeaked, and she smiled fixedly at him to counteract any cowardly impression.

"You can do that, of course, but it will be quite embarrassing."

Her smile faded. "Why do you say that?"

"Because I'll be forced to chase you down and bring you back. I can't imagine that you'll look your best draped over my shoulder as we go through the taproom."

"I'll scream. Ernest won't let you—"

"Won't he?" She'd always thought Leighton smug, but now he fairly glowed with it. "Ernest would not ever interfere, no matter what he heard."

She looked at him, at the openly tigerous satisfaction on his face, and she didn't care. She wanted to run, she *had* to run, she had to try, and she crammed the key into the lock, turned it, and slammed the door back on its hinges.

He muttered, "Damn!" but she didn't look back. She tore out of the room as if . . . as if a tiger were on her heels.

He was. He caught her before she reached the top of the stairs and lifted her with his arm around the waist. She screamed, loud and shrill, but the sound echoed down the stairs and through the obviously empty taproom. Leighton held her there long enough to confirm his prediction. Ernest wouldn't rescue her. She was his wife, and Ernest would leave her to the man he thought to be her husband.

"Satisfied?" Leighton growled in her ear.

She kicked at him, but her heels bounced on his thighs, and without flinching, he swung her around in the narrow hall and headed back for the bedchamber. She twisted, desperately trying to knock him with an elbow, a fist, anything, but she couldn't get to him, and they swept back into the room. Kicking the door shut with his foot, he carried her writhing form to Henry the Eighth's bed and dropped her into the two-thousand-goose-feather mattress. Its softness billowed up around her, stifling her as she tried to leap back at him. He landed on her. Her foot twisted under her and she gave a yelp of pain.

"Stupid girl," he growled, lifting himself and adjusting her leg.

She rammed her knee into his midsection. He doubled

over. She scrambled over him toward freedom. He caught her again and rolled, tucking her under him as he went. "Stupid, stupid girl," he repeated, and she took comfort in the fact that he sounded slightly winded.

Then he kissed her. Last time, she realized, had been playacting. This time, he was angry. He thrust his tongue into her mouth and when she tried to close her teeth on him again, he lifted his head. Looking right into her eyes, he said, "If you bite me, I will retaliate." She flinched and he felt it, lying on top of her as he was, and he smiled using all his white teeth. "And I never make promises I don't keep."

When he put his lips to hers again, she desperately wanted to defy him, but he had made her aware of him and his fury. He was doing it on purpose, she thought, weighing her down with his large body until everywhere she turned, he was there. The scent of fresh air, rain, and heather filled her nostrils, and that was him. The heat of an iron forge covered her, and that was him. The sound of a heartbeat filled her ears, and that was surely him. It couldn't be her own heart that raced so madly, and certainly not because of the way he kissed.

Because she wasn't susceptible to such physical entrapment—at least she never had been before. When he penetrated her mouth with his tongue, she kept her eyes open and her teeth firmly shut.

He didn't seem to mind. He closed his eyes as if she were no threat to him, and it irked her to know it could possibly be true. He explored the inner wetness of her lip, finding untouched places and touching them. His tongue ran the ridges of her teeth and when she tried to shake her head and shake him out, he rapped out one word. "Laura!"

As if she were a child!

Doubling up her fist, she swung at him for his impertinence, but she'd taught him some respect, it seemed, for he caught her wrists in one hand and placed them over her head. She tried to flail away, but the feathers ensnared her and her struggles carried her deeper into the mattress. Her legs churned in useless protest, and panic rose in her. She'd never been so helpless, so out of control, and she didn't want this kiss.

Then he touched her breast, and the kiss seemed innocent in comparison. The wool cloth of her bodice might have been cambric, so little did it protect her from his caress. He explored the lower curve. With each contact, her breath caught. She closed her eyes at last, too embarrassed by such blatant intimacy and the eminent stroke of his fingers against the peak. It must have retained memory of the cold, for it had puckered into that hard little knot. His hand covered it, but not even that warmed it. Then she realized both his hands were busy elsewhere, and she couldn't imagine . . . she ventured a peek *and he had his mouth there.* She froze into immobility. She could scarcely speak, but she managed to choke, "What are you doing?"

He didn't raise his head, but sucked on the cloth until it turned dark and damp. Casually, he said, "I'm making myself happy, and you too, I hope."

"Impertinent!" She took an outraged breath, but that pushed her bosom closer to his face and she hastily tried to make herself as small as possible. Then Leighton, and curiosity, nipped at her, and she asked, "Happy? Why would *this* make me happy?"

Taking the cloth, and the nipple beneath, between his fingers, he rubbed until the friction made her twist to get away, or perhaps to get closer. The lower halves of their bodies pressed together and changes were happening in hers. Changes she didn't want to admit or to have him recognize.

"Can you feel that?" he asked.

"Of course I can," she snapped, pressing her legs together to relieve a sudden, unexplained pressure. "How can I help it when you pinch me?"

"Not here." He cupped her breast in one hand. "But here." And he put his other hand right between her legs! "Doesn't it tingle?"

He pressed his fingers on her mound, then adjusted them to fit closer. If he weren't careful, he'd have one finger in her slot and she'd have to shake him.

One finger . . . two fingers . . . she reached out to shake him, but forgot her intention right before execution. She dug her heels into the mattress, she arched her back, and Leighton murmured, "Deep inside, it should be tight, and maybe you're damp."

"Damp?" She sucked in a breath. "Why would I be—"

A mere adjustment of his fingers brought the dampness he spoke of.

"On the curls between your legs. Can you feel it?"

"No."

"Liar."

She *was* a liar, but she didn't understand what her body was doing or why, and she didn't understand why he remained unaffected.

Or did he? He kept pushing his hips forward in a slow rocking motion, as if he needed to scratch an itch or massage a sore place. She shuddered as some ancient knowledge fought its way up from the depths. She wanted to move like he did, as though she'd danced to that rhythm before, although she never had. When she murmured his name, the way she crooned embarrassed her. "Leighton."

"Keefe," he said.

"What?"

"It's my first name. I freely give my name to you."

Frowning, she tried to understand why his voice resonated with such intention, but he distracted her with those motions. His aggression had modified and her outrage had changed to something softer, and when he put his mouth close to her ear, she shivered.

Gently, he intoned, "Why are you here? Why now? What do you know?"

Her eyes fluttered open, then closed, as she struggled to answer coherently. Then she caught sight of his face. His intelligent gaze was at odds with the passion he simulated, and she realized she'd been duped. He'd been playing her along, and she'd let him. She'd almost betrayed Ronald for a moment's pleasure and a false security.

What was it about this man that made her want to kiss him when all evidence pointed to his guilt? It didn't seem to matter what she knew with her mind, her body still yearned for him. Did she imagine she could find sanctuary in his arms? Did she dream he would protect her from the truth?

Or worse, did she see herself as the tiger's mate? For if she were not careful, she would find herself nothing but a passing meal for that hungry beast.

Venomous as a cobra, she whispered, "I know you killed him. You killed my brother."

He reared back, half off of her, but she didn't make the mistake of trying to run this time. "Are you mad?" he demanded. "Why would I have killed Ronald?"

"You're the leader of the smugglers."

"Is *that* what you think?" Carefully, he lowered himself back down to her and stroked her hair back off her forehead. "Dearest, I'm not the leader of the smugglers. I'm the man who's commissioned to capture them."

She mocked herself for half-believing and said sarcastically, "I would have thought so, once. Brilliant, ambitious, cunning, and brave, Ronald called you."

He half-smiled. "Your brother was an intelligent man."

"Oh, you're all those things Ronald said. When I was notified of Ronald's death, I never doubted you'd help me. He just never realized that you're also wealthy, powerful, well-bred, and"—merciful heavens, she'd almost said handsome—"patronizing."

"I am not"—he struggled, then offered—"patronizing."

"Of course." She mocked him with her tone. "I should have guessed that your campaign to discourage and frighten me was nothing but your way of showing concern for my grief at Ronald's death."

"My campaign to—" He raised himself again and glared. "You've been having delusions."

"Your secretary sneered at me every time I came to you."

His mouth tightened. "Farley sneered at you? I'll reprimand him. What else?"

"When I waited to speak with you, I always saw those young gentlemen going in and out of your office."

"Were they rude to you, too?"

"No, they were most respectful, but sometimes I recognized them skulking about in my neighborhood, and my neighborhood is not a place respectable men visit."

He winced. "You identified them?"

Triumphant, she nodded. "Even in their disguises."

Looking as uncomfortable as she'd ever seen him look, he admitted, "They had instructions to watch over you and make sure nothing occurred which would threaten your safety." He tapped her nose with his forefinger. "You *don't* live in a desirable location, and I intend to change that."

She laughed, her amusement bright and sharp with pain. "Your young men have sold their souls for a cut of the smuggling profits, more likely. Smuggling that takes place on your land."

He struggled with outrage. "Do you credit me with no sense? I'd not be so stupid as to use my own estate."

She stared at him, pressing her lips together and ignoring the tenderness that plagued them. The tenderness he'd caused with his false kisses.

"You don't believe me, do you?" Now he sounded surprised. "What did you think I was going to do to you?"

A vision of Ronald's tortured body flashed through her mind, and she physically felt Leighton wince.

"Kill you? You thought I wanted to kill you?" Cradling her head, he demanded, "Look at me. Really look at me. Do you really think I could ever hurt *you?*"

She saw that the tiger still lurked in his eyes. He wanted to consume her, yes, but for the first time she confronted the fact his meal would be a sensuous one. She swallowed; he watched her throat move and his hunger invoked a like hunger in her.

He wasn't going to kill her. Worse, she no longer believed he killed Ronald. Oh, in her mind she knew he was guilty, but his one flimsy reassurance had lodged in her heart, and she believed in him.

Maybe that explained why she had desired him. She had always believed in him.

He groaned. "Laura." His mouth swooped a necklace of kisses across her throat and placed jeweled kisses on each ear.

He freed her hands and she remained still, horrified by her compliance. Then he kissed her mouth, and it became more than compliance. She kissed him back, opening her mouth willingly. She dared to push her tongue in his mouth and he let her, urging her with his hands as they caressed her shoulders. Her clothing became too tight, then too thick, and when he pushed the sleeves off her arms she helped him.

The cool air of the room struck her overheated skin above her chemise and sanity struck her at the same time. She'd never even been alone with a fully clothed man before, much less one who'd shed his boots and coat, whose scarf had been discarded over the edge of the bed, and whose shirt had miraculously opened all the way to his waistband. "My lord," she whispered.

"My lady." He mocked her.

"This is not proper."

"Most certainly not!" He reared back as if offended. "If it were proper, I would be doing it incorrectly."

She didn't know what to say to that, but when he stripped off his shirt she said, "I will not be a nobleman's toy."

"I never played with toys. I was always too responsible

for that." He touched his finger to her bare chest. "But I think I could learn to play with you."

She stopped breathing. How could she allow her chest to rise and fall when his palm hovered just above, waiting to encourage her transgression?

"We are not married. We cannot share this bed."

His mouth curved in a tender smile. "We will be married."

"Do you think I'm bird-witted?" She laughed shortly, bitterly. "I'm far too poor and you're far too noble."

"Darling, didn't you know? I'm rich enough for the both of us." She didn't believe that for an instant, and he seemed to realize it, for he said, "Look at it from a smuggler's point of view. When we're married you won't be able to testify against me. A wife can't testify against her husband."

She didn't know what shocked her more, his blatant assurance or the speed at which he untied her chemise.

"You are the first woman ever to doubt my integrity," he said.

Hopefully, she inquired, "Does that inhibit you?"

Pausing in his assault on her virtue, he thought, then answered, "Not at all. It liberates me."

She held herself stiff as he stripped her chemise down to her waist and looked on her. His lips opened slightly as he viewed her. Totally without her volition, she imagined his mouth there, and her nipples tightened sharply.

He didn't take his gaze away from her breasts. If anything, she more clearly saw the tiger that lurked behind his façade. But he said, "However, I would not like to think you'll put barriers up against me, not even in your mind." In a tone that disguised the significance of his pronouncement, he said, "I'm the Seamaster."

CHAPTER 3

Laura jumped as if Leighton announced Napoleon fought for England—and indeed, that seemed more likely. Ronald had mentioned the Seamaster over and over again in his diary. The Seamaster directed all the operations in which Ronald had participated. The Seamaster had been bold and daring, intelligent and canny. He was the man Ronald had emulated, the man Ronald had worshipped, and Laura could not imagine that Leighton, with his conservative manner, could possibly be so dashing a figure as the Seamaster.

Then she looked at the man before her. He hadn't been conservative tonight. He'd been as bold as a smuggler, or as the Seamaster himself. The Leighton she'd met in London had been subdued, at least for tonight, by *this* Leighton. This man who used any weapon to get his way. Yes, this Leighton could be the Seamaster—or Jean.

As she finished her contemplations, she realized he now viewed her face with all the interest he had shown her bosom. "You know who the Seamaster is. Your brother wouldn't have told you, so how *do* you know?"

"I'm an eavesdropper." She lied without a hitch, and she was proud of her smooth delivery. But he wouldn't stop staring, using his gaze to scour her mind for guilt. He found it, of course, and she blushed from her waist to the hairs on her head.

Instead of interrogating her, though, he shook his head

admiringly. "An eavesdropper. I should have guessed."

"What do you mean by that?" she demanded indignantly. Then she could have groaned. Of course she didn't want him to think her dishonorable, but better he should think that than realize Ronald's diary rested in her pocket close to his hand.

"I mean"—he pressed a kiss on her mouth—"that you're an incredible woman."

"Please." She pushed at him. "I don't want this."

"Don't you?"

"I've changed my mind."

"As you wish."

He moved off her and she covered herself with her hands, watching him warily. He'd given up too easily, this man who claimed to be the Seamaster. The Seamaster, according to Ronald's diary, had much in common with his namesake. Once he sank his teeth into a situation, he never let go.

Ronald's diary. She glanced down and saw the red leather peeking out of her dark blue skirt.

He saw it, too. His eyes widened and he lifted an inquiring eyebrow. "What is that?"

His hand reached for it, and she caught his wrist. "Nothing."

"Nothing? It's a book." He pulled a long face. "Laura, what are you hiding from me?"

"What do you mean?"

"That book will tell me all your secrets, won't it?"

"No!"

"Everything I desire to know is there." His fingers twitched closer. "It's a novel, isn't it?"

She was so stunned, she could only parrot his words. "A novel?"

"One of those wicked romances." She couldn't restrain him, and he laid his palm on it, preparing to draw it out. "Let me read it, and perhaps I'll learn enough to seduce you successfully next time."

If he read it, he'd learn enough that he wouldn't have to seduce her ever again. If he read it, he'd have all his questions answered, and she still didn't dare trust him. Not with Ronald's diary, nor with the information inside.

He brushed off her effort to restrain him like a bear brushing away flies, and pulled it out.

In desperation she gambled, using her virtue as the stakes.

She laid her hand flat on his bare chest.

He paused in the process of opening the diary. His eyes closed, and her hand rose and fell as he took a hard breath. He wasn't as controlled as she had thought; he still wanted her. It was obvious from the tight set of his mouth and the unmoving stoicism with which he awaited her next move.

Inching her palm down his breastbone, she lingered on a ragged white scar right over his ribs. "How did this happen?"

"Occasionally, someone thinks he has reason to resent the Seamaster, and he tries to do him in." Placing his hand over hers, he stopped her restless movement. "The one who cut me there was luckier than most." Plucking her hand off his chest, he examined it, then folded it within his own. "You are, I believe, inexperienced in these matters, so I will tell you—if you wish for us to remain upright, you should keep your hands to yourself." He put her hand back into her lap and patted it, then advised, "It would be wise to pull your bodice up, also."

His focus went back to the book. Again he began to open it—and she returned her hand to his tanned forearm.

He froze. Nothing moved in his face, nothing moved on his body. He wasn't opening the diary, just as she wished, but she couldn't depend on such inactivity, so she slid her palm up over his biceps. The skin there was lighter, with a finer texture, and she rubbed him with her fingertips. The muscles flexed beneath her palm, and, fascinated, she walked her hand up to his shoulder.

With slow deliberation, he put the book down on the

mattress. When he looked at her, she clearly saw the hunger of the tiger. Imitating her, he placed his hand on her shoulder, then slowly, slowly he pushed her down until she rested against the pillows. "I gave you a chance to think," he said. "Now think no more while I take my pleasure."

His tiger breath brushed her cheek. A slow pounding began in her veins. Her fingertips tingled with it. Her nose, her ears, her toes, every extremity experienced the force of his influence—and he still touched only her shoulder. It frightened her, his power, and she reconsidered her plan of action. After all, he'd put down the diary . . . "Leighton?"

"Keefe," he corrected.

"I don't think we should—"

"No, no." He pressed his finger to her lips. "You aren't allowed to think. You should only feel." Gathering her into his arms, he pressed their bodies together. "Feel this."

Her curves melted onto the firm structure of his chest, and she trembled. Already he was forming her to his desire, taking her sense of individuality and creating a new creature, one composed of man and woman together.

Yet she couldn't allow that. Not yet. She had a mission. She had a duty, and she couldn't allow him to distract her so completely that she failed. She fought to retain her reason and, moving with a care she hoped would fail to alert him, she knocked Ronald's diary off the bed.

It landed with a muffled thump, and Leighton stopped, suddenly alert. Her voice quavered, but she said bravely, "I think I would like it if you kissed me."

He returned his attention to her as suddenly as he had removed it. "Really?" He almost purred with anticipation, and thrusting his hand into her hair, he held her still and kissed her.

After he kissed her, he no longer had to hold her still. For the luxury of his kisses, she would do anything, be anything he wanted, but her compliance didn't seem to satisfy him. If anything, it drove him to a frenzy of touching. He stroked her jaw to the point of her chin, her neck, and her collarbone. He caressed her arms, then linked their hands and brought them up. "Look," he urged. "See the way our fingers entwine. That's how our bodies will be soon."

As he commanded, she looked. Her fingers rested between each of his, spread wide by the width of his knuckles. Clearly she saw his superior strength, his size, the mastery with which he handled her. The precariousness of her plight broke over her. If she allowed this to happen, would she ever recover herself? If she melded with Leighton, could she return to her former shape, or would she always contain a little bit of Leighton in her soul?

Besides—she looked again at the size of his hand, at the size of hers—this would likely hurt. Physically and mentally, this would change her and she writhed in belated panic. "We can't do this. It won't work."

"It will. I promise it will."

Then she became aware of something else. His palm cradled hers. His hand was moving, pressing and caressing the places where the nerves lay close under the skin. He knew how to make her like it; he alarmed her and made her want more all at the same time.

The man was an expert at whatever he did. If he were the smuggler, he would be the best. If he were the Seamaster, he would catch his man. If he were her lover, she would be satiated when they finished.

"Trust in me," he crooned.

"You'll stop if I tell you?"

"I'll do whatever you wish."

After making her wish for him. Slowly, she agreed, "I will trust you—for now."

"That's a start." Loosening his hands, he used them to strip the gown off her hips. Her white pantalettes, tied at her waist, reached below her knees and were so sheer he could see the color between her thighs. She burned when he gazed at her and tried to cover herself with her hands.

"Don't." He took her wrists. "I've fantasized about your body, and it's better than I've dreamed."

Astonished and vaguely offended, she asked, "You thought about this?"

"Of course." He looked right into her eyes. "Didn't you?"

She wanted to refute it. She hadn't thought about it, had she? She'd never imagined what it would feel like if he kissed her. She hadn't thrilled to the thought of his body against her. Yet she couldn't speak the words to tell him so.

His eyes grew brilliant and his nostrils flared like a great cat detecting the eminent collapse of its prey.

The scent of the savage filled her nostrils, and she declared, "I don't think I like you."

"I don't want you to like me. I want no part of such a paltry emotion from you." Her pantalettes loosened under his hands. He stripped them and her stockings from her in one efficient motion.

Her own nudity left her gasping.

His nudity silenced her completely.

In all her life she'd never seen a naked man. Now she knew why. If men like Leighton walked the streets wearing nothing but a smile, women like her would have to join him in the most basic manner. The sight of him made her forget her embarrassment. Fascinated, she touched his chest. Broad, covered with coarse hair that crinkled and rolled, it undulated from the broad, smooth muscles above to the frequent ripple of his ribs. His abdomen rippled, too, strength implicit in the structure beneath the skin.

How did a nobleman build such a body?

She snatched her hand away. By moving barrels of brandy on moonless nights.

He sighed in what sounded like disgust. "You think too much." And he kissed her.

The time for games was over. His intent was clear. He

wanted her, wanted her wanting him, wanted her clinging, panting, ecstatic and mindless. He kissed her softly at first, barely lapping at her lips. Then his tongue sought hers while his hands wandered to her breasts, her stomach, and finally between her legs.

This wasn't like before when he touched her and her gown and petticoats remained between them. Now his fingers tugged at her curls, then intruded between the folds of flesh.

Horrified, she pulled her mouth from his. "Stop that," she hissed.

He didn't answer and he didn't stop. He touched her delicately, using little dabs of rapture.

The weight of her eyelids grew too great, and they half closed. "Please."

"Please what?"

She couldn't remember what, so she just repeated it. "Please."

"Stop?"

Her hesitation amazed her. "Yes!"

"As you wish."

He obeyed her so easily, she should have been suspicious. Instead she breathed a sigh of relief—or was it disappointment?—as he took his hand away.

Then he moved his body over hers and pressed his knee between her legs to separate them. That wasn't what she planned, wasn't what she wanted. It was too intimate, too sexual, too soon.

She couldn't believe this was happening to her. She couldn't believe she was doing this. She dared not struggle, yet everything about it was alien.

She tried to clamp her legs shut. He moved his knee up and spread them wider. The hard muscles of his thigh rocked against her, and she woke to an incredible fact. The subtle probe of his finger had aroused her, but she had feared to move. When he touched her so sensitively, it was as if he were the master and she the painting. But this broad thrust of his thigh encouraged her to find her own pleasure. She left delicacy behind and rode his leg, at first hesitantly, then with increasing assurance, and he encouraged her with just the right pressure.

"That's it," he whispered. "Take what you want. Give all you've got."

Self-conscious, she bit off the whimpers before they could escape her throat.

He didn't like that, and opened her mouth with the thrust of his tongue. "Let me hear everything. I want to know what you feel."

How could he know what she felt, when she didn't even know? She was bursting, ripe, wanting more yet not knowing what more she should desire. She moved ever more quickly, and at last the dampness he spoke of moistened his thigh.

"There it is." He sounded satisfied as he moved his thigh away.

She used a word she'd never admitted to knowing.

"I'll take care of it," he promised, easing himself down onto her. "Hold onto me, and I'll take care of you."

Now his pelvis met hers and renewed the pressure. "Better," she moaned.

"Better yet." He arranged himself and when she thrust, she thrust herself on him.

Her breath caught in her throat. That wasn't better. That was odd, intrusive.

"Do it again," he said.

"What?"

"Like you did before. Take all of me. You're ready. Can't you feel it?"

She could feel nothing else. Grabbing his shoulders, she dug her nails in. She had to stop this madness, but at the same time she throbbed all around him. He didn't stir, although little shudders of strain ran through him. He wanted her to do it all. Like the devil himself, he wanted her to take responsibility for her own downfall.

She hovered for one moment between resentment and amazement. Then her body made its demands. She had to finish it. She had to know.

Bracing her heels, she eased her hips off the bed. He pressed down with the same tension. He met something in her; she retreated, but he caught her hips and held her still and her maidenhead tore before his steady advance. She wanted to rail at him, to tell him of the pain, but she was beyond speech now. She could only meet his gaze with a glare of her own, and when he rested fully against her and all of him was inside her, she bit his collarbone, hard.

He jumped and some of the strain which held him faded. "You are a wild one, and you're all mine." He grinned, his teeth white against the tan of his face. "I'm going to make you very happy."

He started slowly, moving his hips back and forth, bringing himself in and out with a deliberate pace that allowed her to accustom herself to the movement. Excitement returned, building low in her belly. She wanted to move like she had before, but he restricted her, maintaining the pace he had set.

She needed more. She'd thought the effort to speak beyond her, but frustration made her beg, "Leighton, please. Move a little . . . just faster . . . Leighton?"

His pace never changed. "Keefe."

He was killing her. Slowly, with great deliberation, he was killing her. He kept the weapon with him always. He could utilize it at any time. If he didn't win all he wished this time, he'd bring it to bear again, and again, and again.

Still defiant, seeking sensation, she twisted beneath him.

He plunged once, hastily, then stopped and held himself so that they touched in only one place. "Keefe," he said.

Her frustration burst its bounds. "Keefe," she shouted.

The rhythm changed, grew. She lifted her hips to his thrust.

"Keefe," he repeated.

She moaned. "Not again."

"Until you know me. Until I know you'll never forget."

She lifted her head and scowled. "Keefe. Keefe, Keefe, Keefe."

With each repetition, he increased the pace. It didn't help. She only wanted more, seeking relief from the pressure.

"Keep watching me," he said. "Don't look away. I want to see you. I want you to see me."

"Now?"

"Almost."

"Now?"

"Can you feel it?"

The explosive sensation knocked her head back. She arched her spine. She brought her hips up tight against him and fought for every smidgen of pleasure. And when she had finished and rested, panting, against the pillows, he said, "I'm Keefe Leighton. You're my woman now. And I think I'll show you again."

CHAPTER 4

Laura woke with a start and knew she was alone in the bed. Her eyes popped open. Where was he, this nobleman who claimed to be the Seamaster? Who was her lover? She didn't see him, and her heart began to pound in a slow and steady rhythm. Had he seduced her, then abandoned her? Worse, had he got what he wanted from her and even now sought the means to dispose of her? Obviously, her faith in him was a flimsy thing, while her distrust blossomed in the dark.

Then she heard someone prod the fire and saw the tongs and the sturdy brown hand which held them. Leighton was there, sitting on the settle wrapped in his greatcoat. The relief she experienced clearly told her the level of her anxiety, and she put her hand to her chest to still the racing of her heart. Slipping from the bed, she pulled on the robe that hung on the bedpost. The cold floor made her toes curl, but she sneaked toward him, ugly misgivings keeping her silent.

Cautiously she peeked around the high back of the settle and saw him leafing through Ronald's diary.

"What are you doing?" she demanded, her voice cracking like a whip.

Leighton turned his head calmly. He'd known she stood there, she realized. The man was aware of everything around him, with senses heightened by the danger he courted. But did the danger exist because the government sought him, or because he sought the smugglers?

"Why did you keep this from me?" He tapped the diary with his large forefinger. "This contains information Ronald acquired before his last fatal trip, and if I had known . . ."

"If you had known, what would you have done?"

"Jean would not have escaped me." His mouth was a tight line, his brow furrowed, and he sounded sincerely distressed. "This Jean has caused England more trouble than any French rat has the right to cause."

"The smuggling, you mean."

"Smuggling, yes, and . . ." He laughed, short and sharp. "Well. The diary says Jean chose this location to land his contraband not because it is my manor and he knew my identity, but because he has an accomplice in the village." Lifting one brow, he asked, "Do you know who it is?"

"How would I know that?"

"By eavesdropping," he shot back at her.

She widened her eyes at him.

"Don't pretend artlessness," he said. "You're not good at it, to start with, and you revealed too much of yourself when you came to me in London and demanded justice for Ronald. I would have known you were his sister if I had never heard your name, for he talked about your intelligence and bravery, and you have proved to have both."

"So you think it was intelligent for me to have come here to help capture Jean?"

"No! Not that." His hands squeezed the leather binding of the book, then relaxed. "But brave."

"I trembled every moment," she answered honestly.

"But you did it anyway. All my best operatives recognize the dangers, then proceed anyway. If you weren't a lady, I would be hard pressed not to recruit you for our forces."

If you weren't a lady . . . Leighton's words made her realize that he did no more than pay lip service to her. He really didn't consider her anything more than an ornament, a thing to be manipulated. He would discard her when he'd depleted her usefulness, of that she had no doubt.

"You have to understand how important this is to me to capture Jean," he said.

"Will you be commended for your willingness to do *anything* to bring the enemy to justice?"

It was an insult, but he took the blow without flinching, only returning it in kind. "Jean killed one of the best and bravest assistants I've ever had, and I'm interested in revenge. I would think you would be, too, and willing to cooperate toward that end."

It struck her then, the thing that had niggled at her earlier. If Leighton was the Seamaster, he'd sent Ronald to his death. Of course it was worse if he were Jean, the man who'd actually ordered Ronald's death, but surely the Seamaster had known the danger Ronald had courted. He had to have recognized that Ronald could be brutally murdered and his sister left alone, desolate, broken-hearted.

And all for a smuggler. All to stop the flow of French brandy into the country. Rage rose in her. Her cheeks flushed, her hands clenched into fists. Somehow, she wanted Leighton to pay. Somehow, she needed to get out of this room and away from him before he stole her indignation and her heart and left her with nothing but dust and memories.

Intelligent. Ronald had told Leighton she was intelligent, and she needed to prove it now. Leighton was a clever man with no visible chinks in his armor . . . but she guessed he had neglected his duty to tarry with her. True, he suspected she was a source of information and he wanted it, but once he'd seen the diary he could have taken it from her by force. If he hadn't been a tiger, hungry for her . . .

Loosening her fists, she smiled at him. Her lips trembled; he'd said she didn't dissemble well, but this time she hoped to distract him with the promise of another sample of her.

Leighton's eyes narrowed and he considered her as if she were a defendant before the court.

So he was wary. What did loose women do when faced with a dangerous customer? She'd seen enough wenches on her walks from the small shop where she worked to her even smaller living quarters, so she imitated them and shrugged her shoulders in a rotary motion. The movement loosened the front of her robe and Leighton's gaze followed the light material as it slipped back off her chest and opened a narrow gap around her waist.

He said something; it sounded like, "Geminy." A most fervent exclamation for one so dispassionate.

"Come here." Taking Ronald's diary, he put it to the side and held out his hand. "Sit with me and be warm. I don't know what I was thinking, bringing this up when we just now finished with our wedding night."

She wanted to slap him for patronizing her. Instead she bent her head in a parody of obedience and went to him. He brought his knee—his bare knee—out of his greatcoat and she perched there. The worn wool of her robe didn't protect her from his heat, and she feared to melt like a candle exposed to the flame.

But she wouldn't. This was for Ronald.

Tucking his arm around her, Leighton said, "One of my men should be waiting for me in the stable. I'll tell him about the accomplice, and we'll organize a search, but in truth I doubt we have a chance of finding Jean. He's long gone. He'll not remain in the area with so many of my agents here, so I'll have to seek him another way." Reaching his hand inside her robe, he slid his fingers along her ribs until he'd encircled her with his arm and the robe's protection was but a memory. "You'll be safe here. I'll be back for you in the morning, and we'll finish this thing we've started."

Did he plan to kill her, or take her back to bed and teach her how to be an even more satisfactory mistress?

No matter, she was ruined, and she had no intention of remaining when she could escape.

"Oh, Leighton."

"Keefe."

She didn't want to repeat his name, but she did. "Keefe." The word tasted bitter on her tongue. Flinging her arms around him, she pressed her face into his neck to hide her distaste. "You'll be in danger."

His fingers crept along until they rested over the cleft at the base of her spine. Her motion had exposed even more of her, and when she kissed his ear, then outlined it with her tongue, his body shuddered to life.

Sounding both stifled and pleased, he said, "I'll be fine, my dear. I've performed many of these missions and scarcely received a scratch."

"What about this?" Sitting up straight, she pushed his greatcoat off his shoulder and outlined the bare, white scar by his nipple. "You call this nothing?" Her palm grazed him until goosebumps started on his flesh. "You might have been killed."

"Youthful stupidity," he said. "I'm neither so young nor so stupid anymore."

But he was. He had to be. Her plan depended on it, and when she nudged closer into his lap with her hip, she discovered how his truthful body made a falsehood of his words. She tried to hide her triumph and gaze soulfully into his eyes, but he looked suddenly mistrustful and she remembered his claim she didn't lie well. So she mashed her lips on his. He didn't respond at first, but tried to push her away. Not cruelly or emphatically—that he could have done easily. But like a man who feared to hurt her feelings, yet surmised something was wrong. She didn't let go of his neck, and she opened her mouth on his with as much insistence as he'd shown earlier. The hand that she'd used to caress his nipple she slid down his body, opening his greatcoat as he had opened her robe, until she touched the hollow of his thigh just below his stomach. There her fingers hovered, almost in contact with his shaft.

Did she have the nerve to seduce him coldly, for her own purposes? The plan seemed excellent, but the execution was proving difficult. She'd just learned the rudiments of arousal earlier that night, and she had yet to lose the shyness of innocence. Yet she had to concentrate on titillating him rather than on her scheme to escape, for her acting couldn't stand up under his scrutiny. She had to lose sight of the lie and want him again.

After all, that shouldn't be difficult. She did want him again. She'd always wanted him. She recognized the tiger in him, because it corresponded to the tiger inside her. Even if he were the Seamaster and had sent Ronald to his death, even if he were Jean and ordered Ronald's murder, still she wanted him. She'd let him have his way with her and told herself she had no choice because deep inside herself she acknowledged her mate.

The revelation horrified her.

"What?" Leighton asked.

She found herself sitting back on his lap, staring at him.

"Laura, what is it?" He held her as if he thought she would tumble down without his support. "Why are you looking at me like that?"

"I want you." Her voice sounded little and far away, even to her own ears.

Now he looked as stunned as she felt. "I want you, too. I want . . . all of you. I want to talk to you and . . . make love to you and just . . . be with you." The words seemed to struggle from him, from this composed, restrained, thoughtful man, and one of his hands rose to stroke her face. His fingers were trembling. "It's too early, I've done it all backward, but I want . . . I have to ask . . . "

She grasped his penis with her hand and from his grimace, she thought she'd hurt him. Instead he picked her up and rearranged her so her legs parted over the top of his. He put her back down, and the sensation of her bare bottom against his bare legs shocked her back into good sense. He wanted to do this here, now, and if they did she'd have failed. She had to get him back to the bed, and she pushed against his shoulders. "No!"

"What?"

His eyes were glazed with desire, and her denial didn't break through his daze.

"On the bed. Please." She scooted back and he grappled to keep her close. "Please. Leighton. Keefe. The bed. I want to try something . . . exciting."

"This'll be exciting," he said.

"I can't. Not here." He let her slide off the end of his knees, and the pressure made her aware of her own arousal, of how easily she could succumb to his persuasion. "Please." She stood and tugged at his hand. "Come on."

He stood, too, and looked down at her. "I shouldn't," he muttered.

"This won't take long."

He half-laughed. "No, I don't suppose it will."

He stumbled over the edge of the rug as she led him to the bed, and that reassured her. He was still off-balance and at her mercy. As she walked, she untied the belt of her robe and placed it beside the pillows when they reached their goal. His hands encircled her waist to boost her onto the bed, but she twisted quickly away. "No, you get on first," she said.

Tilting his head, he studied her. "You're bold for a fledgling."

"A cub," she corrected. Pushing his greatcoat off, she held it in one fist and promised, "You won't need that." She patted the mattress.

Still bemused, he climbed up and stretched out, a broad, large, handsome piece of male flesh that made her mouth water.

"When you look at me like that . . ."

It was obvious what happened when she looked at him

like that. It was obvious he expected her to cure him, too. He held out his hand just as she found the end of his coat's belt. She dropped the coat to the floor and let the weight of the wool free the leather strap for her use. Then she placed it beside her robe's belt and took his hand.

"You're trembling," he said. "Come up here and let me warm you."

Of course she was trembling. She was scared. Climbing on the bed, she said, "Let *me* warm *you*."

Her voice shook, too, but he smiled at her, all sensuous encouragement. "Have your way with me."

Sprawling on top of him, she threaded her hands through his hair and lowered her lips to his. She pecked at him, then kissed him, then penetrated him with a desperate relish. This would be, after all, the last time he'd want her. If he realized what she plotted, it wouldn't matter whether he were Jean or the Seamaster, he'd extract a terrible revenge. And if she succeeded . . . if she succeeded, she'd have made a fool of him, and no man could bear that.

He responded with quite satisfactory enthusiasm, and she wondered if she might not have a talent for this. Only with Leighton, of course. Leighton was her mate. She ran her hands over his chest, down to his waist, then stroked him as intimately as she knew how. She loved the feel of his skin, the coarse hair over it, the strength of the muscles below it. His arms encircled her, tightened, and he made to roll over to place her beneath him.

"No!" She sat up and pressed her palm into his breastbone. "I want to stay on top."

"Dear heart, I shouldn't even be here on the bed with you. A Leighton never neglects his duty."

"You're not neglecting it, you're postponing it, and besides, haven't you a duty to . . . your wife?" She almost choked on the last two words, and added hastily, "Shut your eyes."

"What?"

"Shut your eyes." Leaning over him, she brushed his eyelids with her lips until they stayed down. "Raise your arms."

His eyes opened again and he directed blue amazement at her. *"What?"*

Taking his muscled forearm in both of her hands, she tugged until his hand was in the vicinity of the headboard. Then she wrapped it around one of the rails. "I want to touch you freely. I want to make you want as fiercely as you made me want." She lifted his other arm and he let her, although he clearly wondered at her. "Is that so strange?"

"I don't understand it," he admitted. "Why would a woman—"

"Give as much as she takes?" Laura lifted a mocking eyebrow at him. "Be generous with her gifts? Seek a sweet revenge?"

His massive arms wrapped around her, hugging her to him, and he held her head while he kissed her fiercely. Letting her go, he raised his hands and grasped a rail in each hand. "Do your worst."

If only he knew!

She didn't demand that he close his eyes again, but instead concentrated on touching him in ways he had touched her. Usually affectionate, occasionally intimate, each caress seemed to affect him more intensely. He waited, almost breathless, for each new contact, and his anticipation built her own. Her body seemed synchronized with his; her muscles tightened when his did, her breath caught with each of his stifled groans.

This was fun. This was fabulous. This was everything she'd promised him, and she had to finish what she'd started. His eyes had closed once in sensual overload, then fluttered open as he struggled to maintain control. She knew she could make him close his eyes. She could make him lose his mind, if only for a moment. She was the female tiger, after all.

She'd used her hands so far, but they formed only part of her arsenal. Now she kissed his body, smoothing the skin of his chest with her lips, then daring to taste his nipple when it came within reach.

He groaned now, right out loud. "Laura." His body shuddered, too, and he twisted on the bed, his eyes tightly shut.

She had him. She'd trapped him. All she had to do was close the trap, but first, she wanted . . . Her mouth wandered to the other side of him while her hands wandered below, and she realized she enjoyed watching him squirm. She liked the power, and she badly wanted to finish the moment.

Not now. Blindly, she reached for the cord of her robe and wrapped it around the rail above his wrists. Not ever. With a quick motion, she used an embroidery knot to secure Leighton to the bed. She was done with love now. She'd never be the Countess of Hamilton again, not in truth or even in her imagination. She wouldn't even dare dream of this.

"Laura?"

His eyes were open now, and he tugged at the knot. She watched the knot tighten, the material stretch, and whipped his leather belt around the other direction to reinforce the restraint. The rail would hold him, even secured as he was to only one. The oak was old and solid, and had no doubt taken greater strains.

"Laura?" He was fully aware now, his gaze shifting from bewilderment to concern. "What are you doing?"

She slid off the bed and looked at him, stretched naked before her. "I'm leaving you."

CHAPTER 5

No woman could tie an effective knot. Leighton knew it, and he jerked on the restraint that held him. Nothing gave, and he twisted to look above his head. The knot, complex and unknown, alarmed him. "Laura, this isn't funny."

"Believe me"—Laura picked her clothing off the floor and began to dress rapidly—"I'm not laughing."

He watched hungrily as she lifted her arms to pull the shift over her head, then jerked his attention away. That was the kind of nonsense that had got him into this dilemma, and his body still spoke to him louder than his common sense. She glanced at him, running her gaze down his form, then looked away, and he guessed the constant changes in his body spoke to her, too. Pleased that he had at least that much influence and still convinced he could persuade her to free him, he asked, "Why would you even want to do this?"

From the corner of his eye, he could see as she pulled on petticoats. "Perhaps you are Jean, the leader of the smugglers, as I first suspected."

Damn the woman! She was a tiny thing, her waist so small he almost spanned it in his hands, with direct blue eyes and curly brown hair, and she was as stubborn and opinionated as his grandmother in one of her matriarchal moods. How could Laura not believe him? Pulling himself up the bed by his wrists, he glared at her. "I *am* the Seamaster!"

Laura nodded without a smile and pulled her dress over her head. "If you are, as you claim, the Seamaster, you sent my brother after these smugglers when you knew the danger he courted. Regardless, you are responsible for his death, and I intend to make you pay."

"Pay? How? By humiliating me?"

She had that stubborn thrust to her chin that he'd learned to recognize. "That, if you're the Seamaster. Or by turning you over to the proper authorities if you're Jean."

The flawlessness of her plan left him speechless with admiration. Admiration, and fury, and an unquenched desire that made him determined to teach her a lesson—when he got untied. He tugged at the knots again and frowned when he saw that the strain only tightened them. Perhaps he could have ripped free from the wool band, but she'd been smart enough to use the leather strap from his coat, and that wouldn't fail. "Now, dear." He kept his voice low and soothing. "This isn't a good idea. If you'd just think about it, you'd realize that. You don't *really* believe I'm Jean, the man who killed your brother. You wouldn't have turned to flame in my arms if you believed that."

She glanced up from her buttons to cast him a look composed of equal parts of alarm and disgust.

"You did, you know. This night has been a rogue's fantasy." That wasn't what he'd meant to say. He didn't mean to dwell on the pleasure of the dark, but the memory of her sweet passion still enfolded him. She'd trapped him by recalling that gratification and promising more, but he should have guessed no woman as inexperienced as she had proved to be would be bold enough to attempt a seduction. Indeed, as he looked at her, she folded her generous mouth tightly and her color rose, and he realized he had embarrassed her. He didn't want to embarrass her now; he desperately needed her to stay so he could convince her to free him. Hastily, he steered back toward the logic he hoped would sway her. "If I'm the Seamaster, as you know I am, then Jean is still loose, still capable of murdering more people as he murdered Ronald. Surely there's more satisfaction to catching him than in gaining a petty revenge on me."

"I'm finding there is a great deal of satisfaction in petty revenge." Pulling up her stockings, she tied her garters around her knee, and he strained to see the turn of her ankle. She lowered her skirts with enough haste to tell him she'd noticed, and she said, "You yourself told me you don't think it's possible to catch Jean tonight, that he's escaped from this area."

He'd told her too damned much. He'd been over-confident, treating her like a woman who would be swept away by the scope of his passion. She was completely dressed now, shoving her extra clothes into the carpetbag she'd hauled from under the desk, and he scowled at her. She should have been swept away by the scope of his passion, damn it. Instead, he'd been swept away by hers. He'd never failed to get his way with a woman before; of course, he'd never neglected his duty for a woman before, either, and that made him uneasy. "Surely you know I'm not a man to falter in anything he sets out to do, don't you? I'm determined to capture Jean, and I will. I'm determined to keep you safe, and I will."

"Probably that's why you remained here with me, wasn't it? To keep me safe while your men hunted this infamous Jean."

It was a indication of his perturbation that he wanted to snatch onto the shameful excuse and agree with her. Only her sarcastic tone kept him sane enough to say dryly, "Oh, yes, I'm that noble. Laura, surely you don't imagine I'm going to keep quiet? I know Ernest. He's been the innkeeper at the Bull and Eagle for years. I'll shout and he'll come to my rescue before you've walked across the taproom."

She grinned at him smugly. "I don't think so. We're married, remember? Ernest won't interfere regardless of what he hears."

The phrase sounded familiar. Then he recognized it. He'd said just that to her when she'd threatened to scream. If he hadn't been in such desperate straits, he would have laughed, but damn the woman! She couldn't leave him here. "When I call Ernest, he'll come."

She nodded thoughtfully. "You're probably right."

As she walked toward the bed, Leighton's heart leapt with triumph. "That's a good, reasonable girl," he said. "You'll see. You're doing the right thing."

Stopping short of the dais, she leaned down out of his sight, and when she rose, she had his clothes gathered in her arms. "Yes, I think I'm doing the right thing, too." Walking to the window, she opened it and threw his clothes out.

"Hey!" His incredulous shout came a moment too late. "How could you?"

She shrugged. "I had to do something. Lack of clothing should slow you down even if you do yell for Ernest."

"Of course I'm going to yell for Ernest." As loudly as he could, he bellowed, "*Ernest! Ern*—where the hell did you get that?"

She'd taken a pistol out of the desk drawer and was checking it in a manner that proclaimed her competence. "From my father. He taught me how to use it. I thought it best if I brought it, for I feared I would meet a villain." Her gaze surveyed him coolly. "I did, but I didn't shoot him."

For the first time, Leighton faced an ugly truth. He wasn't going to get his way. She wasn't going to free him. She was going out into the dark and rain to escape him. And Jean was still free and no doubt bent on mischief. Smuggling was a serious crime, but one the government more often than not turned its back on.

Espionage was something else again. England was at war with France, and secrets leaked from this coast to the French command and into the ears of Napoleon himself.

Leighton knew all about it, because Leighton was the man in charge of maintaining security in the government.

Ronald Haver had worked for Leighton, not as a secretary as his sister originally believed, but to ferret out the source of the leaked information. The son of a career soldier killed serving in India, Ronald had been totally competent, daring, and courageous—a family trait, Leighton had discovered later—and it was Ronald who'd discovered where the information exchange was made.

Leighton hadn't believed it at first. The smugglers landed on the very beaches of his own manor? Did Jean know his identity and mock him by using his home? Or was it simply serendipity, the fact that his beaches had always been and would always be the best place to land with smuggled goods, with caves in the cliffs above to stash the contraband? Ronald's diary had given him the answer he sought, as well as posing a question—who was Jean's accomplice?

"Laura, don't go," Leighton begged. "I'm not the villain you should fear."

"I can take care of myself." She slipped the pistol into her cloth purse and hung it around her wrist. "I've been doing it for longer than I care to remember."

It was true. Ronald had spoken of his sister in glowing terms. He mentioned her competence, her good sense, and her skills, and before he met her, Leighton had formed a picture in his mind of a brusque, broad, homely woman. Ronald had requested that, in case of his death, Leighton care for his sister, and Leighton had been determined to do just that. He'd give her a pension and keep her in comfort for the rest of her life.

Then Farley had ushered her into his office for the first time, and Leighton had been knocked back on his heels. It wasn't that she was gorgeous or sweet. Quite the opposite. She was too short, too thin, too fierce, too . . . right for him. The wanting had shaken him to the core. He'd always kept his passion well in control. He chose mistresses for their experience and he planned to choose his wife for her suitability.

Laura was not particularly suitable. She dressed well, but that was because she was a seamstress. A seamstress! And poverty obviously hovered close. Her father was the younger son of a baron with not even a knighthood to give his name a title. But for Leighton, these matters were trivial compared to his desires. He planned to find and arrest Ronald's killer and present him to Laura as a nuptial gift. She would have him then. That would vanquish the shadow of suspicion from her gaze.

Instead Jean slipped through the trap set for him, and on entering the inn, Leighton had been hailed as Laura's bridegroom by Ernest.

At that moment, his whole life changed. The calm, rational, duty-bound man he was became an opportunist, and he'd forcefully seduced an innocent.

He grinned. And he still couldn't work up one shred of regret.

After donning her redingote, gloves, and hat, Laura walked to the settle and picked up the diary.

At that reminder of Ronald and his fate, Leighton's smile faded. "Laura, please don't do this. Leave me tied if it makes you feel safer, but don't go out tonight."

Going to the door, she twisted the knob. "It's locked again." She glanced back at him in scorn. "Did you instruct Ernest to make sure I couldn't easily escape?"

Bristling, he said, "I can control you without any man's help."

She inserted the key in the lock and turned it, then looked back at him stretched naked and defenseless. "I can see that."

"I'll find you, Laura," he said, and he meant it.

CHAPTER 6

Leighton's promise echoed in Laura's ears as she walked down the hall. *I'll find you.* Yes, he probably would, but not tonight, and that would give her a much-needed reprieve. She'd take a horse from the stable and go to another inn to catch the stage back to London. She'd wiggled her way through the government bureaucracy until she found someone to listen to her concerns, and if they told her Leighton was the Seamaster, well . . .

Oh, he was the Seamaster. What was the use in fooling herself? He was the Seamaster and he no doubt hunted Jean just as he claimed.

But he couldn't get him tonight, and tonight she needed to get away and try to accept the fact she lusted after the man who'd sent her brother to his death. Oh yes, she lusted after him, but she also wanted him to pay with at least a measure of mortification.

Pausing at the top of the stairs, she listened, but heard nothing. Carefully she crept down, avoiding the squeaking step. The fire had burnt to almost nothing in the taproom and the complete and eerie silence spooked her. She wanted to run back to her chamber, to the safety that Leighton represented, but she stiffened her spine. She was, after all, a Haver, and worthy to carry the banner of her father and her brother.

Then a burst of shouting from the kitchen made her

stumble backward and she found herself on the top landing again.

Two men. Ernest and . . . another.

"Those are important papers!" the unknown shouted.

While Ernest answered, "Ye can't have my lord."

Something crashed, glass broke, there was a hoarse cry, then silence. Laura hastily crept down the stairs, keeping to the wall, listening with all her might.

That unknown voice spoke again, this time lower and with enough menace to make the hair stand up on Laura's head. "I can have anything I choose," he said. "Need I remind you that should your beloved Earl of Hamilton discover what you've been doing with me, he'll tack your ears to the stocks?"

Laura put her hands to her mouth to stifle her gasp. Ernest didn't reply to the man's accusation; he didn't rush to deny it. Then she heard an explosion of sound, like air escaping a clogged passage, and someone gasping in deep breaths. She'd seen enough violence done on the streets of London to recognize this. The unknown man had been choking Ernest.

"They took my cargo, those damned government men, and there are some very important papers which I must recover."

Ernest recovered himself enough to croak, "Ye and yer papers! It's all a cover, isn't it, this smuggling? Ye're spying fer the Frenchies, ye are."

Laura made it across the taproom to the doorway by the kitchen in less time than it took the unknown to laugh.

"What if I am?" he said. "You've been well paid for your assistance."

A spy. A French spy. Jean.

Laura leaned against the casement and listened, her heart pounding, her breath short.

"I'm an honest, God-fearing Englishman, I am, and I never agreed to help a Frenchie."

"Honest?" Jean mocked. "Smuggling's not honest."

"In this part of the world, it is." Ernest sounded firm and sure of himself. "My father did it, my grandfather did it, and my great-grandfather did it, but we never—"

"Well, you have now."

Laura heard the click of steel and her hand went to her purse where her own pistol rested.

"Hey!" Ernest's voice rose an octave. "There's no need fer that!"

"We're going to go upstairs now, get your lord, and when we're done with him Leighton will get me my information without a qualm."

"He'll never help ye." Ernest sounded as scornful as possible for a man facing a gun. "A Leighton's honor is above all things."

"Normally I would agree with you," the unknown said. "But Leighton has a lady in that room with him. Her name is Laura Haver, and while I doubt they're truly married—"

"They wouldn't lie to me!"

"—I've seen how Leighton looks at her." The unknown chortled until he snorted. "He'll cooperate with me."

Laura stepped back, shocked. She recognized that laugh. Farley. It was that little worm, Sir Farley Malthus, the one who ushered her into Leighton's London office with such obsequious grace and laughed at her desire to find her brother's assassin. He'd taken her aside one day and told her how ludicrous she made herself, pretending that a mere woman could influence the grand workings of English government. She'd hated him for it at the time, hated him even more for his insinuation she only sought an illicit union with Leighton, but she never imagined such a fussy little gossip could be a traitor and a murderer.

Again she touched the pistol in the purse. But no, that wouldn't do. She only had one shot, and assistance waited in the stable. Quickly and quietly, she made her way to the outer door and eased it open. As she stepped outside, she heard voices in the taproom. Swinging the door almost closed, she fled toward the stable. The mud clung to her skirt and sucked at her boots. Ronald's diary hit her knee and the book came flying out of her pocket.

She didn't stop to get it. It was a memento of her brother, but her brother would have told her to rescue the living, and so she ran harder, right into the dark stable. Pausing, she listened, but she heard nothing behind her. She had escaped without being spotted.

She groped her way along the stalls. A man waited within, Leighton said, but how would she know if it was the *right* man? Might not Farley also have stationed someone in here to take care of any unwanted intruders? She sighed, her breath a frightened exhale, when something small and living hit her from the side. She tumbled over, smacking the wall, and small hands reached for her throat. She knocked them aside as a boy's voice demanded, "Where's m'lord? Tell me what happened to m'lord."

When she didn't respond at once, the boy's hands grappled with her again.

"Ye're a woman!" He sounded disgusted, now. "Are ye that woman he saw on the cliffs?"

"Are you the man he left stationed here?" she countered, wondering what to think.

"What's it to ye?"

Of course, a boy to carry messages would be better than using a man, and it would keep him out of harm's way, too. "If you are," she said cautiously, "he might be in need of help."

The boy sprang off her. "What have ye done with m'lord?"

"I haven't done anything with him, but there are two men in the inn who will hurt him if you don't go get assistance."

"I'll save him myself."

She snagged him as he started to run out the door. "Leighton sent me down here with specific instructions that you're to go for help." It was a lie, but she saw no other way to satisfy him. "He wants me to stay."

"Ye?" The boy sounded scornful. "Why would he want a girl when he could have me?"

"Because I have a gun."

The lad paused, then answered, "That's a choice reason. Do ye know how to shoot it?"

"Indeed I do."

"How do I know ye're telling the truth?"

Laura committed herself to Leighton with her next words. "Because I work for the Seamaster."

The boy's indrawn breath told her of his awe, and he answered, "That's good enough fer me."

He was out the open door like a barn owl swooping toward the open air, and when Laura stepped out she couldn't even see his form as he raced across the heath.

Looking up at the inn, she could see the light from the bedchamber where Leighton lay, tied and naked. This wasn't what she'd imagined when she tricked him. Now she would do anything to have him free because for all her knowledge of firearms and for all of her practice with the targets, she'd never shot a man and feared to do so now. She feared it all: going upstairs, confronting two men bent on murder, seeing the accusation in Leighton's eyes. Because of her, Ronald's murderer might go unpunished. Because of her, he might murder again, and this time it would be Leighton—and she couldn't stand to lose both men she loved to such wickedness.

For just a moment, she covered her face with her gloved hand.

What stupidity, to love a lord when she was nothing but a seamstress and a commoner. He'd made it clear he welcomed her into his bed, but she wasn't stupid enough to swallow his talk of marriage. Now she would go up there, and save his life or die trying, and if he wanted her to remain with him as a mistress, she'd do it. She only had the strength to leave him once, and she'd already tried and made it only as far as the stable.

If she didn't save him . . . well, she knew herself well

enough to recognize all the signs of rampaging infatuation, and she knew she'd die at his side.

Such resolutions made a mockery of her fears, and she tucked her chin into her chest and marched toward the door of the inn.

Crossing the yard, she swerved at the last moment and looked in the windows. The taproom was empty. The door still stood off the latch, just as she'd left it when she fled, and she stuck her head in. Nothing moved. Stepping inside, she left the door open in case the help she'd sent for arrived and wanted to make a quick entrance.

Light spilled down from upstairs and she listened, straining her ears. Voices sounded up there, and moving like a wraith, she crossed the floor.

Farley's voice rang out. "Untie him!"

Grasping the hand rail, Laura climbed the stairs and moved down the hall.

"I'm trying. I'm trying." Ernest sounded surly. "M'lady's quite a woman. These knots are well done."

"You don't have to tell me that." Leighton sounded cool and almost amused. "I've been struggling to free myself ever since the first time I saw her. I doubt I'll ever get free."

Laura paused just beyond the square of light that marked the floor outside the chamber door.

"Cut the damned things!" Farley snarled. "We haven't got time for this nonsense."

"Haven't got a knife," Ernest said.

There was a troubled silence as Farley thought. Then he said, "Here. Use this one."

Laura heard the clatter as he threw it. Someone cursed. Ernest, she supposed, as he scrambled on the floor.

Farley warned, "Don't imagine you can take me out with a puny thing like that knife."

Moving a step at a time through the shadows in the hall, Laura adjusted her position, trying to see in the door.

"I don't see why you're in such a hurry, Farley," Leighton said. "It's not far to the smuggled goods. I could give you directions . . ."

"You'll take me yourself. That's the only way your men will give me what is mine."

Leighton continued as if Farley hadn't spoken. "And I wish you'd stop waving that gun around. What harm do you think I can do to you? My God, man, I'm naked and trussed like a Christmas goose."

Laura winced at the image, then moved far enough around that she had a view of Farley. He stood with his feet planted firmly, the pistol held in both hands in a manner that bespoke great familiarity with it.

He kept the barrel steady and pointed straight at the bed as he said, "I don't trust you, Leighton. You always have a confederate hidden somewhere or another."

It was her cue. Stepping in the door, Laura said, "So he does."

He reacted almost too quickly. The pistol swung at her. The roar of her pistol mixed with Leighton's anguished shout.

One of Farley's legs collapsed. He fell sideways, but even as he landed he was aiming at her again. Leighton came off the bed, severed shreds of her robe tie clinging to his wrists. Laura threw herself on the floor as Leighton smashed into Farley. The pistol discharged, then flew into the air as Leighton knocked it away.

"Laura!" Leighton's shout left her ears ringing, but his hands turned her over as gently as if she were a fragile china piece.

"I'm fine." She wasn't. She'd hit the floor so hard she'd knocked the breath out of her lungs and bruised her elbows, but the bullet hadn't struck her, and that was all that mattered.

Leighton's sharp eyes observed her, then, satisfied, he rapped, "Ernest, secure that blackguard."

"Got 'em, my lord." Ernest's knee rested on Farley's windpipe until, out of air, Farley stopped clawing at Ernest. Examining the oozing wound Laura's bullet had inflicted in Farley's leg, Ernest added, "Nice shot, m'lady."

Wanting to set matters straight, Laura began, "I'm not—"

Leighton picked her up and cradled her in his arms, muffling her protest with his vigor and the impact of his large, bare body. Then he lifted one finger. "Listen."

Outside, she heard the jingle of horses' tack and the movement of their hooves in the mud of the stable yard. Boots pounded through the taproom and up the stairs, and she realized with a rush of horror their rescuers had arrived. Unfortunately, they'd arrived too late to rescue anyone and they'd arrived too early for Leighton to dress himself in a scant semblance of respectability.

Leighton and Laura were compromised.

"Leighton." She pushed at him. "Let go of me!"

"Keefe," he reminded her, and brushed her hair away from her face. "You banged your forehead."

She touched it and brought her hand away, expecting by his concern to see blood. There was nothing, and it ached only a little. "It's fine. I'm fine. You've got to—"

The pounding boots reached the doorway, and a brisk male voice called, "Sir!" A young man Laura recognized from Leighton's London office skidded into the room, pistol raised. He stopped cold at the sight of the naked Earl of Hamilton crouched on the floor with a woman in his arms. "Sir?" The gun wavered.

"Everything's first rate, Robinson," Leighton said. "Put your firearm away."

Someone bumped Robinson in the back, and he stumbled forward.

A boy of perhaps thirteen looked around, spotted Laura, and pointed. "It's her. She's the one who sent me."

"Did you go get help, Franklin?" Leighton asked.

Franklin clenched his skinny fists and placed them on his hips. "Yes, m'lord, the woman told me to."

"You're a good man."

Leighton's praise made the tall lad flush with pleasure. Propelled by the crowd behind him, Robinson moved farther into the room. At least half a dozen men with firearms clustered around him. Laura had seen them all at one time or another in Leighton's anterooms. She had despised them, thinking these respectable men had turned to crime for the promise of wealth. Now, she realized, they were part of Leighton's government operation, catching spies to maintain England's integrity during the war. They all stared, first at Leighton and Laura, then at Ernest and Farley, openly betraying their bewilderment.

"What is going on here?" Robinson demanded.

Ernest stood and dragged Farley off the floor. "Here's yer villain. Ye'd best take him before he bleeds to death."

Obviously the man in charge, Robinson didn't seem to be able to grasp the situation. "That's not Jean," he protested, "that's Farley."

"Your scornful tone explains very well how Farley has been successful in his disguise," Leighton said.

The men murmured while Robinson considered. At last, in a tone that pleaded for credence, he asked, *"That's* Jean?"

The men all looked to Leighton for acknowledgment, and Leighton nodded. "That, my friends, is our spy."

"Oafs." Farley lunged for Robinson and succeeded only in falling to one knee.

Examining him with all the fascination of a boy with a frog, Robinson asked, "What's wrong with him?"

Ernest grabbed Farley by the hair and twisted his head back. "M'lady shot him."

"My . . . lady?" Robinson asked.

"The Countess of Hamilton." Ernest pointed. "There."

Laura moaned. When she'd told her little fib, she'd never thought it would spread so far and provide her with such embarrassment.

"That's not the Countess of Hamilton," Franklin said loudly.

Ernest puffed up like a blowfish. "It is too, ye stupid boy."

Leighton said nothing, but when Laura strove to sit up, Leighton clutched her more tightly and admonished, "You need to be put to bed."

Laura glanced up to see a dozen astonished eyes turned in her direction, and she stopped struggling and hid her face in Leighton's chest.

No doubt just what he planned, for he said, "As you can see, my lady and I require privacy."

"M'lady?" Franklin's round eyes got rounder. "Tell me it ain't so, m'lord. Tell me ye never got married."

Leighton ignored him. "Robinson, if you and the men would take Farley—"

"Ah." Robinson stood as if paralyzed. "Yes, sir."

"Robinson?"

Leighton's voice sounded polite, but Laura looked up in time to see the faint smile which curled his lips. She wanted to hit him, but his reminder seemed effective, for Robinson leaped toward Farley. The other men surrounded the now-helpless spy.

"Franklin." Leighton winked at the boy and nodded toward the men as they hustled Farley out of the room. "Aren't you going to help them?"

"Yes, m'lord." Franklin backed out of the room, his gaze still fixed on Leighton and Laura. Pausing at the door, he shook his head sadly. "I still can't believe ye're married."

Leighton only smiled. "You'll have to imagine the wedding ceremony. *I* did." Raising his voice, he called, "Robinson?"

Robinson popped back into the doorway. "Sir?"

"You know what to do with Farley?"

"We'll do our best to save his wretched life, sir, so he can be questioned. Then"—Robinson's mouth creased with satisfaction—"he'll dance the hemp jig."

"Good man." Leighton dismissed him, and Robinson

took the disgusted-looking Franklin by the shoulder and urged him away.

Now Ernest stood alone in the middle of the room and tried to smile. Leighton frowned back at him, and Ernest wilted. "M'lord, I just want to say that I never knew he was anything but a smuggler."

"I know, Ernest." Leighton clutched at Laura as she again struggled to scoot away. He whispered, "You're the only thing keeping me decent."

Bustling over to the fire, Ernest knelt beside it and built it up. "If ye can see yer way clear not to arrest me, I swear I'll not have further dealings with spies."

"Nor smugglers," Leighton said.

Ernest sighed. "Nor smugglers." He brightened. "I've built up my stock of brandy, anyway." Seeing the bottle of wine sitting on the table, he walked to it and, using the corkscrew he kept at his belt, opened it. Taking two cups out of his pockets, he set them beside the bottle, then stepped back with a flourish. "I'll leave ye, then, m'lord and m'lady, to finish yer honeymonth."

With a start, Laura realized she was about to be left alone with a very naked, possibly vengeful Leighton. He wasn't the wicked smuggler or the ruthless murderer, but when she looked closely she still saw the twitch of a tiger's whisker and the gleam of a tiger's sharp tooth.

She needed to get away. She needed to get out *now*. Trying to slide away from the clutch of his paws, she said, "I'll just leave with Ernest so you can dress."

His query jerked her to a halt. "In what?"

A vision of his clothing soaking in the mud ripped through her mind, and she said feebly, "Perhaps Ernest can find something"—she glanced toward the door—"that you can wear." It was closed.

The room was empty except for a tiger and his prey.

CHAPTER 7

"He's gone!" Laura didn't know why she was surprised. Ernest showed a talent for disappearing just when she needed him.

"He probably realized I would want to commend your bravery in private."

Again she tried to ease away from Leighton. This time he let her. Raising a brow, she inquired, "Commend?"

"You did save the life of one of His Majesty's most important agents."

"So I did." Perhaps getting away from Leighton hadn't been such a clever idea. True, it was a relief to escape his embrace, but now she had to look at him. All of him. Especially the part that towered over her when he rose to his feet and stalked toward her.

"You captured a known spy," he said. "I don't even know why my men and I bothered to come to this event."

She backed toward the desk. "I don't think you're being fair."

"Fair? Why should I be fair?" He smiled at her with every evidence of courtesy, but she couldn't relate his society civility with his naked body. It was amazing how large he appeared when stripped of his clothing. Much larger than when his shirt, breeches, and coat gave him bulk. Now she could clearly see the breadth of his shoulders, the ladder of his ribs, the muscles of his thighs.

His legs were longer than hers, too, but he didn't move

more quickly than she did. If anything, he seemed to be enjoying the chase, taking care not to overcome her.

"Of course, you did need me." His mouth twisted. "I served you admirably as bait, did I not?"

"I did not tie you to the bed as bait."

"That's true." He nodded genially. "It was revenge, I think you said?"

The desk bumped her thighs and she grasped the edge with her hands. A sense of déjà vu overcame her—they'd done this before. "Revenge seemed like a good idea at the time."

"Not now?"

"You're not tied, now."

"You are a very astute woman." He loomed over her and took her chin in one hand. "Did it never occur to you I would, one day, be untied?"

"I didn't expect to be here when it happened."

"Bad planning, but I'm grateful." He tried to embrace her, but she shrieked and ducked under his arm.

Skittering toward the door, she tried it and wasn't surprised to find it locked. Ernest had proved himself quite handy with the key.

She turned, expecting to find Leighton behind her. Instead he was pouring wine into the cups and smiling genially. "You're nervous," he said.

"Have I reason to be?" Her tone was a challenge, but she retreated toward the fire.

"A woman as courageous as you should never be nervous. Wine?"

"I don't think—"

"After all, you threw yourself into danger to save my life." He walked toward her, still unashamedly nude, and offered the cup.

At first she didn't want to accept it, but the need for some artificial fortitude overcame her. Taking the cup, she took one sip, then drained it in one long, cleansing swallow. Handing it back to the startled Leighton, she squared

her shoulders. "I didn't do it for you, I did it for Ronald.
You were just in the way."

"For Ronald only?"

"Anyway, I promise I will never rescue you again."

"I agree." He placed the cups on the floor. "You won't."
He efficiently began to strip her of her clothes. "Because
I'm going to tie you to the bed until you've learned better."

Now he allowed her to see beyond the cordial smile
and play of hospitality. He was, she realized, truly aggra-
vated with her. When she tried to struggle, he treated her
like a two-year-old, overcoming her physical objections
with plain, overbearing competence.

"This is not acceptable!" she exclaimed, trying to hold
the hands that roamed over her so effectively.

"Having my wife step in front of a bullet is not acceptable either." He wrestled her out of her gown, her petticoats, and her shift, and apparently decided he could
leave the stockings and garters.

"All right! I'm sorry I told Ernest I was your wife. I
didn't know you'd ever find out about it. I certainly didn't
know you'd take unfair advantage of a woman traveling
alone."

He chuckled. "Why not? You took unfair advantage of
me."

"I most certainly did not!"

Swinging her into his arms, he said, "It's quite unlike
you not to take responsibility where you should."

She wanted to answer him tartly, but in the place where
their flesh met, she experienced a sensation not unlike the
one she'd discovered earlier in the evening. Horrified, she
muttered, "You've imprinted yourself on me."

"What?"

"I said"—she tried to regain control of herself, at
least—"I admit I'm responsible for coming here and trying
to find Ronald's killer, and I admit I'm responsible for
telling Ernest I was your bride, but of what crime can you
accuse me?"

He dropped her on the bed and the feather mattress poufed up around her. Leaning over, he trapped her between his arms. "Of stealing my heart."

"Don't joke about these things."

Coming closer, and closer still, he touched her lips with his. It wasn't a kiss, not really. More of a suggestion, or a promise. With his lips still on hers, he said, "I'm not joking."

She wanted to ask for clarification, but as she told him, she was a coward.

When she didn't speak, he straightened and rubbed his hands together. "I've never done this before, and you took all the ready material the first time. What shall I use to bind you?"

Bouncing up, she said, "Don't be ridiculous."

"Look at this." He lifted his scarf off the floor. "Lucky for me, you must have missed it when you threw my clothes out the window."

"Lucky."

"Now lie back down again." He crawled onto the mattress to enforce his command. "And put your hands up by the railing."

In frustration, she asked, "Are you always reduced to tying your mistresses?"

"Not my mistresses, no." He straddled her. "But I've never had a wife before. It would seem they're a little harder to subdue."

"I'm not your wife."

"You will be."

He looked quite serious as he lifted her hands to the rails over her head, and she realized that it wasn't that she thought he would dishonor her. It was that she objected to being a part of his obligations. "You're doing this for Ronald."

His look of surprise lasted only until he looked her over, naked and waiting. "Believe me, your brother is the last thing on my mind right now."

"I'll not be married out of duty. I'd rather be your mistress."

Throwing back his head, he laughed until she stung with embarrassment and wrestled away. "Whoa." He caught her immediately and tried to regain a respectable amount of gravity. "That is an offer I will treasure. However, I won't marry you out of duty."

He fit the scarf over her wrists and tied them to the rail, and she stared at him in frustration. "Then why?"

"Tug on your hands," he instructed.

She did as she was told. He'd managed to wrap that scarf around securely enough to keep her in place, yet gently enough the circulation still flowed.

He sighed with pleasure. "That's a relief. I'd hate to think you'd shot the spy *and* tied a better knot than I. It would be such a blow to my ego."

He wasn't going to answer her. He wasn't going to tell her why he proposed marriage when he could have her for so much less, and that made her think that it was duty, or his promise to Ronald, or some other stupid, manly honor thing that reduced her to an obligation and made a mockery of her love. She turned her face away.

He sighed, his breath a faint feather on her skin. "You'll never forgive me, will you?"

"For what?"

"For sending Ronald to his death."

"Oh." She shrugged. "That."

He paused, then complained, "You tie me naked to the bed and leave me for anyone to find in revenge for your brother's death, then you say, 'Oh, that'?"

She could almost have laughed at his disgruntled tone. Almost, if only he weren't pressed so close against her, torturing her with what he offered and withholding so much. "If you'd only told me that Jean was a spy for France, I would have understood. Once Ronald had a chance to work for England, no one could have kept him from it."

"Ahh." He kissed her, a light comforting press of the lips on her cheek. "You knew him well."

"It's the curse of being a loyal soldier's child. We'll all fly into danger for Mother England." She mocked herself and her courage. "It was the thought of Ronald dying for something as trivial as French brandy that made me angry."

"If that was angry, I'd hate to see you furious." He tugged at the scarf. "Not even this would keep me safe, I suspect. So if it's not anger, what is it that keeps you from having me?"

Placing his hands on her wrists, he ran them down her arms. She didn't want to feel anything, but his caress made her squirm. "Laura," he called softly. Never lifting his hands, he smoothed them over her breasts, down her stomach, along her thighs to the garters at her knees. "I should take these off," he said. "But I like them. They remind me of you. You're lying here gloriously nude, exposed, trusting me enough to let me tie you, yet not trusting me enough to tell me your secrets. Yet I can tell you mine." Holding her lips, he laid on her, giving her his warmth. "I love you, Laura Haver."

Startled by his words, his fervency, his need, she turned her face to him and stared.

"You're going to marry me because I'm not going to give you a choice. I've compromised you in front of my men and in front of Ernest."

She wiggled, wanting to grab him by the ears and make him talk. "Never mind the compromising. What about the love?"

"I can't 'never mind' the compromising. My grandmother knows everything that goes on on this estate, and when she hears about this, she'll take a switch to me. You, too, if you won't marry me."

"Love?" she urged.

"You'll learn to love me." He kissed her cheek, then nuzzled the place behind her ear. "You already like to make love with me, I could tell, and that'll just get better and better." His hands stroked a long, slow line from her hips to her throat. "Say you'll marry me, and I'll demonstrate."

Something like a shiver slid up her spine. "If I don't?"

"I'll demonstrate anyway." He kissed one breast, then grinned at her wickedly. "I'll demonstrate to you the same way you demonstrated to me . . . earlier."

He'd make her want him, then leave her unsatisfied. Her eyes widened as she heard his purr of amusement. No wonder she had seen sparks of the tiger in him. Beneath that placid façade hid a man determined to have his own way and ruthless enough to do anything to get it.

Well, she wanted her own way, too, "I'll marry you," she said.

Taking her nipple between two fingers, he rolled it. "Why?"

Pressure sprang up between her legs, and she pressed her hips toward him to relieve it. But he moved away, still touching her, and she mumbled, "I love you."

His eyelids drooped, then he fixed her with his interrogational gaze. "What?"

Louder, she said, "I love you."

"Truly?"

"I love you truly."

He looked at her carefully, not quite believing her, and she lifted her head and kissed him. Kissed him with her lips and tongue and with the force of her passion.

When she finished, the grave shadow had gone from his eyes and they gleamed with gratification and a wicked touch of elation. "I love you truly, too," he said.

"I believe you." She shifted impatiently. "Now untie me."

Peeling himself off of her, he looked her over from her stockinged feet to her wriggling hands. "No."

Indignant, she struggled to sit up. "You promised—"

Licking his thumb, he circled her navel until the damp

brought a chill to her skin. Observing the goosebumps that covered her, he grinned into her face.

He hadn't promised to untie her, she realized. He'd only promised to withhold satisfaction if she *didn't* marry him. Rubbing his cheek on her stomach, he moistened her skin with his tongue.

"Leighton." She used her fiercest voice, but he paid no attention. He only slipped farther down her body and wrapped one arm around each one of her thighs. "Leighton!"

He corrected her, "Keefe," and dipped his head between her legs.

She shrieked his name. "Keefe!"

Lifting his head, he said, "You can make as much noise as you wish." Then he nuzzled deep in the cleft between her legs. "No one interferes between a man and his wife."

"I can make a lot of noise," she snapped. Looking down she could see only the forehead and eyebrows. His tongue licked at her in the first sharp, glorious step to gratification. Leaning back, her mouth curled in the anticipation of satisfaction. "But the door is locked, so we won't have to worry."

MELTING ICE

STEPHANIE LAURENS

CHAPTER 1

"If you believe the family will continue to countenance such profligate hedonism now that you've stepped into your poor brother's shoes, you are fair and far out, sir! *You—will—marry!* Soon. And well!"

With his great-aunt Augusta's words ringing in his ears, to the tune of emphatic raps from her cane, Dyan St. Laurent Dare, most reluctant fourth Duke of Darke, sent his gray hunter pounding along the woodland track. Outlier of the New Forest, the wood was thick enough to hide him. The pace he set was reckless, a measure of his mood; the demon within him wanted out.

The gray's hooves thundered on the beaten track; Dyan tried to lose himself in the driving rhythm. After an entire afternoon listening to his relatives' complaints, he felt wild, his underlying restlessness setting a dangerous edge to his temper.

Damn Robert! Why did he have to die? Of a mere inflammation of the lungs, of all things. Dyan suppressed a disgusted snort, feeling slightly guilty. He'd been truly fond of his older brother; although only two years had separated them, Robert had seemed like forty from the time he was twenty. Robert's staid, conservative personality had shielded his own more robust and vigorous—not to say profligate—character from their exceedingly strait-laced family.

Now Robert was dead—and he was in the firing line.

Which was why he was fleeing Darke Abbey, his ancestral home, leaving his long-suffering relatives behind. He had to get out—get some air—before he committed a felony. Like strangling his great-aunt.

Tolerance was not one of his virtues; he'd always been described as impatient and hot-at-hand. Even more critical, he had never, ever tolerated interference in his life, a point he was going to have to find some polite way to make plain to his aunts, uncles—and his great-aunt Augusta. Naturally, they still saw him as his younger self. They had descended on the Abbey, intent on impressing on him the error of his rakehell ways. They all believed marriage would be his salvation; presumably they thought securing the succession would be a goal in keeping with his talents. They had made it plain they thought marriage to some sweet, biddable gentlewoman would cure him of his recklessness.

They didn't know him. Few did.

Jaw setting, Dyan swung the gray into a long glade and loosened the reins; the heavy horse plunged down the long slope.

He'd only just arrived back at the Abbey—for the past ten years, India had been his home. A decade ago he'd left London, intent on carving out a new life—that, or dying in the attempt; even now, he wasn't sure which of those two goals had, at the time, been his primary aim. His family had been relieved to see him go; the subcontinent was reassuringly distant, half the globe a comforting buffer against his scandalous propensities. Under India's unrelenting sun, his recklessness had found ample scope for danger, intrigue, and more danger. He'd survived, and succeeded; he was now a wealthy man.

On being informed of Robert's death and his ascension to the title, his initial reaction had been to decline to be found. Instead, a nagging, deeply buried sense of responsibility had goaded him into liquidating his assests, realizing his investments—and disengaging from the clinging embrace of the Rani of Barrashnapur.

By the time he'd reached London, Robert had been dead for well nigh a year; there'd seemed no need to rush into the country. He'd dallied in town, expecting to slide into the indolent life he'd enjoyed a decade before. Instead, he'd discovered himself a misfit. The predictable round of balls, select parties, and the pursuits of *ton*nish gentlemen engendered nothing more than acute boredom, something he was constitutionally incapable of tolerating.

Worse, the perfumed bodies of discreetly willing ladies, as ever at his beck and call, completely failed to stir his jaded senses. For one who, for the past ten years, had had his every sexual whim instantly and expertly gratified, abstinence for any measurable time was the definition of pure torture.

And self-imposed abstinence was the definition of hell.

Reluctantly, knowing his family was lying in wait for him, he'd returned to the Abbey, his childhood home. Only to be met by the family's demands that he marry and ensure the succession without delay.

It was enough to send him straight back to India.

And the Rani of Barrashnapur.

Memories of golden limbs, all silk and satin, wrapped around his senses; gritting his teeth, Dyan shook them aside. The end of the glade was rapidly approaching, the gray all but flying over the thick grass; Dyan hauled on the reins. Slowing the huge hunter to a canter, he turned into the bridle path that led from the glade.

He was searching, still searching, as he had been for years. Searching for something—an elusive entity—that would fill the void in his soul and anchor his restless passions. His failure to discover that entity, to fulfill his inner need, left him not just restless, but with his wildness—that demon that had always been a part of him—champing at the bit.

His predator's instinct was to focus on his target—then seize it. To be unable to define what his target was left him directionless. Like a rudderless ship in a storm.

Drawing rein in the clearing that marked the next bend, he sat still, breathing deeply, letting the gray do the same.

Through the trees, lights twinkled. Shifting to get a better view, Dyan saw that the entire ground floor of Brooke Hall was ablaze. His childhood friend Henry, now Lord Brooke, and his wife, Harriet, were obviously entertaining. From the extent of the lights, a house party was in progress.

Hands relaxed on the pommel, Dyan stared across the fields. Wisps of conversations caught during his stay in London wafted through his brain. Allusions to the Brookes, and the house parties they gave. A vision of his relatives' faces, particularly his great-aunt Augusta's, if he failed to show for dinner—failed, indeed, to return at all that night—rose in his mind. His long lips lifted, then curved.

He hadn't seen Henry and Harriet in ten years; it was time to renew old friendships. Twitching the reins, Dyan swung his hunter toward Brooke Hall.

"I realize it's inconvenient, but I would like to speak to Lady Brooke, please, Sherwood." Her bag at her feet, Lady Fiona Winton-Ryder tugged off her gloves, and ignored Sherwood's scandalized expression.

"Ah . . . indeed, Lady Fiona." His calling coming to the fore, Sherwood relocated his butlerishly impassive mask and turned.

The drawing room door opened; Henry, Lord Brooke, looked out. "What is it, Sher—" Henry broke off, his gaze sweeping Fiona, taking in her travelling bag and her pelisse. He stepped into the hall, firmly closing the drawing room door. "Fiona!" Plastering a smile over his transparent surprise, he advanced. "Is there some problem at Coldstream House?"

"Indeed." Lips firming, Fiona lifted her head. "Edmund and I have had a falling out—the most *acrimonious* disagreement! I have *sworn* I will not stay at Coldstream another hour—not until he apologizes. So I've come to beg houseroom until he does."

Henry's jaw slackened.

Fiona swept on: "I realize the timing's inconvenient." A regal wave referred to the drawing room and the sounds of the gathering therein—in reality, she had planned her arrival to the minute, for just before dinner, so Henry, with guests waiting, would be hard pressed to argue. "But I know you've plenty of room." She smiled confidently; Henry couldn't contradict her—she'd known this house from her earliest years—she knew very well how many beds it held. More than enough.

"Ah, yes." Henry lifted a finger, easing the folds of his cravat.

Squirming—as well he might; Fiona fought not to narrow her eyes. If she had her way, Henry would squirm even more before the evening ended. The doorbell pealed; assuming it was a late-arriving guest, Fiona did not turn as Sherwood bowed and moved past to the door. Her gaze firmly fixed on Henry's face, she waited, brows raised in polite question.

"I suppose—" Henry began, then he blinked and stared past her.

"Good evening, Sherwood."

The deep, rumbling voice sent Fiona's eyes flying wide.

"Good evening, my lord—er, Your Grace."

Fiona's heart stopped, stuttered, then started to race. She stiffened; shock skittered down her nerves and locked her lungs. She spared one instant in pity for old Sherwood, stumbling in his surprise. She'd known Dyan would eventually return to take up his brother's mantle—but *why* did he have to turn up *now*?

She resisted the urge to whip about; slowly, regally, with all the cool haughtiness at her command, she turned, her composure that expected of an earl's daughter—only to discover Dyan almost upon her.

His eyes met hers instantly, the dark, midnight-blue gaze more piercing than she recalled. Her heart in her throat, she lifted her chin—a necessity if she was to continue to meet his eyes.

She'd forgotten how tall he was, how intimidating his nonchalant grace. Large, lean, and distinctly menacing, he prowled—there was no other word to describe the languid arrogance of his stride—to her side. His name rhymed with lion; she'd always thought of him as a dark jungle cat, black king of the predators. Dark brown hair, black except in bright sunlight, one thick lock falling rakishly over his forehead, contributed to the image, as did the hard, austere, planes of his face, set in an arrogantly autocratic cast.

The years in India had changed him. She was struck by that fact as he drew closer and her gaze took in the alterations, some obvious, others less so. Gone was all vestige of youth, of innocence, of any lingering softness; his features, now heavily tanned, had been stripped to harsh angularity, leaving them more dramatically forceful, more compelling than she recalled. His gaze, always sharp, was more penetrating, his intelligence more obvious in his eyes. His expression was world-weary, more deeply cynical; his movements were slower, more languid, more assured.

Gone was the youth, the young man she had known. In his place was a black leopard, mature, experienced in the hunt, in the full flush of his masculine strength. India had honed his dangerous edge to lethal sharpness.

He was dressed with negligent grace in buckskin breeches and a dark blue coat, his Hessians gleaming black, his linen faultless white. His expression was studiously impassive.

He halted by her shoulder; his presence engulfed her.

Her gaze locked with his, Fiona discovered it took real effort to breathe. "Good evening, Dyan." She raised her brows haughtily. "Or should I say, Your Grace?"

A frown flashed in his eyes. "Dyan will do." His accents when irritated were as clipped as she recalled. For one instant longer, he stood looking down at her, at her face, then he switched his gaze to Henry. And smiled, effortlessly charming. "Evening, Brooke."

The devil-may-care grace worked its magic, as it always had. Henry relaxed. "Dyan." Smiling, he held out his hand. "We hadn't heard when you'd be back. What brings you this way?"

"My relatives." Dyan grasped Henry's hand. "Or," he drawled, as he released Henry and turned to gaze, rather speculatively, at Fiona, "should I say my great-aunt Augusta?"

Henry frowned. "Your aunt?"

"Great-aunt," Dyan corrected him, his gaze still on Fiona's face. "Believe me, there's a difference."

"Don't have any, myself, but I'll take your word for it." Henry tried unsuccessfully to catch Dyan's eye. "But what's this great-aunt done?"

"Driven me from my home." Deserting Fiona's stubbornly uninformative countenance, Dyan looked back at Henry. "And my bed. I wondered if I might prevail on you to put me up for the night?"

"Certainly," Henry gushed—then glanced at Fiona.

Who smiled winningly. "Perhaps," she suggested, "if you summon Harriet—"

Harriet didn't need to be summoned—she slipped out of the drawing room at that moment, carefully closing the door before turning to see who was keeping her husband from his guests. When she saw who it was, she paled—then flushed—then paled again.

Dyan viewed the reaction with acute suspicion. It wasn't, he knew, due to him. Finding Fiona Winton-Ryder here, a bag at her feet, had shaken even him—more deeply than he could credit. Despite not having done so for fifteen years, despite his firm conviction Fiona was no longer any business of his, his immediate, almost overpowering impulse was to grab her by her honey-gold hair, haul her out of the house, give her a thorough shake, then throw her up to his horse's back and cart her straight home to Coldstream House.

Given what he'd heard of the Brookes' house parties, and having a more than academic understanding of the subject, he was not just surprised to find Fiona here, he was—the realization was a shock in itself—shocked. For one unholy instant, his mind had reeled with all manner of visions—visions of Fiona. But, as he'd looked deep into her eyes, all hazel-greens and golds, he'd seen, clear and true, the same girl he'd known years before. Relief had hit him like a blow, right in the center of his chest.

She hadn't changed. Not in the least.

Which meant she was up to something.

That conclusion was borne out by her next speech.

"Harriet, dear." Smiling serenely, Fiona opened her arms to Harriet and they exchanged their usual kiss. "I fear I am come to throw myself on your hospitality—as I explained to Henry, Edmund and I have had a falling out and I've refused to stay at Coldstream until he apologizes."

Dyan frowned. He knew Fiona's explanation was a lie, but why the devil was she staying with her brother at Coldstream House? Where was Tony, Marquess of Rusden— her husband? He looked at Fiona, but she avoided his eye. Harriet's reaction to Fiona's tale was more revealing. She blushed fierily—and glanced helplessly at Henry. Who, muffin-faced, looked helplessly back.

"Ah . . ." Wide-eyed, Harriet stared at Fiona, who smiled encouragingly; Dyan knew the precise instant Harriet inwardly shrugged and bowed to fate. "Yes, of course." Her words sounded like the capitulation they were; a fleeting frown tangled Fiona's brows, then was banished. Wringing her hands, Harriet continued, "I'll get

Sherwood to show you to your rooms." She smiled weakly, but with a hint of hope, at Dyan.

He smiled reassuringly and held out his hands. "It's been a long time, dear Harriet, but I, too, am claiming refuge from my relatives. I hope you can find a pallet somewhere."

"Oh, I'm sure we can." Harriet's smile turned to one of relief. She took his hands; under cover of planting a kiss on his cheek, she squeezed them warningly. "We'll have to reorganize a trifle but . . ." Shrugging lightly, she turned aside. "Sherwood—"

Harriet's hope—her relief—had communicated itself to Henry. Leaving Harriet to issue her orders, he faced his unexpected guests and fixed Dyan with a significant look. "Well! Just like old times—isn't it?"

Dyan studied Henry's face; so, he noticed, did Fiona. "Old times" referred to their joint childhoods, when, as a small army, he, Fiona, Henry, Harriet, and an assortment of others—all children of the local gentry—had roamed far and wide through the New Forest. He had been their leader; Fiona, two years his junior, had been his second-in-command, the only one of them all who would, without a blink, argue, remonstrate—simply dig in her heels—if some escapade he suggested was too wild, too reckless, too altogether dangerous. She had jerked his reins any number of times, usually by invoking his conscience, a sometimes inconvenient but surprisingly forceful entity.

Conversely, he, as far as he knew, was the only person presently alive who had ever succeeded in managing Fiona, mettlesome, argumentative female that she was. Dyan surmised it was that aspect of their "old times" of which Henry was attempting to remind him. Which confirmed his guess that the entertainment Henry and Harriet had planned for this evening would not meet with Fiona's approval. But that still didn't tell him what had happened to Fiona's husband.

"Indeed," he drawled, politely noncommittal.

Fiona flicked him a quick, suspicious glance, but said nothing.

"If you'll follow Sherwood," Harriet said, gesturing towards the stairs, "he'll show you to your rooms."

Smoothly, Dyan offered Fiona his arm; she shot him another suspicious glance but consented to rest her fingers on his sleeve. In silence, they followed the stately Sherwood up the wide stairs; a footman followed with Fiona's bag.

Dyan held his tongue as they ascended—for the simple reason that he couldn't formulate a single coherent thought. His predator's senses were well-honed, acutely sensitive. They were presently screaming, far too adamantly to be ignored. Their message left him reeling.

Fiona, strolling haughtily beside him, was, indeed, the same girl he'd known before. Unchanged. Untouched.

Unmarried.

He knew it—felt it—deep in his bones. One glance at the fingers of her left hand, presently residing on his sleeve, confirmed it—no band, not even any lingering trace.

As they reached the top of the stairs, Dyan hauled in a not-entirely-steady breath. The foundations of his life had just shifted.

He couldn't interrogate Fiona in front of the servants. Forced to hold his tongue, he slanted her a glance as she glided regally on his arm. She was of above average height—her head just topped his shoulder. Her hair, lustrously thick, was pulled back in a chignon; her face was a perfect oval rendered in ivory satin. Her glance, delivered from large hazel eyes set under finely arched brown brows, still held the same directness, the same uncompromising honesty—the same uncompromising stubbornness—that had always been hers. That last was obvious in the set of her full lips, in the elevation of her chin.

He squinted slightly—and saw the band of freckles

across the bridge of her nose. She was exactly as he remembered.

So what had happened to Tony? And why was she here?

He frowned. "How's your brother?" In Sherwood's wake, they turned down a long corridor.

Fiona kept her eyes forward, her chin up. "Edmund's in perfectly good health, thank you."

The urge to shake her returned; Dyan set his jaw and held it back. They'd reached the end of the wing. Servants were scurrying everywhere.

The rooms Harriet had assigned them were next to each other—Dyan suspected for a very good reason. A maid appeared and Fiona, with a haughty nod, disappeared into her room.

"I've brought some fresh cravats, Your Grace." Henry's valet hovered at Dyan's elbow. "If you'll let me take your jacket, I'll have it brushed."

His gaze on Fiona's closed door, Dyan nodded. "You'll need to be quick."

He was waiting for her when she came out.

Lounging in the shadows, his shoulders against the wall, Dyan watched as, unaware of his presence, Fiona exited her room. Looking down the corridor, she closed the door. Hand still on the knob, she cocked her head, listening. Light from a nearby sconce bathed her in golden light.

Dyan's chest locked. For a long minute, he couldn't breathe, couldn't drag his eyes from the figure robed in turquoise silk poised before the door. This was a Fiona he'd glimpsed only briefly, in the ballrooms of London ten years ago. Guinea-gold curls fell from a knot on the top of her head, a few shining locks artistically escaping to frame brow and nape. The smooth sweep of her jaw and the graceful curve of her throat were highlighted by delicate aquamarine drops depending from her earlobes; the expanse of ivory skin above her scooped neckline played host to the matching pendant. Dyan fought to draw breath, fought to ease the vise locked about his chest; her perfume reached him, violet and honeysuckle—the scent went straight to his head.

His blood rushed straight to his loins.

Before, in London, seeing her only through breaks in the crowds surrounding her, he'd never been able to let his gaze dwell on her, as it was dwelling now. Dwelling on the ripe curves of hips and derriere clearly outlined as she leaned slightly forward; when she relaxed, letting go of the doorknob and straightening, another set of curves came into view—her breasts, full, Rubenesquely abundant, positively mouthwatering.

Desire ripped through him—hot, strong, violent.

Abruptly, Dyan straightened and pushed away from the wall. Fiona heard him and swung around. And frowned.

Dyan strolled forward. "Now we're alone, perhaps you'd like to explain what you're doing here?"

Up went her pert nose; down came her lids. "You heard." Turning, she started down the corridor. "I had an argument with Edmund."

"And pigs flew over the forest this morning."

"I *did*." Fiona heard the tartness in her tone. Trust Dyan to thrust in his oar. "You've been away for years—things have changed." They hadn't spoken in fifteen years, but here he was, as usual, trying to take her reins.

"Try again," he advised, falling into step beside her. "It takes generations, not mere years, to change a man like Edmund. I'd believe he's got a mistress stashed away in the north wing of Coldstream House faster than I'd believe he'd waste his time arguing—*attempting* to argue—with you."

"*Be* that as it may, I assure you—"

"Fiona."

She only just managed not to shiver. The three syllables of her name were infused with steely warning—a warning she recognized only too well. The stairs were in sight, but she knew she'd never make their head—not unless she told Dyan the truth. She knew his propensities; minor considerations like her dignity—or the possibility of her screaming—wouldn't stop him. She drew in a deep, much-needed breath. "If you *must* know, Harriet spoke to me last week, when she came to tea."

She kept walking; the less time she spent alone with Dyan, the more certain her goal would be. "She told me about these house parties Henry organizes." She paused, conscious of the blush rising in her cheeks. But it was, after all, Dyan she was talking to. She lifted her head. "About the activities the guests Henry invites delight in. Expect. Engage in."

Beside her, Dyan blinked. "*Henry's* guests."

Fiona nodded and started down the stairs. "Precisely." Sherwood was waiting by the dining-room door; leaning closer to Dyan, she lowered her voice. "You know what Harriet's like—she's got no gumption at all. I decided the least I could do was come and support her. At least that way she won't have to spend the entire time in fear for her virtue."

"Fear for her . . . ?" Dyan was stunned. He stepped off the stairs in Fiona's wake. "Fiona—" Blinking, he refocused—and discovered her forging ahead. "Here—wait a minute." Striding after her, he caught her arm and halted her, swinging about so his body screened her from Sherwood. "Listen—"

Fiona looked down, at his fingers wrapped about her elbow.

"I don't know what Harriet claimed, but that's not—"

"Dyan—let go. *Right now.*"

Dyan did. Instantly. The quaver in her voice momentarily threw him.

Fiona didn't look up; she stepped back but didn't meet

his eyes. "I didn't expect you to agree with my views—I don't expect you to help." Her chin firmed. "Just don't try to stop me."

With that, she whirled from him. Lifting her head, she swept into the dining room.

Dyan cursed, and strode after her.

He crossed the threshold just as Sherwood opened his mouth to announce Fiona. Dyan planted his boot on Sherwood's foot.

Sherwood cast him an anguished, somewhat reproachful glance. "Miss Winton," Dyan hissed, and removed his boot.

With commendable aplomb, Sherwood announced Miss Winton and His Grace of Darke.

Dark was precisely how Dyan felt as he stalked up the table. Harriet had left two seats vacant, next to each other in the middle along one side. Equidistant, Dyan noted, from Henry at the head and Harriet at the foot. Chairs scraped as the gentlemen hurriedly stood; all heads turned to assess the late arrivals. With the single exception of Henry, every male reacted similarly as their gazes connected with the vision that was Fiona—their eyes widened, taking in her abundant charms; their lips lifted in anticipatory smiles. More than one reached blindly for their quizzing glass before recalling where they were.

Following on Fiona's heels, Dyan fought back a scowl. He was peripherally aware of the response his own appearance was provoking—the flaring interest that lit many feminine eyes, the sudden increase in attentiveness, the subtle preening—the slithering tendrils of sexual excitement that reached for him. He ignored them.

He waved the footman back and held Fiona's chair. His logical mind patiently reminded him that she had rejected him—very thoroughly—fifteen years ago; she was no responsibility of his. The lecture fell on deaf ears. Seeing one so-called gentleman reach for his monocle under cover of the general re-sitting, Dyan caught his eye—a second later, the gentleman flushed; letting his monocle fall, he turned to the lady beside him.

As he waited for Fiona to settle her skirts, Dyan looked down the table; Harriet met his saber-edged glance with an imploringly helpless look. Dyan swallowed a furious oath, and sat.

"Such a *pleasure*, Your Grace, to see you here." The lady on Dyan's left, a handsome woman with almost as much bosom on show as Fiona, leaned closer and smiled warmly. "I hadn't realized you were acquainted with the Brookes."

"Childhood acquaintances," Dyan informed her tersely, and turned to Fiona.

Only to discover a soup tureen in the way. She was helping herself, apparently concentrating. Finished, she held the ladle out to him, still refusing to meet his eyes. He reached for it—and caught it in midair; she'd let go before his fingers touched it. Frowning, Dyan helped himself to the thick oyster soup, then waved the footman away.

"Did you hear about the party old Rawlsley held at that manor of his in Sussex?"

The other guests, well ahead of the two of them, were spooning up the last of their helpings and starting on the next phase—tossing conversational balls about the table.

"Gillings said he'd pop up tomorrow—he had to stay in town until his wife retired to Gillings Hall."

By keeping his eyes on his plate, Dyan avoided the many waiting to capture his attention. Fiona, too, kept her eyes down. He shot her a sidelong glance; lashes decorously lowered, she sipped her soup. Looking back at his, Dyan frowned. What had happened in the hall?

Deaf to the conversations about them, Fiona breathed deeply, steadily, and ate her soup. And struggled to settle her nerves. Dyan's touch had jerked her back fifteen years—to that moment when he'd kissed her in the forest, and her world had stopped turning. Just a simple touch— and her knees had gone weak; she'd felt like crying for all her lost dreams, dreams that had come to nothing, that had turned to dust. Forcing the old memories into the deepest mental drawer she could find, she slammed it shut—there was no point letting their past torment her.

Gradually, a measure of calm returned; she could actually taste the soup.

Beside her, Dyan had been frowning at his, absent-mindedly stirring it; apparently reaching some decision, he lifted the spoon and sipped. "You're obviously as stubborn as ever." Glancing sideways, he caught her eye. "You're on some damned righteous crusade, aren't you?"

Fiona raised a haughty brow. "Better than a licentious one."

The riposte stopped him in his tracks—for all of half a minute. "Fiona, can I at least suggest—just introduce the idea to your mind—that Harriet might not be *quite* as innocent as you're supposing?"

Fiona's lips compressed; she fought to hold back her words, but they tumbled out, acid and tart. "You may suggest what you like, but I would hardly accept your word on the matter. I know you find it difficult to distinguish between a virtuous lady and a lightskirt."

Dyan's brows snapped together. "What the hell's that supposed to mean?"

Fiona shrugged. "You confused me with some wanton scullery maid years ago."

"What?!"

It was just as well the rest of the table were loudly enthusing over the dishes comprising the next course, which Sherwood and his helpers had just set forth. Fiona merely raised her brows and took another sip of her soup.

The turbulence to her left didn't abate, although Dyan lowered his voice. "I *never* confused you with anyone."

His words were harsh—and bitter. Dyan frowned ferociously and viciously stirred his soup. He'd never confused any other woman with Fiona. "What the *devil* are you talking about?"

He glanced up in time to see Fiona color delicately. She shot a brief glance his way, then looked down and carefully laid her spoon precisely in the center of her plate. "When you kissed me in the forest. You've probably forgotten."

Forgotten? Dyan stared at her. One didn't forget major turning points in life. He bit the words back; jaw clenching, he looked away. He had an exceptional memory, particularly when it came to Fiona. In the blink of an eye, he was reliving that scene in the forest—something he'd not allowed himself to do for over ten years. Nevertheless, it was easy to go back—to the clearing where they'd stopped to rest the horses after he'd deliberately lost Henry. Too easy to hear the hot words Fiona had heaped on his head the instant he'd released her and she'd been able to draw breath. *"Don't you dare confuse me with some wanton scullery maid!"* She'd paused, and looked briefly, expectantly, at him—stunned and stung, he'd simply stared back. Then she'd drawn a second breath, and a tirade had tumbled out—a scornful, scathing, hurtful denunciation. She had dismissed the incident, tarnishing it, rejecting what should have been—hell, *had been* to him—a glorious moment.

Dyan frowned; he glanced at Fiona. "I didn't think you were—or confuse you with—a maid. Or any other woman."

"Oh?"

Her haughty disbelief hit any number of nerves.

"No." The single syllable vibrated with suppressed fury. "I didn't."

A footman reached between them to clear their plates—Dyan looked away, ostensibly scanning the guests, in truth seeing nothing more than a blackly swirling haze. The old hurt was still there—unhealed, throbbing, and raw. He could still feel his shock, feel the totally unexpected pain. Taste the bitterness that had flooded him.

"Excuse me, Your Grace."

Fresh plates were laid before them; stiffly, her expression a polite mask, Fiona served herself from the already plundered dishes. With an effort, Dyan forced himself to do the same—he supposed he had to eat, or at least preserve the appearance.

"Here, my dear Miss Winton. Allow me." The gentleman on Fiona's right held a large platter for her inspection; Fiona rewarded him with a brief smile. As she made her selection, the gentleman's eyes strayed downward—an instant later he looked up, blinking dazedly. Dyan gritted his teeth—and jabbed his fork into a slice of roast beef.

Other gentlemen and ladies, too, were exceedingly helpful; Dyan blankly refused all invitations to interaction. Beside him, he felt the cool wall of Fiona's hauteur slide into place, deployed between her and any too-overt advances.

Sherwood hovered between them. "Wine, Your Grace?"

Dyan nodded curtly. Sherwood filled his glass, then Fiona's. She was still making her selections; as she finished with each dish, she slid it toward him. Grimly, Dyan piled food on his plate. From the corner of his eye, he saw Fiona lift her head and scan the table, then imperiously wave up one last dish. Eagerly, gentlemen reached to pass it to her; she smiled benignly and accepted it—then handed it wordlessly to him.

Frowning, Dyan received it; he looked in—pork in wine sauce. Fiona hated pork, but the dish was one of his favorites. With a grunt, he helped himself, glancing at her from under lowered brows. She was calmly eating—she didn't look his way; he wasn't sure she even realized what she'd done.

The simple act helped him get his temper back on its leash. Picking up his knife and fork, he growled through still-clenched teeth: "I didn't kiss you all those years ago because I thought you were some sort of loose woman."

Fiona slanted him a suspicious, slightly wary glance. "Why did you kiss me then?"

"Because I wanted to." Dyan sliced into the roast beef.

"Because I wanted to kiss *you*. Not just any woman, but *you*. Strangely enough, I thought you'd enjoy it—that I'd enjoy it."

"And did you?"

"The kiss, yes. The rest—no."

The rest—the words she'd heaped on his head, had used to flay him—was engraved on her heart. Watching him from beneath her lashes, Fiona shifted in her chair. Dyan never lied. He could bend the truth with the best of them, but he never directly lied. Lips compressed, she chased peas around her plate. "I thought . . . that you were just seizing opportunity." Without looking up, she shrugged. "That it was just because I was there—a willing female."

"*Not* so willing." A pregnant moment passed, then he said, his voice very low: "I *never* thought of you like that."

Her world was tilting on its axis; Fiona couldn't believe she'd read him so wrongly. Her stomach lurched, then sank; her heart contracted. Her mind rolled back through the years, through all her hopeful, hopeless dreams; gradually, she steadied.

She hadn't been wrong. She'd given him opportunity enough to tell her if he felt anything for her—had, indeed, all but asked him outright for a declaration, a clear statement that she wasn't just a wanton scullery maid to him, that she meant more to him than that. He hadn't made that statement—not then, nor at any subsequent time. She'd waited, telling herself she'd surprised him, asked for too much too soon. But she'd already been so far gone in love she hadn't been able to believe he, always the leader, was not; that he didn't feel for her as she did for him. So she'd waited through the years while he'd been away at Oxford; he hadn't even come home for the vacations. He'd been laying the foundations for his future career while she'd been deluding herself in Hampshire. But she'd learned the truth—*seen* the truth—when she'd gone up to town. Oh, no—she couldn't forget all her wasted years, the rivers of wasted tears. Lifting her head, she reached for her wineglass. "If you found it so enjoyable, I'm surprised you didn't seek to repeat the exercise."

"*After what you said?* I'd have had to don armor."

Fiona humphed and set down her glass. "You could at least have come up to me in London and said hello—not just nodded vaguely over a sea of heads."

"If you'd looked my way just once, I might have."

"*Once?*" Swivelling in her chair, Fiona stared at him. "*Once?* If I'd looked at you any more, a blind scandalmonger would have noticed!"

Dyan opened his mouth—Fiona held up a hand. "Wait!" She closed her eyes, like a seer looking into the future, only she was looking into the past. "Lady Morecambe, Mrs. Hennessy, and the Countess of Cranbourne." Opening her eyes, she glared at Dyan.

It took him longer to place them—three of his mistresses from that time—the Seasons both he and Fiona had been in London. Disconcerted, he snorted, and eyed her suspiciously. "How did you find out? Not from watching—I was never that obvious."

"*You* weren't—*they* were." Her expression mutinous, Fiona skewered a broiled shrimp. "They made themselves ridiculous, trying to hold your attention. So if *you'd* actually looked *my* way just once—"

"Heslethwaite, Phillips, Montgomery, Halifax, and, of course, Rusden—I can go on if you like."

Her most assiduous suitors. Turning, Fiona stared at him.

Narrow-eyed, Dyan met her gaze. "Why the hell did you think those ladies had to work so hard to hold my attention?" He spoke softly, through clenched teeth. "Because it was forever wandering. To *you*! When I think of the contortions I went through to hide it—"

"It would have been more to the point if you'd thought to look at me while I was looking at you." Shaken, Fiona swung back to her plate. "Well,"—she gestured wildly with her knife—"you could even have made the *huge* effort of crossing the floor and asking me to dance."

"What? Fight through the hordes to secure a place on your dance card?" Dyan snorted derisively. A moment later, he added: "Aside from anything else, I never got to balls early enough."

"You could have made an exception—made a real effort."

"Oh, undoubtedly—and set every gossipmonger's eyes alight. Just think—the notorious Lord Dyan Dare actually turning up to a ball early just to get his name on Lady Fiona Winton-Ryder's dance card. I can imagine what they'd have made of that."

Fiona sniffed disparagingly. "You could have paid a morning call—although I daresay you never even saw the mornings, having to recuperate from the nights before."

"My recuperative powers are rather stronger than you suppose. I don't, however, believe your parents would have appreciated a morning call from me. One whisper of that, and the gossip mill would have cranked with a vengeance. Besides—*if* you recall—I had every reason to believe my advances were unwelcome."

The undercurrent of bitterness in his tone was impossible to ignore; Fiona didn't believe him capable of manufacturing it. She bit her lip, and studied her half-empty plate. "I really didn't think you'd be that easily discouraged—not if you were in earnest."

Chest expanding as he dragged in a deep breath, Dyan sat back and reached for his wineglass. If they had the scene in the clearing to play again—and she said what she'd said then? He forced himself to consider it, to study her words as dispassionately as he could. Fifteen years on—so many women on—her words held a different ring. No, he was forced to concede, he wouldn't be discouraged—not now—understanding as he now did how women often reacted, their uncertainties and fears, the bees they sometimes got in their bonnets. But then? Slowly, he exhaled. "Well, I was."

He made the admission quietly, looking back down the years. He'd been seventeen, just getting into his stride with women. And Fiona had been . . . well, he'd always thought she'd been—would always be—his. He'd thought she'd welcome his advances. When she'd spurned him . . . *That* had been a blow from which he'd never quite recovered.

Frowning slightly, he shifted and set down his glass. A point that had forever puzzled him nagged for clarification. "Incidentally, what was that nonsense about you not being able to waltz? I taught you to waltz myself."

Fiona set down her knife and fork. Picking up a dish of sweetmeats, she turned and handed it to the gentleman on her right. Bemused, he took it. Fiona smiled encouragingly—and didn't turn back. Dyan, after all, had answered his own question. She couldn't waltz *because* he'd taught her.

All the other dances she'd managed perfectly well; none required the degree of physical contact—familiar contact—necessitated by the waltz. Luckily, she'd discovered her problem at a small, informal dance party before she'd made her come-out, where they'd been permitted to practice the waltz. When Dyan had taken her in his arms, she hadn't had the slightest problem; when her partner that night—a perfectly innocent young gentleman, brother of one of her friends—had tried to do the same, every muscle in her body had locked. Not from fright, but from a type of revulsion. She'd tried to fight the reaction and had ended by swooning. After that, she hadn't tried to waltz again. Her veto had driven her mother to distraction, but she'd held to it; she'd never waltzed with anyone but Dyan.

She could feel his gaze on her half-averted face—any second he would press for an answer. She glanced about, but the other diners, having finally accepted their disinterest, were all engrossed in their own conversations; there was no one free to rescue her. Fiona tried to ease the knots in her stomach—tried to breathe deeply enough to calm herself and think.

At the end of the table, Harriet stood; heaving an inward sigh of relief, Fiona grabbed her napkin and placed it by her plate.

Dyan frowned down the table at Harriet—her timing had always been woeful. To his experienced eye, she looked slightly tipsy, her inhibitions nicely softened by the heady wine she'd ordered served. Fiona, thankfully, had barely taken two sips.

Rising with the rest of the gentlemen, he drew out Fiona's chair. As she turned, he blocked her way. "For God's sake," he whispered, "develop a headache." He caught her eye—and poured all the emphasis he could into the instruction: *"Retire early."*

She studied his eyes, his face, clearly considering his words, and his motives.

Dyan opened his mouth to clarify both—

"My dear Miss Winton—I'm Lady Henderson."

Fiona's polite mask, all assured confidence, slid into place. As she smiled and shook hands with Lady Henderson, an older blonde, Dyan inwardly cursed. Forced to stand back, to let Fiona escape, he couldn't help wonder how long it would be before one of the guests realized that Fiona's innately gracious, lady-of-the-manor airs were just a little *too* assured for plain Miss Winton.

With a last, cool, noncommittal glance for him, Fiona fell in beside Lady Henderson; head high, she left the room. Beneath his breath, Dyan swore. Grimly, he resumed his seat.

And prayed that, for once in her life, Fiona would simply do his bidding.

CHAPTER 2

Fiona grasped the few minutes as the ladies milled in the hall to try to bring order to her suddenly chaotic thoughts. Only to conclude that making head or tail of them was presently beyond her—the only point of which she felt certain was that Dyan had interpreted her words in the clearing as rejection. Rejection—the dolt! How could he have been so blind? So deaf? *"Don't you dare confuse me with some wanton scullery maid,"* was what she'd said, having already heard of his exploits with at least two of the species. And then she'd waited—for him to reassure her that she was special to him. That she was his love, as he had been hers.

The stupid man hadn't said a word. He'd stared at her blankly, then let her pour her hurt scorn over him. *Then* he'd gone off to consort with countless beautiful women, as if to illustrate that she was nothing special to him.

And *then* he'd gone off adventuring in India and left her behind.

Well! What was she supposed to think?

The impulse to brood darkly on that point was almost overwhelming, but she hadn't forgotten she was here on a mission.

Realizing from some lady's startled glance that her lips were grimly set, Fiona forcibly relaxed them into a serene smile. She fell into line as the ladies trailed into the drawing room.

Pausing beyond the threshold, she scanned the room, noting the groups of ladies deploying about its gracious expanse. One group broke apart, laughing immoderately; the raucous note jarred on her ear. The wisest strategy seemed clear—deal with Henry's guests, protect Harriet, then retire gracefully at the appropriate time.

Then she could deal with Dyan.

"Excuse me, Miss Winton."

Fiona turned as Lady Henderson, who had been chatting with some other ladies, came up. Her ladyship—Fiona placed her in her forties—smiled, genuinely friendly. "You seem somewhat lost, my dear—I do hope you don't mind me mentioning it. Is it your first visit here?"

Supremely assured, Fiona smiled back. "Indeed no— I've known Henry and Harriet for . . . quite some time." Sherwood—she presumed at Dyan's behest—had concealed her identity; there seemed no reason to bruit it abroad. "But," she added, looking over the room again, "this is the first time I've attended one of these house parties."

Lady Henderson blinked. After a slight hesitation, she asked, "Pardon my curiosity, my dear, but do you mean the first time at Brooke Hall—or the *first time* altogether?"

The note of concern in her ladyship's voice drew Fiona's gaze back to her face. "I've attended many house parties, of course. But I have to admit this is the first of this . . ." she gestured airily, "ilk."

"Oh, dear." Her ladyship, concern clear in her face, stared at Fiona. Then she glanced across the room to where Harriet was holding forth by the chaise. "What *is* Harriet thinking of?" Looking back at Fiona, Lady Henderson placed a friendly hand on her arm. "My dear, if you truly are not . . ." With her other hand, she mimicked Fiona's earlier gesture. "In the way of things, then I would really not advise this as the place to start. The evening revels here can get quite . . . well, quite *deep*, if you take my meaning."

Despite not being "in the way of things," Fiona suspected she could. She looked across the room. "Perhaps I'd better speak with Harriet."

"Perhaps you had." Lady Henderson removed her hand. "But just so you know how things progress should you decide to join us, once the gentlemen return, we take about half an hour to choose our partner—or partners, if you decide on more than one. Then the games start. Sometimes there's a specific goal to begin with—like who can make a lady reach ecstasy first. But before very long, things just naturally evolve."

Again, her ladyship's hands came into play; Fiona, her expression studiously blank, nodded. "I see." Drawing a deep breath, she turned toward Harriet. "Thank you, Lady Henderson." With a regal nod, she glided away—straight to Harriet.

Whether or not Dyan was right about Harriet, retiring early, as he'd advised, *before* the gentlemen returned, would clearly be prudent. Fiona fetched up by Harriet's side.

"And then his lordship declared I was quite the best—" Harriet, highly animated, glanced up—and jumped. "Oh!" She paled, then smiled weakly at Fiona and gestured about the circle of ladies. "This is my dear friend, Miss Winton. Ah—" Eyes wide, Harriet scanned the room. "Pray excuse me, I must speak with Mrs. Ferguson." She swept the circle with a wavering smile, sent a startled glance at Fiona, and fled across the room.

Fiona watched her go through narrowing eyes.

"Miss Winton, I declare you must tell us all you know about Darke." A lady sporting a profusion of red ringlets laid a familiar hand on Fiona's arm.

Forsaking Harriet's retreating figure, Fiona fixed the lady with a decidedly cool glance. "Must I?"

"*Indeed* you must!" another of the laughing ladies assured her. "Harriet told us you know him better than she does, and, of course, here we always share." The lady smiled, archly coy. "You really must warn us—is he as *vigorous* as he appears?"

"Or even *half* as inventive as his reputation?"

"Does he prefer a slow waltz—or do his tastes run more to a gallop?"

The smile Fiona trained upon the circle of avid faces was a study in superiority. "I'm afraid," she murmured, her tone drawing on centuries of aristocratic forebears, "that there's been some mistake. *I* do not share." Her smile deepened fractionally; inclining her head, she smoothly moved away.

Leaving a stunned silence behind.

Fiona scanned the crowd—and saw Harriet's startled-rabbit face peeking out from behind an ample matron. Harriet promptly ducked; eyes narrow, lips firming, Fiona set out in pursuit.

She knew the routine of *ton*nish house parties to the minute; she had plenty of time before the gentlemen arrived. Time and more to catch Harriet and give her a piece of her mind, before retreat became imperative.

But Harriet didn't want to be caught. Shorter and slighter than Fiona, she used her status as hostess to flit from group to group. Disgusted with such craven behavior, Fiona gave up the chase. Sweeping around to head for the door, she spied Lady Henderson. On impulse, she stopped by her ladyship's side.

When her ladyship glanced her way and smiled, Fiona smiled, rather tightly, back. "I just had one question, Lady Henderson, if you would be so good as to humor me."

Her ladyship inclined her head and looked her interest.

"Who signed the invitation that brought you here?"

Lady Henderson's eyes opened wide. "Why, Harriet, of course. As usual."

Fiona's smile grew steely. "Thank you."

She turned to the door—

It opened, and the gentlemen streamed in.

. . .

Thanks to Henry, garrulously eager for his approval, Dyan was among the last to enter the drawing room. The first thing he did on crossing the threshold was scan the room; the second thing he did was swear, volubly if silently, his gaze fixed on Fiona, trapped at the center of a crowd of eager gentlemen.

Dyan gritted his teeth. Even if she'd come to her senses and swallowed her pride enough to take his advice, she wouldn't have expected them back so soon. Given the number of males present, it shouldn't have been possible to pass a decanter around in less than thirty minutes—so Henry had had three smaller decanters placed along the table. The guests had quaffed the wine—understandable, given its quality.

And so here they all were, back in the drawing room, blocking Fiona's retreat.

Disguising his interest in her, Dyan prowled idly down the long room, his heavy lids at half-mast, concealing the direction of his gaze. If Fiona had managed to slip away, he'd have followed; upstairs, in the seclusion of their rooms at the end of the wing, they could have sorted out what had really happened fifteen years before—and all that had, or hadn't, happened since. Instead, here she was, acting honeypot to a swarm of bees.

He shot her a glance as he drew level; she was looking down her nose at one impulsive gent—a Mr. Ferguson, if he remembered aright. Even from a distance, he could see the chill rising as she acidly requested Mr. Ferguson to remove his foot from her hem.

It was an old trick; Mr. Ferguson, startled, stepped back and looked down. Fiona smoothly turned, giving him her shoulder.

Dyan's lips twitched; his brows quirked as he continued his prowl. Lady Arctic had been Fiona's nickname among the more sporting rakes in town; it had been said no man could melt her ice—he'd die of frostbite first. Right now, Lady Arctic looked to be holding her own. He'd half a mind to retire and let her weather this alone.

Then again. Eyes narrowing, Dyan swung back, studying those gathered about Fiona.

"Your Grace!"

The title was still unfamiliar; it took Dyan a moment to recognize what the two ladies bearing down on him were after. Him.

"I was just speaking to Miss Winton," the possessor of myriad red ringlets informed him. "She quite sang your praises, my lord."

Dyan raised his brows. "Indeed?"

"Your efforts left her utterly prostrated, she said." The redhead leaned closer—any closer and she'd have pressed her breast to his arm.

"So we've come to offer our services in her stead." The second lady, a sultry brunette, drifted close; her musky perfume rose like a cloud—Dyan fought not to wrinkle his nose.

"I fear, madam, that I'm already spoken for." With a nod, he stepped aside and turned away.

"But you *can't* be!" the redhead protested. "You've only this minute walked into the room."

Dyan glanced back, cynically dismissive. "I'm here to consort with an old friend."

Leaving the two ladies whispering vituperatively, he strolled languidly on, not stopping until he'd reached a wing chair placed in one corner of the room. He lounged in its comfort, long limbs sprawling; a nearby ottoman caught his eye—he nudged it closer, then propped both booted feet, ankles crossed, upon it.

And fixed Fiona, on the opposite side of the room, with a dark and brooding gaze.

He needed to talk to her—fully intended to talk to her— but he was obviously going to have to wait until she learned the truth of Harriet's innocence the hard way.

Turning his head, he searched for Harriet and discovered her chatting blithely—too blithely—with a Lord Pringle. His lordship already had his arm about her waist. Well on the way. Inwardly shaking his head, Dyan looked away. Why on earth had the witless wanton painted herself to Fiona as an injured innocent? The outcome—the present imbroglio—was all too predictable. Fiona had always been a loyal friend, steadfast and true. A friend one could rely on, with a strong, very forthright character. It wouldn't have occurred to her to doubt Harriet's word.

"Might I interest you in a wager, Your Grace?"

Dyan glanced up—a well-developed blonde smiled seductively down at him. Deliberately, she leaned forward, bringing the ripe swells of her breasts to eye level.

"I'm sure," she purred, "that we could think up a most *satisfying* challenge—and an even more *satisfying* reward."

"I've been informed by my great-aunt that, having succeeded to the title, such endeavors are now beneath me." Dyan waved dismissively. "Something to do with my dignity."

His great-aunt Augusta might as well be useful for something; she had, indeed, made such a comment. Taken aback, the blonde blinked and straightened, then, seeing his gaze once more fixed across the room, tartly shrugged and walked off.

A shrill shriek cut through the rising hum; Dyan recognized it—so did Fiona. She stiffened. The glance she threw Harriet—an ice-bolt—should have transfixed her; their hostess, well away, clinging to Lord Pringle, didn't even notice.

Fiona's chin went up another notch; her expression turned a touch colder, a touch haughtier. His gaze fixed on her face, Dyan narrowed his eyes. Perhaps fate wasn't being unkind—with any luck, Fiona would be so incensed, so distracted by Harriet's perfidy, he'd be able to learn what he desperately wanted to know without being too obvious. Perhaps even without showing his hand.

"I declare, my lord, that my legs are quite *exhausted*." Artistically flicking a fan, a gorgeously arrayed brunette paused beside him, her large eyes greedily surveying his long frame. She licked her lips. "Perhaps I could—"

"No." Dyan spoke quietly, coldly. His fingers closed around the woman's elbow before she could swing about, her clear intention to plant her lush derriere in his lap. His eyes, cold and dark, trapped hers. "If your limbs have weakened so soon, dear lady, there are chairs by the wall. I suggest you avail yourself of one."

He withdrew his hand and his gaze, leaving her to retreat with whatever dignity she could muster. She left with a heated glare, but not a single word.

His expression growing grimmer, Dyan looked again at Fiona—at the gentlemen still surrounding her. Some, sensing the state of play, had drifted away; only the most determined remained. Four—four too many for Dyan's liking.

He'd studied the male company over the port; they were not of his circle; none were familiar. More importantly, they were not of the *haut ton*, the rarefied elite to which Fiona was accustomed.

She'd been presented at eighteen, and had instantly attracted the very best of attention. The most eligible gentlemen had flocked about her; she'd never lacked for suitors. Dyan's frown deepened; the single most important question he had for Fiona resonated in his head. Why hadn't she married Anthony, Marquess of Rusden, as he'd fully expected her to?

A quick shake of Fiona's head had him tensing. She turned from one gentleman, imperiously dismissive; the man frowned, hesitated, then strolled off. Three left. Dyan forced himself to relax—at least outwardly. Despite the Seasons she'd spent in London, he doubted Fiona would find her remaining suitors-for-the-evening quite so easy to dismiss. Her very presence would be interpreted as a declaration that she was available. Beneath his breath, Dyan swore. It was just as well he was here to haul her out when she got in over her head. Then she'd have to be grateful.

As well as distracted. Fleetingly, he raised his brows. Perhaps there was hope yet?

He wasn't, however, enjoying the situation. Another lady swanned close—he froze her with a glance. She quickly changed tack and swanned out of his sight. Dyan glowered at Fiona. He felt like a dog watching over a particularly juicy bone—or a wolf over a particularly bountifully endowed sheep.

Fiona saw his glower—and inwardly glowered back. Her face felt stiff, having been held in a distant, impassive expression for too long. She was beginning to wonder how much longer she could maintain it, along with her hold on her temper.

"You really need to relax, my dear Miss Winton." Sir Magnus Herring, on her left, inched closer. "A little flirting's so innocent."

Fiona fixed him with a severe glance. "That, my dear sir, is hardly my style." Earl's daughters didn't flirt, but she couldn't tell him that.

Sir Magnus inched closer; regally, Fiona waved the two would-be cicisbeos on her other side back and started to stroll. "A little fresh air would be more to my liking." The French windows behind Dyan's chair were open to the terrace and the soft shadows of the evening outside.

Not that she had any intention of setting foot on the terrace. She was heading for Dyan. He might be annoyed enough to look like a human thundercloud, a reincarnation of Thor, the god of war and lightning, his dark hair falling, rakishly dangerous, over his forehead, his eyes dark and stormy—but for her, he represented safety, security; he wouldn't let her down.

Her three encumbrances clung like barnacles as she glided over the parquetry. She was used to dismissing unwanted advances—Mr. Moreton and Mr. Coldthorpe she was sure she could handle. Sir Magnus was a model cut from a different cloth. A bluffly genial, heavily built, and handsome man, he was, she sensed, used to success.

He wasn't going to accept failure easily.

She'd blocked a score of his subtle advances, turned aside a host of glib propositions—and still he persisted.

"Perhaps," he murmured, holding fast by her side, head bent so the others couldn't hear, "we could view the moon together, my dear? Moonlight, they say, can have a quite liberating effect on a lady's passions."

Fiona met his warm gaze with a blank look. "There's no moon tonight." There would be, but much later; she doubted Sir Magnus would know.

The chagrin that showed fleetingly in his pale eyes said he didn't; the flash of something else Fiona glimpsed—an almost grim determination—brought Lady Henderson's timetable forcibly to mind.

She looked ahead—and saw a band of ladies—the red-head, two brunettes, and two blondes—descend, in a froth of silken skirts, on Dyan.

Fiona blinked. Then, plastering a bright smile on her lips, she headed for the melee. She swept up as Dyan, scowling blackly, was fending off two females by main force.

"Enjoying yourself, my lord?"

Her cool query, ringing as it did with the assurance of old friendship, made all five women pause. Dyan grasped the moment to set aside his two tormentors. "As always, my dear." Carefully, he reset his cuffs.

The undercurrents between them ran deep; they always had. Mr. Moreton and Mr. Coldthorpe, the hopelessness of their cause evident, opted for second best. With glib and ready charm, they moved in on the disappointed ladies.

Lady Henderson had been right—all the ladies, some with last, disgruntled glances at Dyan, accompanied by Mr. Moreton and Mr. Coldthorpe, headed off to join the large group of couples gathering at the center of the room.

Sir Magnus did not follow. He studied Dyan, still lounging with no overt show of interest, then turned to Fiona, and smiled. "Well, my dear, shall we?" He lifted a suggestive brow. "Would you rather the terrace or are the bright lights more to your liking?"

Fiona raised her brows. "Neither holds any appeal."

Sir Magnus's smile deepened. "Ah, but you see, you really must choose." With a nod, he indicated Dyan stretched beside her. "I rather think it's me—or Darke." His teeth flashed; smoothly, he slid an arm about Fiona's waist. "Now tell me—which would you rather?"

Fiona froze—literally. Her spine locked; every muscle in her limbs clenched. Her gaze, cold before, turned as chill as hoarfrost. When she spoke, her words froze the very air. "You are mistaken."

Watching, even Dyan fought back a shiver. He had never seen Lady Arctic in action. Knowing Fiona as he did, he could hardly credit the transformation—but he recognized the look in Sir Magnus's eyes instantly.

Braving the ice, Sir Magnus leaned closer. "I don't believe you understand, my dear." Teeth clenched, presumably to stop them chattering, he spoke softly. "You have no choice *but* to make a choice."

Dyan didn't think—he reacted; the next instant, Fiona was safe in his lap. He met Sir Magnus's surprised gaze over Fiona's curls. "Unfortunately, Herring," he drawled, settling his arms comfortably about Fiona's waist, "it's you who have, as Miss Winton said, made a mistake." A languidly bored expression on his face—and a fell warning in his eyes—he smiled urbanely at Sir Magnus. "Miss Winton and I made our choices long before we arrived tonight."

Sir Magnus's face set. He hesitated, looking down on them. Safe in Dyan's lap, Fiona looked coldly ahead and refused to even glance at Sir Magnus, leaving him with no option but to accept defeat. With a curt nod, he turned and strode away, toward the congregation at the room's center.

The instant he moved off, Fiona drew a long breath. *"Well!"* Incensed, she glared after him. "Of all the *coxcombs*—"

She'd always had a good line in tirades. Dyan listened with half an ear; she was as incensed as he could have wished.

"It's outrageous! What sort of friends are these for Henry and Harriet? Old Lady Brooke would turn in her grave! That hussy with the red hair and the blonde in the green—do you know what they asked me?"

The question was rhetorical; Fiona didn't pause for an answer but swept straight on.

Leaving Dyan to consider the sight of her, the feel of her, as she sat across his thighs, his arms loosely about her, and railed at the company. She was distracted, certainly; she was also relaxed—with no hint of the frigid rigidity that had attacked her the instant Sir Magnus had touched her.

Experimentally, Dyan tightened his arms; she shifted within them, but otherwise didn't seem to notice. He raised his brows, and pondered, then grasped her waist and lifted her, ostensibly settling her more comfortably in his lap.

She threw an absentminded frown his way, but didn't even focus on him. She didn't so much as pause for breath—her tirade continued unbroken.

As the weighted heat of her seeped through his breeches, Dyan gritted his teeth. Lady Arctic wasn't freezing him. Far from it.

He let her ramble while he toyed with that discovery. And considered how it fitted with her past. The next time she paused for breath, he asked: "Why didn't you marry?"

Startled, she looked at him.

He raised his brows, his expression as innocent as he could make it. "I was sure you'd accept Rusden."

So sure, he'd gone to India. He'd met Tony, an old and valued friend in White's; Tony had been bubbling over with his news. He'd come from Coldstream House; he'd made a formal offer for Fiona's hand and was waiting for the summons to return. For Fiona to accept him. No one, least of all Tony, had doubted that she would. He had already succeeded to his father's estate; as a Marquess, he could offer Fiona far more than most others, and she'd made it clear she approved of his company. She'd always had a bright smile for easygoing Tony.

Which was a great deal more than she'd bestowed on Dyan.

He'd been at White's to meet with a merchant trader keen to find a partner to finance a venture in India. The trader had got more than he'd bargained for—a partner, but not a silent one.

He'd left for India on the next tide.

And had never, in his infrequent letters to his brother, asked about Fiona—never asked about the children he imagined she would have with his good friend Tony.

Fiona shrugged and looked down at her hands, loosely clasped in her lap. With Dyan so close, it was easy to remember those lonely days in London, when she'd finally closed the door on her youthful hopes. Witnessing him and his ladies, she'd been forced to concede she had no future with him. So she'd done the right thing and considered her earnest suitors—Anthony, Marquess of Rusden, had been the outstanding candidate. Remembering Tony, and his easy smile, Fiona shook her head. "He was too nice."

"Too nice?"

Too nice for her to marry—to let him give her his heart, without having anything to give in return. That had been the definitive moment when she'd finally accepted the truth. She'd given her heart away long ago—it was no longer hers to give. She hadn't been able to offer any softer emotion, not even sincere wifely duty. Her unfailing re-action to any man touching her, especially with amorous intent, had made marrying a man who required an heir an impossibility. So she'd refused Tony as gently as she could, turned her back on marriage, and come home to be her brother's chatelaine. Fiona shrugged. "My parents died soon after, so I had Coldstream to manage—you know Edmund couldn't do it on his own."

His gaze locked on her face, Dyan drew a slow, even breath. Edmund was going to have to learn.

Fiona drew breath and straightened, then leaned back against his shoulder. After an instant's hiatus, she softened, and sank against it. Against him. Dyan only just squashed the impulse to close his arms fully about her. Her fingers trailed across his arms; he forced himself to remain still.

From their long-ago past in London, he let his mind roll forward through the years, through the inglorious, notorious events of his life. Through all the loneliness. All sprang from the loss of Fiona from his life. Even his characteristic wildness was driven by a sense of incompleteness—a void that had come into being fifteen years ago.

And now? Now he was jaded—he'd drunk of life's well until it was dry. He no longer felt anything—unless it be a mild distaste—for the perfumed bodies so readily offered him. He could walk away from it all—from the women, the adventures—without a backward glance. Indeed, he'd already done so, which was why he was here.

Here—searching for his elusive something. Who he'd discovered in the Brookes' front hall. And who was presently warming his lap.

He focused on Fiona, although he couldn't see her face; his senses reached for her, wrapped around her. In glee, in joy, in a giddy rush of lust—and something far more powerful. His feelings for her were not jaded at all; they sprang from a different well.

She was different. She'd always occupied a special place in his life, the only woman of his generation he'd dealt with person to person, intellect to intellect, heart to heart. She'd been the only woman in his life fifteen years ago—she was still the only one.

Dyan felt her topmost curls, soft as down, against his jaw. And wondered how to tell her.

The fact that she was sitting on a man's lap, his thighs hard beneath her, his arms loosely but quite definitely about her, his shoulder and chest a pillow behind her, took some time to seep into Fiona's mind. And when it did, along with a nagging niggle that she really should stand up—Sir Magnus was long gone and there was no overt danger to excuse her seeking shelter in Dyan's arms—she promptly dismissed it. The man in question was, after all, Dyan—and she was still in Harriet's drawing room, a place she no longer considered safe without close escort.

Besides, she felt comfortable—safe, secure, and pleasantly warm.

Precisely how warm she felt, how relaxed and at ease, how much she was luxuriating in the sense of rightness that held them—that knowledge unfurled slowly, a dawning revelation.

And when it finally burst upon her that she was not rigid, not frigid, that the vise that normally locked her every muscle was simply not active, the answer seemed obvious. This was Dyan, her one and only love, although she'd never acknowledged that except in her heart. She never reacted that way when he touched her. Through the years, they'd wrestled, fought, shared saddles—she'd never frozen at his touch, as she did with every man but him.

Her senses, fully alive, it seemed, for the first time in fifteen years, registered the heat of him, the steely strength surrounding her, the subtle scent of sandalwood. Without conscious thought, she shifted, sinking deeper into his light embrace. The swell of her hip slid over his thighs; her leaping senses registered the hard ridge now pressed against her.

Her breath caught; for an instant, she thought she might freeze. Instead, a warm flush spread through her, insinuating heat just beneath her skin. A tingle of excitement skittered along awakening nerves. Her lungs abruptly resumed their proper function, a little faster than before.

Fiona blinked. And considered an unexpected prospect.

Despite the fact she'd stopped listening, she was aware that the tone of the evening's entertainment had turned overtly salacious. Bordering on the shocking. Then again, none of the guests knew who she was. And Dyan was here, holding her in his lap, holding everyone else at bay.

The unlooked-for prospect teased and tantalized. Dyan hadn't married; the county grapevine had already spread that news. Was she game to seize opportunity and, even if only for one night, take what she'd always felt should be hers?

She took precisely one minute to make up her mind.

Lips firming, Fiona sat up and twisted about to face Dyan. Halfway through the maneuver, punctuated by a *sotto voce* curse from him, a familiar shriek made her glance up.

She froze.

With shock.

"*My God*! Just *look* at Harriet!" Fiona's eyes flew wide. "Great heavens! How *can* she? And where's—"

Dyan kissed her—much as he'd kissed her fifteen years before. His lips closed over hers—more confident, perhaps, more assured; Fiona felt a funny lick of heat unfurl and flick in her belly.

Then he drew back.

"—Henry got to?" Fiona frowned at Dyan. "Why did you do that?" Had her thoughts somehow shown in her face?

His expression studiously innocent, his eyes veiled by his long lashes, Dyan answered truthfully. "To see if you tasted the same." Did sweet innocence have a taste? He rather thought it did.

Fiona frowned harder. "And did I?"

Dyan smiled. "Yes, and no. Just as fresh, but . . ." His lids lifted; he trapped her gaze with his. "Sweeter." He leaned closer, his gaze dropping to her lips. "Riper."

When his lips closed over hers again, Fiona fought

down a shivery sigh. It was surprisingly easy to sink into his arms, into his kiss—then again, she'd long ago given up physically fighting Dyan. He was too strong; right now, she reveled in that strength, discovered a whole new aspect of the characteristic as he drew her deeper. Deeper into his arms, until they locked, steel bands, about her; deeper into his kiss, so that she forgot where she was, forgot who she was, forgot everything beyond the subtle pressure of his lips, the artful caress of his tongue as it swept her lower lip.

She had no idea why she parted her lips; it simply seemed the right thing to do. When he surged within, she stilled, then quivered as excitement gripped her. He slowed, but his languid possession never faltered; deep inside her, embers glowed. Caught in the game, she tentatively returned the caress—and felt, unmistakably, the rush of desire that surged through him.

Muscles that were already hard became harder; he shifted, turning and drawing her down beside him, so they were locked together in the chair, breast to chest, his hips to her thighs. Fiona wasn't about to protest. This time, she wasn't going to ask him if he loved her. This time, she wriggled her arms free, twined them about his neck and kissed him back with a fervor no wanton scullery maid could possibly command.

Dyan took all she had to give, drank it in—wallowed in the heady taste of her. Her flagrant encouragement prompted him to deepen the kiss; a minute later, he swept one hand up her side, then closed it gently over her breast. And felt the jolt of passion that rocked her, heard her soft moan. Her nipple hardened to a pebble against his palm; he felt confident in interpreting that, too, as incitement.

So he stroked, and fondled.

She responded with an ardency that nearly stole his mind.

His fingers were drifting to the closures of her gown, eager to release her abundant charms to all his senses, before he recalled precisely where they were. Although he'd swung her around so she was shielded from the room by his body—and the room was shielded from her—Harriet's drawing room was no place for a seduction.

At least, not this seduction.

Intent on removing to a place of greater privacy, he drew back.

At precisely that instant Harriet's unrestrained shriek lanced through the room.

It startled them both. He, however, recognizing the tone, knew better than to look. Unfortunately, before he could stop her, Fiona, eyes wide, peeked over his shoulder.

Her jaw dropped; her eyes grew even wider—then wider still. Glued to the spectacle, she tried to speak—but no words came out.

Reluctantly, Dyan glanced over his shoulder; it was, if anything, even worse than he'd expected. With a not-so-muffled curse, he shoved the ottoman aside, stood, then scooped Fiona up into his arms.

She clung to him readily, twining her arms about his neck. She was still too shocked to speak, her face blank, as if she hadn't yet decided on her expression. Dyan didn't wait for her decision; he strode to the door to the terrace, mercifully ajar. Shouldering it fully open, he swung Fiona through and headed around the house to the library.

As he'd expected, that room had been prepared for the use of guests; its French doors stood wide. Fiona's breasts swelled mightily as he pushed into the room. *"Did you see . . . ?"* Her expression was horrified.

"Unfortunately, yes." Dyan's jaw set. "Just forget it." He crossed the candlelit room swiftly, pausing in the shadows of the open main door to scan the front hall. It was empty.

"Forget? How can I possibly forget seeing Harriet like that?"

An unanswerable question. "Sssh." His eyes on the drawing-room door, through which the sounds of the orgy they'd just escaped clearly permeated, Dyan strode, as silently as his bootheels allowed, across the tiled hall. To his relief, Fiona held her fire until he'd climbed the stairs.

"And where the devil was Henry?" she demanded.

Up the redhead. Thankfully, engrossed with Harriet's misdemeanors, Fiona had missed seeing that.

"How *could* they?" she asked—and looked at him as if he ought to know.

Dyan narrowed his eyes. "Strange to tell," he said, as he swung down the long corridor leading to their rooms, "there's a certain code of behavior us rakes-of-the-first-order abide by." The scene he'd glimpsed before they'd left the drawing room replayed in his mind; jaw firming, he shot Fiona an affronted glare. "If you're harboring any notion that I ever behaved like that, forget it. I may have indulged in my share of wild antics, but my standards preclude public performances."

She humphed, but seemed to accept his reassurance, just as she'd accepted him carrying her all this way. Knowing Fiona, it was safer to carry her—that way, she could only argue, not try to elude him and mount any action on her own. He couldn't see any reason to put her down. Yet.

"They're married," she stated as they neared their rooms. Her tone rang with matriarchal disapprobation—it would have done credit to his great-aunt Augusta. "They've two beautiful children asleep in the nursery." A gesture indicated the floor above. "How *can* they behave like that—consorting with others openly? Don't they have any pride?"

When he made no answer, she humphed, and tightened her hold about his neck. "I can't understand it."

Dyan decided she was right—he couldn't understand it either. But he was no longer concerned with Henry, or Harriet, or what they were getting up to in the drawing room. His predator's soul had finally sighted his ultimate target—he was about to seize it.

Fiona was the solution to all his problems—his relatives, his great-aunt Augusta—and even more importantly, the wild restlessness in his soul. She'd filled that need before—provided an anchor, a focus for his passions. She would do so again.

It was time—past time—he melted Lady Arctic.

"Hypothetically speaking," he said, "if we married, would you be faithful?"

The wary frown Fiona slanted him was not what he'd expected. "I'd consider it," she eventually replied.

Stopping outside her door, Dyan frowned back. "What's to consider?"

"If," Fiona said, sticking her nose in the air, "you would reciprocate in like vein."

"And if I would?"

She smiled and lightly shrugged. "What's to consider?"

Dyan grinned. Wolfishly. "So will you?"

Fiona's frown returned. "Will I what?"

"Marry me."

Her heart leapt; Fiona fought to calm it. He was teasing her—he couldn't possibly be serious. Not here. Not now. Not like this. She narrowed her eyes at him. "Dyan, I am not going to marry you just so you can get your great-aunt Augusta out of your house."

He sighed. Deeply. She felt it all the way to her toes. "All right." He juggled her in his arms. "But you will remember I asked, won't you?"

With that, he walked on—to the door next to hers. His. Fiona's frown dissolved into blank astonishment. "What are you doing?"

Dyan opened the door, walked in, then kicked it shut behind them. He looked down at her. "Seducing you."

CHAPTER 3

"Dyan—" Beyond that, Fiona couldn't think what to say. Her earlier thoughts of claiming her due returned with a vengeance, but *she'd* intended to direct the enterprise, not the other way about. She'd run in his harness too often not to know how dangerous that could be. She tried a frown. "Stop funning."

His brows rose. "Funning?" He held her gaze for an instant, then hefted her in his arms and strode forward. "The fun, Lady Arctic, has not yet begun."

Lady Arctic? "What—?" Alerted by the glint in his dark eyes, Fiona looked ahead. The room was lit by a single candle, helpfully left on the bedside table. Its flickering flame only partially illuminated the quilted expanse of satin coverlet spread over the massive bed. With said bed drawing rapidly nearer, she didn't look further. "Dyan— this is silly. You don't want to seduce me."

"I've wanted to seduce you for fifteen years."

Fiona stared at him. "Rubbish! You went to India, remember?"

Fleetingly, his eyes met hers. "I left on the day your engagement to Tony was supposed to be announced."

Fiona blinked. "You left . . ." She studied the harsh, tanned planes of his face. "But I didn't accept Tony."

Dyan stopped by the side of the bed. His heavy lids lifted; the expression in his eyes stole her breath. "When

I think of the tortures I endured, imagining you in his arms, in his bed . . . swollen with his child."

The planes of his face shifted as he grimaced. "I should have known better."

He tossed her on the bed.

Fiona shrieked. Dyan followed her down, landing half beside her, half over her. Fiona struggled, totally ineffectually, to hold him back. He ignored her efforts; one hard thigh trapped hers. Deliberately, he leaned into her, his weight pressing her into the bed, anchoring her beneath him. He didn't bother with her hands but instead framed her face.

And kissed her.

No gently savoring kiss, but a commanding, demanding incitement—a ravishing challenge—tempting in the fire it offered, tantalizing in its sensual promise. His lips were hard, hungry, ruthlessly insistent. It took no more than two heartbeats for Fiona to react. Winding her arms about his neck, she kissed him back.

Fervently. With all the long-denied ardor in her soul.

She wanted him—she could hardly miss the fact that he wanted her. For now—for tonight—that was enough. He'd spoken already of marriage; she wasn't so innocent she didn't know they hadn't reached the end of that discussion. But such matters—and all others—could be left until the morrow.

Tonight she would be what she'd always longed to be.

His.

Dyan didn't wait for any further encouragement. Drawing his hands from her face, he deepened the kiss, locking her lips apart so he could plunder unrestricted. His weight held her immobile; he had no intention of doing the gentlemanly thing and easing back. Instead, he set his hands skimming over the smooth skin of her upper arms to her delicately molded shoulders, partially covered by the tiny silk sleeves of her dress. The interference registered, but he wasn't yet ready to deal with that; his first priority was to fully appreciate the sensation of her silk-clad body, all soft womanly curves, trapped and yielding beneath him.

Sensual gratification was a wondrous thing.

He let his mind absorb the impact of her lush breasts, soft stomach, rounded hips, and delightfully firm thighs, as well as the length of her long, slender legs. Only then did he set his hands moving again, deliberately tracing those selfsame curves.

Her breasts filled his hands—and more. Their softness firmed at his touch. He kneaded, then went searching, capturing each nipple, rolling them to tight, aching buds.

Her breath hitched; she pressed her head back into the bed, breaking their kiss. Dyan shifted his attention to the long curve of her throat, exposed like an offering. Her breathing stuttered as his roving tongue found one pounding pulsepoint; he laved it, then sucked lightly and felt her melt—just slightly—beneath him.

Inwardly, he grinned devilishly. She was going to melt a great deal more. He released her breasts and let his hands quest further, fingers widespread, tracing her ribs, then the sides of her waist, his thumbs following her midline. When his thumbs reached her navel, she arched lightly beneath him, her hips lifting wantonly against him.

Dyan grinned in earnest; he let his lips drift lower, to pay homage to the ripe swell of her breasts exposed above her low neckline. Simultaneously, he slid both hands lower—and lower—tracing her body all the way to her knees. Then he reversed direction.

His thumbs came to rest in the hollow between her thighs; he rotated them, one just above the other.

Fiona's startled gasp filled the room. Driven by the sound, Dyan caught the fine silk of her neckline with his teeth and tugged it down; one tightly pearled nipple slipped free of the confining bodice. He fell on it—hotly— swirling his tongue about the ruched peak, then drawing it into his mouth to taste, to suckle, to torment.

The muted scream Fiona gave was music to his ears. Her fingers, on his shoulders, flexed, then sank deep. She arched, offering herself to him in flagrant invitation.

Dyan tormented her some more.

Long before he dragged the silk from her other breast, and tortured that nipple as he had its mate, Fiona was convinced she would soon lose her mind. Surely women didn't normally have to withstand this . . . this heated torture—not every time they mated. How could they?

Her wits were whirling, her mind awash with sensations: from the hardness of his hands locked about the tops of her thighs, to the heavy weight of him—so peculiarly welcome—to the heat that welled within her, washing through her, in response to the heat of his lips, his mouth, his tongue. He was hot, too—she could feel the heat of him wherever they touched. His clothes muted the sensation; if they were removed, his skin would scald her.

The thought made her shiver; his rotating thumbs pressed deeper and she shuddered, then gasped. Of its own volition, her body arched, offering. One thumb slid still deeper and pressed, then caressed—her breathing stopped, then started on a fractured, shuddering, almost silent moan.

His hands left her, his weight anchoring her completely once more as he lifted his head and recaptured her lips.

His fingers busy with the closures of her gown, Dyan spared a moment to consider the next phase. Still kissing her, he opened his eyes and checked the light—it wasn't good. When he bared her, he wanted to see her clearly. Half shadows would not suffice. Evocatively plundering her soft mouth, tempting her to match him and meet him, he skated through his recent memories; there were candlesticks on the mantelpiece.

Accepting the inevitable—given he was not about to accept anything less than the ultimate experience tonight—he drew back from their kiss.

He looked down at her—she was panting only slightly. When he saw her eyes gleam beneath her lashes, he trapped her gaze in his. "I'm going to get up for a moment. *Don't move.*"

Enforcing his edict with a warning look, he levered away from her, then sat up and got to his feet.

There was another single candlestick and a three-armed candelabra on the mantelpiece. Dyan lit the candles, then quickly positioned furniture about the bed. One single candle on either side and the candelabra at the end threw an acceptable amount of light upon the coverlet. Upon Fiona, still lying as he'd left her, a dazed expression in her hazel eyes, her lips swollen from his kisses.

The sight sent a surge of sheer lust through him; Dyan shackled it, trapped it—he'd let it loose later. First, he was going to sate his senses—all his senses—in enjoyment, in the sheer pleasure of enjoying her.

Shrugging off his coat, he flung it on a chair and returned to the bed.

Sitting on its edge, he removed his boots and stripped off his stockings. Turning his head, he caught Fiona frowning at the candelabra. Inwardly grinning, he clambered back on the bed.

As he settled beside her, one hand going to her waist, then sliding around to the laces along her side, Fiona transferred her frown to him. "Is this to be some kind of exhibition?"

Dyan toyed with various replies while his fingers loosened her laces; he finally settled for: "More like a demonstration." Flicking the last knot undone, he trapped her gaze. "Consider it a learning experience."

He was going to learn her—all there was to know of her. Tonight he'd know her on every possible plane.

Fiona studied the dark blue of his eyes, and could see nothing beyond brutal candor. He might be teasing her, just a little, but . . . Then he shifted, his weight trapping her again, his hands rising to tug the tiny puffed sleeves of her gown down—and she saw the reason for the light. "Dyan, I don't think the candles are such a good idea."

She tried to catch the sleeves, but her dress, which she'd surreptitiously hiked back up, was steadily moving down.

"First lesson," Dyan said, his gaze fastening on her freed breasts, concealed only by her tissue-thin chemise. "You don't think. That's my role—you stick to yours and we'll get on just fine."

The gravelly note in his voice, the heat in his eyes, roaming her barely veiled body as he drew her gown down, set desire coiling insidiously through Fiona. She caught her breath—and wasn't at all sure she'd done the right thing in not resisting. She'd remained on the bed because she hadn't believed her legs would support her, because she'd known Dyan's reflexes were lightning fast and he would catch her long before she reached the door. And because she'd wanted, beyond anything else, to be his tonight.

She suddenly realized she didn't have any real idea of what being his entailed. Not to him. "Ah—" She had to moisten her lips before she could ask, "My role—what's that?"

The answer came back so quickly her head whirled. "To *feel.*" The deep purr of his voice slid under her skin and vibrated through her bones. Drawing her gown free of her legs, he tossed it aside and turned to her, his hands sliding up her body, his touch laden with possessiveness, his eyes no less so. He cupped her breasts; Fiona lost her breath.

"To lose every inhibition you ever had."

His eyes glinted darkly as he surveyed what he held, then they flicked up to hers. Deliberately, holding her gaze, he lowered his head—and licked; first one aching nipple, then the other; long, slow licks that dampened the thin silk and left it clinging. He observed the effect with transparent satisfaction.

Then, lowering his long body to hers, he kissed her deeply, until her head spun and her senses whirled. He ended the kiss and waited, his lips a mere whisker from hers, his breath another form of caress. When Fiona caught up with reality, his hands had left her breasts to slide beneath her, cupping her bottom. As she made that discovery, he gripped her and lifted her, tilting her into intimate contact with the rigid length of his staff.

Deliberately, he rocked against her, the heavy fullness riding between her thighs, over her mound and across her taut belly.

"To do everything I ask," he breathed against her parted lips. "To be *everything* to me."

Fiona hauled in a desperate breath. "Dyan—"

"Stop arguing."

She had to, because he was kissing her. Quite when it was she gave up all resistance, Fiona couldn't have said—the whirling, swirling maelstrom Dyan called forth was beyond her strength to fight. It came from him—it also came from her. A deep, compelling desire to be one, to shed the outer, peripheral trappings that society placed between them—not just their clothes, but their inhibitions as well—to lose themselves in the vortex, each holding the other fast, relying on the other to give all that they needed, to assuage the driving, inchoate desire—the desire to know and be known.

As simple as that, and even more powerful.

When Dyan drew her chemise from her, Fiona was ready to let it go. She was a-simmer, her skin heated and skittering, aching for his touch. When it came, bare hand to bare skin, she gasped and held him closer. Their lips met as his hands roamed—and he learned all he would.

Naked on the satin coverlet, her hair loose, a silk pillow about her head, she wantonly let him touch her—as he would, where he would. She parted her thighs and let him stroke her, probe her, tease her. Until her body ached with urgent longing, a mass of overheated skin and straining, overstretched nerves—of slick heat fueled by some inner furnace his relentless caresses ignited. And when his knowing fingers called the constellations crashing down upon her, leaving her waltzing with the stars, her body arched, bowed, and ached—for him.

He left her only briefly; when he returned, she'd regained enough wit to register his nakedness. Enthralled, she would have stopped him, held him back so she could admire the lean length of him, the heavy muscles banding his chest, the taut, ridged abdomen, narrow hips, and long, strong legs. And the flagrant maleness gilded in the candles' golden light—fiercely strong, rampantly male, urgently possessive.

She would have taken time to absorb it all, but he was in no mood to dally. His face hard, set, the dark planes etched with desire, he brushed her questing hands aside and came to her, lowering his body directly upon hers, nudging her parted thighs wider so his hips settled between. As she slid her arms about him, reaching as far as she could to hold him close, Fiona understood. She tipped her head back and he took her lips, her mouth, instantly; he was ravenous.

He felt as hot as the sun, and as loaded with primal energy, his every muscle heavy with it, sinews taut and tight.

Pressing beneath her, his hands slid down the long planes of her back, down over her hips, then fastened, his grip firm and strong, fingers sinking into the softness of her bottom.

Again, he lifted her, tilted her. This time when he rocked, he pressed into her.

Fiona tried to gasp but couldn't; as she felt the thick, steely strength of him invade her, stretch her, she tried to pull back from their kiss.

Dyan wouldn't let her. He held her trapped with his kiss, held her immobile with his hands—and relentlessly, inch by steady inch, claimed her.

Fiona shuddered, and gave herself to him—opened her arms and held him tight, opened her body and let him come in, opened her heart and let him take possession of what had, for so long, been his.

She was so hot, so slick, so *tight*—Dyan had to devote every last ounce of his considerable control to holding himself back. He felt the resistance of her maidenhead; a second later, it vanished. She remained so softly pliant beneath him, so welcoming, he wasn't sure she'd even felt it. He surged deeper—and felt her instinctively rise. He pushed deeper still, then slowly withdrew, then returned, more strongly, more forcefully. Filling her.

She took him—took him in, scalding him with her wet heat, with the inner furnace of her desire. Beneath him, she rose to each thrust, her breasts caressing his chest, her thighs cradling his hips, her long legs tangling with his. He set a slow rhythm—he saw no need to rush; her body was a heaven he wanted to savor for all time. He used his tongue to teach her the beat; once she caught it, he drew back from their kiss and, straightening his arms, held himself over her.

So he could see her—see her in all her glory, totally, wantonly his. See her breasts rock with his thrusts, the sheening ivory skin delicately flushed, rose-red nipples engorged, erect. See her hands, clutching spasmodically, fingers sinking into his forearms as he plunged deeper and pushed her higher. See, looking down, the gentle swell of her belly, taut with desire as he filled her deeply, completely. See the fine thatch of bronzy hair that veiled her soft center merge with his darker curls.

See the ridged length of him, slick and gleaming with her wetness, thick and heavy and hard as oak, slide, again and again, into the hot heaven that was her.

And, at the last, see the mindless wonder infuse her face as her body clenched around him and ecstasy took her.

The gentle ripples of her climax gradually died; her breathing slowed. Her features relaxed; her hands fell from his arms as she drifted into paradise.

Dyan looked his fill, then closed his eyes, let his head

fall back, and, with three deep thrusts and a long, shuddering sigh, joined her.

She was his.

She woke to the sensation of the sheet sliding away, to the cool caress of night air on recently flushed skin. Lifting her weighted lids was an effort; the candles had guttered—the room was in darkness, except for the wide swath of moonlight lancing in through the uncurtained window. It fell across the bottom half of the bed, illuminating the rumpled sheets, sheening the folds of the crumpled satin coverlet, and revealing two pairs of legs.

Hers, skin white and pearlescent in the silvery glow; and his, darker, rougher, long muscles etched in shadow. As she watched, his legs shifted, sliding over hers.

In the same instant, the sheet whisked away completely, slithering over the side of the bed. Hard hands replaced it—hot, urgent, and demanding—roving her skin, every curve of her body, possessively claiming, stroking, stoking her furnace again.

He shifted her onto her back and surged over her, covering her; his body, hard, rigid, taut with sexual promise, settled heavily on hers. His lips captured hers in the same moment; the embers of their earlier passion flared, then caught flame.

She felt the fire rise, felt the conflagration take her, cindering the last remnants of inhibition, leaving her heated and panting—wantonly, recklessly his. As his lips left hers, streaking fire down her throat before moving on to her naked breasts, to her nipples tight with yearning, she gasped—the only thought her reeling mind could grasp. "Again?"

"And again." He took one aching nipple deep into his mouth; when he released it, it ached even more. "You've melted for me—now I want to see you *burn*."

She struggled to blink, struggled to catch his eyes—but

he wasn't interested in conversation. He surged over her again, taking her lips, her mouth, devouring greedily. In the same movement, he took her, pressing into her again, relentlessly surging inward until he filled her.

Until she thought she would fracture from the sheer joy of feeling him a part of her. She tilted her hips and took him in; he pressed deep, then withdrew, and returned. This time, he didn't lift from her, but remained, moving heavily, erotically, upon her. The friction, the seductive rasp of his hard, ridged, hair-dusted body over her soft flesh, quickly set her afire. She wrapped her arms about him, locking his hard frame to her; she squirmed beneath him, seeking to assuage the heat spreading beneath her skin, flowing through her veins, flooding her belly, flaming where they joined.

For one crazed moment, she thought she'd never get enough of him. Then she felt the tingling, tightening sensation—the coalescing of her heat—the first heralds of that volcanic sensation that had rocked her twice before. She felt her body tighten, straining to capture his; she gave herself up to the deep rhythmic rocking, the steady, relentless possession.

His. Only his. His and no other's.

The refrain filled her—her mind, her heart, her soul. He impressed it upon her with every slow, deliberate, harnessed thrust, with every urgently ravenous kiss. Their lips melded, parted, and melded again. And the fever built.

Panting, her mind awash with glorious anticipation, her body striving for that magnificent surcease, she reached for it—

Abruptly, he drew back. Lifting from her, he sat back on his ankles, hands on his thighs. Stunned, she stared at him. He was breathing hard, his chest rising and falling dramatically, his eyes dark pools glinting in the faint light. The moonlight fell across him; he was flagrantly aroused—as aroused as she.

She blinked—he reached out and caught her hands.

"Come." He hauled her up. "Like this."

He dragged her to her knees, then positioned her, kneeling in the moonlight facing the end of the bed. The bed end was a high one, carved oak, its knurled top not quite level with her waist.

"Hold the bed end."

Dazed, heated, aroused to her toes, she obeyed; his hands, locked about her hips, prevented her from shifting her knees—to grasp the bed end, she had to lean forward.

Immediately her fingers clamped around the cool wood, she felt him behind her.

The next second he was inside her.

She gasped; he withdrew and slowly, deliberately, speared her again.

She shuddered and looked down; bracing her arms against the driving thrusts, she struggled to think—but her mind, her senses, refused to focus on anything beyond his relentless possession. He held her hips—his grip like a vise—and repeatedly penetrated her, each thrust deliberate, probing, complete.

Her senses locked on the continual invasion, on the hard, hot strength that claimed her again and again. She gave up all effort to think and instead surrendered—to the compulsion to let herself enjoy this intimate pleasure and the deep driving joy of feeling him sink into her.

She was open to him, flagrantly, wantonly, without any pretense of restraint. Her breaths coming in panting gasps, she heard again the refrain, louder now, each syllable emphasized by the leashed force behind every steely invasion.

His. Only his. His and no other's.

She had known that all her life; he was demonstrating it now, in a way she would never forget.

As if sensing her acceptance, he shifted slightly, and released her hips. The steady, regular penetration continued, but his hands now roamed, at first lightly, tracing the curves of her bottom and hips, the sensitive sides of her torso, the bountiful fullness of her breasts, the quivering tautness of her belly. Then his touch turned hot, and more sensual—his hands sculpted, then possessed, even as he continued to fill her.

Increasingly intimately, he caressed, fondled, and probed; she gasped and threw back her head, hands gripping the bed end tightly.

Behind her, he shifted, then she felt his chest against her back, his thighs and knees more definitely against hers. He drew her up and back slightly, and closed his hands over her breasts, greedily filling his palms, fingers kneading.

His hips still thrust against her bottom as he held her, trapped, before him.

"Open your eyes." His voice, so low and gravelly she could hardly make out the words, grated beside her ear. "Look across the room."

She did—and saw them reflected in the large mirror on the dresser. The sight stole the last of her breath.

Her body was all shimmering ivory, her hair a tousled swatch of pale silk hanging over one shoulder. Her head was high, thrown slightly back, her lids heavy, her lips parted. Her breasts, swollen and aching, sumptuously filled his hands. Her thighs were widespread, knees sinking into the bed. Her hips rocked suggestively, then rotated, slowly, heavily, as, buried inside her, he ground his hips against her.

Then he withdrew and resumed his steady rhythm. He was a dark presence behind her, his tanned hands and fingers clearly visible as they kneaded her breasts. Dark head bent, he concentrated on each thrust, each deep penetration; what she could see of his face was all hard angles, harsh planes etched with passion. He didn't look up.

The sight that held him so enthralled slowly filled her mind—of his staff, hard and hot, passing between her thighs, between the twin hemispheres of her bottom, claiming her. Possessing her.

His. Only his. His and no other's.

He was her lover, her rightful lord, the phantom of her secret dreams—dreams she had not allowed her waking self to know.

He filled her—over and over—and she was his. Completely. Wantonly. Irrevocably his.

The refrain swelled and filled her, even as he did. Caught in the relentless repetition, she gasped and closed her eyes.

And felt the vortex grab her.

It lifted her; she felt her body tense and tighten, closing intimately about his.

With his next thrust, he pressed deep, holding her to him, then withdrew from her.

Her eyes flew wide—but before she could speak, a fat pillow appeared before her. Followed by another. And another.

He flipped her around and tumbled her onto them, then, scooping her to him, drew her and the pillows up the bed, away from its end. Releasing her, leaving her heated, frantic, and thoroughly dazed on her back in the middle of the bed, he rearranged the pillows, piling them beneath her hips.

"The bed end—hold onto the railings."

She blinked and looked up and back at the wooden fretwork at the end of the bed. Her hands were reaching, slim fingers sliding between the slats in the woodwork and gripping tight, before the thought had formed in her mind. As her hands fisted about the cool wood, she felt his hands on her thighs, felt him grip them and spread them wide.

With a gasp, she looked back and saw him—on his knees between her thighs, hard hands anchoring her hips— slide into her. He surged in, and in, until he was embedded in her softness. Then he leaned forward, into her. She gasped and arched, feeling him deep within her. She felt him groan, the sound harsh and deep.

"Oh, yes—there's more."

The pillows held her hips high against him; reaching

back, he lifted her legs and wound them about his waist. Then, planting his hands flat on the bed, one beside each of her shoulders, he braced his arms and, still leaning heavily into her, started to move.

She was frantic from the first, already tight and tense— each deep, impaling stroke drove her relentlessly on. On into a land of selfless passion, where nothing existed beyond the wild heat that gripped them, the wild force that filled them, where their writhing, panting bodies became mere vessels for their greedy senses.

A wild cry escaped her; she lifted against him, head back, fingers tight about the wooden rails. He lowered his head and laved her breasts, his tongue a burning brand. Then he trapped one nipple and suckled—fire arced through her; she cried again and tried to draw back, away from the forcefully intimate probing of his body sunk so deeply into hers.

Before she moved an inch, he caught her, coming down on his elbows to grasp her shoulders and anchor her beneath him. The sudden movement brought his weight more fully upon her, forcing him even more deeply into her.

His next compelling thrust drove the air from her lungs.

She gasped desperately, and felt him surge powerfully again. Her eyes flickered open; his heavy lids lifted and he met her gaze. Of their own volition, she felt their bodies ease, then forcefully fuse; lost in his midnight gaze, she felt the flames rise.

"Now burn," he said. "And take me with you."

He surged again; she closed her eyes and heard the flames roar.

She let go and let them take her, and him, burning away all the past, all the barriers; all their pride, their vulnerabilities—everything that had ever stood between them. Burnt, too, were the wild, stubborn children they'd once been; the trappings of their youthful love caught fire and exploded, then rained down, ashes on the forest floor.

Leaving only their naked selves, locked intimately together in the moonlight, clasping each other as the flames roared on.

Their lips met, parched, dry, and hungry; they drank from each other and clung closer still.

And then it was upon them, a bright pinnacle of ecstasy that flared like the sun, then fractured, hurling them into a heated darkness where the only sound was that of two thundering hearts.

She screamed, a gasping, keening cry, as the moment shattered about them; she felt him gather her closer still, felt the final powerful fusion, the ultimate joining of his life and hers.

And then it was past. The moment slowly died, the ecstasy faded, yet neither moved. They lay locked together; the moon shone softly upon them, a gentle benediction.

Nothing any longer lay between them; there was nothing to interfere with the selfless, compulsive communion of their bodies, and their souls.

She heard the refrain as she slid into sleep, his breath a gentle caress against her throat.

His. Only his. His and no other's.

Dyan awoke to find the muted light of dawn sliding into the room. In his arms, Fiona slept, her back curved against his side. He'd fallen asleep with the sound of her ecstasy ringing in his ears.

The memory warmed him.

He turned on his side and gathered her close, letting her silken warmth fill his senses. The result was inevitable; he was long beyond fighting it. He wanted her, needed her— and the ache was too new, too fresh, too excruciatingly sensitive to let it go unassuaged. And after last night, when her maturity had entirely overwhelmed her innocence, he felt no compunction in gently easing her upper thigh high, and sliding his fingers into her hot softness.

He had loved her well, stretched her well, yet she was still very tight. He found the bud of her desire and stroked, caressed. Soon she was slick and swollen, his fingers sliding easily into her soft channel.

It was the work of a moment to withdraw his fingers and, easing over her, replace them with his throbbing staff. Gently, very gently, he eased himself into her.

All abandoned innocence, she was fully open to him; luscious and hot, her soft flesh closed about him. Dyan closed his eyes tight and held back a groan as he sank deeper into her heat.

And felt her awaken, felt that single moment of shock—then she melted about him.

Fiona awoke to the indescribable sensation of being intimately invaded—of feeling Dyan's body, hard and strong, surround her—of feeling him, hard and strong, fill her completely. She felt every inch of his slow slide, of the steady, relentless invasion.

And felt within her a glorious well of feeling rise up and swamp her. She closed her eyes, as if to hold it in, and felt his arms close about her. Felt his chest against her back, felt his jaw brush her shoulder.

"All right?"

She smiled and nodded. And felt his spine flex, felt him move within her.

She said nothing more, did nothing more, but simply lay there—his—and let him love her. Let him fondle her breasts, each caress gentle, long-drawn, heavy with wondrous feeling. Let him fill her gently, riding slow and easy, with no hint of the mindless urgency that had overtaken them in the night.

After last night, she had no doubt that her body would satisfy him. When, at the last, he'd collapsed in her arms, he'd been beyond words, thought, or deed. He'd been sated so deeply he'd not moved for ages; she'd felt the difference in his muscles—the complete loss of tension.

The same tension that was slowly coiling within him

now; he pressed closer, tightening his arms around her, splaying one hand across her belly, under the sheet. Holding her steady as he moved more forcefully, but still with the same lazy rhythm.

His jaw rasped her shoulder; his breath tickled her ear. "The others—the wanton scullery maids?"

"Hmm?" Eyes closed, Fiona smiled, concentrating more on his movements than his words.

"They were just practice—all of them."

Her smile deepened. "Practice?"

"Practice," he averred, and rocked deep. "For this."

"Ah." Eyes still closed, Fiona felt the shudder that passed through him. She concentrated on the feel of him, slickly sliding within her.

"Practice for *you*." He nipped her ear, as if aware she wasn't listening. Fiona giggled, and tightened about him. And heard the hiss of his indrawn breath.

He gripped her more tightly. "No man likes to come to his love inexperienced, unprepared." He shifted within her, then sank deep. "I wanted to be able to give you . . . *this*."

This was a slow, rolling climax that washed over her like gentle sunshine, a flush of heat that spread from where they joined through every vein, every limb—leaving her weighted with the most delicious languor, her senses spinning with delirious joy, and her heart filled with a heady rush of emotion.

Tears sprang to her eyes as the sensations peaked. She felt Dyan stiffen behind her, then felt the warmth as he flooded her.

Fiona closed her eyes; her smile slowly deepened. Regardless of what he thought, Dyan had given her much more than *this*.

CHAPTER 4

Five minutes later, or so it seemed, Dyan hauled her from the bed.

"Come on." He pulled her up to sit on the bed's edge, then bullied her into her chemise.

Yawning, Fiona frowned. "I'm sleepy."

"You can sleep later—at home."

"Home?" She yawned again. Her bag had miraculously appeared in the room; Dyan, fully dressed, was rummaging in it.

He turned, with her carriage dress in his hands. "Here—put this on." He pulled it over her head.

Emerging somewhat irritated, Fiona, left with little choice, pushed her arms through the sleeves. "What's the time?" she grumbled.

"Late enough."

Fastening the dress, Fiona looked up, and saw Dyan cram her turquoise silk evening gown into the bag. "Dyan! You'll crush it!"

She started forward; scowling, he pushed her back. "Never mind about your gown—we've got to get moving. Where are your stockings?"

They found them under the bed. Still dazed, half-asleep, Fiona pulled them on. "But what—?"

"Here." Dyan bent and slipped her shoes on. Then he stood and scanned the room. "That's it. Let's go."

He hefted her bag, grabbed her hand and towed her to the door.

"Where are we—"

"*Sssh!*" Opening the door, he glanced out, then hauled her through.

Swiftly, he strode along the corridor. Muttering direfully under her breath, Fiona hurried beside him, too occupied with making sure she didn't stumble to utter any further protest.

They tiptoed down the stairs. Reaching the bottom, Dyan paused to peer through the open drawing-room door; behind him, perched on the last step, Fiona whispered in his ear, "Why are we acting like a pair of thieves?"

He turned his head and glowered at her—and didn't answer. Instead, with long, swift strides, he towed her across the front hall, down the side corridor and into the garden room. A male guest, collapsed in a state of considerable disarray in a garden chair, snored noisily; Dyan tugged Fiona past, shielding her from the sight.

The next instant, they were out of the house and striding for the stables. Long inured to Dyan's method of covering ground—and his habit of hauling her along with him—Fiona valiantly scurried to keep up. If she didn't, he'd been known to toss her over his shoulder; she didn't think India had changed him all that much.

As they rounded the corner of the house, she caught a glimpse of his face—grimly set. "Do you always wake up in such a delightful mood?"

The glance he sent her was fathomless. "Only after orgies."

"Oh." Fiona glanced back at the house. "Was that what that was?"

"Take my word for it."

Dyan's bootheels rang on the stable cobbles. Sleepy grooms blinked wearily; Dyan waved them away. "I'll get my own horse."

The grooms turned back to their duties, glad to be spared, but remained too close for Fiona to question Dyan further.

Left holding the head of a magnificent gray hunter while Dyan saddled the beast, Fiona gradually woke up, gradually recalled all that had taken place in the night. Grateful for the crisp morning air, and its cooling effect on her red cheeks, she gradually remembered all that had passed between them—and all that had not.

By then, Dyan had the saddle on, and had tied her bag behind it. He mounted, then, urging the gray forward, managing the beast with his knees, reached down and plucked her from the cobbles. The next instant, she was crammed between him and the pommel.

She immediately wriggled; he stiffened and hissed, "Sit still, dammit!"

"I used to fit," Fiona grumbled, still wriggling.

Cursing fluently, Dyan lifted her, and resettled her with one knee about the pommel. "That was years ago—there's rather more of you now."

Fiona sniffed; there was rather more of him, too. The most interesting part was pressing into the small of her back. Ignoring it, she clung to the arm that wrapped about her waist. He clicked the reins and the gray clattered out of the stable yard. Dyan turned him toward the forest, and the track that led to her home.

Yawning again, Fiona sank back against him. "Was it really necessary to sneak out like that?"

"What did you plan to do—stay for breakfast?"

Fiona raised her brows. "Do they serve breakfast after orgies?"

Dyan humphed and didn't answer.

Comfortable enough, and secretly glad to be safely on her way home, Fiona relaxed in his arms, smiling softly as the familiar scenery slipped by. She felt a twinge or three, but that was a small price to pay for the glorious sensation of fulfilment suffusing her. She was going to enjoy reveling in it, studying it from all angles—and managing what came next.

She was deep in plans when the roof of Coldstream House rose through the trees. She sighed, and straightened. "You can drop me off by the shrubbery—I'll walk in from there."

She felt Dyan's glance, then he looked ahead again. "I'm coming in."

Fiona blinked, then she turned and looked into his face. "Why?"

His glance was so brief she couldn't read it. "I want to talk to Edmund, of course."

"Of *course*?" A dreadful, not-at-all appealing suspicion unfurled in Fiona's mind. "Which course is that?"

"The course I intend to follow—to wit, to ask for your hand."

"My hand?"

"In marriage."

"Marriage?"

"I did ask, remember?"

"But I didn't agree!" Fiona glared at him. She could see his direction now—it didn't fit with her plans.

Turning into the drive, Dyan glanced down at her, the set of his jaw all too familiar. "As far as I'm concerned," he growled, "you agreed—a *number* of times—last night."

"Rubbish!" Fiona ignored her blush—this was definitely no time for maidenly modesty. "You seduced me!"

"And you allowed yourself to be seduced. *Very* enthusiastically."

Glancing ahead, at the stables drawing rapidly nearer, Fiona grimaced. "But that was just . . ." She gestured vaguely. *"That*! It wasn't about marriage."

"It was as far as I'm concerned—and I suspect Edmund will agree."

Fiona set her jaw. "He won't be up."

"He's always up at cockcrow. Buried in a book, maybe, but he'll see me."

Fiona drew in a deep, very determined, breath. "I am *not* marrying you." Not yet. Not until he'd answered the question she'd asked fifteen years ago. Fifteen years was a *hell* of a long time to wait for an answer; she'd be damned if she let him wriggle out of giving her that answer now.

And, oh, she knew him well. If she gave any sign of agreement, of being ready to countenance any announcement of their betrothal *before* she'd convinced him to say the words, she'd never hear them! Given last night, this was her last chance; avoiding him physically would be impossible—the only thing she had left to bargain with was her agreement to their marriage.

The stable arch loomed before them; Dyan slowed the gray to a walk. "Fiona, if I ask, and Edmund gives his blessing, what are you going to do? Refuse?"

"Yes!" She was quite definite about that.

Dyan snorted derisively. "Of all the *buffleheaded* females!"

"I am *not* buffleheaded!" Fiona swung to face him as they entered the stable yard. "It's *you* who can't think straight!"

His face set, Dyan looked past her, at the groom who came running. "Where's his lordship?"

"He's unavailable!" Fiona informed him.

Dyan kept his gaze on the groom. "In the library?"

Fiona swung about and, ominously narrow-eyed, stared at the groom, who cravenly kept his gaze fixed on Dyan's face—and nodded.

Damn, damn, *damn!* Inwardly seething, Fiona swallowed the vitriolic words that burnt her tongue—she might swear at Dyan, but she would not curse before her brother's servants.

She had to wait while Dyan dismounted. She tried not

to notice the fluid grace, so redolent of harnessed masculine power, with which he accomplished that deed, tried not to notice how easily he lifted her—no mere lightweight—from the saddle. Lips shut, she allowed him to tow her, her hand clasped firmly in his, out of the stables.

Just like him to race ahead, to recklessly cram his fences. But she'd hauled on his reins before; she was determined to do so again. To hold him back, until they got things straight—clearly stated—between them.

There was no way she'd wait another fifteen years to hear what she wanted—*needed*—to hear.

She had to wait until they gained the relative privacy of the gravelled walk up to the house before she could reassert her intransigence.

"Why all this rush over marrying me?" She darted a glance at his set face, and tried to slow her steps. "You've waited fifteen years and now you can't wait another day?"

His grip on her hand tightened warningly; if anything, he strode faster. "One, I seduced you." He flicked a measuring, too-arrogant-by-half glance at her face. "Quite thoroughly, if I do say so myself."

He looked ahead, neatly avoiding her dagger glance. "Two, you need someone to ride rein on you—Edmund demonstrably can't. Three, my great-aunt Augusta will approve of you and consequently take herself, and all the rest of the family, off home. And four—" He drew her relentlessly up the terrace steps. "I've grown exceedingly tired of my cold ducal bed—you can come and warm it. Particularly as the exercise appears to meet with your approval and you don't seem to have anything better to do with your life."

As a proposal, it lacked a certain something. From Fiona's point of view, it lacked a great deal. Jaw set, teeth clenched, she set about demolishing it. "For your information, *Your Grace*," she uttered the title with relish—she didn't even need to look to know it brought a scowl to his face. "At my age, I do not consider a quick tumble—even three long tumbles—to be sufficient reason to tie myself up in matrimony."

"More fool you," Dyan growled, and dragged her through the open morning-room French doors. "I know you've always been stubborn, but don't you think this is overdoing it—even for you?"

"Furthermore," Fiona said, rolling over his interruption with positively awe-inspiring dignity, "as I have survived the past fifteen years quite comfortably without anyone riding rein on me, I can't see that your assistance in that sphere is of any particular advantage."

"Yes—but has anyone else been comfortable? What glib lie did you feed Edmund for your absence last night? Do you imagine he believed it?"

It was an effort not to answer that, but Fiona ignored her blush, stuck her nose in the air and forged on: "And I do not at all see that the notion of saving you from your just deserts—to wit, the attention of your great-aunt Augusta—should in any way influence me in such an important decision."

"That's because you haven't recently met her." Dyan ruthlessly towed her down the corridor to the library. "When I tell her I want to marry you, she'll be over here in a flash—you'll marry me quick enough to be rid of my great-aunt Augusta."

Fiona's eyes kindled at the thinly veiled threat. "And as for your last inducement to marriage, while last night was enjoyable enough in its way, I do not feel any overpowering urge to repeat the exercise anytime soon."

To her surprise, Dyan halted; the closed door to the library was two steps away. Slightly behind him, Fiona stepped up, intending to peer into his face. He turned in the same instant.

And the wall was at her back—and his lips were on hers.

One hand framing her jaw, holding her trapped, he voraciously plundered her mouth. He leaned into her, letting her feel his muscled weight, letting her sense her vulnerability, her helplessness. Letting her sense the instant desire that raged through him—and her.

His chest crushed her breasts—they promptly swelled and ached. She felt her body soften, felt her limbs weaken, felt all resistance melt away. Felt his other hand press between their bodies, sliding down to evocatively cup her, felt his hard fingers search, and find her. Felt the skittering thrill that raced through her as he stroked, even though his touch was muted by her skirt.

And felt, within seconds, the slick wetness he drew forth. For one aching instant, he pressed more firmly against her; his tongue probed the wet softness of her mouth with a now familiar, deliciously deliberate rhythm while through her skirts, he stroked the wet softness between her thighs, probing her to the same evocative beat.

Then he drew back from the kiss.

Dyan continued to stroke her, feeling her heat scorch through the cambric, sinking one fingertip between the luscious, slippery folds. He looked down at her face and waited for her lids to rise. When they did, revealing her eyes, all stunned hazel and gold, he cursed softly; driven, he took her mouth in a last, ravenous kiss—then drew back. "You'll melt for me, Lady Arctic—anytime, anywhere. Believe it." He growled the words against her lips—then forced himself to release her. He took a step back, supporting her against the wall. The instant he judged her legs capable of holding her upright, he caught one of her hands; flinging the library door wide, he tugged her over the threshold.

The room was a large one, rolling away down the wing. Edmund's desk stood at this end, perpendicular to the door. A massive, dusty-looking tome lay open upon the desk; Edmund—a large, heavily built gentleman in a soft tweed jacket—was poring over it. He looked up as they entered. His expression mild—deceptively vague—he smiled gently and sat back, removing the thick-lensed pince-nez balanced on his nose.

Dragging in a quick breath, her eyes wild, her hair still loose about her shoulders, Fiona wrenched her hand from Dyan's. He let her go; she threw him a mutinous look, then marched across the room.

Dyan closed the door—and remained in front of it.

Brows lifting slightly, Edmund shifted his mildly bemused gaze from Dyan to his sister, now pacing furiously before the fireplace.

Color high, Fiona swung to face him. "Edmund—I do not wish you to listen to a single word Dyan says—not one!"

"Oh?" Looking even more bemused—in fact, faintly amused—Edmund looked back at Dyan. "Good morning, Darke. What was it you wished to say to me?"

"*No!*" Fiona wailed.

"By your leave, Edmund, I wish to—"

"*Don't* listen to him!"

"—Apply for Fiona's hand—"

"Edmund—he's entirely out of order. I don't want you to pay any attention—"

"—In marriage." Eyes locked with Edmund's, Dyan ignored the seething glare Fiona hurled his way.

Edmund blinked owlishly, then looked at Fiona. "Why shouldn't he ask me that?"

Still pacing, Fiona folded her arms beneath her breasts. "Because I don't wish to consider the matter at present."

"Why not?"

"Because it's too soon."

Edmund blinked—very slowly—again. "Too soon after what?" His gaze slid back to Dyan; he raised a quizzical brow.

"I suspect she means too soon after last night, which she spent in my bed."

"It *wasn't* your bed!" Fiona hotly declared.

Across the room, Dyan met her gaze levelly; he could still see the last remnants of the gloriously distracted look that had filled her golden eyes in the corridor. And last night. "The bed I was then inhabiting." He glanced at Edmund. "At Brooke Hall."

Edmund met his gaze and nodded once, in understanding. Still utterly unperturbed, he again looked at Fiona, now pacing even more furiously. It was Dyan's firm opinion that Edmund, ten full years Fiona's senior, had been born unflappable—which, given his sister's propensities and the adventures he himself had led her into, was probably just as well.

After a long moment, Edmund asked, still in the most reasonable of tones, "How long should Darke and I wait before we discuss this matter?"

Fiona stopped. Lifting her head, she stared at Edmund. Then her eyes blazed. "I don't want you discussing it *at all!* Not until I give my leave. I don't want you to discuss *anything* with Dyan—if he has anything to discuss he can discuss it with me."

Edmund merely opened his eyes wider. "And how long are these discussions between you likely to take?"

Fiona flung her hands in the air. "How the hell should *I* know?" She threw a furious glance at Dyan. "Given his progress to date, it might well be another fifteen years!"

Uttering a barely smothered, distinctly unladylike sound, she whirled on her heel and stalked down the long room to another door to the corridor. She flung it open and left, slamming it shut behind her. The sound rang in the silence of the library. Both men stared at the door.

"Hmm," Edmund said, and reached for his pince-nez.

Dyan blinked. He watched as Edmund settled his spectacles back in place and refocused on his dusty tome. Dyan frowned. "You don't seem overly concerned. Or surprised."

Edmund's brows rose; he continued to scan his page. "Why should I be concerned? I'm sure you'll sort it out.

Never was wise to get in the way of either of you—and as for getting *between* you—a fool's errand, that." Reaching for a ruler, Edmund aligned it on the page. "And as for surprise—well, that's hardly likely, is it? The entire county's been waiting for years for the two of you to come to your senses."

Dyan stared. Oblivious, Edmund went on, "Only real surprise is that it's taken you so long. Fiona's the only one who's ever hauled on your reins—and you're the only one who's ever rattled her." He shrugged. "Obvious, really. Of course, with you in India, no one liked to *say* anything . . ." His voice was fading, as if he was sinking back into his tome. "Presuming you don't actually *want* to wait another fifteen years, she's probably taken refuge in her office— it's the room that used to be Mama's parlor."

Dyan continued to stare at Edmund's bent head for all of thirty seconds—then shook his head, shook himself, opened the door and went off to track down his obviously fated bride.

Who obviously hadn't expected to be found. The stunned look on her face when he walked in the door was proof enough of that. Coldstream House was a rambling mansion; she should have been safe for hours. Realizing Edmund had betrayed her, she stiffened, lifted her chin, and edged behind a chaise.

His eyes on her, Dyan closed the door. Noting the tilt of her chin, the flash of ire in her eyes, he turned the key in the lock, and calmly removed it. He hefted the key in his palm, watched her gaze lock on it—then slid it into his waistcoat pocket.

And started toward her.

"Dyan—" Fiona lifted her gaze to his face, and retreated fully behind the chaise. She frowned at him. "What do you think you're doing?"

"I'm about to get your agreement to a wedding—ours."

Not entirely under her breath, Fiona swore. He was going to avoid saying the words—she *knew* it. But she'd be damned if she married him after all this time without that—without a clear, straightforward declaration.

"I'm not simply going to agree to marry you." She fixed her gaze on his face, on his eyes, waiting to read his direction.

"That much, I'd gathered." His gaze lifted; his eyes, deep midnight blue, locked on hers. "What I don't yet know is what's going to change your mind."

Snapping free of his visual hold, Fiona, suddenly breathless, realized he was rounding the end of the chaise. With a half-smothered shriek, she turned and raced around the other end. "Words," she said, and glanced over her shoulder.

He followed in her wake, unhurriedly stalking her. "Which particular words would you like?"

"Reasons," Fiona declared. "Your reasons for marrying me." She scuttled behind the second chaise, facing the first on the other side of the fireplace. As long as he didn't pounce, they could go around and around for hours.

Something changed in his face; he looked up and again caught her eye. Fiona fought not to let him mesmerize her. "I don't want you to marry me for any stupid, chivalrous reason—like saving my reputation."

His brows rose; his eyes glinted wickedly. "I didn't know your reputation needed saving." His lips quirked. "Other than from me, of course."

Fiona glared, and slipped around the second chaise. "I *meant* because of attending what I have on excellent authority was an orgy at Brooke Hall."

"I think," Dyan said, head to one side as if considering the matter, "that you'll discover you didn't attend any orgy—in fact, I seriously doubt anyone will remember seeing you there at all. But," he said, steadily tracking her, "if that's what you're bothered about, you may put it from your head. I'm not marrying you to save your reputation."

"Good. So why, then?" Fiona returned to the safety of the first chaise. "And if you tell me it's to get rid of your great-aunt Augusta, I'll scream."

"Ah, well." Dyan surreptitiously closed the gap between them. "You are going to get rid of great-aunt Augusta for me—there's no doubt whatsoever of that. However," he conceded, swiftly lengthening his stride as he neared the chaise, "that's not, I admit, why I want to marry you."

"So why?" Safe behind the chaise, Fiona turned; Dyan caught her and hauled her into his arms. "Dyan!" She struggled furiously, but he'd trapped her arms instantly. Furious, she looked up, a blistering tirade on her tongue—

He kissed her, and kept kissing her, until she couldn't remember her name. She couldn't think at all; she could only feel—feel the ardor in his kiss, the deep, long-buried yearning, the soul-stealing invitation that she'd first tasted fifteen years before.

And her answer was there—all she needed to know of why he wished to marry her—it was all there in his kiss. He laid himself bare—showed her what was in his heart. Not simply passion, though there were clouds of that aplenty; not just desire, though the hot waves lapped about them. And not just need, either, although she could sense that, too, like a towering mountain planted at the core of his being.

It was the emotion that rose like a sun over it all, over the landscape of their bound lives.

That was why he would marry her.

The heat of that sun warmed her through and through; Fiona shed her icy armor. Softening in his arms, she wriggled her own free and draped them about his neck. He instantly drew her closer, deepening the kiss, letting the feelings intensify—the passion, the desire, the need—and that other. Fiona gloried in it. Dyan shifted; she didn't realize he was backing her until her hips hit the edge of her desk. He gripped her waist and lifted her, balancing her bottom on the very edge of the desk.

Almost instantly, she felt the cool caress of the air as he lifted her skirts—pushed them up to her waist and tucked the folds behind her. Then he slipped one hand under the front edge of her chemise. Balanced as she was, with his hard thighs between hers, she was open to him; within seconds she was shuddering.

Dyan broke their kiss and trailed his lips down the long curve of her throat. Fiona let her head fall back, her fingers sinking into his shoulders as he slid one long finger past the slick, swollen, pouting flesh throbbing between her thighs, and reached deep. He stroked; she moaned.

Satisfied, Dyan withdrew his hand and went to work on the buttons of his breeches.

"And," he whispered. Fiona lifted her head and their parched lips brushed, then parted. "If you haven't yet got the message—or you've suddenly been struck blind and can't read it—how about I'm marrying you because . . ." Even now, he couldn't resist teasing her. Dyan studied her face, her gloriously distracted expression; his lips twitched. "You might, even now, be pregnant with my heir."

Her lids flickered; beneath her lashes, her eyes glinted. Her lips started to firm—Dyan kissed them. "And," he murmured, wrestling with a button, "if you aren't, I fully intend to come to you, day and night, and fill you at every opportunity—until you swell and ripen with my child."

Her lips parted—he immediately covered them. "How about," he said, the instant he released them, "that I'm marrying you because, without you, the rest of my life will be as empty as the last fifteen years."

That, he could tell from her eyes, was almost accepta-ble.

The last button refused to budge; he was so aroused he was almost in pain. Dyan bit back a groan. Fiona, noticing his problem, reached down to help. Her smaller fingers dealt deftly with the recalcitrant button; his staff, engorged, erect, sprang forth, into her hands.

Dyan groaned again—louder—as her fingers closed

about him. "How about," he ground out, quickly pushing her hands away, "that I'm marrying you because I need to be inside you—you and no other—or I'll go insane."

She looked up and, one brow rising quizzically, caught his eye—he was clearly getting very close to achieving his goal. He was also getting very close to—

"Dammit, woman, *I love you*! I've loved you forever, and I'll love you forever. Are *those* the words you want to hear?"

"Yes!" Fiona's face turned radiant. She flung her arms about his neck and kissed him passionately. She broke off as he grasped her hips, anchoring her on the very edge of the desk. "Anyone would think," she said, wriggling a little as he pressed between her thighs, his staff urgently seeking her entrance, "that saying those words was painful."

Dyan knew what was painful—he found the source of her slick heat and thrust deep. She gasped, clung tight, and melted—not an iceberg but a volcano, all heat, around him. He wrapped his arms about her and, with an aching shudder, sank deep. "Am I to take it that's acceptable? That you can accept that as a suitable reason for our marriage?" He knew she loved him—had known it for confirmed fact the first time she'd parted her thighs for him; she was, after all, Lady Arctic—and he was the only one who'd ever melted her ice.

All he got in answer was a sigh as he embedded himself fully within her. "For God's sake, woman—say yes!"

Fiona tipped back her head; a glorious smile curved her lips. She met his dark eyes, almost black with leashed passion; deliberately she arched, and drew him deeper still. *"Yes."*

She said it, panted it, screamed the word at least six times more, before all fell silent in the office.

He took her in his arms and filled her heart, gave her life purpose, completed her. She took him in her arms and held him, filled the aching void within him, and anchored his wild and reckless soul.

They were married two weeks later; Dyan's heir was born a bare nine months after that. His great-aunt Augusta, for quite the first time in his life, was pleased to approve.

WEDDING KNIGHT

CELESTE BRADLEY

To sisters.
And to never having to go it alone.

CHAPTER 1

England 1813

The graveyard echoed silence but for the sound of running feet and her own straining breath. Kitty Trapp stopped to gasp for a moment against a tall marker stone, one carved with cherubs and the word "Beloved." The morning sun had yet to rise above the London dwellings surrounding the churchyard, making the shadows dense and undefined.

There. White flashed between two tall stones—a mere translucent wisp as insubstantial as fog—then it was gone.

Again. The early morning light brightened through the mist to glimmer for an instant on a pale figure. Kitty dodged a headstone and dashed to the side of one of the great mausoleums, regretting her sedentary existence in an entirely new way as her side clenched in a stitch. She clutched her waist tightly with one hand while holding up her hem with the other—and kept running. *Faster.*

With a last burst of speed that she hardly knew she was capable of, Kitty burst through a decorative hedge that separated the rich from the not so rich even after death. With one hand stretched before her, she reached out—

And caught her sister's sleeve before Bitty could make the largest mistake of her life.

It took a moment for Kitty to gather enough breath to speak. "Bettina Melrose Trapp! Get back in that church this instant! What can you be thinking to race through hallowed ground? And on your wedding day!"

Bitty let free a sob while struggling to pull away from her twin's grip. Kitty, however, had years of experience in getting her way. She might be the ever so slightly younger and the ever so slightly less attractive and the much less financially desirable twin, but she was also ever so slightly taller and much, much meaner.

Bitty only struggled harder, surprising Kitty with her willingness to possibly damage her wedding gown. Kitty didn't dare ease her grip, however. Behind them was a church full of influential people, including the Prime Minister and half the members of the House of Lords.

Thinking again of Mama's eagerness to impress the imperious Lord Liverpool, Kitty began to drag her twin back through the gravestones to the tiny room off the nave where they'd been sent to await the first strains of the wedding march.

"But I don't want to!" Bitty struggled harder, although Kitty noticed that she kept her wails muted. "I don't want to wed him in front of all those people!"

"Well, you ought to have considered that before you accepted Mr. Knight's proposal." Reaching the old arched door of the back exit off the nave, Kitty towed her twin inside. She only released Bitty when she'd closed the oak door on its thick iron hinges and thrown the great latch once more.

In his small alcove off the nave, Mr. Alfred Theodious Knight paused in the act of adjusting his cravat. The hollow echo of a door slamming somewhere in the church distracted him. He waited a long moment, but no further uproar ensued. Good. Hopefully, events would continue as scheduled.

Not that he was in a hurry to wed the Trapp girl. She hardly inspired hot-blooded urgency. When one examined the match logically—and Knight examined everything logically—the girl would suit him well enough. Unexceptional looks, if not precisely pretty. Blond, which was pleasant but scarcely necessary. Of flawless reputation—aside from one recent blunder—and possessing an unobtrusive demeanor.

This last was important, for Knight wanted no torrid stories floating about concerning his marriage. He'd had a lifetime of living down the outrageous antics of his shameless mother. He'd not tolerate such nonsense from his own wife.

Further, the girl was of adequate family, with surprisingly high connections. Figure: landing somewhere between pleasingly plump and overindulged. Taste: excruciating, but that had already been dealt with. Inheritance: large enough to inspire interesting possibilities but not so large as to eclipse his own.

And finally, but in his mind the most important, wedding Bettina Trapp would erase a possible stain upon his family's name. If only it were this easy to erase all the misdeeds of Knight's younger half brother, John Tuttle.

Born out of their shared mother's affair with a horse trainer hired to develop the blood stock, John Tuttle had never felt the need to live down his origins as Knight did. In fact, John seemed intent on broadening the spectrum of sins painted upon the family history by the late Mrs. Knight.

Several weeks ago Tuttle had decided to line his pockets with Miss Trapp's inheritance. With characteristic Tuttle treachery, John had proceeded to lure the naïve Bettina Trapp onto a balcony during a ball and had there leaped upon her like a hungry hound. Only the happenstance of Bettina's sister coming upon the scene had prevented a scandal that would have rocked London.

Upon reflection, Knight realized that he had never seen his bride's sister. By John's furious and drunken description just before Knight had ordered his half sibling boarded onto the next ship to the West Indies, the other Trapp girl was a proper witch.

Typical of younger siblings, Knight was sure.

The wedding march ought to play soon. With habitual calm, Mr. Alfred Theodious Knight firmly squelched his boredom and returned to adjusting a cravat that was already tied to perfection.

Standing with her back to the only escape from the tiny cell, Kitty folded her arms and regarded Bitty with fond exasperation. Bitty never could accomplish anything without a fuss and flurry, even something as simple as walking down the aisle. Melodrama was as much a part of Bitty as was her indecision and her basic timidity, although Bitty's essential lack of will was the only thing that made Kitty able to live with her pampered and narcissistic twin.

Not that it was entirely Bitty's fault. Kitty thought that she might herself have been as malleable as Bitty if she'd been the focus of her parents' social ambitions for her entire life. Instead, she'd had to fight every day of her life for the slightest notice from her family.

Perhaps that was why Bitty was so prone to theatrics, as a sort of outlet for her own desires and dreams. Although Kitty couldn't imagine why. As far as she knew, Bitty's desires and dreams coincided entirely with Mama's ambitions for her.

Until today, that is.

"If you didn't want to have a grand wedding, why didn't you say something weeks ago? Or yesterday, for that matter? What will Mr. Knight say?"

"Oh, I cannot bear to think on him. So grim—so *dark*!"

Kitty blinked at that. "You don't fancy his looks? Then why did you accept him?" Astounding. She had seen the gentleman on the day when he'd come to offer for Bitty, although he hadn't seen her. The landing on the stairs was a lovely place to spy on someone in the entrance hall. In Kitty's opinion, the stern and silent Mr. Knight was quite ideal, at least in his even features and fine dark eyes.

Bitty only shuddered in response. "I don't want to talk about it."

"Again, something best brought up in conversation before today," muttered Kitty. She threw out her hands. "The poor man is standing out there right now waiting for you! The world is standing out there waiting for you!"

That had been the wrong thing to say. Bitty shrank back, then unbelievably, reached behind her neck to begin undoing the tiny buttons that ran down her white silk-clad back. "No, no, no—" Then she began to tug the tightly fitted sleeves down, right there in the church with half the world waiting outside the door!

"Bitty, what are you doing?" Kitty rushed around behind her to do her up again, but Bitty twisted away to tug at the costly beaded silk as if it were a filthy rag.

"No!"

Kitty was astonished at the vehemence in her sister's voice. Bitty was choosing *now* to exhibit a spine? Kitty tried a new tack. "Bitty, wait," she said in a soothing tone. "Think on it. This is your wedding day. Everything is just as you wished. The church is the one where Mama wed Papa. The flowers are just as you dreamed. Your gown . . ." Well, to be truthful, the gown was a horror, all tucked and beaded and beribboned with not one inch unadorned. In Kitty's opinion, Bitty had never had one smidge of taste, nor had Mama.

Kitty abandoned soothing to go straight to entirely livid. "Bettina Melrose Trapp, put your wedding gown back on this instant!" All to no effect. Bitty stripped the dress off and tossed it ruthlessly over the back of a heavy carved chair.

A tap came at the door that led into the church. "Girls?"

Kitty closed her eyes. *Mama*. Things were about to go from bad to disastrous. Bitty dove behind the dressing screen. *The coward*.

Mrs. Beatrice Trapp, society matron and patroness of everything socially advantageous, entered the room like a lavender ship under sail. "Kitty? Where is your sister?" She spotted the dress tossed unceremoniously aside. Her eyes widened in appalled surprise. "She isn't yet dressed? The vicar is expecting us now!"

Kitty saw a scene in the making, what with Mama's ambitions colliding with Bitty's theatrics—a long, loud, and potentially very public scene indeed. Quickly, she stepped in.

"Mama, you must stall the ceremony." She wrapped one arm about her mother's stout waist and steered her back to the door. "A minor hair mishap, that is all. We only need a moment."

Beatrice Trapp looked over her shoulder at the limp and empty wedding gown. "But don't you need my help to get Bitty dressed?"

Kitty sent her mother out with a small push, just to build up her momentum. "Don't worry, Mama. You'll have a bride to marry off in mere moments."

One way or another.

There were several hundred guests in the church. That meant nearly a thousand eyes turned Kitty's way when she took her first hesitating step on her father's arm down the aisle.

This is a dreadful plan. Kitty's conscience seemed to beat against the barrier of her lie like a trapped moth. *Don't do this!*

Firmly she squelched the inner protest. 'Twas no great problem. She would simply do this one thing for Bitty, and for her parents, and no one need know but Bitty and herself. After all, it wasn't as though they hadn't done it time and again in their childhood.

Mr. Knight stood tall and imposing next to the vicar. Heavens, had his shoulders always been so broad? Kitty's veil—*Bitty's veil*—hung mistily between herself and the groom—*Bitty's groom*—

Kitty shook herself firmly back to the subject at hand. She need only make it through the ceremony, trot home to undress, and stuff her sister into the very fine traveling suit awaiting her, and kiss Bitty good-bye as she left on her honeymoon.

It was only that . . . when she'd dreamed of this moment in her life, she'd never thought it would be a farce, an unworthy prank. What should have been her first and only time taking this journey had been twisted. Now Kitty didn't know if the purity of her own walk down the aisle could ever be returned to her.

So when she arrived at the altar and turned to face Mr. Knight, there were very believable tears in her eyes.

Knight tried not to heave a visible sigh of impatience at the slow intonations of the vicar. The pomp and symbolism that was wrapped around what amounted to a business transaction never ceased to amaze him.

His bride wept beside him. He hoped she would not turn out to be sillier than most. Unfortunately, he'd yet to see evidence of any brain at all in Bettina Trapp. The one report he'd had of her led one to believe she hadn't the sense to get herself in out of the rain. His impression upon first meeting her on the day he'd proposed had not been favorable, for she'd merely blinked at his offer with wide brown eyes, then paled, then nodded.

Still, Knight retained a hope of finding some sort of intellect beneath the vapid exterior. A long and intimate future with a completely brainless woman didn't bear thinking about.

He took his bride's hand in his at the appropriate moments, said the expected litany, vowed forever away to this creature whom he truly didn't know at all.

Wedded bliss, the vicar said. Knight didn't see it as anything of the sort. Simply a business transaction, after all.

The entire party had arrived at the Trapps' home for the wedding breakfast. The moment Kitty could manage it she ran for her room. It would only take a few moments to change, especially if Bitty had everything ready as they had arranged.

It wasn't until Kitty had neared the top of the stairs at a run that she realized that never once—not before, during, or after the ceremony—had her parents asked after her . . . er, Kitty. Pausing at the door to her room, she fought down the hurt that no one had noticed Kitty's absence from the festivities.

Flinging herself into the room, she pasted on a bright smile, ready to give Bitty every detail of the last hour—

There was no one in the room, or in Bitty's room. Or in the bathing chamber, or in the small sitting room attached. Worse, much worse . . . Bitty's traveling things weren't anywhere to be seen.

Bitty was gone.

Kitty slumped on her bed, unmindful of crushing the priceless satin of her gown—Bitty's gown.

What was she to do? She was tempted to change back to Kitty and merely report to her parents that Bitty was gone . . . but then she'd likely have to tell them of the deceit they had perpetrated. And if that deceit ever became public knowledge . . .

Kitty swallowed. If she'd thought the scandal of a reluctant bride would have been bad, the scandal of a runaway wife would be ruinous to the entire family! And she herself would be publicly branded a liar and mischief maker of the worst sort. Her parents would be dragged into it, there'd be no avoiding that. Mr. Knight might very well sue them or have them charged with something criminal!

"Oh, Bitty," she breathed. "What have we done?"

Feeling dizzy and more than a little sick, Kitty stood up to reach to the buttons of the gown she was fast beginning to hate with a thick and choking passion. It wasn't easy, but she managed to get herself out. Luckily, she hadn't had to wear the corset beneath it, for Bitty had added a bit of weight during her engagement.

For the first time, it occurred to Kitty that her sister had been unhappy all along. Kitty tried to remember if Bitty had attempted to communicate that unhappiness at any time.

She couldn't pin down any one moment, but now that she thought about it, Bitty had been very quiet lately, at least when she wasn't planning details of the wedding.

Kitty always tried to be brutally honest with herself and she could see now that she had been more than a little jealous of Bitty's nuptials. She herself had avoided talking to her twin soon after the engagement, although she had told herself it was because hearing about the lace on Bitty's veil for the hundredth time was not terribly interesting to her.

She ought to have remembered that an unbearable Bitty was an unhappy Bitty. Now it was too late. Bitty had flown, but Kitty had no idea where to. Surely she wouldn't hide with any of the families they knew, for no one would assist a young woman in her own ruination. Yet where could she have gone? When would she be back?

And why had she left Kitty in the lurch? Bitty was profoundly self-absorbed, that was true, but surely she must know that Kitty couldn't keep the secret forever? What had been the point of this wedding farce if Bitty had never planned on behaving as a proper wife should?

Clad now in her chemise and stockings, Kitty began to pace the room. She must order her mind, that's what Aunt

Clara would say. Aunt Clara was Lady Etheridge, wife of the Prime Minister's adviser. She was also a famous political cartoonist who feared nothing and no one.

Kitty wished Aunt Clara were here now, but Lady Etheridge had begged off the wedding breakfast, admitting her lack of appetite that morning.

Kitty picked up her silver hairbrush and began to undo the hasty twist she had put her hair into to fit beneath the veil. A small bark of laughter left her lips at the sight of the pile of pins on the dressing table.

Before disappearing, Bitty had taken the time to undo the elaborate mass of braids and ribbons that Kitty had spent hours putting into her hair this morning. Not truly one of her duties, but Bitty had insisted on having her sister with her and had disdained the help of a maid.

Kitty had been flattered at the time, and quite willing to oblige, but now a dark thought twisted through her mind. Had Bitty *planned* this outrageous flight? Had she herself been purposely maneuvered into taking her sister's place at the altar, like some sort of ancient sacrifice?

No, surely not even Bitty would do something so unworthy. This morning's panic had been unfeigned, Kitty would swear to that. Bitty had simply worked herself up further and had fled her own exaggerated fears.

Surely.

Bitty would be back, Kitty dared be in no doubt of that. Her sister would come back as soon as she had calmed, and the switch could still take place. There was no need to alert Mama and Papa yet. Mr. Knight need know no differently at this point.

She could continue the charade until Bitty returned, likely tonight or perhaps tomorrow. Even Bitty would not push the bounds of propriety by staying too long on her own. One night might be covered, two would be harder, and anything after that would require the help of the entire family and staff—which meant the gossip would get out, one way or another. No, Bitty would be home in two days at the latest.

Of course, that didn't exactly clarify what Kitty should do tonight.

The wedding night.

CHAPTER 2

As Kitty hugged her mother good-bye, Beatrice Trapp leaned back to take a long look at her. Kitty ducked her head to toy with the embroidered frogs of her spencer. Her bonnet covered her hair, which was ever so slightly lighter than Bitty's, but she no longer had the veil to hide her face. Mama wasn't impossible to fool even now, but she was one of the most difficult. "Kitty will be at her friend's house for a few days, Mama."

Beatrice nodded. "Darling, are you sure you feel well enough to go away just now? You've had a trying day. I'm sure Mr. Knight can be prevailed upon to wait until tomorrow." Beatrice turned to the man who stood beside Kitty. "What say you, Mr. Knight? Will you allow me to keep my daughter for another day?" This was said lightly, almost flirtatiously, in the way that Mama usually spoke to socially advanced gentlemen, but Mr. Knight did not answer in kind.

"As she is no longer your daughter, Mrs. Trapp, but yet my wife, I believe it is upon me to look out for her welfare now." His deep voice sounded bored and a tad impatient. Kitty didn't look at him, but she was aware that he had moved a step closer to her.

The man thought himself her husband. He would not tolerate being brooked in his will, that was already apparent. Kitty looked up just long enough to shoot her mother one of Bitty's small refined smiles, careful not to show her teeth the way Mama so disliked in Kitty's usual grins.

"I shall be fine, Mama," she said in Bitty's soft tones. "Mr. Knight will take good care of me, I am sure." She wasn't sure of any such thing, but she had the knife Aunt Clara had given her tucked in her bodice and more knowledge of the vulnerabilities of the male anatomy than any respectable young girl had a right to. She could take very good care of herself, thank you.

Mr. Knight's carriage awaited outside, and a footman wearing the black and silver Knight livery helped her into it. Mr. Knight followed, seating himself across from her in the rear-facing seat, as any gentleman would. He seemed well mannered, if somewhat arrogant. Kitty cursed her own pride that had withstood learning more about her sister's fiancé. She should have had a wealth of second-hand information from Bitty by now, if she'd not been so caught up in her own bitter feelings.

Yet if her family had wanted to include her in the plans and discussions, they had given her no hint of it. Mama had sometimes literally shut Kitty from the room during such times.

And when she'd asked Papa about the dispensation of Bitty's inheritance from Grandmama Melrose, Papa had jovially patted her on the head and told her not to trouble herself over matters that didn't concern her.

True, Bitty's inheritance wasn't strictly Kitty's business, since Grandmama, who had died just before the twins' birth, had most clearly specified that her wealth should fall to the eldest daughter.

Eldest by no more than half an hour. The inequity of this had been part of Kitty's awareness for as long as she could remember, since she and Bitty had heard their parents discussing it in one of their many excursions into eavesdropping. From that day forward, Bitty had never allowed Kitty to forget it. Every argument was lost, every squabble dispensed with, when Bitty would draw herself up and say grandly, "Yes, but *I* am the heiress."

Not that Bitty hadn't had some trouble as well, from one fortune-hungry fellow in particular who had tried to coerce her to his own advantage. But beyond John Tuttle and his friend Wesley Merrick, there had been charming men, and stolid respectable men, and even one impoverished baronet calling upon Bitty.

Yet Bitty had chosen Mr. Knight, who as far as Kitty knew had never once danced attendance on her sister. He had simply presented himself one day with his offer in hand, had spoken to Bitty privately for a moment, then had taken her acceptance into Papa's study to finalize the matter.

Tipping her bonnet slightly to see around the brim, Kitty examined the man across from her. His profile was in evidence as he gazed out the small window in apparent boredom. His brown eyes were very nearly black in their intensity, and Kitty had to admit once more that the chiseled cut of his jaw conformed to her own masculine ideal.

As if he felt eyes upon him, he turned his head to look at her with one eyebrow raised in query. How irksome. Couldn't he spare enough words to ask his own wife what she was thinking? Need she respond to mere gestures like a well-trained hound?

In irritated response, she mirrored his own expression directly back to him. He blinked, then gazed at her levelly for a moment longer. Then, as if he couldn't be bothered, he turned his attention back to the window.

She'd annoyed him. Kitty reminded herself that she was supposed to be portraying Bitty. Despite Bitty's sharp battle instincts in the war of sibling rivalry, with anyone outside the family Bitty was nigh unto speechless with shyness. Especially strange men. In particular, gruff, unsmiling men like the one seated across from her.

Dear Lord, Bitty, what were you thinking?

Kitty began again. She pressed her lips into one of Bitty's smiles and injected that breathy quality to her voice that Bitty used to apparent advantage.

"Mr. Knight?" There was no response. They were supposedly married now. Perhaps something a bit less formal? Alfred Theodious Knight, the vicar had named him in the ceremony. "Alf—"

He interrupted her with a black glare that made her shrink back against the cushions.

"I do not enjoy being addressed by my given name, Bettina. Nor do I appreciate any derivative thereof. As I informed you before, I do not tolerate Alfred, Alf, Alfie, Theodious, Theo, and most especially not *Teddy*. My familiars call me Knight. As my wife, you may address me as Mr. Knight." He gave his cuffs a tug. "I trust we need never have this conversation again."

Conversation? When she'd only been allowed half a word? What an appalling man. "Alfred the Odious, indeed," Kitty muttered under her breath.

"I beg your pardon, Bettina?"

She smiled sweetly at him. "Merely taking note of your wishes, Mr. Knight."

He subsided into his previous pose of boredom with one last suspicious glance. "Very well. See that you do."

Kitty leaned back onto the cushions and turned her gaze to her own window, hiding behind her bonnet brim once more. Good heavens, if this was to be Bitty's life, Kitty vowed she would never envy her poor sister again.

Knight helped his bride from the carriage with his own hand this time. He was feeling a tiny stab of regret for the harsh tone he'd taken with her earlier. Yet she had already disregarded his very specific instructions regarding his address. If she turned out to be defiant beneath her mild exterior, they were going to have a very rough road.

Willful and intelligent might be somewhat interesting. Willful and foolish could not be borne.

On the steps of his house, his servants stood in a line to welcome their new mistress. He hadn't very many dependents, for he disliked the disruptions of a full house-hold, but neither did he consider himself difficult to work for. All he demanded was that his wishes be met immediately and completely. In return, he paid well and provided security for all.

All very simple and direct. Knight wished above all for his life to be orderly. Obtaining a wife shouldn't play too much hell with orderly, if he managed her well.

Night had fallen, making the candles glow brighter up in the spacious "Madam's" chamber where Kitty had been led by a young but purposeful maid. She had spent the last hours penning desperately cheerful notes to all of Bitty's acquaintances, thanking some for appearing at the wedding, forgiving others for not. She signed them "Mrs. Knight" and added a postscript to each one.

"Should you happen across my sister, please tell her that I was sorry not to see her at the wedding breakfast and that I hope she recovers from her complaint soon."

Not precisely clever, but it was the best she could do. Some of Bitty's circle were less friends than they were competitors. Kitty didn't know all of them well enough to know who Bitty would trust.

After sending the footman to post the letters, Kitty realized the hour. It was so late she'd missed dinner, absently refusing while concentrating on her mission. Now it was her wedding night and her "husband" would be expecting a willing bride.

In a sudden burst of panic, Kitty dug through the trunk for Bitty's oldest and warmest flannel nightdress. It would cover all but her neck and her hands. Bitty's new maid glanced askance at Kitty's choice of nightwear.

"I believe the master had something other in mind for you, madam." The girl went to the chest to retrieve something filmy that fluttered as she walked back to Kitty. "This is what he purchased." The maid held up the gown by the scant shoulders of ribbon and let the length of sheer silk fall to the floor.

Kitty stared. *He* had chosen such a scandalous night-dress? Why, it was naught but a spider web with a bit of lace on the hem! And the neckline—heavens, she'd spill from it like an overloaded bushel basket of French melons! Kitty took a step back from the horrifying item even as a part of her admired the beauty and elegance of the Grecian design.

If I were a true bride, receiving my true love in our honeymoon bower . . .

Well, enough of fantasy. Her objective was to fend off Mr. Knight for as long as possible. She wouldn't like her chances of fending off an elderly half-blind vicar while clad in *that*. Kitty raised her chin. "I'll wear what I have chosen."

The maid looked doubtful. "The master said—"

"The master may wear that if it pleases him so," Kitty said firmly as she began to change. Honestly, the man was a blasted tyrant. Best he learn from the beginning not to push a Trapp about. "I, on the other hand, intend to wear what pleases me."

"The master won't like it."

Indeed, the master didn't like it, not one bit. Kitty could see it from his expression the moment he stepped into her chamber a few moments later. The maid took one look at his glowering face and made herself entirely scarce.

Even Kitty felt the force of his disapproval. Why had she ever thought him severe and unreadable? His disappointment and distaste were so evident to her that they very nearly distracted her from the fact that he wore only his dressing gown loosely tied over a pair of trousers.

Broad male chest flexed before her very eyes. *Heavens.* So broad. So male. Her mouth went very dry and she swallowed her indignant words with a convulsive contraction of her throat. Without the formality of coat and cravat his dark good looks lent him the air of a wild and untamed pirate . . . or a sultan.

She took a small step toward him, frankly staring at his magnificence. Yes, in his dark garnet silk dressing gown that revealed his glorious chest and his rippled stomach he was like a desert prince, striding into her tent to ravish his captive princess.

Her heart stuttered and her mind quite nearly stopped working.

Ravish me.

Better than that, stand very still and let me ravish you . . .

"Bettina," he began—and woke her from her desire-tinted daze with a dash of cold reality. She forced herself to look away, at the wall, at the floor—at anything but him or the wide bed that awaited them. What was she thinking? He was Bitty's groom. He was Bitty's grim and tyrannical husband, and she was Bitty's loyal and loving sister.

Blast it.

Knight looked at his bride with her frumpy gown and her demurely downcast eyes and felt his momentary interest subside. When he'd walked in she'd gazed at him with what he would have interpreted as desire if he hadn't known the realities of the situation. No, the woman before him had no more interest in him than he had in her.

Which was why he'd selected such a revealing night-dress in the first place. When the modiste had blushingly held it up for him, he'd decided that almost any woman's desirability would be improved by that gown and perhaps a bit of dim lighting.

And a great deal of wine. Hence the two bottles now standing opened and breathing on the night table.

A moment ago, he'd quite astonishingly decided that he didn't need the wine, and that he wouldn't mind at all if the candles remained well lit. That spark had faded, unfortunately.

"Bettina," he said again, almost hoping she would look up at him with that gleam in her brown eyes—but of course she did not. Good God, would this be the story for the rest of their lives? He would speak and she would keep her eyes locked to the stitching of the carpet? He fought back the creeping horror of never-ending boredom to try once more. He took a step toward her, pulling from deep within him that endless male fascination for all things female.

He would coax a bit. Although he hadn't planned on bothering with seduction—after all, he was within his rights and she'd wed him willingly enough—part of him wanted to discover whether that bit of fire that had flashed behind her eyes had been naught but wishful thinking on his part. So he walked around this still and silent woman with her downcast eyes until he stood directly behind her.

"Wife," he whispered in a breath that stirred the hair by her ear. He was sure she shivered in response. Too bad he couldn't tell if it was from fear or temptation. "Why aren't you wearing my gift?"

"Oh, is that what that was?" Her voice was very soft, but Knight swore he could detect a note of . . . sarcasm? From Bettina Trapp, the blandest female who ever drew breath? His interest stirred once more. He moved closer, until her bottom almost nestled in his lap.

"Wear it for me."

"No-thank-you-kindly-I'm-utterly-fine-in-this." She stepped away. He followed. She was moving in the general direction of the bed and he was growing steadily more interested in consummating this marriage of inconvenience.

He raised his hands to her shoulders, keeping her still. His fingertips hesitated on the soft skin of her neck, then he allowed himself to stroke gently. Her skin was actually quite lovely, white and fine. His groin underwent a slight stirring. He leaned closer to draw in a breath of her.

Warm sweet air rose from her hair and her neck. Was

that flowers or fruit she made him think of? Or did he care? No, his rising desire decided it for him. He didn't care as long as he could keep filling his senses with sweet soft skin.

He opened his eyes to gaze down at her. The view down the neckline of her dowdy nightdress was frankly tantalizing. The male animal within him was having more success pushing aside the logical gentleman than Knight would ever have suspected. What just moments ago had seemed overly plump now seemed nicely ripened. What had seemed plain and undesirable now showed hints of satin and fire . . .

He bent to press his lips to the ivory silkiness of the back of her neck. He thumbed the shoulders of her gown aside to reach more delightful skin. The neckline resisted him, so he tipped her head to one side while he nimbly unfastened the row of tiny pearl buttons that locked away those plump treasures.

Kitty's toes were curled tightly in her slippers and her knees had gone to pudding. All she could think was that Mr. Knight had the warmest lips she had ever imagined. Warm, damp kisses on her sensitive neck, on her exposed shoulder . . . The heat radiated directly through her, right to her belly and below.

When his fingers parted the bodice of the gown and pulled the warm flannel open, Kitty very nearly lost her sense of up and down, light and dark. Cool air wafted over her skin for a brief moment, then hot hard palms pressed gently over her breasts.

Oh, heavens.

Those fiery palms pressed her backward until she leaned gratefully upon something sturdy and wide. Heat seeped through the back of her gown. His heat, radiating from that magnificent chest. The man was afire and Kitty felt her own flames being fed by his touch.

Gently, her heavy breasts were hefted and caressed, his touch spiraling in from the outer flesh to the more sensitive inner skin. Kitty's hands fisted at her sides as the slow torture of his progress began to make her hips squirm of their own volition.

Touch me. Please.

"I am." The warmth of breath on her neck only sent her further into these new and mystifying sensations. The deep voice continued, murmuring softly alongside her ear.

"So responsive, aren't you, darling? Who would have thought there was so much fire inside?"

He touched her nipples at last, his fingertips wrapping around the aching points. He gently rolled them in his fingers, every tiny twist sending bolts of lightning to a spot directly between her thighs. Kitty inhaled sharply and pressed back against him further. Someone was making the most outlandish little animal noises. It was only with distant surprise that Kitty realized it was her.

"So very delicious," that deep voice murmured into her neck. "I must have a taste, Bettina."

Kitty's eyes flew open. Bitty's husband! Naked breasts! She squeaked and shot from his grip like a ball from a cannon.

Knight was left standing with his hands wrapped around empty air and his erection straining his trousers. With more agility than he would have credited her with, his previously quivering bride bounded onto and over the bed to stand warily on the other side with her gown twisted closed.

Knight's hands felt empty. He didn't like it. Not ten feet away there was warm female flesh to be savored, warm female secrets to be discovered. Dimly he recalled that he was a civilized man, a gentleman of refinement and restraint. He strove to be all that was gallant.

But not at this moment.

Now, he wanted *more*.

Kitty's flesh tingled as if he'd branded her with hot coals. As irresistible as the pull was, more powerful was the need to pull away. She gathered her undone gown about her more tightly. This wasn't going well at all. He was being rather persistent—actually, he was being quite devastatingly primitive—and she was finding it painful to resist him.

She tamped down her desire to face her tormentor. "I'm not going to."

He stopped in the act of raising one knee to the mattress, apparently quite prepared to pursue her around the room until she dropped. A sort of haze dropped from his expression and his gaze sharpened on her face.

"Not going to what?"

Kitty blushed but kept her stance. "Not going to—" She waved at the bed between them. "You understand?"

He went very still but Kitty had the impression that he might yet leap across the bed to capture her. Pin her down and ravish her like a beast. *Heavens.* A shiver went through her at the thought. A shiver of revulsion, of course.

Oh, is that what they are naming it these days? I thought it was called bald wanton lust.

"Why not?"

For a moment, Kitty actually had to wonder if she'd hurt his feelings. Then she reminded herself that cold and grim Mr. Knight had no feelings. She folded her arms more tightly. "I'm afraid I—" Oh, dear. How to buy some time?

He straightened slowly. The sharpness left his expression and he shrugged. "Ah. You need a bit more time to accustom yourself to your new home. Very well, I shall not press you tonight." With that, he turned and strode from the room. His open robe flapped loosely about his trouser legs, making him look for all the world like a disgruntled sheik.

Kitty gaped for a moment at his abrupt departure. Then she flew across the room to press home the latch that locked his adjoining chamber from hers. Breathlessly, she leaned against the finely carved wood. Her knees were shaking with relief . . . or was that disappointment?

He thought her fearful, properly virginal and timid. Unfortunately, that was not as true as it should have been, at least the timid part. Yet entirely useful, on further consideration. She could play upon it, if it would buy her enough time to recover Bitty, and then all would be right. She would be back with her parents, Bitty would be here, and Knight would have his wedding night as he desired.

Abruptly she became angry. This was not fair. Her first kiss, her first feelings of true desire, her first experience of the heat of a man's hands on her skin—and none of it was truly hers. All rightfully belonged to Bitty, who apparently didn't want them.

As she bent to blow out the last candle before she climbed into the large and empty bed, Kitty wondered how she was supposed to go home to her parents after this charade was over and continue acting the part of an oblivious maiden. Especially now that she had felt the warmth and hardness of Alfred Theodious Knight's magnificent bare chest.

CHAPTER 3

The next morning, Kitty awoke to the sound of a muffled thump in her room. She rolled over in the tangled bedding to peer at Bitty's maid—what had she said her name was? Oh, yes, Martha—who was latching up Bitty's dress trunk.

Kitty sat up in bed and stretched her toes deeper under the covers. Bloody Knight and his bloody chest. She'd hardly slept a wink, and when she had, she'd dreamed of sheiks and pirates and highwaymen, all with Knight's intense dark gaze.

Time to dress, unfortunately. Bitty's trousseau was a horror, all ruffled gowns and bead-encrusted slippers. Bitty was very proud of it all. Kitty wasn't looking forward to wearing any of it.

However, the wardrobe held not a single item of Bitty's. Instead there hung within it an array of exquisite gowns, tasteful outerwear, and amazing day dresses. Stunned, Kitty clambered off the bed to step forward, reaching to stroke the bodice of an amber silk evening gown that very nearly glowed in the morning light.

"The master chose it to match your eyes," the maid said happily. "There's ever so much more coming. Bags and gloves and shoes to match, and the underthings—oh, madam, wait until you see the underthings!"

The girl turned toward the large chest of drawers by the window. Kitty watched her go, but felt her eyes drawn back to the lovely gowns. Walking dresses of crisp peppermint stripe, spring green, and even one of most impractical ivory. There was a summer cape of wool so fine it seemed almost a silk, and a winter one trimmed in ermine. There was even a riding habit, for heaven's sake, of a deep chocolate velvet that shimmered under Kitty's touch.

She'd have to learn to ride, just for the pleasure of wearing it—but it was not hers to learn to ride in. Kitty blinked. She felt as if the room had suddenly come back into focus. Before her stood a wardrobe full of lovely tasteful things, but none of it was to Bitty's taste. In fact, Bitty would loathe them and call them plain and dull.

Yet Bitty would never be able to withstand a glowering Knight the way that Kitty had. One glance from those disturbing eyes and Bitty would silently comply . . . and wear something she hated every day for the rest of her life.

Kitty looked about her. Where had Bitty's carefully chosen things gone? Even as she had the thought, a tap on the door gave way to an expressionless footman whose eyes never strayed to Kitty in her dressing gown. The young man hefted the empty trunk to his shoulder with a puff of exhalation, as though it were heavy. Or full.

She gasped. "Hold there!" The footman only increased his pace from the room. Kitty ran after him into the hallway. She tugged at his sleeve, causing him to stop instantly. "Are those my things?"

The footman was obviously trying to be respectful and not gaze at her in her dressing gown, but he was also trying to answer her direct question with respect. He settled on bobbing his bowed head repeatedly. "Yes, madam."

"Where is the rest of it?"

"In the attic, madam."

"Bring it back at once. All of it."

"But the master ordered it, madam." To his credit, the fellow seemed honestly torn.

"Well, am—am I not your mistress now? Do you not obey my orders as well?"

"Yes, madam."

"Then I order you to return this trunk to my chamber, along with all the others. Immediately!"

"But madam, the master said—"

Kitty grabbed hold of one of the trunk pulls with determination. The footman resisted.

"I. Don't. Care. What. The. Master. Said." She punctuated each word with a tug. She didn't notice the horrified stillness that had befallen Martha and the footman until a pair of polished black boots entered her lowered vision.

"Of course, that would be Mr. Knight," she breathed.

"That would be quite correct, Mrs. Knight," a deep voice responded.

She looked up to see him standing before her in a chocolate brown riding coat of superfine and a snowy shirt of linen. Buff jodhpurs were tucked into the high boots. A riding whip twitched against one boot top, making an entirely inappropriate thought pop into Kitty's head. He looked completely delicious, even with the scowl.

A distant portion of Kitty's brain imagined how wonderful she would look beside him in the matching riding habit . . . *on matching white steeds, riding away into a sunset.*

"Mrs. Knight, have you a gastric complaint?"

Kitty's fantasy disappeared. She was back in the chilly hallway in her dressing gown and tangled hair, playing tug-of-war with a footman. "I beg your pardon?"

Knight's scowl deepened. "You had a very odd expression upon your face. Are you ill?"

"No." That much she was sure of. The rest took a moment to come back to her. Then anger swept away her discomfort and embarrassment. Lovely thing, anger. Good thing she always had a bit of it on tap.

Without letting go of the trunk, she aimed her glare at Bitty's thoughtless and overbearing husband. "Have you any idea how much deliberation and expense went into this trousseau?"

Mr. Knight swept the trunk with a dismissive glance. "Inferior choices and wasted expense."

"Yet it was B—it was my choice and expense, not yours. These are my things, to do with as I please. I please to hang them back up in that wardrobe. And I please to wear them!"

Dark distaste crossed Mr. Knight's face. It made him very nearly frightening. "I desire that you do not raise your voice in this house." His voice was deadly cold. "I'd have thought you had more restraint than this."

Bitty would have. Bitty would never squeak at this high-handed treatment. Right there in the hallway, with her hands still wrapped around the brass pull of the trunk, Kitty saw clearly what Bitty's life would be like under this tyrant. Well, not if she could bloody help it. Let him just try to control her, just let him dare. "Then you do intend to refuse me my things?"

"I do. You have much finer replacements in your chamber." He checked the watch in his pocket, obviously considering the matter closed. "I suggest you don them—"

Kitty cut loose with a wail guaranteed to peel the paper from the walls. She let go of the trunk to cover her face with her hands, leaving a sliver of visibility between her fingers, of course.

The look on Knight's face was priceless. Pure horror, with a tinge of fear. Perfect. Kitty wailed louder, and shook off Martha's attempt to comfort her. "You—don't—like—me—anymore!" The words came out in earsplitting gasps.

Hmm. Judging by the glimmer of comprehension on Knight's face, she might have gone too far. Ah well, nothing to do but press on. "I want to go h-h-home!" Kitty broke into a run, bursting through the half-circle of three appalled spectators. Without once removing her hands from her face, she pelted down the stairs and headed for the front door.

In the front hall, she had to slow a bit to let them catch up. Honestly, were they going to let her dare the street in her dressing gown? She almost giggled. Knight was about to get a great deal more than a raised voice if he didn't—

A large square hand planted itself on the door before
her. "What the bloody hell are you about?" Knight roared.

With a great deal of satisfaction, Kitty lowered her
hands to clasp them primly before her. "Tut-tut, Mr.
Knight. I desire that you do not raise your voice in this
house."

He went white. Then red. Then purple. "Intriguing,"
Kitty murmured. Then she turned her sweetest smile on
the footman. "What is your name, dear man?"

The fellow actually looked to Knight first. Goodness,
they were all entirely loyal to the master, weren't they?
Grudgingly, Kitty had to admit that spoke favorably on
Mr. Knight's behalf. The master didn't speak, apparently
too enraged.

Finally, the footman shrugged. "My name's Watt, madam."

Kitty increased the syrup in her smile and fluttered her
eyelashes. "Watt, will you be a darling and bring all my
pretty things back to my chamber?"

Watt looked to the master again, but there was no coun-
termand this time. Knight seemed quite lost in his ire. Watt
shrugged again and nodded. "Yes, madam." He left with
Martha trailing in his wake.

Mr. Knight began to inhale and exhale once more, although they were great heaving breaths. At least his rage
wasn't going to cause asphyxiation. Kitty tilted her head
at him. Should she stay and twist him up once more?

She eyed the large hands clenched at his sides. Ah,
perhaps not. With a twitch of her dressing gown, she was
running back up the stairs. It was a shame to replace all
those lovely things with Bitty's horrid trousseau, really.

Still, it was a matter of principle.

Knight was forced to return to lessons of long ago as he
stood alone in the entrance hall. Breathe. He forced his

emotions to quiet, pulled them back within him and stoppered them once more. The tumult inside stilled, then seeped away. Cool, safe reason ruled once more.

He felt solid once more, steady. Yet how had he ever been shaken from that place he had so carefully built all those years ago? Not since his boyhood had he been so lost to temper and passion. Unless one counted last night.

Knight turned his gaze up the stairs as if he could see through walls. She would be changing into one of those awful frocks, he knew. He thought of the glances she would draw, the supercilious brows she would raise, even the whispers that might ensue. The laughter.

Yet this battle was the least of the problem. That maneuver—threatening to run into the street—had been outrageous and impulsive, not to mention clearly manipulative. Everything he did not want in a wife.

Knight felt very much as if he'd paid top price for a blooded carriage horse and been handed the reins of a zebra. There was no predicting the actions of such a creature. He hardened his jaw. Very well, then, he'd been had. Yet all was not lost. People could be trained, even as he had trained himself to still his own passions—to behave with utmost rectitude. Much could be done with the lot he had been handed.

Life in the Knight household was not going to be quite what the new mistress expected. Her challenge would be met and her cause most certainly lost. There would be propriety.

Yet there was no denying that even as Knight turned to set his plan into motion, he was feeling more alive than he had in years.

In her new chamber, Kitty secretly bade a mournful goodbye to the elegant contents of the wardrobe as Martha exchanged the lot for Bitty's trousseau. Ruffles it would be, all in the name of sisterly loyalty. Perhaps when Bitty returned, she would consider disposing of those lovely things into more appreciative hands.

And if a few of the worst things became soiled or damaged before Bitty returned, all the better. Cheering at that thought, Kitty donned a purplish silk morning dress that made her bosom look like a hearth mantel and her skin fade to deathly pale. It was the worst of Bitty's inventions. Kitty felt it her bounden duty to ruin it before noon.

Martha left the room to supervise the storing of Mr. Knight's selections and came back twisting her hands nervously. "I beg your pardon, madam, but Mr. Knight has ordered us all from the house."

Kitty stopped in the act of tucking a stray wisp of hair away. Turning from the mirror, she blinked at Martha in dismay. "From the house? He's not sacked you, has he?"

"Oh no, madam. Much the opposite." Martha looked away. "He said we was to take our days off, madam."

"We?"

"The staff, madam. We're all to go." The girl stepped forward earnestly. "I don't want to leave you, madam."

Kitty was beyond confused. "Nor do I want you to."

"Thank you, madam. I know the master planned to travel soon. But I thought I was to go along on the honeymoon in your service."

The honeymoon. A few weeks at Mr. Knight's estate in the Cotswolds, Bitty had bragged. Oh, dear. She'd forgotten completely about the honeymoon. "Where is Mr. Knight now, Martha?"

"Waiting for you at breakfast, madam."

Kitty brushed past Martha, absently patting her shoulder as she passed. "You must follow your master's orders, dear." Not having a maid would be the least of her worries if she was going to be dragged from London before Bitty could return.

Mr. Knight was indeed at breakfast, although he hadn't

waited for her. He sat in the bright breakfast room with his newssheet and a nearly finished plate of kippers and eggs. He didn't so much as look up as she hesitated outside the open door.

Kitty tried to think. How to delay this disaster? She needed something altogether reasonable in order to convince him, she was sure. Reasonable and intelligent.

She was entirely the wrong woman for the job, then. Still, there must be something she could say to dissuade him from leaving town. Bitty wouldn't be able to follow and they couldn't switch places for weeks. Weeks in which Mr. Knight would certainly demand a few of those fascinating, dangerous marital rights.

"We cannot leave London!" The words burst from her, born of panic. She strode into the room to face him across the table.

He rose, lifting a napkin to his lips for a moment as he considered her coolly. Then he placed it carefully next to his plate. "We are not."

Kitty felt as though she'd missed a step. "W-what?"

"Mrs. Knight, we are not leaving London."

Kitty waved a hand in the general direction of her room. "But Martha said she'd been dismissed for days."

"Indeed she has. As have Watt and Fenster and my cook, Mrs. Till. Only my driver remains." He stepped away from his chair and rounded the table. "If you cannot allow me to be master over my own staff, then we will have to make do with no staff." He raised a brow. "That is, *you* will have to make do with no staff."

No staff? He was punishing her, teaching her not to defy his orders to the servants. She felt a twist of humiliation within her. She'd misbehaved again, she'd stepped out of line—

Wait a moment. She had merely defended Bitty's right to wear clothing of her choosing. Now he was punishing shy, timid Bitty for it. At that moment, uncertainty turned to steel. Take the high hand with her sister, would he?

This man needed training if he was going to be a good husband for Bitty. Kitty almost hoped Bitty would stay away for a few days.

To Alfred the Odious, Kitty turned wide eyes, blinking rapidly. "N-no staff? B-but who will cook for me and button me? Who will carry my purchases?"

His expression became positively smug. The rat. "You'll cook for yourself and tend to your own wardrobe. As for purchases, I don't believe you'll be needing any pin money for the next few weeks, do you?"

To be truthful, Kitty had a reticule full of banknotes upstairs. Mama wasn't fond of letting Papa know too much about her expenditures. Contrition was easier than cajoling, Mama always said. Kitty was certainly learning the truth of that statement.

But Mr. Knight didn't need to know that.

"Oh, dear!" She brought a theatrical hand to her cheek. "No pin money?" She almost rolled her eyes at the satisfaction that crossed his expression. Delicious physique or not, this man was pure evil. By the time Bitty returned, changes needed to be made. And Kitty was just the woman for the task.

She was going to make him wish he'd never been born.

He'd obviously been born for the task. Knight watched his stunned bride flee the room, her waywardness quite erased, he was sure. That had been quite simple. Really, a stern offensive was best for all concerned. He seriously doubted she would ever go against his will again.

He smoothed his waistcoat with a tug. The flash of humiliation that had crossed her expression bothered him. Damn it all, he hadn't wanted to crush her. He'd simply wanted her to realize that he would brook no opposition, and he'd done just that. He'd won the day.

So why, when he remembered the hurt in those big brown eyes, did he feel a sense of defeat?

• • •

Kitty stopped running the moment she'd turned the corner in the hall. Her stomach rumbled, a reminder that she'd not yet broken her fast. Remembering Mr. Knight's single plate at the table, she guessed that he'd not ordered anything served for her.

Grinning, she wandered the large house until she stumbled upon the stairs down to the kitchen. It was an orderly place, obviously well kept, but the cook was nowhere to be seen. A bowl covered by a checked cloth revealed dough rising. Kitty smirked. Mr. Knight obviously knew nothing about women, if he'd ordered his cook to walk away from her baking.

The dough looked as though it had a good while to go yet. Kitty wandered into the larder. Shelves of lovely things awaited. A pudding sat cooling in a crock, and a number of pies with golden and sugary crusts met her delighted gaze. A ham sat on a plank for slicing, and a flick of another checked cloth revealed a number of meat pastries just waiting for someone hungry to come along.

"All for me," sighed Kitty. She set about making a feast with a slice of ham, a wedge of pie, a morsel of cheese, and a pear from the bowl on the great worktable. She ate slowly, enjoying the warm morning sun that dripped like honey through the small window over the dry sink. She popped the last bit of cheese into her mouth and sighed aloud. "Poor Mr. Knight. No cook, no maid, no footman. How will he get by?"

CHAPTER 4

Knight had very little work to do, since he'd tied up all his affairs for his honeymoon. Once he'd finished his duties and sent his driver off with his post, Knight realized he hadn't seen his bride for some time. She'd been bustling to and fro all day, distracting him mightily. He'd never known when he might be treated to a view of rounded bottom raised as she dusted beneath a table in the room across the hall, or catch a glimpse of delicate ankle as she stepped on a footstool to dust a high shelf.

Of course, he hadn't seen all that from behind his desk, but it was amazing what a man could find to do about his front hall when he had the time.

Feeling oddly without direction now, Knight walked the halls of his own house with his hands stuffed into his pockets. Without servants to direct or calls to make, it hardly seemed as though he had any sort of work to do all.

Was that all his days amounted to? Orders and talk?

What nonsense. He was a man of great industry, well on his way to securing a substantial fortune and a certain influence in the world. The name Knight had come to mean something in the past ten years, finally erasing society's tendency to equate it with shocking behavior and tawdry tales.

Speaking of shocking, where was that wife of his?

Kitty dusted off her hands and examined her work with satisfaction. The house gleamed. She'd spent a very busy afternoon doing the dusting and the baking. The baking because she wanted to eat tonight. The dusting because she was going mad waiting for some sign from Bitty.

Unfortunately, the post had already come. She had checked it eagerly after using her own money to pay the deliveryman. Her fishing expedition had reeled in no results. Not one of the letters mentioned "Kitty" but for some bewildered responses that they had not had any reason to see her.

So there remained nothing to do but wait. Should she go to Mama and Papa? She flinched as she imagined the sheer volume of the scene which would ensue.

But what if Bitty was in serious trouble? A woman could disappear in London if she wasn't careful. Still, girlish delight in horror stories notwithstanding, both she and Bitty were usually most careful.

Kitty certainly hoped no one had harmed her sister, especially since she reserved that right for herself. "Come back, Bitty," she whispered to the silent house. "I can't hope to fool him forever."

Dinner. Knight sniffed appreciatively. The smell of baking had warmed the house for the last hours. Knight had missed his tea. He hoped his bride would be preparing a decent meal.

What if she couldn't cook? Perhaps dismissing *all* the servants had been hasty. So many ladies were never required to step foot in their own kitchens—why would the Trapp household be any different? But the scent of bread reassured him. When he entered the dining room, he sat expectantly at his place.

Bettina entered soon after, bearing a full plate. Knight perked up at the sight of thick slices of ham and fried potatoes. Simple food to be sure, but he would be sure to compliment her nonetheless. It was important to reward good behavior—

She set the plate down opposite him and sat down. With a flourish, she opened the napkin over her lap and set to. Knight sat openmouthed as she cut a dainty bite of ham and popped it into her mouth. He cleared his throat. She looked up and smiled in a friendly manner, but kept chewing. The appreciative sounds she made caused his own stomach to growl in response.

The sound echoed through the silent room. The clink of her knife and fork ceased. He looked up from his envious examination of her dinner to see that she had become quite crimson of face.

Good. She deserved to be embarrassed, failing so miserably in her wifely duties. Then he heard a snicker escape her full mouth. With affront he realized that she was not embarrassed, she was *laughing* at him!

Kitty tried with all her might not to laugh, but the look of mingled yearning and infuriation on Mr. Knight's face was too much to bear in silence.

With a fierce scrape he pushed back his chair and strode from the room. Kitty heaved a happy sigh and took another bite. He wouldn't find the best of the larder, she'd made sure of that.

After she'd had several more lovely mouthfuls, Mr. Knight strode back into the dining room to slap a plate onto the tablecloth with such force that she feared for the fine bone china. "If you break that, you'll get shards in your cheese," she pointed out helpfully.

For cheese and a torn hunk of bread was all he'd mustered from the stripped larder. It was his own fault if he hadn't thought to check the cupboard beneath the stairs. "Men," she sighed. "Helpless in the kitchen."

"Women," came the growled reply. "Spiteful in every way."

She put down her fork to fold her hands before her plate. "*I* did not dismiss the servants out of spite. *I* did not tear the cook from her kitchen purely to starve someone into submission." She considered his plate. "In fact, it is thanks to me that you've bread at all."

She could see the battle within as it shadowed his face. A gentleman would thank her for her efforts, and compliment the results. A tyrant would not. It was as though she could see a clock pendulum casting to and fro within him. *Gentleman. Tyrant. Gentleman. Tyrant.*

She took pity on his dilemma. "It was not meant to be a poser, Mr. Knight. You may eat my bread without thanking me for it."

Of course, now he truly ought to thank her for her understanding. She sat back to enjoy the play of irritation and dismay across his face. Really, the man was too easy. There was little fun in such conquest. But Kitty was never one to pass up a little fun.

Knight finally managed a very grudging nod of thanks, but he wasn't able to do much more than pick at the meal he'd worked so hard for. This woman he'd married was his worst nightmare come to walk the earth. A stubborn and unpredictable creature with much too high an opinion of her own opinion. Of course, there was the fact that he'd never been less bored by a female.

But bored was surely preferable to such constant conflict and insecurity. She needed taming. As Knight considered possible measures, it occurred to him that there was one ground where he undoubtedly held the advantage. While not a promiscuous man, he had a certain amount of experience in matters of the bedroom. What he needed was to gain influence over her. Intimidation was not working. But what of seduction?

He hid a grin behind his napkin. Yes, a proposal with benefits for all. He'd take it out on her hide—that lovely silken hide. She be at his feet by midnight.

Knight prepared to ride into battle. He combed his hair. He bathed lightly in the basin in his chamber. He splashed a bit of oil of sandalwood on his neck and chest. Then he tied his velvet dressing gown over nothing but trousers. Eyeing himself in the glass, he remembered how his bride had shown a certain interest in his chest. With a dry tweak of his lips at his own reflection, he opened the dressing gown a bit more.

All was fair in love and war and marriage, it seemed. He laid one hand on the latch of the door between the master's and the madam's chambers. The door stuck tight. Locked, of course.

A man on a mission should always be prepared. He reached into the pocket of his dressing gown to retrieve the key. With a thrust and a twist, her key fell from the other side of the lock and the door opened under his hand. Knight stepped through quickly and bent to sweep the other key from where it had fallen.

Bettina sat at her dressing table, half turned on her stool to stare openmouthed at him. A hairbrush hung from her grip and Knight was treated to the stunning sight of his wife's hair hanging smooth and shimmering down her back. It was spun gold in sunlight. Beautiful. He suddenly wanted to feel it draped over his bare flesh.

While he stared at her crowning glory, she took advantage of his distraction to jump to her feet and dash to the other side of the bed. She stood with feet braced apart, wielding the brush before her like some sort of blunt, bristly knife.

She was wearing another example of flannel gone to seed, he noticed, though fortunately she hadn't gotten around to buttoning up the bodice yet. What treasures! It occurred to him with great satisfaction that those were his treasures, to do with as he wished. As master of the house and of his wife, he could take full advantage of ownership any time of the day or night.

The thought of exposing those full globes to the light of day . . . oh, perhaps in his study sometime during a break from his business affairs. She might bring him tea and he might pull her into his lap and let down that magnificent hair to fall about him as he tugged her neckline down to satisfy an entirely different appetite.

Hmm. There might just be a few unrecorded benefits to these marriage shackles. All that was needed was a bit of persuasion. With afternoon gains in mind, he started forward.

"Stop just there, Mr. Knight!"

The authority in meek and mild Bettina's voice surprised him from his lustful reverie. He stopped despite himself.

"Now turn around and return to your room."

He glanced at her weapon of choice. "Or you'll groom me to death?"

She scowled at him. "Anything can be a danger if one knows where to strike."

That surprised a grunt from him. So she had learned a lesson from her past lack of caution. This was not a problem, however. He had no doubt he could manage against her feeble defiance. She had given him the key to her defenses the previous night.

"I won't force you, Bettina."

She lowered the brush slightly. "No, I don't believe you would." Then she raised it defensively once more. "But you can be a little too convincing, once you get within arm's reach. I have no intention of letting you get close enough."

"You are my wife," he coaxed. "This cannot go on forever."

She muttered something under her breath. It sounded like "I don't need forever."

"You should resolve yourself to your state now." He took a deep breath to draw her attention to his bared chest. He saw her gaze waver and the tip of her tongue cross her lips for a brief flicker. He allowed his attraction to her show on his face. "I can be quite persuasive, you know."

She gave her head a brief shake at that, as if forcing herself from a reverie of her own—then burst out laughing. "And your actions today are your idea of persuading a woman? Trying to take away her possessions, banishing her servants, and canceling her honeymoon?"

Knight stiffened. "Well, when one says it so—"

"It matters not how one says it. The fact is that you haven't the slightest idea who your wi—who I am, and you've so far shown no interest in finding out. The way to a woman's bed is through her heart, not just her eyes!"

He tightened the belt of his dressing gown with a frustrated yank. "So you wish empty compliments and forced endearments?" he said derisively. "That only makes a woman seem foolish to me."

"Oh, the compliments had best be full to the brim," she said with her eyes narrowed. "Go on, try it. Attempt to say one blasted complimentary thing about me."

He looked at her, then looked away. He shoved his hands into his pockets, then removed them. "You have lovely skin," he mumbled to the carpet.

She leaned nearer, her head tilted as if to hear better. "So sorry, didn't catch that."

He heaved a sigh of irritation. "You have beautiful skin," he barked. "Like bloody ivory satin!"

To his shock, she actually colored prettily. "Why thank you, Mr. Knight," she replied with a small curtsy. When she dipped low, Knight was treated to a view into the valley of delights. She took a pointed step closer.

Very rewarding. Perhaps there was something to this compliment thing. He cleared his throat and tried again. "Your figure is most attractive. Especially your—" He halted, frozen with indecision. He couldn't continue, no gentleman would, yet the challenge in her eyes wouldn't allow him to stop. "Especially your . . . décolletage."

"Hmm." She considered him for a long moment. Then she moved forward another step. "I believe you have potential, sir, although we must work on your delivery."

She was only a few inches from the edge of the mattress. If he could tempt her closer, she would be forced to mount the bed linens. Whereupon *he* could mount *her*.

An objective was a lovely thing for a man to have. It gave structure to his imagination, focus to his every thought. He took a deep breath, prepared to win the day. "You are very witty."

She took a step back. "Point to me," she said briskly. "You're lying now."

"No!" He thought furiously. "Elegant! I meant elegant!"

She narrowed her eyes. He waited, his breath caught in his chest. She stepped back again.

"Bloody hell! I told you what every woman wants to hear! What more do you want?"

"Every woman does not want to hear that she is witty and elegant, Mr. Knight. Every woman wants to believe that *you* consider her witty and elegant."

"But I—" He stopped, frustrated. If he claimed it was so, he'd cross even his own boundaries into lying. "Blast it, you are the most frustrating female on the face of this earth!"

A sad smile tweaked her lips. "That was honest, at the very least. But—" She took another step back, until she was standing where she had begun. "Match quite lost, I'm afraid."

"Bloody hell," roared Knight, and fled the field in defeat.

Kitty didn't allow herself to breathe freely until the door had closed. He'd taken the blasted key of course, but she didn't believe he'd be back tonight.

Another night away from her home. Another night with which to ruin her reputation and future forever. Another night with Bitty lost to the cobbled wilds of the city.

It was a good thing Knight had left the room, for she

was just starting to realize how delicious he'd looked with his dressing gown spread open over his virile chest. She closed her eyes to preserve the memory of that dark tracing of manly hair that rode the hard contours of his chest and trailed down to a most fascinating and forbidden land beneath his navel.

He was entirely perfect. And he was Bitty's.

Kitty covered her face with her hands and heaved a great sigh. She was truly beginning to dislike Bitty for the first time in her life.

The next morning as Knight dawdled over his papers, his bride breezed into his study in a truly horrid gown of orange and purple striped silk. Since Knight had just been adding imaginative details to his favorite new daydream concerning his study, it took him a moment to realize she wasn't merely an overdressed version of his fantasy.

Of course, he would never imagine such a gown. She stood gazing at the filled shelves with her fists upon her hips. "Perhaps if I dust all the books, I can somehow irreparably damage this awful dress," she muttered.

"I've a tinderbox if you'd like to burn it," Knight offered.

She whirled in surprise. Her full lips formed a perfect O. Marvelous what that expression did for a woman's appeal. Primed for a kiss.

Abruptly, Knight tired of fantasies and midnight tests. He tossed aside the newssheet he'd not been reading and stood. With two long strides he was close enough to pull her into his arms. Bettina gasped as he drew her hard against his chest.

There was that O again. He covered it with his own mouth, taking her lips forcefully. A voice within him warned him that he was being too rough, that she was too timid and innocent to bear such handling.

Then she kissed him back.

CHAPTER 5

Kitty had never dreamed a man's mouth could be so hot within. He tasted of tea and tobacco and Knight, and she wanted *more*. She wriggled her arms free of his grasp without ever taking her mouth from his. She wrapped her hands around his neck and drove her fingers into his thick dark hair to pull him down closer to her.

His grip tightened. She loved it, loved the secure feeling his strong arms imparted, loved the way it pressed his hips tighter to hers. His tongue slid between her lips, dipping into her like the first taste of an Italian ice.

How vulgar. How wicked. How *wonderful*.

He pulled her back with him until he'd seated himself in his chair and her on his lap. Never once did their lips part. Kitty felt delightfully tiny against his strength and wriggled as close to him as she could, pressing her breasts hard to his chest to ease the outrageous tingling they suddenly suffered.

His hands were now free to roam her body and they did. Hard hands on her bottom, hot hands covering her bodice. Dear God, how many hands did the man have?

Not enough. She wanted more.

He was fumbling with her buttons in the back. His clumsiness might have been charming if she hadn't been in a bloody hurry to feel his hot hard hands on her bare flesh. Uncurling her own fingers from their death lock on his hair, Kitty reached behind her to push his hands away and do it herself.

He wasn't patient enough. With adorable urgency, he tugged at her neckline, pulling it down to expose the tops of her breasts. Kitty's hands went limp on her own buttons when his mouth met her flushed skin. Oh, heavens. Oh, *yes*. She arched her back to press her breasts closer to his searching lips and tongue. She felt him tugging harder to free her completely from her bodice.

The buttons gave and the silk dropped low around her waist. Kitty only laughed and wrapped her fingers into his hair again as he dove face first into her bosom with a groan. The buttons didn't matter, the gown didn't matter. She'd been wanting to ruin it anyway before Bitty saw it again—

Bitty's buttons. Bitty's dress.

Bitty's husband.

With a cry, Kitty flung herself free of Knight's lap, his hot mouth, and his hard searching hands.

Knight sat there, his expression dazed and his hands still reaching. "Wh—Bettina?"

With both hands, she pressed her bodice high to cover herself as she backed away. "I am a terrible person. Oh, dear God, forgive me!"

She wanted to run, trailing hems, torn buttons, and all, back to her chamber. Away from Knight, but most of all, away from the wicked, wicked woman who was herself. But what help would that be? She was still the wrong woman in the wrong house, the wrong woman in his embrace.

This last refusal had evidently pushed Mr. Knight too far, for he flung himself to his feet. "What do you mean by this—this *performance?*"

Kitty took one instinctive step away from his black scowl, then stopped and raised her chin. "I apologize for forgetting myself, Mr. Knight."

He shoved his hand through his hair. "It wasn't the forgetting that I minded, it was the remembering," he muttered.

Kitty was fairly sure she wasn't supposed to hear that. The truth was, she couldn't agree more. How lovely it might have been if she had not remembered that she was writhing half-naked on the lap of her sister's husband.

Somehow she didn't believe that explanation would soothe Mr. Knight. Yet how to explain away her swift reversal? She pushed a lock of fallen hair behind her ear, keeping one hand holding up her bodice.

He looked rumpled and confused and quite delicious with his customary aloofness shattered at his feet. He gazed back at her, his jaw working and his face flushed. Yet for all his temper, she was not afraid. In fact, she preferred him flustered and upset to cool and remote. Unfortunately, she also felt quite guilty about causing his state.

He turned away, letting free a small growl of frustration as he tugged his waistcoat back into place. "Mrs. Knight," he said without turning. "Would you care to explain your reasons for not consummating our union?"

Oh, dear. Alfred the Odious was back. Kitty sighed. She must convince him to withhold his advances, just a bit longer, just until Bitty returned. She took a deep breath. "I was very sheltered, Mr. Knight."

He nodded sharply. "Of course you were."

Kitty went on, feeling her way. "Our short engagement did not give me time to prepare myself." That at least was the complete truth.

"And?"

Ah. Hmm. "And . . . well . . . that is all?" She hated the querying note in her voice but it was too late to take it back. She was a terrible liar, plain and simple.

He sent a dark glance over his shoulder, then looked away once more. "So you are not reluctant because of . . ." He cleared his throat. "That is to say, no past experience has turned you sour on . . . on relations?"

Heavens, he seemed to be struggling even more than she. Kitty frowned slightly. He couldn't know of Bitty's encounter with that awful Tuttle character, could he? No, no one knew but herself and two very close friends. "N-no," she replied, hoping she was speaking rightly for Bitty. "Nothing like that. It is only that . . ."

Oh, to blazes with it all. She threw up her hands, then slapped one back to her chest when her bodice began to slide. "You said you didn't like outrageous behavior, didn't you? I'd think a wrestling match in the study chair qualifies as outrageous by anyone's standards!"

He turned in surprise. Understanding mingled with a very annoying sort of assumption crossed his handsome face. Kitty waited warily, for surely some Odious statement was coming her way.

"But Bettina, your passion is wonderful when applied properly." He smiled reassuringly in a superior way. "It is merely that you apply it to every moment of your life, which I cannot permit in a wife."

Kitty blinked. Her prediction had been correct. "What are you saying? That as long as a woman saves her outrageous and impulsive nature for your exclusive pleasure but hides it at all other times, you will allow her to retain such a nature?"

His brows drew together. "Well, when you say it so—"

Kitty sighed her frustration. "Mr. Knight, I could spend the rest of my life translating you for yourself, but let me simplify things now. You cannot reform a person without their cooperation. If you wish something from someone, I recommend that you simply *ask*." Kitty looked down at her ruined gown. "While you ponder that outrageous and impulsive statement, I believe I ought to go change." She turned to leave the study.

Knight cleared his throat behind her. "Bettina . . . if you would . . ."

Kitty turned back, surprised. His tone had been almost courteous. "Yes, Mr. Knight?"

"I would very much like to see you wear one of the

gowns I chose for you." He seemed to struggle for a moment. "Please."

There was nothing she'd like more. "I would be happy to." Kitty smiled and shook her head at him. "Now was that so hard?"

Encouraged, he went on to ruin her good impression. "I had planned to call upon a friend this afternoon. Perhaps the red striped gown?"

"Choosing for me, Mr. Knight?" Kitty narrowed her eyes. "Do not press your good fortune."

His eyes darkened in irritation. Ah. Perhaps she had best not press her own fortune. Kitty smiled gaily at his annoyance and danced from the room, still clutching the ruined bodice tightly to her bosom.

It took a very long time for Knight to regain composure this time, but he managed. By the time the clock rang noon, he was once again a man in charge of his passions.

When Bettina returned downstairs, she was not wearing the red stripe, but her choice of pale green was entirely appropriate. He was pleased to see that it suited her coloring beautifully, making her pale skin glow ivory and rose and her pink lips look very ripe and inviting. At least, he was fairly sure it was the gown causing that effect.

In fact, he'd never seen her look better. It seemed he'd happened into taking a pretty wife after all. Perhaps he ought to try polite requests more often. He might be able to get her into more such suitable fashions.

Feeling very pleased with his new strategy, Knight didn't wait until the carriage had pulled around to make his next polite request. "I would very much appreciate it if you'd abandon your usual manner and behave with decorum during this visit. Please. Mrs. Arden's husband was a close friend, and I help her keep an eye on her business affairs. I shouldn't want you to do anything embarrassing in her presence." He hesitated for a moment. "Please."

Bettina blinked at him slowly. Then she smiled most prettily. "Perhaps you should write down what you want me to say?"

Excellent. The new strategy was working beautifully. He waved expansively. "No need to worry. Simply do precisely as I tell you."

Again the dimples flashed. "Nothing would make me happier, sir."

Knight helped her into the carriage, silently congratulating himself all the while.

Mrs. Arden was a widow, Kitty realized. A lovely, elegant widow whom Mr. Knight seemed to know all too well. Kitty couldn't pin down any one thing, but the ease he exhibited as he greeted Mrs. Arden—as opposed to his polite bow to the other ladies present—and the warmth of the lady's reply—well, it was quite disturbing, that's what it was!

Mistress? Perhaps not. Even Kitty could see no present undercurrent of attraction, and she was bloody well looking. Of course, Mr. Knight was married now, at least in his own mind. He might be a rigid, unbearable tyrant, but he seemed an honorable one. Kitty would wager Bitty's inheritance that Knight was at least as demanding of his own behavior as he was of others', if not more.

So why did she find the invisible bond between Knight and Mrs. Arden so painful? Possibly it was the unmitigated approval that he bestowed on the widow, approval that had never come her way and likely never would. Never come Bitty's way, she meant. Of course.

Perhaps that was why the devil came knocking when Mrs. Arden turned to her with a kind and welcoming smile.

"Mrs. Knight! How lovely to meet you at last. Please, won't you sit down?"

Kitty stood quite still. Mrs. Arden hesitated with her

hand still raised to wave Kitty to a seat. Knight glared at her. She merely blinked at him expectantly.

"Sit, Bettina," he growled.

Kitty sat so promptly the other ladies rose an inch from their cushions. One of them tittered. Kitty merely gazed amiably at all present.

"Ah . . . Mrs. Knight, have you enjoyed our pleasant weather this week?"

Knight watched as his bride sat with her hands in her lap and made no move to answer. Knight saw the glances exchanged between the other ladies. She was making a spectacle of herself. He felt the old familiar nausea rise. He stepped around to the back of the sofa and bent his mouth to Bettina's ear. "What are you doing?"

"Precisely as you tell me."

Knight felt his fingers close on the back of the sofa until his knuckles had surely turned white. "Converse with Mrs. Arden."

Bettina promptly turned to her hostess. "No, Mrs. Arden, I have not."

Obviously taken aback, Mrs. Arden blinked. "Have not what, Mrs. Knight?"

"Have not enjoyed the pleasant weather this week."

"Do you not favor the sunshine, Mrs. Knight? I find it very invigorating after so much rain."

"I adore sunshine, Mrs. Arden. Mr. Knight simply has not let me step foot out of doors in days."

The other two ladies present exchanged knowing glances. One of them erupted into high giggles, quickly hidden behind her gloved hand. Knight distinctly heard someone whisper, "Newlyweds!"

Bettina continued to smile blandly at her hostess. If one didn't know better, one would think her brainless. Knight wasn't going to fall for that again. She was no fool. She was bloody devious!

Mrs. Arden recovered her poise and turned her attention to him. "How has your health been, Mr. Knight?"

Knight opened his mouth to reply but his bride raced him to it. "Mr. Knight has been suffering some indigestion. I fear he does not bear his own cooking well."

"His own cooking? Have you lost your cook, then, Mrs. Knight?"

"Oh, no," replied the she-devil. "He sent all the servants on holiday. He wanted us to be alone in the house."

Muffled snorts came from the other ladies. Even Mrs. Arden seemed to be having difficulty maintaining a polite expression. Knight leaned down once more.

"What are you doing?" he hissed.

"I am conversing with Mrs. Arden, sir," she replied in normal tones.

Mrs. Arden gave a light laugh. "So formal, Mrs. Knight. Do you always address your new husband thus?"

Knight tensed. Not the harmless change of subject his hostess believed.

Bettina shook her head. "Oh, no, Mrs. Knight. I also call him Alfred Theodious."

She said his second name oddly, almost like—

Alfred the Odious. Knight felt a flush rise. One of the other ladies began to frankly bray. Mrs. Arden herself erupted into giggles that she valiantly tried to cover as a ladylike coughing spell.

"Mrs. Knight," he managed to say past gritted teeth. "Pray *stop* conversing with Mrs. Arden."

"Certainly."

Mrs. Arden caught up her composure, but the visit was over as far as Knight was concerned. As he pulled Bettina to her feet a bit too briskly, Mrs. Arden leaned close.

"I like her, Knight," she whispered. "I believe she'll do you good."

"I believe she'll do me in." Knight barely managed to convey the usual pleasantries as he hustled his wife from the house. Behind him he could feel the gossip flaring like the heat of a flash fire on his back.

. . .

The carriage pulled into traffic with a jerk. Kitty let the momentum carry her sprawling back on the cushions while she laughed out loud. "Oh, my, that was enormous fun."

His face showed stark anger. "That was inexcusable."

"Oh, pooh, Knight. What did I say that was so terrible? I told the absolute truth."

"You know precisely what you did! You—they believe—"

"They believe I'm a bit dim and that you are a veritable stallion. Not so far from the truth, I'd wager."

"You are anything but dim," he snarled. "You are as clever as hell."

Kitty blinked. "Truly? Do you think so?" She smiled at him. "That's the nicest thing you've ever said to me." Her smile dimmed slightly. "Of course, it's practically the only thing you've ever said to me, if I don't count the orders you've given."

"That's not so."

"Oh, yes," she told him. "It is so. I sincerely doubt you like me at all. Why did you wish to marry m— Why did you propose?"

He scowled at her. "You know why."

Of course, she didn't. But supposedly Bitty did. "Hmm." Kitty looked away from him.

"You really are the most impossible woman!"

In spite of her efforts to be just that, she was hurt. Bitty truly would be the wife he wanted. She would never oppose him nor would she misbehave in public. Bitty was a lady, through and through. At some point in the past few days, Kitty had ceased to be a caricature of Bitty and had begun to be herself.

And I am an impossible woman.

It was a good thing she would never be his wife in truth. She'd either drive him mad or be locked away herself.

She crossed her arms and made herself grin back into his scowl. "You really are the most overbearing man."

He seemed taken aback. "I am not. I am a most reasonable man."

She rolled her eyes. "Everyone considers themselves reasonable, particularly if they are not."

Mr. Knight opened his mouth to retort, but what could he say that would not prove her point? She waited, but he only huffed a great sigh of irritation and turned to face the window.

Heated silence invaded the carriage, making Kitty uncomfortable. As enjoyable as baiting the bear had been, now she regretted it. She'd thought he needed to be shaken from his stolid ways, but now she had the feeling there was much more to his aversion to public spectacle.

Unable to fight the feeling that she had gone too far, she turned to him. "Mr. Knight, I am sorry," she said sincerely. "It was not my intention to hurt you." His dark eyes fixed on her face. Encouraged, Kitty took a breath. "Perhaps if I knew why you recoil from a bit of tittle-tattle so—"

Knight jerked his gaze away and pounded on the trap above his head. The coachman flipped it open. "Stop here," Knight barked. "I've a need to—to purchase something."

The carriage pulled up before a tobacconist, but Knight leaped from it before it came to a complete stop. Kitty watched him flee her innocent question with new unease. Once again, she realized how little she knew of this man she was lying to with her every breath.

Unfair. So unfair, to him and to herself. If Bitty did not come today, she was going to have to tell Knight the truth.

In the meantime, she couldn't leave it like this, with him thinking her so uncaring and devious. The look on his face when he'd leaped from the carriage . . .

Such a fine face—a fine man. What was she doing? To toy with him, trick him like this, was against everything she believed in. What mad impulse had led her to walk down that fraudulent aisle to him, as if he were no more than a fleshless, heartless statue of a man? What selfish moment had led Bitty to allow it?

Kitty gazed morosely out of the carriage window. For a moment, she eyed her own reflection in the tobacconist's window, a pale face in a darkened square opening in a fine and shiny carriage. Her bonnet was a tad off center but she didn't care.

A woman pedestrian stopped to check her own bonnet in the glass, her face appearing slightly lower than Kitty's. The bonnet was expensive but gaudy. Orange silk ribbon decorated bright scarlet flowers. Absolutely awful. Kitty glanced idly into the woman's reflection, then away.

Then back.

Oh, God. The other woman raised a hand to tuck a free strand of blond hair away, then froze as her gaze met Kitty's in the glass. Matching brown eyes went wide.

Bitty Trapp turned from the window and ran even as Kitty twisted open the handle to the carriage door. Nearly falling to her knees as she leaped from the carriage, Kitty swept past the driver to follow her sister at a dead run. She was barely aware of Knight exiting the shop as she passed the door and frankly ignored his bewildered call.

Bitty's bonnet bobbed on down the street. Kitty tried to keep the scarlet flowers in view as she ran. It wasn't easy, as the heads and shoulders of other pedestrians blocked her line of vision. Damn her height and Bitty's! Was everyone in London taller than they?

Kitty stopped at a collection of crates at the entrance to an alleyway in order to clamber up onto one of them. Frantically, she searched for those scarlet flowers. She could see down the street for nearly a block, but Bitty's distinctive bonnet was nowhere to be seen.

A clatter and a high feminine yelp echoed from down the shadowed alleyway. Kitty's eyes narrowed. Only Bitty would be silly enough to flee down a dark alley. Kitty hopped down from her perch and strode down the narrow passage to investigate. When she caught up with her sister she was going to murder her.

Kitty halted in shock at the sight that met her eyes. Bitty—and it was indeed Bitty—stood caught between three rough characters who had blocked her way. The awful bonnet had been pulled from her head and lay discarded. The three characters did not look as though they regretted its demise.

It seemed everyone had homicidal intentions toward her twin today.

"P-please," stammered Bitty. "Let me by."

Kitty slid one hand into her bodice to touch cold steel. She slipped the knife from its narrow sheath and held the blade between her fingers. She was too far away for accuracy, unfortunately. Hiding her hand in the folds of her skirts, she hustled forward.

"Bitty, darling! Time to go, dear!"

Forceful assurance usually worked better than cowering fear, and this time was no exception. The three fellows instinctively took steps backward. Kitty barreled onward to grasp Bitty by the elbow. "Mr. Knight is waiting right out there on the street, dear."

That message was to warn the ruffians. Unfortunately, Bitty took it quite the wrong way. Kitty was dragged to a stop just when they were about to make it out of arm's reach. "No, Kitty! I—"

Kitty turned on her sister with a fierce smile. "Bitty dear, we can discuss this later. Now it is truly *time to go.*"

The pause had given the men time to recover from their surprise. "Ah, now don't go," one of the men said with a sly smile. "Looks like we got ourselves a matched set, lads!"

Bitty finally caught on, for she shrank against Kitty in fear. It was too late. The third man, a great hulking fellow with hands like shovels, now blocked their way back to civilization.

"Bitty," Kitty whispered into her sister's fallen hair. "Do you have your knife?"

Bitty made a tiny helpless noise. "I only carry it to balls!"

"Oh, for pity's sake!" Kitty shoved her sister behind her and faced Shovel-hands. "We are awaited," she warned him. "Someone will be along to find us at any moment. It would behoove you to let us pass." She nudged Bitty with her elbow. "Give these men your reticule, dear. I'm sure that will more than make up for their time spent."

"Why don't you give them yours?" sniffed Bitty.

Kitty bared her teeth in a falsely patient smile and said only, "I left mine in the carriage, dear sister. Give these gentlemen your reticule *now.*"

Behind her back, Kitty felt her sister's shoulders sway as she tossed the bag to one of the ruffians. She glanced over her shoulder to see the leader, a rat-faced fellow lacking most of his teeth, digging eagerly through Bitty's things.

"Oy, there ain't but a shillin' here!" He angrily flung it to the grimy cobbles and advanced on them. "What you playin' at?"

Oh, damn. "Bitty, did you forget Mama's first rule of economics?"

"No! But I spent it already, on the bonnet."

"Bloody hell!" said the leader.

"My sentiments exactly," muttered Kitty. She braced herself for battle. "I am getting tired of rescuing you, Bettina Trapp," she whispered. "When are you going to begin rescuing yourself?"

"Wedding Mr. Knight was *your* idea, Kitty," came Bitty's hissed reply. They pressed their backs together as the three men circled in closer. Kitty felt Bitty bend quickly and looked back to see that her sister had picked up a bit of alley litter—a broken piece of wood no more than a few inches long, but with a lovely splintered end.

Still, if they were doomed, there was no reason not to have the last word. "Bitty, you've caused the most awful mess with your Mr. Knight."

Bitty snorted and took a swing at a grimy groping hand with her wooden sliver. "You've been sharing his bed for two nights, *Katrina*. I'd say by this point he is *your* Mr. Knight."

Kitty ground her teeth together. "I only went home with him to avoid a scandal! Why did you run away?" She raised her knife high enough for their attackers to see. It caused a bit of a stir, but apparently their blond feminine helplessness was more convincing than their meager weapons. The predatory circling did not abate.

Bitty kicked out at one who came too close and jabbed her splintery dagger at another. "I didn't run away— *Ow*."

Kitty felt Bitty take a blow from one punishing fist that rang through both their bodies. She spun them both to face her sister's assailant with blade poised. She was now facing up the alley toward the street, but she could see little past the giant Shovel-hands. "What do you mean?" she said over her shoulder. "Of course you ran away!"

"No." Bitty's speech was slurred. The bastard had struck her sister in the mouth. Kitty had plans for Shovel-hands. Oh, yes.

"I didn't run," Bitty went on. "I eloped."

CHAPTER 6

Knight was frantic. Bettina had disappeared from one moment to the next. He'd followed her when she'd passed him but the throngs of Londoners enjoying a bit of afternoon shopping had concealed her petite form almost immediately.

When he'd retreated into the shop it had occurred to him that she was quite right. If he told her of the embarrassments and humiliations he'd suffered in his past, she would be much more likely to conform to his wishes. After all, she was not cruel. In her finer moments, she was very nearly agreeable. A slight smile had crossed his face when he'd thought of dinner the previous night. If nothing else, she was stimulating company.

He would tell her just as soon as he could find her. He'd thought he'd glimpsed her standing a bit above the crowd, looking for him, but then she'd disappeared once more.

This wasn't the most dangerous section of the city, but neither was it perfectly safe. The very people who were attracted to spend their blunt here became the attraction themselves to those who did not wish to work for their wages. Cutpurses and pickpockets abounded, while even more unsavory characters moved in the shadows and alleyways.

As Knight hovered near where he had last seen Bettina, he noticed just such an alleyway. But his sometimes overly clever bride would never enter such a perilous place. He would have wagered his estate on it—until he heard her voice, high and angry, coming from just that alleyway.

"You *eloped*?" Despite Aunt Clara's lessons, Kitty dropped her defenses to spin around in shock. She realized her mistake immediately, but Shovel-hands was faster. His thick arm came around her throat.

As much as she wanted it, vengeance on Bitty would have to wait. A girl had her priorities. Like breathing. Kitty swept her knife upward in a blind slash. The giant twisted sideways and she hit nothing but air. She tried again, but her throat was in agony and her knees had developed the oddest weakness. Through bulging eyes, she saw Bitty overwhelmed and disarmed by the other two men.

The two ruffians pulled Bitty farther down the alley, into the shadows. Kitty squirmed in the giant's grasp, but she couldn't seem to connect with anything meaningful, although at one point her knife did come back streaked with crimson.

Bitty's squeals rose to a fever pitch. Kitty's sight was beginning to dim. Swift and queasy certainty struck—she and her sister were not going to survive.

A demon came roaring down the alley. A darkly handsome demon with eyes of obsidian and rage.

Knight grabbed a handful of the brute who was choking his woman and spun the bastard around. Bettina staggered away, stumbling to her knees, chest heaving. Knight's need to run to her vied with his urge to kill something. The giant chose for him.

With great fists like hams, the ruffian swung at Knight. He ducked most of the blows, took one jarring knock to the shoulder, and managed to get in a few right hooks of his own. He'd expected worse, from the size and roughness of the man. It was almost as though the fellow were holding back, as if he were waiting—

"Knight! Behind you!" Bettina's hoarse cry led him to duck aside just as two more ruffians ran from the shadows at him. Her warning had cost the three an easy victory. One of the men kicked at her crouching form as he passed. She cried out in pain and fell once more.

Knight took him down with one heartfelt blow. The man lay still on the filthy cobbles, jaw askew. Bettina sat up and sent Knight a wobbly nod, her hand still at her throat. He saluted her quickly, then dove back into the fight.

The other newcomer eyed his comrade lying among the alley litter and took precautions, stooping to pick up a crusted plank. Knight stepped back warily, for the length of the timber beat his own reach. He kept moving, trying to keep both men well in sight.

The giant charged. Knight bent to take the impact on his shoulder. They both went down. The man was enormous, a strong and dirty fighter. Knight got in a few blows that sent the great square head rocking backward, but in the end the ruffian got him in a hold that threatened to snap his back.

Kitty watched with horror as the two men began to overwhelm Knight. He needed help—her knife! She'd dropped it in her daze. Disregarding the filth, she scrabbled madly across the floor of the alley. The light was dim, the knife was likely grimy now as well—bloody hell, where was the blasted thing?

Her fingers closed on the hilt. Swiftly she wiped the blade on her ruined dress. It wouldn't do to miss because of a slimy grip. She hefted it and focused on the fight, limping around the three men as the smaller ruffian began to beat the immobilized Knight with his plank.

"Coward," she hissed, but he wasn't her target. She must get Shovel-hands. The ratlike leader was nothing without the giant. She couldn't get a clear target. She moved in closer. Knight was still struggling, but she could see him growing weaker. Then he kicked out fiercely, catching Rat-face squarely in the groin.

Slowly and without a sound, the man dropped to his knees. Then, with a great helpless gasp in, the fellow's lungs were primed. The resulting howl of agony gave even the giant pause. In that moment, Kitty had her shot. Knight saw her then, knife poised. His eyes widened. "Knight, down!" she cried. Without hesitation, he ducked in the giant's grip.

The blade went spinning through the air. It was the best throw she had ever made. Deep into the giant's shoulder went five inches of razor-sharp steel. The man's left arm went limp at once. He dropped Knight and staggered back, looking down at the hilt in disbelief.

Then, stupidly, he pulled it from his flesh. Kitty swallowed. Oh, dear. Blood, and a great deal of it. In dim-witted horror, the giant grabbed his profusely bleeding shoulder with his good hand and took off at a run.

Knight rose to his feet breathing heavily. With eyes burning with incipient tears, Kitty saw that he was unhurt. Why was it that she only cried when events were over? Most unladylike.

"Are you well, darling?"

The endearment made the tears rise higher. She wished it were true, so wished that she were his darling. With shaking knees, she stepped forward to move into his embrace. Then she saw Rat-face rise behind him.

"No!" But this time she was too late. The swinging plank struck Knight across his head and sent him spinning into the brick wall of the alley. He slid limply to the cobbles.

Rat-face threw down the plank and stepped toward her, nearly purple with rage. "You'll pay for this, you will. You'll—"

Thud. The man dropped like a stone at Kitty's feet. Too stunned to move, she looked up to see Bitty with the plank hefted in two hands. "Pig!" Bitty snarled down at her victim. "Nasty bloody *pig!*"

Kitty felt the world as she knew it shift around her. Bitty striking a blow? Bitty cursing? Bitty *never* cursed!

A muffled groan came from beside her. Knight was slumped against the brick wall of the alley. Kitty limped to kneel beside him.

"By the way." Bitty bent to pick up her ruined bonnet. "I'm Mrs. Wesley Merrick now. Married in Scotland, right and proper, Kitty, and there isn't a thing you and Mama can do about it."

Kitty jerked her head up in shock. "But—but that's bigamy! You're married to Mr. Knight!" Betrayal lanced her chest. "And what of me? I took vows in your name!"

Bitty lifted her chin. "Yes, *you* took those vows, because you couldn't leave it alone. Why did you want to force me to marry someone I loathed?"

Kitty laid a protective hand on Knight's shoulder, as if to shield him from Bitty's scorn. "How can you say you loathe him? He's the finest man I've ever known!"

Bitty glared. "Don't you know who he is? He's John Tuttle's brother, blood of the man who tried to force me in order to get my inheritance! Mr. Knight came to finish the job, threatening to expose the entire story if I didn't agree to wed him!"

"Impossible," Kitty said flatly. "He said no such thing."

Bitty flipped her tangled hair over her shoulder. "Well, he certainly *implied* it, if you ask me. Standing there all dark and imposing, telling me his family name depended upon my accepting him. Reminding me of *Tuttle.*"

Kitty was stunned. All this because Bitty thought Knight had blackmailed her? Her sister's lingering fear and hatred of John Tuttle must have poisoned the few moments she had spent in Knight's company, for her to believe any such thing of this wonderful man. "But—but you eloped with Wesley Merrick? He *helped* Tuttle that night!"

Bitty folded her arms. "He apologized. Very prettily,

too. We've been corresponding for weeks. Tuttle made him do it, you know. Poor Wesley can be a tad too easily influenced. I've taken him in hand, however."

In hand? Bitty was the leader of the two? Merrick must be easily influenced, indeed. Kitty shook her head. "Bitty, we may look alike, but I have never understood you less. How could you do this to me?"

"I simply wanted a head start, with no one trying to stop me."

"You might have told me!"

"I tried, truly I did. But I was afraid you'd tell Mama, and then I would have given in. I'm not like you, Kitty. You always know what you want. I'm never sure. And even when I am, people start talking at me, and talking at me, and soon I'm all turned around!"

Kitty nodded. It was true.

Bitty looked away. "So I left you to take care of it for me." Then her gaze returned to Kitty's. "I thought you'd raise the alarm immediately. I didn't think you'd go away with that—that *man!*"

Kitty could see her sister meant every word, and something in her eased at the knowledge. Bitty's actions had been thoughtless and cowardly, but not malicious. "Well, I did. Now you must come home with us to talk to Mama and Papa," Kitty urged. "We must sort this out."

Bitty's face crumpled. "I cannot face them, Kitty! Not yet!" Her gaze flickered down to the unconscious Knight and she retreated a step. "He'll be so *angry!*" She turned away, obviously ready to flee.

"Bitty, wait! You have to help me with Knight. He's hurt!"

"You help him. I want nothing to do with the man." Bitty ran from the alley, trailing scarlet petals of silk behind her like falling leaves.

Knight stirred, then lifted a shaking hand to his head. "Ow," he breathed. Kitty sat directly in the muck to get a look into his eyes. He seemed dazed, but she didn't believe he was going to lose consciousness again. He tried to rise. She braced him, helping him to stand.

He blinked rapidly, finally focusing on her face. "Bettina," he said, as if checking his own ability to identify her. Then he took a great deep breath, letting it out with a short laugh. "At least now I'm only seeing one of you. For a moment there I could have sworn you were two."

Mingled relief and chagrin twined through Kitty's gut. He didn't remember clearly. He was dismissing seeing Bitty and her together as part of the blow to his head. She didn't have to tell him just yet.

But tell him she must. Just as soon as she got him home safely. She wrapped her arms about his waist. He draped his over her shoulders. Together they limped and staggered to the end of the alley, out into the daylight, and into the capable hands of Knight's coachman, who stood stoically by the carriage still.

Back in the kitchen of his house, Knight poured steaming water into the teapot with one hand while he used the other to press a cool cloth to his aching head. The tea leaves within the pot swirled unpleasantly, making him look away. His vision had finally stopped spinning but the pounding was only now beginning to abate.

Knight turned to see his begrimed bride carefully wiping her hands with another cloth and dabbing at the impossible stains on her gown.

He carried the teapot to set it on the table close to her. "There's no hope of survival, I'm afraid, my dear. You may happily toss it into the rubbish bin."

Knight was stunned to see tears in her eyes as she looked up at him. "It was so beautiful," she said mournfully.

He blinked. "I thought you found it awful."

A half-sob, half-laugh escaped her. "No. I never found it awful. It was the loveliest dress I've ever worn."

Carefully not jarring his head, he sat beside her. "Bettina, I don't understand a single word you're saying."

She looked away, then down. "Mr. Knight, I—"

He put his hand on hers. "Please don't call me that any longer."

She looked up at him in surprise. Her lashes were damp and spiky and her brown eyes were large in her grimy little face. "What should I call you then, sir? You said I mustn't use your Christian name."

Knight winced at this reminder of his own pomposity. "I cannot imagine why I thought it mattered. Call me whatever you wish—although I'd rather not be 'Alfie,' if you don't mind."

She smiled so sadly it pulled at him inside. "I shall simply call you 'Knight,' then. It suits you."

"Not Alfred the Odious?" His teasing didn't have the desired effect. Her face fell once more.

"I've been horrible to you, haven't I?"

He curled his fingers over hers and lifted her hand to lie inside his. "I've been no prize myself." He looked away. It was time she knew. He ought to have been forthright about his past sooner, even before his proposal. But the tea was ready.

He poured for them both and pressed her steaming teacup into her hands. "Drink this, it will steady you."

Tell her, you coward. Trust her.

"Bettina, I have to—"

"Knight, there's something you need to know."

He laughed. "I'll go first, shall I? My story has been waiting a bit longer, I believe."

He told her everything, sparing his family no quarter. The anger, the vicious quarrels. Then his mother's abandonment and the subsequent gossip and shame.

How Mrs. Knight had lived openly with her lover in London and how Knight had watched the gossip embitter his father. The scrapes against the other boys when he could bear the name-calling no more. How not a week went by without some new titillating nugget of news for him to discover in the worst way. Hearing that he had a brother. Realizing that his mother loved her new son more.

He paused to gaze seriously at Bettina. "Now do you see why I can never allow that to happen again? You must show more restraint. Our children cannot be put through such a nightmare. Do you agree?"

She blinked, then nodded slowly. Knight reached to push aside a tangled curl from her brow. "So, no more knife fights in the alleyways, then?"

She bit her lip and looked away, then nodded once more. Satisfied, Knight went on with his story.

Childhood became adulthood under the stain of rumor, until he had begun to make the name of Knight stand for acuity and respectability once more. That is, until John Tuttle's active pursuit of further scandal, ending with his attack upon her at her ball.

"The story came to me through one of Tuttle's friends," he told her, "who felt guilt over his part."

She nodded. "Wesley Merrick."

Knight was surprised. "Why, yes. At any rate, I cornered Tuttle about it and finally got an accounting of the entire affair. In the end, he wasn't even trying to deny it. He was too busy blaming your sister for foiling his master plan."

She was listening carefully, as she had all along, with her chin propped on one fist. "So that's when you came to B—to propose, in order to make an honorable attempt to right Tuttle's wrong?"

"Don't mistake me," he said ruefully. "After I packed John off on a ship to the West Indies, I proposed in order to preserve the family name."

She frowned slightly. He found it quite attractive, the way her light brows arched together. "But Knight, you have no family."

"I—" He halted, stunned. If he had no family, then what

did his family name mean? Nothing? Then he remembered and sent her a small twist of his lips. "I have you. You are my family." For some reason, that sounded just right.

She blinked. "Oh, Knight. Oh . . . no. You don't want me, remember? I'm an impossible woman, you said so yourself. I—I make trouble. I oppose you constantly. I carry a *knife,* for pity's sake!"

Knight threw back his head and laughed out loud. It felt wonderful, despite his headache. It felt free. He gazed at her fondly. "Well, I can't say that I minded it, just this once."

She smiled slightly, then looked away. "Now I must tell you—"

"You're shivering!" Knight tightened his grip on her hand to still its quivers. "You'll do nothing before you take a hot bath."

"But—"

"Are you opposing me again, darling?" He smiled to let her know he was teasing. He felt like smiling a great deal suddenly.

Her breath caught slightly and her bottom lip quivered. Knight stood quickly and pulled her to her feet. "On to your chamber, my lady. I'll be your footman and draw your bath."

She nodded limply and turned to go. Then she turned back. "After that, Knight, we must talk."

"As you wish, my lady. Now go."

CHAPTER 7

Upstairs in her chamber, Kitty stripped off the once beautiful green silk, then held it carefully in her hands for a moment. There truly was no saving it. Perhaps someday she'd have another like it—although once the scandal ignited, she'd never find a husband to buy her one.

Bitty had her man, one she seemed quite satisfied with. As a properly married woman, although she was at the heart of the scandal along with Kitty, she would escape mostly unscathed.

As had no doubt been her plan all along. Kitty was seeing Bitty in a clearer light now than ever before. The helpless one, the silly one, the witless one—yet perhaps the clever one after all. It was not Bitty standing here in this intolerable fix. It was not Bitty trapped somewhere between lies and loyalty. Bitty had chosen—and was still choosing—to follow her own heart and no one else's.

Kitty clutched the gown to her breast. "As for me, I would choose Knight," she whispered. In all his stuffy dignity, in all his obsession with the past, in all his longing for the warmth and acceptance he'd never had.

A seed of thought planted itself in her mind. Perhaps she could have him now, every bit of him. After all, neither of them was rightly married. They could take new vows, make promises of their own. If they acted quickly—and if secrecy held—she could be safely married to him before the gossip began, which would take most of the salacious pleasure from it. *It will still be quite horrible,* a voice within reminded her. *The very thing he's always dreaded.*

Surely she could make it up to him. Somehow.

Pipe dreams, stated the little voice flatly.

The door opened and her new footman came in laden with steaming buckets. He'd stripped off his filthy shirt and now wore her favorite sultan's dressing gown. She laughed and jumped forward to pull the copper tub from its hiding place behind the dressing screen. "I cannot wait," she cried. "I smell like the bottom of a shoe!"

Knight laughed deeply as he poured the hot in, then mixed it with a bit of cold. "You smell better than I do," he said. "I believe the giant came home with me."

Kitty swished her fingers through the water. The perfect warmth of it made her bruised body ache with longing. "I'm going to wash my hair," she said fervently.

Knight reached to tangle his fingers with hers beneath the water. He pulled her up to stand close to him. "Let me wash your beautiful hair," he whispered. His warm breath in her ear sent quivers through her and his offer made her toes curl on the carpet. *Choose*, her heart demanded. She chose.

"If you wish," she whispered back haltingly.

"I wish." His wet hands came up to pull apart the ribbon tie of her chemise. She felt the heat of his fingers through the dampened fabric and her shivers increased.

"You're shaking." His hands stilled. "Are you cold or frightened?"

"Neither," she said softly. "Quite the opposite."

"*Good.*" Intensity made his deep voice rumble directly through her. He spun her around in his arms, releasing her by the waiting tub with a fierce hug. Then he stripped her chemise from her with greedy delight and stood back to admire her.

She stood shy and proud, quite nude before him. For the first time in her life, she felt beautiful and wanted. Then she saw his face fall.

"You're covered in bruises!"

"So are you, no doubt." She grinned and stepped into the warm water. "But I promise to be kind."

She sank into the heat, so grateful for the bath that she found herself near tears once more. Then when she felt Knight gently pouring warm water over her filthy hair, she closed her eyes and allowed them to leak down her face with the water. He scooped a fistful of soap from the dish he'd brought and began to rub it gently through her hair.

"Do you know that last night was the first time I ever truly saw your hair?" His voice was low and soothing. His hands were sensual magic. "I had no idea it was so beautiful. Like gold." He laughed at himself. "I'm no poet, as you can tell. But it was all I could think about after I left you. I dreamt of golden hair and you."

He poured another pitcher of water over her scalp. Kitty let her head fall back, then sat up to allow the rest to stream down her bare back. She pressed more water out with her hands, then wiped the water and the tears from her eyes. Knight was sitting back on his heels watching her, the pitcher hanging unnoticed from his fingers. His eyes had gone quite black. "You're a goddess, do you know that?"

Kitty twisted to lay her folded arms on the edge of the tub. She dropped her chin on her arms and gazed at her filthy, bath-splashed handsome Knight. "I am when I'm with you."

He leaned forward to kiss her. She lifted her face. But he pulled away, grimacing. "The reeking giant lives on," he said.

Kitty laughed. "Then change places with me and we'll put him to rest at last."

Knight was more than willing. He wrapped a large piece of toweling about her, stealing a caress or two while he did so, then eagerly climbed into the still hot water.

But Kitty found it very hard to concentrate on washing his hair. Her eyes felt as round as saucers, but she couldn't help it. That had been such a sight, when he'd stripped his trousers and drawers off—

"Darling, you're pouring water on the rug."

She blinked and changed the angle of the pitcher. "Um, Knight? I was wondering . . . how does it work, precisely?"

"Ah, you saw that, did you?"

"Hmm-mm." She rubbed the soap into his thick hair. It slid through her fingers like black silk. He groaned and slid further into the tub. His hair-speckled knees rose from the froth. He had very nice knees, but Kitty was interested in something else entirely.

Supposedly Bitty had been educated in bridal knowledge. She, however, had been kept in girlish ignorance. Very annoying. "Is it . . . ? Will I . . . ?" She gusted a frustrated sigh as she rinsed his hair. "I don't even have words!"

"Then stop talking." Knight erupted from the water and stood naked before her.

It was her turn to sit back on her heels and become breathless. Her mouth was too dry to speak anyway. He was a masterpiece of male flesh. His flawless form rippled in hills and valleys that dizzied her as her eyes traveled him hungrily.

And those were still very nice knees.

He stepped dripping from the tub and plucked her from the floor, trailing towel and all.

"My pocket goddess," he murmured. Kitty felt the bed linens at her back but her gaze was locked with Knight's. "My Knight," she whispered back.

He kissed her then, finally, thoroughly, and she returned it without reservation. The toweling was tugged away and then she was covered by warm, damp man. He lay upon her with one knee between her thighs and arranged her wet hair upon the pillow, spreading it about in a wanton manner. "There, just as I pictured it."

Kitty bit his chin. "Stop talking."

Hot skin on her skin. Hot hands on her body. Scalding lips on her flesh. "I'm in heaven," she whispered to him.

"I've only begun," he whispered back. "Now be quiet."

She didn't say another word, but she wasn't quiet, not at all. When he rolled her rigid nipples with his fingertips, she sighed. When he did it gently with his teeth, she moaned. When he did the same to the sensitive nubbin between her thighs, she squealed.

Then he entered her with his fingers. *Yes.* She wanted . . . something . . . so badly. She was so empty she ached. He stroked her deeply, until a spark came to life in her belly and her thighs quivered around his shoulders. He kissed and stroked, until she drove her fingers through his hair and cried out loud with the pleasure.

Limply, she let her knees go slack and her legs fell from their hold on his shoulders. "Oh, *heavens,*" she gasped. "I never knew."

He moved up and over her. "You still don't."

She blinked as she felt a hard blunt presence between her thighs. "Oh. Now?"

"Yes, my love. Now." He kissed her deeply as he pressed within. Kitty squirmed a bit, but he captured her hips with his big hands. "Trust me," he whispered into her hair.

She ran her hands up to lock loosely over the back of his neck. "I trust you." He kissed her once more. She put her whole heart into the kiss. He filled her slowly. She felt a brief instant of pain which she studiously ignored. She stretched as far as she could, then she stretched more.

"Now, you see?" she gasped. "This is what I was talking about."

"All done talking, my love." He kissed her quiet. "Feel."

Kitty let her head roll back on the pillow and felt. The fit wasn't quite as tight as it had been. The fit, in fact, was marvelous. Knight withdrew, leaving her aching for him. But he returned, again and again. Pleasure came back, outrageous and unbelievable. "Oh, *Knight*."

Each stroke felt like a thousand caresses deep inside her. That spark came to light again in her belly, but grew larger and brighter than before. She opened her eyes to see Knight's large body moving over her. His eyes were black, watching her. She shied away from the intensity of his gaze.

"Look at me," he said, his voice deep and roughened. "I want to watch you ignite."

She wasn't so lost in pleasure that she didn't hear the thread of lonely need in his voice. She opened her eyes, shyness be damned. Her gaze never left his as he deepened his thrusts in response.

His jaw hardened. Her back arched. Their quickened breath mingled. They burst into flame.

Together.

A sound echoed through the empty house, waking Kitty. She sat up, then winced at the stinging ache between her thighs. The candles had gone out, but the coals still glowed. She turned to look beside her, but Knight was not there.

"I hope you're getting us some food, Mr. Knight," she murmured to the empty room. "It has been an eternity since breakfast."

She felt sticky and uncomfortable. The cooled tub still stood by the fire. Kitty scuttled across the chilly room and knelt to hold a candle stub to the coals. Mama hated when she did that, for the wax dripped evermore off center. Kitty grinned. This was not her mother's house. In a matter of days, it might even be hers.

The candle flared and Kitty plunked it next to the tub. The cloth still dangled on the side. Kitty repaired what damage she could, then turned to pull a nightdress from the chest. The Grecian gown beckoned. Kitty weighed her soreness against possible benefits. The decision took no time at all. She pulled the lovely thing on over her head and let the hem drift to the floor. It was nothing more than a moonlight shimmer on bare skin. Perfect.

Perhaps she ought to go surprise Knight in the kitchen. The thought of the vacant house beckoned. All those empty rooms! Feeling very wicked, Kitty pulled her wrapper over the decadent nightdress and ventured down the stairs. She had just turned toward the kitchen when she heard another noise from behind her.

"The study, Mr. Knight? I certainly hope you're planning a carpet picnic." She turned back the other way. Then she heard something breaking, shattering like glass. She jumped, then pressed her back to the wall. That couldn't be Knight. Only an intruder could cause such a noise. She stepped back until she was around the corner, then she ran for the kitchen.

Knight wasn't there, either. What if the intruder had harmed him? He could be in the study right this moment, bleeding like the giant! Desperately, Kitty grabbed a knife from Mrs. Till's drawer.

The study was at the front of the house, with a street-facing window. Anyone could break the glass and enter, if they wanted to brave the ten-foot drop to the walk.

She moved to the study door on silent bare feet. Years of practice sneaking past Mama's bedchamber were certainly coming in handy. The sounds from within—the scraping sound of drawers being roughly opened, the clatter of their contents being tossed about—led her to think that the intruder either didn't know she was at home or didn't care.

She could hide. The house was large. She was small enough to fit in any number of places. But what if Knight needed her? Not to mention the idea of hiding in the dark, the chill horror of waiting while the burglar came closer and closer . . .

Kitty pushed open the study door, knife poised at her shoulder, slightly concealed by her hair. The man digging through the desk jerked in surprise and whirled to face her. Tall, if not as tall as Knight. Handsome in a weak-chinned fashion. Very much thinner and more haggard than when she'd last seen him. Tattered finery now too large and filthy boots completed the picture of a rich man gone bad.

"John Tuttle."

Tuttle blinked at her, then snorted. "I thought you'd be on your honeymoon with Knight, Bitty. Or should I say 'dear sister'?"

"I suggest you say good-bye."

A sneer crossed his face. "As if I would listen to you." His eyes narrowed. "Unless, that is, you had something useful to tell me?" He began to move slowly toward her. "I need money. Tell me where Knight keeps his cash and I'll go."

"Stay back, John."

"Why? Don't you want to take up where we left off?"

Kitty almost hoped he'd rush her, so that she could lodge her knife somewhere defenseless. "Your wits are as dull as ever, John. Don't you recall what will happen to you if you ever touch a Trapp again?"

"Yap, yap." He rolled his eyes. "All the influential ladies of London will hang me out to dry on the social hook. Your sister made that quite clear." He moved closer with a grin. "But she's the strong one, isn't she, Bitty? You're the silly timid sister, and you won't tell a soul that I've been here. Will you, Bitty?"

Kitty felt her lip lift in contempt. "You unbelievable snot! I ought to—" She stopped, considering. Knight wouldn't be happy about her skewering his brother, she was sure. Ah, well. "So be it." She poised the knife in proper throwing position. "Say good-bye to any little Tuttles you had planned."

John's eyes widened in sudden recognition. *"Kitty?"* But it was too late. The knife flew.

CHAPTER 8

Knight froze in the doorway of his study when steel shimmered across the room. He'd stepped out back to wake the coachman and send him on a mission to bring back Mrs. Till at once. There was nothing in the house to eat but crusts of pie and yesterday's bread.

John's screech broke Knight's shock. He lunged forward to support his falling half brother. John clutched at him in horror. "She's unmanned me! She's mad! She—"

"She missed." Bettina's dry comment pierced John's babbling. Knight looked down to see that she was quite correct. John's trousers would never be the same, but there was no blood. The knife had entered an unoccupied area of fabric provided by John's lost pounds.

Knight looked up at Bettina in surprise. She shrugged. "What can I say? Kitchen knives aren't quite as accurate."

He stood, dropping John to snivel on the floor. "Did he attack you?"

"It crossed his mind." She was watching him warily. He felt much the same about her. Saving the day in a back alley was one thing. Flinging knives at family members seemed somewhat—

"Mad!" John was furious now that he'd realized his assets were still intact. "She's a raving lunatic, Knight! I came for a visit—I didn't want to wake anyone so I waited for you in your study—"

Knight merely cast his gaze around the chaos in the

room. John cut the lie off in mid-sentence. "So I was looking for a bit of blunt to tide me over, what of it? The
blokes I paid to get me off that ship you set me on took
all I had. You're my brother, remember?"

Knight lifted a brow. "How could I forget?"

Encouraged, John went on. "I was just leaving when
she ran in and attacked me!"

Knight nodded slowly, then slid his gaze sideways to
his wife. She seemed calm and blessedly unharmed. "Bettina, why don't you tell me—"

"Bettina?" John's derisive howl drew Knight's attention quickly, but not before he saw Bettina flinch.

John laughed loudly, then seated himself on top of the
desk with a genuine smile on his face. Knight watched
him, puzzled. John, still grinning, shook an admonishing
finger at Bettina. "You've been very naughty, haven't you,
my dear?"

Knight was in no mood for John's games. He glanced
at his bride apologetically—only to see her eyes were wide
and frightened and her face was as pale as a ghost. He
stepped toward her, alarmed. "Bettina?"

John giggled. "I never tire of hearing it," he said.

Knight turned on him in fury. "What the bloody hell
are you going on about, John?"

John sighed in disappointment. "Honestly, Knight, you
have no patience." He shrugged. "If you must spoil my
fun, I'll tell you."

He hopped off the desk and paced behind Bettina, who
stood still and shivering, her gaze locked on Knight's.
"Please, Knight—I was going to tell you—" she said.

Knight watched in disbelief as she closed her eyes and
swallowed. She looked so—

Guilty.

He moved to stand before her. "Tell me what?"

She licked her lips. John leaned over her shoulder. "Tell
him!" he sang lightly into her ear with a grin.

Knight was truly worried now. "Bettina—"

John clapped his hands together sharply. "Wrong answer. To the back of the class!"

Knight flinched. "What is this, Bettina?"

She put one hand behind her to shove John away and took a deep breath. "I am not—"

John slung his arm around her shoulders. "Did your fiancée ever mention that she was a twin, Knight?"

Knight blinked. "Twin? I knew she had a sister . . ."

John shook his head. "Not just a sister. A twin. As in two peas. Both blond, both bosomy, both with terrible taste. Bettina and . . ." He gave her a cordial squeeze. She seemed quite frozen. "Katrina. Kitty to those of us who know her well." John looked down over her shoulder and plucked her wrapper aside for a peek. "And from the looks of that nightdress, you do know her well."

Knight couldn't seem to wrap his thoughts around what was happening. He could only stare at his bride's white, guilty face. "Darling?"

John spun away in glee. "Oh, this is so rich! This is a moment I've waited for all my life." He plunked himself down in Knight's chair and crossed his legs. "Big brother tarnished at last. The shock! The scandal! Society will feed on it for years." He smiled and linked his hands over his sunken stomach. "At least they will when I get through with them."

She moved then. Bettina—no, Katrina—Katrina rounded the desk and approached John. "No you can't! He didn't do anything! He didn't know!"

John smiled happily at her. "I know. That's what makes it so lovely." He sent Knight a darker smile. "See, dear brother? Do you see how sometimes these things just happen to a man?" John shook his head sadly. "Tsk-tsk, Alfie."

Knight could not take his gaze from her guilty face. "Even the wedding was a lie, wasn't it? That was you, not your sister?" Knight closed his eyes as the truth finally began to sink in. He wondered what they would call him now. The Dupe? The Fool? Whatever, it would be cruel and cleverly unforgettable, he was sure.

She rose—*Katrina*—and came to stand before him. "Oh, Knight, I'm so sorry—"

"Answer the question," he barked.

She flinched, then nodded. "It was I at the altar."

"The vows are meaningless then. Unless there was a signed proxy?" She only looked away from him. "I see. Did it not bother you to lie before your church and family? You are—and I can scarcely bear to state something so obvious—not who I thought you were."

Her chin jerked up. "I know I hurt you—"

"Hurt me, Miss Trapp? You have destroyed me."

John raised his hand in a wave. "I helped!"

She cast John a withering glance. Knight pondered the pot calling the kettle black. Black as her heart, no doubt. "Tell me, Katrina, was tonight the last piece of the puzzle?" He laughed, the sound spiky in his own throat. "Was the attack in the alley staged? And the other girl—I did see her, didn't I? Bettina was a player as well, of course. You could never have pulled it off without her."

She looked at him with those lustrous brown eyes. "It wasn't a play, Knight. I only meant to get through the wedding for Bitty. She was so nervous—"

She looked down at her hands. "No, that's not true. I don't believe she intended to marry you at all by then. I believe she might have planned for me to step into her place. Kitty to save the day, as always." She looked up and shrugged helplessly. "She knows me all too well."

"You're lying again," Knight said calmly. "I can tell because you're speaking." The ice was moving in, stilling the pain, driving it deep and quiet. He turned away. "There is no more need for fairy tales, Miss Trapp. I have ruined a woman of good family. I must marry her." He went to the door, then spoke to her without turning back. "Do me the small favor of returning to your home until I can make the necessary arrangements—"

"No."

Kitty couldn't take her eyes from the stark pain on his face when he turned back to her. He likely thought it quite controlled, but she could feel it burning her from across the room. She couldn't take back what she had done. That was a burden she would carry forever. She could not allow him to carry it, as well. He looked back at her with dead eyes. "You will not go home?"

She wanted to wrap her arms about him, to stand between him and those who would hurt him. Yet how could she when it was she who wielded the greatest weapon? "I will go home, Knight. But I will not marry you."

He did not react, but merely nodded. "That, of course, is your prerogative. My honor demands I offer." He turned back to the door.

"Mine demands that I refuse," she whispered. But he was gone.

John leaned back in his chair. "Now that was truly enj—"

In one swift motion, Kitty bent to retrieve the kitchen knife and sent it spinning once more. John jerked in shock at the hilt that suddenly erupted between his thighs. "Bloody *hell*," he wheezed.

"Get out of Knight's house," Kitty said coolly as she left the room. "And never come back."

CHAPTER 9

Three days later, Knight stepped from his silent and gloomy house into pearly gray daylight. There were a few people on the street and he felt their eyes on him, every one.

The last thing Knight wanted to do was enter society. He remembered all too well how it would be. The sudden quiet when he entered a room. The amused glances, or worse, the pitying ones. The tongue-tying rage at the titters and the innuendo and the certain knowledge that much worse was being said behind his back.

But Helen Arden's accounts were due back to her and Knight refused to dawdle. When he arrived at her house, he was quickly shown into a small side parlor, for the large front one was in the full throes of morning calls. Even with the door closed between, he could hear the interwoven exchange of high voices coming from the other room.

Something certainly had them all in a lather. Knight was fairly certain he knew what it was. Or rather, who. The sound scraped his nerves raw and started his head thumping anew. He put one hand on the lump that still graced his skull. Another bloody reminder of *her.*

Helen entered almost immediately and carefully shut the door behind her. "My apologies for the to-do," she said. "I cannot seem to slow their discourse. You are bearing up well, I hope?"

Knight avoided her warmly inquiring gaze to shuffle

through the leather-bound file he'd brought to her. "I've made a great deal of progress. You'll see here where your properties have begun to bring you much better rents—"

"Bother the accounts. Knight, what are you going to do about Katrina Trapp?"

The documents swam before Knight's gaze. "What can I do? She's refused me, more than once." He closed the file and rubbed his aching head with one hand. "She wants no more to do with me than I do with her."

Helen chewed her lip. "She was jealous that day you visited, you know."

He snorted. "I doubt that."

She smiled sadly at him. "I don't. Women can tell these things. She knew at once that you and I are fond of each other. I knew at once that such a thing mattered to her."

Knight stuffed his hands in his pockets and stared at the carpet. "She's a vicious schemer. She played me for a fool and now—now it has all begun again, just like before."

Helen raised a brow. "Yes, just like before . . . but for the part where you are nine years old and defenseless."

Knight jerked his head up at that. She was quite right. He was not powerless this time. He barked a short laugh. "So forthright. You sound like my w—like Katrina."

Helen folded her arms and gazed at him with profound exasperation. "Really? Can a person truly be both forthright *and* a vicious schemer?"

Knight closed his eyes against the truth in her words. None of it mattered. The true problem here was that Katrina would never be the kind of wife he needed. He wanted a woman who would keep her opinions to herself, who would behave with perfect decorum, who would never become the object of gossip—

Dear God, I'm bored already.

He turned abruptly. "I cannot discuss this further," he said to Helen over his shoulder. "I must go."

In the hall, Helen's butler appeared with his hat and

gloves. Knight was tugging on the gray gloves when two women exited the teeming parlor in full tête-à-tête.

"Well, what did you expect from a family like that?" one was saying. The other woman tittered. "I heard his mother was quite shameless—" They saw him and halted in dismay.

No, not defenseless at all. Knight bowed deeply. For the first time in his life, he knew precisely what to say. "Ladies, I wish you good afternoon." He smiled dryly. "A terrible thing, scandal. Contagious, don't you know? I do hope both your families have their skeletons safely hidden."

Then Knight turned his back on them and left the house wearing his hat at a cocky angle.

The Trapp house was in an uproar, and for the first time in her life, Kitty had no intention of fixing any of it. The last three days had been laden with pleading and recrimination, but none of it had been hers.

Another note from Knight had come yesterday. Another cool and polite offer of matrimony to save the family name. Kitty wasn't sure anymore if he meant hers or his own. The Trapp name had suffered, quite true. Bitty had left an ugly mess, costing Papa a great deal of money and future favors to unwind her from the legalities of two marriages. Kitty had been called to testify that she had indeed spoken the vows to Knight and not Bitty, but she wasn't quite sure she'd been believed.

Nevertheless, Kitty was glad for her sister. Wesley Merrick might be as passive and spineless as a pudding, but he slavishly adored Bitty, who seemed a veritable Amazon in comparison. Bitty was happy, living her own dream at last.

At least one of us is.

"Well, once you marry Mr. Knight in truth," Mama was saying with forced assurance, "it will all die down. It isn't nearly so interesting to gossip about the happily married."

"Oh, I believe I will be of interest for a long time to come," replied Kitty. "I refused Mr. Knight."

Beatrice gaped. "But *why*? It solves everything!"

"Everything for you and Papa, to be sure. It even smooths Bitty's way. But Mr. Knight does not want me. Do you truly wish me to tie myself for life to a man who thinks me an embarrassment? I would suffer a lifetime of hiding my feelings, stifling my thoughts, curbing every action for fear of causing that poor man one more moment of mortification. I doubt very much that would make either of us happy."

"Will being a scandal for the rest of your life make you happy?" Mama was livid. "Ruining us all?"

"If you're ruined—which I doubt—then I am sorry. But truly, how long can it last? Bitty is happy in her lot and I wish her well. Papa has influence and power that has nothing to do with me. You have connections of your own. Aunt Clara would never allow you to be ostracized. You may hear whispers for a time, but if I am out of sight they'll soon take their gossip elsewhere."

Kitty crossed her arms. "What matters to me is for all to know that Knight behaved with nothing but honor and integrity, and that it was I who refused his offer. If you'll make sure of that, Mama, then I can go with good will."

"You—you're going away?" Mama's eyes filled with tears. "I'm to lose you both?"

Surprise washed through Kitty at her mother's emotion. This was not theatrical excess. Beatrice was truly sad. Kitty relaxed her militant stance to take her mother into her arms. "Oh, Mama, please don't be upset. I cannot stay now, but I'll likely be back. Perhaps after Mr. Knight marries in truth—"

She couldn't finish that thought. Too painful. Too forceful a pressure on her newly won resolve. Knight would marry someday. He would choose a perfect lady to be the perfect accessory to his perfect gentleman. Someone who would never ever appear in the newssheets or on the lips of gossips. Someone who—

The front door knocker clanked downstairs. That alone was a rare occurrence at the moment. There was nothing like scandal to clear one's parlor. Kitty parted from her mother and sat Beatrice down with a fresh handkerchief in hand. She went to the top of the stairs. It wouldn't be Knight, she told her naïve and hopeful heart. She'd been adamant in her last refusal.

It seemed to be merely a delivery, although Kitty couldn't imagine why it hadn't been taken to the service entrance. She couldn't see who brought it, but if she sat down on the top step, she could see Rogers the butler as he started up the stairs with a paper-wrapped parcel. When he lifted his eyes to see Kitty squatting there like an eavesdropping child, he gave no reaction. He merely continued his leisurely dignified way up the stairs.

"Rogers," Kitty said. "Who is it for?"

"It has come from Knight House. It is addressed to you, miss."

Kitty lunged for the package. Rogers merely braced himself as she took it and ran back to her room. Beatrice looked up from her sniffling as Kitty dropped to one knee on her bed and ripped into the paper covering the parcel. "Who is it from? Someone showing support in our time of trouble? Someone influential?"

Kitty opened the last layer to reveal a beautifully inlaid box. Expensive. Her heart fell as she realized that Knight was still trying to do his duty by her. Yet jewels or baubles would not sway her, she promised herself. Then she opened it anyway.

Inside, the box was formed into six compartments, each lined in purple velvet. In each individual compartment lay a single gleaming throwing knife. Unable to breathe, Kitty lifted one lovely leaf-shaped blade into her hand. The balance was exquisite. She could unman an army of Tuttles with knives like these.

"Oh, dear," murmured Beatrice. "Is that some sort of threat, do you think?"

Kitty returned the knife to its place with a lingering caress. For the first time she noticed that the hasp was carved with two letters. *"KK"*—*"Katrina Knight."* Her throat tightened. He was sharing his name. "No threat," she whispered. "This is a celebration."

"Of what?"

Kitty closed the case, stroking the rich satinwood of the top with a tender caress. "Of me," she said softly. "Just as I am."

Then she sprang from her seat and dashed to the hall. "Rogers! The delivery, who—"

"Mr. Knight is waiting right downstairs, miss," came the laconic reply.

And he was. He stood there tall and breathtaking, just as she'd seen him that first time—with one amazing difference. Kitty halted midway down the stairs, stunned by the light of love and approval that gleamed in his intense gaze.

"Hello, Katrina."

She'd missed his voice. Her soul seemed to vibrate in tune with the deepness of it. Still frozen on the landing, she could not answer him. She'd dreamed of him looking at her so. Now that he was, she couldn't bear to trust it.

Knight reached one hand up toward her. "Katrina, come down."

She hesitated. "Knight, I am still quite impossible."

He smiled. "I know. I find I prefer you that way."

Her body warmed from the inside out. "But they'll be talking about us forever."

He nodded. "I imagine they will. I foresee a great deal of gossip about how insufferably in love we are." He held up both hands and tilted his head. "Now come home."

Kitty grinned. This was no time for decorum. With the nimbleness of long practice, she hiked herself to sit on the stair rail. Speed was paramount—for her marvelous, steadfast, handsome Knight awaited her.

"Wheee!"

THE PROPOSITION

LESLIE LaFOY

For the Wichita Junior Wind Hockey Moms

The best in the game.

CHAPTER 1

London, England
April 30, 1877

Julia Hamilton looked at her reflection in the ladies' room
mirror and wondered when she'd started to look old, when,
precisely, the weariness had begun to settle into her bones.
She tried smiling at herself, but it only deepened the lines
at the corners of her mouth and made her blue eyes look
even more faded and dull. Brides-to-be were supposed to
be radiant and bubbly.

Radiant she definitely was not. As for bubbly . . . Julia
sighed. She'd never been fond of parties; had never liked
all the noise and bright lights, the meaningless conversations, and the silly competition among the women. It was
all such a monumental waste of time and energy. And
tonight's affair somehow seemed louder, brighter, more
meaningless and wasteful than most.

At least, Julia consoled herself, glancing around at the
half-dozen women primping before the other mirrors, she
wasn't considered part of the competition anymore. Her
engagement last month had not only effectively removed
her from that particularly unpleasant fray, it had also made
her largely invisible. It was a small mercy, but she was
exceedingly grateful for it. She'd be even more grateful
when her fiancé found her and announced that it was time
to leave. Unfortunately, it would be quite some time yet

before she could hope for such a deliverance. Lawrence had business to conduct. As he'd announced just after they'd greeted their host and hostess and just before leaving her alone ten feet into the ballroom.

"You'll never guess who's here!"

Julia turned with everyone else to consider both the breathless young woman standing in the doorway and the riddle she'd posed. The way her hands were pressed to her midriff suggested the news was fantastic enough that the girl had sprinted to the ladies' room to share it. The sparkle in her eyes suggested that it might well be the arrival of royalty. The girl glanced around the room and then, before anyone could hazard a guess, blurted, "Rennick St. James!"

Julia's heart tripped end over end, catching her breath and sending her pulse racing. Rennick was back in England? He was here? In her mind's eye she could see him; the rakish quirk to his smile, the mischievous sparkle in his dark eyes, the chiseled planes of his jaw. And she could see herself, too. Running to greet him, laughingly throwing herself into his strong arms and letting him pull her hard against his massive chest.

Her heart hammering wildly, her blood heated, Julia ruthlessly stamped out the impulse. How could she even *think* of doing such a thing? Simply speaking to Rennick in public courted scandal. To actually throw herself at him on the ballroom floor . . . London would never forget, Lawrence would never forgive, and Giles would roll over in his grave. And her children . . . Her heart tripped again. Thank God Christopher and Emma were away at school, that they couldn't reasonably know that Rennick had returned. They so adored him. Just as Rennick adored them in return. How relentlessly they'd argued for her to wait for him. How deeply they didn't understand why she couldn't.

"Have you actually seen him?" she vaguely heard someone ask.

"Yes," the young woman replied, advancing into the room. "He'd just handed off his hat and gloves and was greeting Lord and Lady Wells when I came in here."

"How do you know it was him?" someone else asked.

"My father said it was and that I was to stay well away from him," the girl supplied, leaning over Julia's shoulder to peer at herself in the mirror. Pinching her cheeks, she added, "Papa said that if he asked for a spot on my dance card, I was to find a polite way to refuse."

Julia gathered her reticule and fan, then rose, letting the young woman have the mirror to herself. Rennick never asked for a spot on a dance card. Most of the time he simply took the card, grinned wickedly, tore it to bits, and took as many dances as he pleased. Which was typical of the way Rennick went through life. How she'd missed him the past three years. Life was always so interesting, so delightfully unpredictable, when Rennick was about. Even parties were endurable when he attended.

Yet another young, breathless voice asked, "Is he as handsome as everyone says he is?"

"Oh, yes," the girl sighed, then mashed her lips in a futile attempt to make them look fuller and darker.

"I wonder why he's come back to London all of a sudden."

"His father's health is failing, you dolt," someone on the far side of the room answered. "Don't you pay attention? The earldom is going to be his before the year's out."

Lord Parnell had begun to decline? Julia blinked, stunned by the news. How had she not heard of it before this moment? The answer came quickly and on a sad wave of realization. Robert St. James, the Earl of Parnell, had been one of Giles's friends, a man of similar age. With her husband's passing, the world of his friends had slowly drifted beyond her awareness.

"Well, it's a good thing your father warned you away from him," said a girl with large breasts and a green silk bodice that barely covered the peaks of them. "I'd so dislike having to trample you on my way to his title."

"As though a man like Rennick St. James would be interested in the likes of you."

Julia arched a brow and considered each of the young women in the room. Unless he'd changed a great deal during his exile, there wasn't a single one of them that Rennick would rebuff. At least not until he'd sampled as deeply as he could push them to allow. The odds were that at least two or three of them would allow him everything they had.

"I have a perfectly good lineage to offer."

"Rennick St. James isn't the least bit interested in lineages," announced a familiar voice from the doorway. Julia smiled and sat on the upholstered couch as Anne Michaels advanced into the room with her usual air of calm authority. "Unless you're willing to hand him your virtue on a silver tray, he won't notice that you exist."

"Perhaps I am," countered the girl whose father had forbidden her to so much as dance with Rennick.

"You certainly wouldn't be the first," Anne laughingly admonished, easing down beside Julia. "But if you think he'll ask to marry you in the morning, you're sadly mistaken. And you won't be the first woman in that queue, either. He's absolutely notorious."

"And all the more attractive for it, in my opinion," the girl in the green dress offered, fluffing the curls that framed her face. "Imagine the accolades in being the one to finally settle him down."

"He'll never settle down," Anne countered, echoing Julia's thoughts perfectly. "He may marry for the sake of producing a legitimate heir, but pity the woman he chooses. She'll be a brood mare and nothing more. He'll never be faithful to her. He's incapable of such restraint."

And she'll die of a broken heart, Julia silently added, her throat tightening. Opening her fan, she fluttered a breeze across her suddenly too warm face and breasts. The movement caught Anne's attention.

"Julia, darling," she cooed, tweaking one of the silk roses that cascaded over Julia's shoulder. "I was quite surprised to see you come in this evening. I thought you would have declined Lady Wells's invitation out of sheer exhaustion. I know I would have."

She'd tried. No less than three times, but Lawrence had refused to hear of it. Julia managed a weak smile. "Lawrence maintains that parties are the perfect pretext for doing business after regular office hours."

"And he couldn't very well attend without you," her friend supplied knowingly. "Not without inviting speculation regarding your upcoming nuptials." She adjusted the trail of a grosgrain ribbon, asking, "How are your plans coming along?"

The Plans. She'd come to hate the very thought of them. Yet another very non-bridal tendency of hers. "As of this afternoon," she replied, summoning what she could of a smile and hoping it passed for serene, "all the details have been not only decided, but carved in stone. I desperately hope that the next four days can pass without a crisis of one sort or another. It may be an effect of my age, but I honestly don't remember this much work attending my first marriage ceremony."

Anne chuckled softly. "I wonder what Rennick will have to say about your plans."

It was the most amazing, perplexing, disconcerting thing: part of her blood ran cold at the look she could well imagine on Rennick's face. Which set the other part burning molten through her veins. She quickened the tempo of her fanning and decided that the best course lay in trying to be at least outwardly circumspect. "I doubt very much whether he's aware of them. And, even if he is, I can't see any particular reason why he'd consider them worth comment."

"He was a good friend of your late husband. God rest his soul."

He'd been her friend as well, but sharing that bit of

information wasn't in the interest of maintaining appearances. "Rennick will no doubt, at the first opportunity, offer his condolences at Giles's passing, but I can't imagine that we'll have anything to talk about beyond that."

"Good," said the girl in the green dress as she stepped back from the mirror and tugged her bodice even lower. "I would so dislike having to trample you, too, Lady Clayburn."

"I shall stay well out of your way," Julia promised. "And wish you—all of you—the best of luck."

As Julia knew it would, the offering spurred them to action. With a barely controlled smile, she watched the girl in the green dress eye the door and the other young women who lay between her and a quick exit. The others discreetly did the same. And in the next second they were all moving in a flurry of bouncing bustles, swishing fabric, rustling silk flowers, and streaming ribbons and feathers. In the doorway, the girl with the bouncing bustle and breasts put an elbow into the ribs of the one who had selflessly shared the news with them all.

Anne laughed as the last trailing hem disappeared from the room. "Like moths to the flame."

"And not a one of them even slightly capable of fending him off," Julia added, shaking her head. "As welcome-home gifts go, he'll be delighted."

"Might I offer an observation, Julia?"

"Concerning?" she asked warily, knowing well her friend's penchant for honesty.

"Life, I suppose."

Julia braced herself, quickening the speed of her fanning and desperately trying to think of an excuse to bolt from the room. And go where? her rational mind posed. Out to where Rennick would see her? Out to where she would have to face temptation in evening attire? God, no man ever looked better in a suit than Rennick St. James. It was so deliciously, decadently easy to imagine what he'd look like stripped out of it.

"Lawrence Morris might indeed be a Knight of the Realm," Anne said softly, "and the keenest financial mind in the empire, but you're settling, Julia Hamilton. You can do ever so much better."

And she most certainly could do worse, too. "In what respect? I'm not interested in titles and social status. You know that. Or at least you should."

"That's not what I'm talking about at all," Anne instantly countered. "Lawrence is very much like Giles was. Except considerably younger and less personable. Don't you want more out of your second chance at marriage?"

Her stomach oddly turned to lead even as her rational mind took control and offered the patent explanation. "No, not really. There's a great deal to be said for the comfort of the predictable and the steadfast familiar."

"There's also a great deal to be said for Rennick St. James."

Her pulse skittered and her throat tightened again. Instinctively she quickened her fanning and then, aware of the nervousness the effort betrayed, snapped it closed and laid it in her lap. "I'm thirty-three, Anne," she pointed out, pleased that her voice didn't sound as breathless and panicky as she felt. "I'm far too old to be a reliable brood mare. And far too prideful to stand by and watch my husband carry on affair after affair."

Anne waved her hand dismissively. "Thirty-three is not too old, Julia. My mother had four children after that age. And, that issue aside, he could well have changed in the last three years. He might be quite ready to settle down and be a good husband."

"Rennick?" she laughingly scoffed. "Never. You said so yourself not five minutes ago. Whether he dies a young man or an ancient one, his end will come in the bed of another man's wife and we all know it."

"And the pity," her friend said, rising from the couch, "is that you're not adventurous enough that it would be your bed."

"Anne!"

Her arms akimbo and her smile broad, Anne gazed down at her with an arched brow. "Oh, for heaven's sake, Julia. Are you the only person on earth who doesn't know that Rennick was Giles's friend largely because he hoped to seduce you?"

Oh, Lord. How hard she'd worked to keep the distance, to keep their relationship proper so that no one would ever have the slightest reason to suspect the quality of her character and the happiness of her marriage. Had it all been for nothing? Had everyone been whispering behind her back for the last thirteen years?

"Oh, not to worry," Anne offered gently, her smile taking on a patient patina. "No one ever once thought he had the slightest chance. You're the epitome of perfectly proper. Everyone always knew that for Rennick it was the attraction of the impossible conquest."

"I am not perfectly proper," Julia protested. *Not if waking thoughts and restless dreams count against me*, she silently added.

"Ha!" Anne challenged. "We've known each other all of our lives. Name one time when you didn't sweetly accede to the expectations of others. Name one time when you deliberately—or even accidentally, for that matter— took a step that could have led to the tiniest bit of gossip."

"Why would anyone want to create a scandal?"

"Scandal? Julia, my dear, you don't even know how to begin to inspire gossip. A scandal would be utterly beyond your abilities."

"And I should be ashamed of that?" she asked, for some inexplicable reason feeling deeply wounded.

"No, not at all," Anne replied gently. "I'm simply suggesting that when Rennick St. James offers his condolences on Giles's passing, you really ought—just the one time—to take a tiny chance and see if there might be something more the two of you have to talk about."

She knew what Rennick would want to talk about.

She'd seen it shimmering in his eyes countless times over the years, heard it ripple beneath the surface every time he said her name. And she knew how it all affected her, how very dangerous being around him was. "I'm to be married in five days, Anne. It's a little too late to be entertaining Rennick's notoriously less than honorable attentions."

Anne sighed heavily and shook her head. "Who cares if they're honorable, Julia? And too late is when you're legally Lady Morris. For God's sake, do you want to spend the rest of your life wondering what it would be like to make love with Rennick St. James?"

Julia stared up at her, stunned that somehow Anne knew the darkest, most secret of her private torments. Did everyone know? Was she that transparent? "I can't believe," she stammered, clinging to pretenses, "that you're even suggesting that I do such a thing."

"If it helps any, my dear friend . . ." Her smile faded. "Were I in your shoes tonight," she said somberly, "I'd have Rennick flat on his back before he could sputter so much as a single word of condolence. Life is for living. And boldly is better than safely and timidly. For once in your life, Julia Hamilton, dare to live boldly. Even if it's for only a few short hours."

And with that pronouncement, that taunting challenge, Anne Michaels turned and walked away, leaving Julia alone in the ladies' room, stunned and reeling. And frightened.

She opened her fan and slowly moved the blade back and forth as she considered the road that had brought her to the horrible dilemma in which she now so unexpectedly found herself. She'd been seventeen when her father had arranged her marriage to Giles Hamilton. He'd been thirty years her senior, a widower without children, and the most considerate, doting, wonderful man she'd ever met. She'd been content as his wife, the mother of his children, the mistress of his various estates.

And then thirteen winters ago Giles had come back

from a business trip to London with Rennick St. James in tow. She'd met them in the foyer and from that single moment life had never been the same. She'd looked into Rennick's eyes and an arc of heat had leaped between them, searing through her breast and down to her womb before filling the core of her soul. She'd literally hiked her hems and fled as soon as she politely could. It had taken no more than a few seconds, but running away had accomplished nothing; the effect had been inescapable and forever.

She'd never believed in such foolishness as love at first sight. She had refused then to accept that that was what had happened to her. She'd studiously avoided him and immersed herself in being a devoted wife and mother. She'd focused on the contentment of her existence and ruthlessly quashed the powerful, troubling feelings that the mere sight of him stirred in her. When Giles came to her bed and made love to her, she kept her eyes open to remember that it was him, to keep Rennick St. James from invading their intimacy.

And then one night, during the height of the next season, he'd cut in on her dance with Giles and she'd had no choice but to face the truth. He'd smiled down at her and whispered her name and, like some giddy, starry-eyed debutante, her knees had all but given out. She hadn't been able to speak, hadn't been able to meet his gaze after that. She'd finished the dance with him for the sake of propriety, because she needed the time to gather her scattered wits and find a way to keep the tears at bay.

He hadn't spoken, either. Not until the notes of the music faded and she began to step out of his embrace. *"I'll wait for you, Julia. For as long as I must."*

No words had ever terrified her more. She loved her husband, cared for him deeply and would never hurt him. But she loved another man, too. A notorious, unrepentant rakehell. In a way that wasn't the least bit sane or wise or explicable. She wanted him with a passion unlike any she'd ever felt for her husband, with a consuming desire she hadn't known existed.

And so she'd done the only thing she could have; she'd lived a careful lie, always pretending that she didn't know the truth, always protecting Giles and the genuine sweetness of their companionship, always pretending that Rennick was nothing more to her than a friend.

Now Giles was gone. And out there, somewhere in the glittering chaos of the ballroom, was the man who had promised to wait for her. The rake to whom no sane woman would ever be foolish enough to hand her heart.

It had been three years since she'd last seen him. Since he'd been called out by an enraged husband and had to flee the country for dueling. He might have changed, Hope wildly suggested. In the passage of those years, he might have lost interest in pursuing her, might have forgotten the promise he'd made so long ago. And if, when he looked at her next, there was no spark in his eyes she might be free of her feelings for him.

But if the spark was still there . . . She had to go home. Before she found herself facing Rennick and the impossible temptation he'd always been. Julia snapped her fan closed and rose from the couch, her course clear. She'd spent thirteen years imagining what it would be like to make love with Rennick St. James. What was another thirteen? What was a lifetime? Especially when weighed against the certainty of a broken heart.

She poked her head out of the ladies' room and, not seeing Rennick, made her way along the back of the ballroom, keeping in the shadows of the palms as much as she could. Part of her felt ridiculous for the furtive scurrying. The other part felt dangerously exposed and vulnerable and fervently wished that Lady Wells had thought to bring even more plants from her greenhouse. She slipped behind a mercifully full specimen and surveyed the wall along which the smoking and gaming rooms had been set up for the men. It took several long, torturous minutes, but finally a door opened and Lawrence stepped out with two other men.

She glanced about and, still seeing no sign of Rennick, seized a deep breath and stepped from concealment. It was no great feat to summon a distressed expression as she approached her fiancé.

"Lawrence, dear," she began without preamble or acknowledging his companions. "I'm wondering how much longer we'll be required to stay. I have the most hideous headache and would truly like to go home."

He cocked a brow and withdrew his pocket watch. Studying the face of it, he replied, "I'm to meet Denham in the card room on the moment and can't leave now. He has some accounts he wants to move and there would be hefty administrative fees for the man who acquires them." He put the timepiece away and looked at her to smile thinly and add, "Perhaps Lady Wells has a powder she can give you."

Only a magic powder would save her. A magic powder that could make her disappear into thin air. "I'll speak with one of the maids," she said, her stomach churning with dread.

"Or perhaps you could take a walk in the evening air. Lady Wells's gardens are reputed to be quite well designed. Rumor has it that she pays her gardener an obscene monthly wage."

The gardens! Yes, of course. As an alternative to leaving, they would do nicely. They were huge and she could easily hide there. "That's an excellent suggestion, Lawrence. Thank you. Best wishes to you on your negotiations with Denham."

He bowed slightly at the waist and she took her leave, making a line straight for the opposite wall and the doors that led out onto the balcony and the sweeping stairs down to the darkness of the sprawling gardens.

Julia stepped out and pulled the door closed behind her, then glanced up at the half-moon. All right, so the gardens weren't going to be as dark as she had hoped, but at least she'd made it this far without encountering Rennick, and surely she could find some deep shadows in which to hide. The night air was cool and she hadn't thought to bring her wrap with her, but she'd survive. Lord knew she didn't dare go back inside to retrieve it.

Her skirts in hand, she skipped down the steps and turned to her left, intending to make her way out to the boxwood maze. She took only a single step before she froze in her tracks, her heart lodged high in her throat and pounding furiously.

"Hello, Julia."

He smiled and her knees melted.

CHAPTER 2

For a horrifying second Rennick thought she might fall, but even as he reached to catch her, she stiffened her back, squared her shoulders, and took a step that put her beyond his fingertips.

"Rennick."

Her voice was as hesitant as her smile, both tremulous and tentative enough to make his heart ache. God, what had happened to her in the years he'd been gone? She'd grown thin and her eyes had a haunted, lonely look to them. His every instinct but one urged him to take her in his arms and kiss her, to promise that he'd never leave her again. The voice of restraint whispered that in pushing her too fast and too far he'd lose what precious little chance he had.

It took all the self-control he possessed in that moment to keep his arms at his sides and jauntily ask, "Did you come out here hoping to hide from me?"

He saw her force herself to swallow, heard the shakiness of the breath she drew before she found another weak smile and replied, "No, not at all. I just needed some fresh air. Welcome home. How long have you been back in London?"

Patience, he cautioned himself. *Patience*. While Julia was always wary at the start, it never took more than a few minutes for her to relax, to forget that she was afraid of what had always existed between them. "Just a few days," he answered. "I went directly to the country house on my return. I've been there the better part of two weeks."

"How is your father?"

"Failing," he supplied bluntly, knowing there was no reason to put a soft light on the truth. Not with Julia. "I would have been to London sooner, but he had a particularly bad spell and I couldn't leave. The doctors, after this last episode, have given him no more than three months."

"I'm truly sorry to hear that, Rennick," she said, the tightness—blessedly—easing from her voice. "I know that you haven't always been on the best of terms, but that beneath the contest of wills, you've respected each other."

Rennick nodded and sighed. "He figures he has me over the proverbial barrel with his death approaching and all. He's using guilt and family obligation as leverage to get me to marry. Preferably before the week is out."

She laughed, genuinely and fully, and there was the tiniest sparkle in her blue eyes as she countered, "Assuming that you're interested in accommodating him, it shouldn't be all that difficult to accomplish. The talk in the ladies' room this evening centered around who was in danger of being trampled in the rush to be the next Countess Parnell."

Relief flooded through him. Beneath the sadness and wariness, his Julia was still there, still bright and real like no other woman he'd ever known. Their dance was an old and familiar one, and that she was still willing to step into it with him . . . He grinned, sensing that everything was going to be all right at the end of the course. "I've had more dance cards waved under my nose in the last ten minutes than in the last ten years combined."

"Oh, how you must be suffering," she offered dryly, fighting a smile.

He snorted. "All they want is my title."

"And all you want are their bodies," she instantly countered, her smile broad and as dazzling as ever. "As the pursuit of noble purpose goes, neither you nor they have any claim to high ground."

He again tamped down the impulse to reach for her. "Oh, how I've missed you, Julia. No one else is ever so brutally honest with me."

She shrugged and caught her lower lip between her teeth for a second before changing the subject by brightly asking, "Where have you been the last three years?"

"I spent the first one in France. The last two in Ceylon. I've learned quite a lot about the cultivation and production of quality tea."

"Well, that will give you something to talk about in the late afternoons," she observed cheerily. "Parlor talk can be so very dicey. Especially when you're facing a prospective mother-in-law across a tea cart."

"Is that the voice of recent experience?" He regretted the words the instant they were off his tongue and it was too late to call them back. He regretted them even more deeply when her smile evaporated.

"So you know."

God, he'd blundered and broached the subject before the timing was right. There was nothing to do now but square up to it all and make the best of the situation.

He nodded and clasped his hands behind his back. "The banns are published in the paper, remember? Father has the *Times* sent to him on the daily post. He pointed out the notice the first day I was back and used it as his opening into the subject of my own matrimonial sacrifice."

"He certainly didn't waste any time, did he?"

"Apparently you didn't, either," he gently but pointedly countered.

"Giles has been gone well over a year, Rennick," she rejoined just as smoothly. "I've offended no one's sense of propriety in becoming engaged to Lawrence."

"No one's except mine."

She arched a brow and crossed her arms over her midriff. "And precisely how does my engagement offend you?"

Rennick blinked, surprised by the sound of steel in her voice. The Julia he'd left behind had been always easy-going, always quiet and gentle in her resistance. Had being a widow, having to make her way alone in life, changed her? If only he'd known of Giles's passing at the time. He'd have come back for her then and damned the consequences for dueling.

"I thought," he explained, watching her carefully, "I'd made it clear that when you were free, I'd like a chance to gain your favor. I rather thought I'd earned it, as well."

"You've been gone for three years, Rennick. I had no idea where you were and if you'd ever return."

She had to have known that he'd be back someday. He was destined to be a damned earl. He didn't have any choice except to come back to England. He sighed and reined in his irritation. All he'd wanted for thirteen long years was to take her in his arms, kiss her senseless, and lose himself in the wonder of making love with her. Arguing was not part of his fantasy and he wasn't about to let frustration get the better of him. He expelled a long breath and decided to start over.

"Are you cold?" he asked.

"I'm fine. Thank you."

She was lying. Somehow it was reassuring to know that she hadn't gotten any better at that since he'd been gone. He unbuttoned his coat and shrugged out of it. Slowly closing the distance between them, he draped it over her shoulders and drew it around her. Moonlight bathed her face as she looked up at him. "You couldn't wait for me, Julia?" he asked softly, his lapels lightly fisted in his hands.

"You couldn't write?"

Releasing her and stepping back so that she didn't feel threatened, so that he didn't have to think and battle temptation at the same time, he asked honestly, "And what would I have said? That I remembered a hundred times a day the feel of you in my arms the night I left the country? That I dreamed every night of someday getting more than one chaste kiss from you?" He smiled wryly. "Giles would have had my gizzard."

She surprised him yet again by chuckling softly. "In the first place, you could have written a version of that letter to any one of a hundred women. And in the second, you might have penned a note every few months or so to simply say that you were still alive."

He stared at her, stunned. "You thought I was dead?"

"Given your proclivities, Rennick, Giles and I both considered it a distinct possibility. Especially as time wore on and there was no word from you or of you. It seems that you didn't write to your mother, either. I know because I asked her."

It was the way Julia had always set him back on his heels; gently but ever so firmly. Some women pouted to make their point or get their way. Others either screamed or went stone-cold silent. He adored Julia for her ability to do battle—and consistently win—with unfailing gentleness and grace.

"All right. I was remiss in my misery and I'm sorry," he granted, thoroughly, properly chastised and just as determined to leave the past behind them. "But I'm back now. We still have a chance to be together."

"If you read the banns," she countered calmly, "you'll have noted that I'm to be married in five days."

"I'll take them."

She slowly shook her head. "I'm not offering them, Rennick. I've pledged my fidelity to Lawrence."

"Not legally," he pointed out happily. "There's no civil contract between you. Not yet."

"You are drawing, in your usual fashion," she countered, "a fine line that truly doesn't exist. I'm engaged. I cannot entertain offers from any other men."

"No matter how attractive you find them?"

"Rennick, I'm not—"

"Don't you dare even try to lie to me, Julia," he gently interrupted, knowing what course she was about to take. "We've been friends for far too long and I know you all too well. You're attracted to me. Just as deeply and for as long as I've been attracted to you. We both know that. We've known it for years."

"Be that as it may, I can't—"

"Four nights, four days," he pressed, buoyed by the fact that she'd given him even a tacit admission of her feelings. "That's all I ask. If you decide on the afternoon of the fourth day that you'd prefer a life with your boring banker, I'll let you go."

She sighed and tilted her head to consider him. The moonlight gilded the high arcs of her cheekbones, glinted in the golden strands of her hair. "Simply for the sake of satisfying my curiosity . . . What would happen on the fourth day if I decided I didn't want to go back to Lawrence?"

Then Rennick would be the happiest damn man in the entire British Empire. That she was so much as thinking ahead to the possibility thrilled him. "You'd marry me. After the scandal of leaving Morris had died down a bit, of course." He grinned and added, "Unless you don't care any more about those sorts of things than I do. In which case, we can slip off to Gretna Green and simply let the scandal explode without us."

Both her brows arched higher and a smile tickled the corners of her mouth. "And how long do you think it would take for one or the other of us to regret the decision to marry? A week? Perhaps two?"

"I'd never regret it."

"Well, I would," she countered, chuckling. "The first time I saw you dash off in pursuit of a swaying skirt."

"It wouldn't happen. I'd give up all other women for you," he promised, knowing even as he offered it that his past gave Julia every reason to doubt his word.

She laughed outright, the honest, joyous sound strumming over his heartstrings, reminding him of how utterly empty his life had been without her and affirming the course he'd chosen the second he'd laid eyes on that piece of newsprint. It was going to be a long contest; he knew Julia. But he also knew himself and that he was going to win it one way or the other. She wasn't, by God, going to marry Lawrence Morris. Not as long as he had breath in his body.

"Intentions and declarations don't make reality, Rennick," she said. "You couldn't give up chasing women if your life depended on it. You thoroughly enjoy the hunt. And I'm not the least interested in spending the rest of my life with a philandering husband. We'll simply have to be content with being friends."

He disagreed, but wasn't willing to be distracted from his more immediate purpose to discuss the man he'd been for thirty-four years and why. He'd explain it all to her later. Right now, though, the seconds were ticking away and he wasn't inclined to waste them. "I spent the better part of ten years being your friend, Julia, and I never was content with it. Resigned to enduring it, yes, but never content. And I'm not about to go placidly back to that arrangement." *There*, he thought, *I've given her fair warning.*

"I'm afraid that the only choice you have is to be my friend or to be someone I once knew."

He couldn't really blame her for thinking that she could lay down such an ultimatum and have him accept it. In all the years he'd known her, he'd allowed her to get away with it every time she had. But that had been before. As of tonight, there were new rules. "No, Julia," he said patiently, shaking his head. "There's a third choice. Be my companion for the next four days. Give me a chance to prove myself. You owe me that much."

"I *owe* you?"

Ah, the steel was back in her voice. But this time, rather than being perplexed and troubled by it, he found it delightfully stimulating. He reached out and trailed a fingertip along the line of her delicately curved jaw. Her breath caught and even in the paleness of the moonlight he could see desire flickering in the depths of her eyes.

"The simple truth, Julia, is that I could have forced the issue long ago. I easily could have stripped away your good virtue and tumbled you happily onto your back any number of times. But I didn't. I respected your marriage to Giles and kept my hands to myself."

Pleased that her breathing had become shallow and ragged, he trailed his fingertip up from her chin to trace the fullness of her lower lip as he softly added, "If, in the end, you choose to marry Lawrence Morris, I'll respect your vows this time, too. But before you march back up the aisle and relegate me to the periphery of your life again, I deserve a chance to make my case. I've earned it."

He saw the newly planted seeds of doubt begin to grow, saw the temptation in her eyes. And then he saw her draw a deep breath and summon resolve. She turned her head, breaking their physical connection. Only when he let his arm fall to his side did she look back at him.

"Unfortunately, Rennick," she said softly, her smile tinged with sadness, "you've also earned—a thousand times over—the reputation of a rake. Being seen in your company has ruined countless women. Lawrence would be mortally embarrassed to have my name linked to yours in the days before our wedding. I wouldn't blame him at all if he wanted to call it off."

"Oh, now that would be a pity," he offered wryly.

"In fact, I've tarried too long out here with you already," she went on, slipping his coat off her shoulders. She held it out to him. "Thank you for the loan of your jacket, Rennick. I really must be getting back inside before we're seen together and the whispers begin to fly."

A gentleman would take the jacket, respect her concerns, and let her go. So would a rogue certain of the outcome and with the time to be patient. "To hell with the whispering," he said, stepping past her outstretched arm to slip his around her narrow waist. "Let's give them something actually worth talking about."

Rennick heard his jacket fall onto the grass at his feet the second before she pressed both hands flat against his chest. He smiled and paused, knowing that his heart was pounding against her palms, filling her, warming her, enticing her own to match the cadence and join him in the dance. Lord Almighty, was there any woman on earth more beautiful, more luscious, than his Julia? Had he ever wanted any woman more than he did her?

Her eyes fluttered closed and on a ragged sigh she whispered, "Rennick, please."

Oh, he did please. With every fiber of his being. He had for as long as he could remember. He bent down and captured her lips with gentle resolve, tasting her as he'd so long dreamed, savoring the softness of her lips and the soft whimper of her surrender as her arms slipped up to encircle his neck.

The long smoldering embers of his desire burst into flames. Starving, burning, he pulled her closer and deepened his kiss. She melted into him, and when he touched the seam of her lips with his tongue, she acceded. At the slow sweep of his invasion, she moaned, low and hard, and the sound of her pleasure, the passion of her acceptance, rippled through him, fanning the flames hotter and brighter.

The voices of reason and conscience cried as one and he obeyed. He broke their kiss, but didn't let her go. Holding her tight, he tucked her head under his chin, and grinned off into the night gardens. God, his heart was racing and he could hardly breathe. Actually making love to her would probably kill him. Lord knew, though, that if he had to die, that was definitely the way he wanted to go.

"Tell me," he whispered, nuzzling his cheek into the golden curls piled atop her head, "that Morris makes you moan like that when he kisses you."

She started and tore herself out of his embrace.

"You're a scoundrel," she accused, backing toward the stairs, her breasts rising and falling in a cadence every bit as winded as his own, her lips deliciously ripened from his kiss.

"You've always known that," he pointed out, smiling and advancing toward her, keeping the distance between them constant. "It's part of what draws you to me. Deep in your good little heart is a wanton who desperately yearns to be set free. You know that I can do that for you."

"Good night, Rennick," she said firmly, lifting her hems and moving up the stairs sideways, her gaze riveted to his.

He stopped at the bottom and leaned against the railing, watching her go. Her eyes . . . Lord, the life was back in her eyes again. And that was all the sanction he needed. "I'm not giving up, you know."

She faltered and then stopped. "Please do. Spare us both the torment."

Rennick shook his head in silent refusal.

Her breasts rose as her breath caught. Her eyes wide, she hiked her hems well above her ankles, turned her back to him, and raced up the stairs, calling out as she went, "Good night!"

Rennick chuckled as she reached the top and disappeared from sight. She'd said good night. Not good-bye. There was a significant difference between the two. A difference he had every intention of exploiting. He glanced up at the moon and marked the hour. Before it set, Julia Hamilton was going to be back in his arms again. And he wasn't going to let her run away next time. No, as of tonight, there were new rules.

He scooped up his jacket and, pulling it on, headed for the end of the house and the line of waiting coaches.

That Lawrence considered interior coach lamps both a fire hazard and an unjustifiable expense was a good thing, Julia concluded as they rolled through the night. Had the little space been lit, she would have been compelled to smile and carry on something approximating cheerful conversation. In the darkness she didn't have to bother with either. All she had to do was sit quietly in her seat, listen to the hoofbeats against the cobblestones, and note as they passed under the occasional street lamp that Lawrence was using the light and a stubby pencil to scribble notes in a little leather-bound book.

She closed her eyes, grateful that the evening was finally coming to an end. And because she hadn't decided what to tell him about Rennick if he asked, she was even more grateful that her husband-to-be was otherwise occupied. She arched a brow as it occurred to her that Rennick St. James wouldn't spend a carriage ride making notes and ignoring a woman in the opposite seat. No, if he were the one seeing her home, he wouldn't be on his seat at all and she'd probably have her skirts rucked—

Julia choked back a gasp and banished the image from her mind, checked to be sure Lawrence hadn't noticed her start, and then drew her shawl closer across her breasts. Heaven help her, she silently moaned. If such wanton imaginings overtook her senses when she was awake, she didn't dare sleep tonight. Not that she had much hope of it, anyway, she had to admit as the coach slowed and drew to a stop at the curb in front of her townhouse. The question of what to do about Rennick hadn't left her mind since she'd left him at the base of the balcony stairs.

As the springs shifted and the driver climbed down to open the door for them, Lawrence carefully poked his pencil into the spine of his book, closed it, and then slipped it into the breast pocket of his coat. "I realize that I've been poor company, dear Julia," he said as the door opened. "But I needed to capture some thoughts before the details escaped my memory. I hope you understand."

He didn't wait for her to murmur a demure acceptance.

Or bother to see if perhaps, just this once, she might throw a tantrum over being ignored. No, he rose from his seat and stepped out, turned around and with a smile offered her his hand.

Julia took it as she always did and allowed him to help her down the steps. And, as she always did, she accepted his arm and let him lead her up the walkway toward her front door. The steps and porch were dark this evening, she noted. Apparently Paul had either forgotten to light the lamp or to check the oil level before he did. She'd have to speak with him about the oversight in the morning. At the moment, however, she really needed to think of something to say to Lawrence. The silence was becoming decidedly noticeable and, at least on her side of it, awkward.

"Did your meeting with Denham go well?" she asked, recalling the only other exchange they'd had that evening.

"Exceedingly," he replied, his voice buoyant as they climbed the short flight of stone steps. "His current account manager is in Watford. Denham and I will travel there in the morning, retrieve the books, and then survey several of his holdings before we return to London."

He was leaving town? Julia knitted her brows, not at all sure how she felt about his departure. "How long will you be gone?"

"Five days," he supplied crisply, withdrawing his arm and leaning around her to open the door. Light spilled out from the foyer as he added, "Six at the most, I should think."

Julia sat unceremoniously on the stone balustrade, both stunned and hurt. "Our wedding is in five days, Lawrence. Four, actually, since it's now past midnight."

He started. "Oh, yes. Of course," he hastily offered. "Then I shall be back late the evening before."

No apology, she noted. Not that that was at all unusual for him. But for some reason tonight it irritated her. "Would you prefer to postpone it?" she asked. "We can if you have more important matters to attend."

Lawrence shook his head emphatically. "No, no," he assured her. "The expense of changing the date at this point would be unconscionable. I'll simply have to plan around it. What I don't get done before, I'll see to immediately after."

The expense? "Will you be staying for the reception," she asked tightly, "or shall I instruct that one less meal be served and save a few shillings?"

He blinked and rocked back on his heels, his eyes going wide and the color seeming to drain from his face. "Were you not able to find a powder for your headache, Julia?"

"No, I wasn't," she answered, thinking that if she could find one now it would be a magic potion to make *him* disappear into thin air. Or, better yet, to Watford. Forever.

"And the walk in the gardens didn't help, either?"

"For a while. As it turns out, it was the best part of the entire evening," she answered testily, wondering why men always assumed that female anger had to be the cause of some malady rather than the natural consequence of thick-headed male behavior.

"I hope you'll feel better in the morning."

She sighed at the sincere concern she heard in his voice and her anger drowned beneath a wave of guilt. He did care for her in his own rather bumbling and distracted way. "Thank you, Lawrence. I think I'll sit here for a while and see if some fresh air doesn't improve it."

He nodded and moved toward her, saying, "Then I'll—"

"No, please," she interrupted, shooing him back. "You have a busy day tomorrow and it's very late. You need to get your rest. Please go and don't worry about me. I'll be fine."

"Well . . ." He sighed and then shrugged. "Good night, dearest," he said, leaning down to brush a kiss over her cheek. "I'll send word to you when I return."

"Travel safely and enjoy the journey," she called softly, watching him walk away. He waved over his shoulder without looking back and his little book was back in his hand before he vaulted up the carriage steps.

Julia closed her eyes and shook her head as the coach rolled off. He was so predictable, so dedicated to his work.

"My," drawled a familiar, dry voice, "such unrestrained passion."

CHAPTER 3

"Rennick, you're a cad," Julia declared as he came up the steps.

He grinned and dropped down beside her on the balustrade. "I know. It's by deliberate choice, too."

"How long have you been skulking in my shrubbery?"

"I wasn't skulking," he replied cheerfully. "And I wasn't in the shrubbery. If you'd bothered to look as you were coming up the walk with Sir Galahad, you would have seen me standing off to the side. Where, I might add, I've spent the better part of the last two and a half hours waiting for you to come home. When did you become such a late-night reveler?"

"I'm not a reveler," Julia corrected, enjoying his presence beside her and wishing she didn't. "Lawrence had business to conduct."

"Was the time in the garden really the best part of your evening?"

And it had been the worst part of the evening, too. Just as having him a part of her life had always been the very best and the very worst of it. "Oh, Rennick," she said softly, not knowing what she should do.

He leaned to the side and playfully bumped her shoulder with his. "Come away with me, Julia. Let me show you what a proper good-night kiss should be like."

It was no wonder he'd bedded half the women in London society. He knew just what to say and how to say it.

It was impossible to be truly and righteously indignant with him. He was so charming, so disarming. So very, very appealing. "There's absolutely nothing proper about your proposal, Rennick St. James. Nothing."

"Granted. But it is tempting, isn't it?"

Yes, God help her, it was. She sighed and looked over at him. "You're not going to give up, are you?"

His grin was soft. Not quite victorious, but decidedly knowing. "I told you I wouldn't."

"Do you intend to camp on my doorstep?"

His eyes sparkled with heart-tripping devilment. "Actually, I intend to bribe your footman into letting me in the house."

She wouldn't put it past him. "You're without conscience."

"I can't afford the luxury," he admitted with a quick shrug. "That cold fish is going to be your husband in four days if I don't make my claim rashly and boldly. If you want me to court you with poetry and flowers and mildly flirtatious parlor talk for the next six months, then call off the wedding and I'll fall into line. But if you're not willing to do that, then you can either agree to freely give me the next few days and nights or you can spend them fending off one outrageous meeting after another."

The fact that he was here with her now suggested that he wasn't making idle threats. Thank goodness Lawrence hadn't seen him waiting for her. That would have been a most unpleasant scene.

"And fair warning, darling," he added, leaning close, "at some point someone's bound to notice my persistence. Especially since I'm willing to make quite a public spectacle of it. Personally, I don't give a damn about embarrassing Morris, so if you want to protect his sensibilities . . ."

Her jaw went slack and she turned on the stone railing to stare at him. "That's . . . that's . . ."

"Blackmail," he supplied blithely, nodding again.

"Come away with me and I'll spend the next three days apologizing for it."

She turned away, fixing her gaze on the pool of light spilling out through the open doorway. What did it say, she wondered, that he was keeping better track of the passing time than her betrothed? What did it say that she could hear Anne Michaels's voice urging her to live boldly? And why, of all the men in the world with whom she could have fallen in love, did it have to be the only one certain to break her heart? "Rennick . . ."

"Have mercy on me, Julia," he said softly, gently. "Please say yes."

She could walk into her house, close the door, and refuse to open it until the time came to meet Lawrence at the church. Or she could walk in the front door, out the back, and take refuge in the homes of any number of her friends. They would hide her, vouch for her virtue. And if she took either of those courses, she'd spend the rest of her life wondering about what might have been, what she might have had. She closed her eyes and swallowed down the curious tide of tears and elation. "You don't leave me with any other choice."

"That was largely my intention," he admitted, bounding off the railing to step in front of her and extend his hands.

Julia hesitated, knowing instinctively that if she reached for him, if she put her hands in his, she would not only be committed to the folly, but she'd be forever changed at the end of it. And that, as frightening as that prospect was, she was undeniably drawn to it, to him. She lifted her hands from her lap and deliberately placed them in his. "I'm not promising you anything beyond amiable conversation, Rennick."

His fingers gently curled around her hands and the tension visibly ebbed from his shoulders, from the edges of his smile. Slowly drawing her to her feet, he murmured, "I'll accept whatever you choose to give and ask for nothing more."

The warmth and strength of his hands enveloped her, wrapping around her heart and soul, comforting her, enthralling her. *Like moths to the flame.*

He wouldn't have to ask, Julia realized, panic seizing her. She hadn't thought this through as thoroughly as she should have. She'd made assumptions and with Rennick that was always a dangerous thing to do. She'd thought she had the strength to hold him at bay. Good God, she should have known better. "Where shall I meet you?" she asked, desperate to escape. "When?"

His brow shot up and his smile quirked. "Meet me? I know you, Julia. You're having second thoughts already. If I let you go, you'll disappear into the nearest rabbit hole and I'll spend the next three days in a maddening version of hide-and-seek. Consider ourselves met as of this moment."

"But . . ." she stammered, glancing into the foyer of her house. Her sanctuary.

"You can send your staff a note in the morning." He shifted his hold on her right hand, lacing his fingers through hers, and then released his claim to the other to reach out and silently close the door, to close off her avenue of escape. "If you want them to know where you are, you can swear them to secrecy and tell them. If you don't, we'll make up some suitable tale and no one but you and I will ever know."

"At least let me pack a few necessary things."

"You'll want for nothing," he assured her, drawing her down the steps and out into the yard. "I promise."

Rennick could feel the frantic beat of her heart, could see the apprehension in her eyes, in the tightness at the corners of her mouth. He kept her moving and kept the gentle, reassuring smile firmly on his face. And with every beat of his own heart he resisted the temptation to pull her into his arms and kiss away her doubts.

He'd won the first battle in their contest; the second was just beginning. And the rules had changed yet again.

He wanted forever with her and now the safest strategy for gaining that wondrous prize was to employ just the right amount of enticement tempered by just the right amount of patience.

Lord knew she inspired the former and deserved the latter. Thirteen years was a very long time and denial and evasion were difficult habits to discard. Three days weren't as many as he'd like to have for the task, but if it proved long enough to get her to call off the wedding, he'd count himself fortunate and the effort a magnificent success.

"Where are we going, Rennick?"

Their immediate destination was his carriage, parked in the alley behind her house. But he knew that wasn't what she really wanted to know. And since it wouldn't do to tell her at this point that he was taking her to one of his hideaways, he opted for a generality. "Heaven."

"More likely to hell in a handbasket."

She'd wanted to sound disgruntled and concerned, but the vibrancy of her voice belied the attempt. "If it turns out that way," he assured her, gently squeezing her hand, "we'll have a grand time getting there, darling. A grand time. I promise."

"I can't help but notice that you seem to have added a new word to your vocabulary."

They reached the coach and he pulled open the door. Handing her into the dimly lit interior, he explained, "Calling you 'darling' didn't seem like the thing to do when Giles was alive. I thought it might create a problem or two we'd be better off to avoid if we could."

"Actually, that wasn't the one I was referring to," she said as he dropped down on the facing seat and pulled the door closed. "I've heard you call countless women 'darling' over the years. But I don't recall having ever heard you utter the word 'promise' before tonight."

It was one of those he'd always considered to be perilous to use in the company of women. If inadvertently used in proximity to other words, it could well result in being snared, skinned, and served up as the main course on the altar of Holy Matrimony. That he'd used it with Julia without so much as a conscious thought . . . "I'm not quite the same man who left here three years ago." *Or who returned here two weeks ago for that matter,* he silently amended.

"Is that good or bad?"

He knew it was for the better, but also knew just as well that simply proclaiming it wouldn't convince her. "You'll have to be the judge of that."

The carriage rolled forward and he sighed in something akin to contentment. Julia hadn't fought him for nearly as long or as hard as he'd feared she might. Largely, he knew, because Lawrence Morris wasn't the great love of her life. No, her heart still belonged to him. If only he could get her to freely, openly give it. If only sitting there drinking in the wondrous sight of her would be enough for her to know how deeply and forever he loved her.

"You look as though you're desperately searching for something to talk about."

He shook his head and confessed, "I have so many questions to ask you, so many things I've been wanting to share with you for so long . . . I'm trying to decide where to begin."

"You could just blurt out the first thing that comes to mind."

"All right," he said crisply, surrendering himself to the tide of hope. "How's Christopher? How's Emma? Are they both well and happy? Where are they?"

Julia smiled. Of course he'd start with her children. They both considered him something between an older brother and a fun-loving uncle. And in the time before he'd had to flee, he never came through the door without some sort of little present for them, without a hug for Emma and a wink for Christopher. "They're both fine," she supplied. "Christopher is at Eton. Emma is off to Bath this week with her classmates on holiday."

He cocked a brow. "Isn't she just a bit young to be charging about the country?"

Julia chuckled, thinking that he sounded positively paternal and how he'd wince if he could hear the notes of it himself. "She's fourteen, Rennick. In just a few years she'll be presented and she'll be a wife within a year or two after that."

"Fourteen? Somehow, in my mind, she hasn't aged one day since I last saw her."

"Well, she has. And you'd hardly recognize her. She doesn't look much like a little girl anymore." Julia watched his brows knit. And then he blinked, looked stunned for a second, horrified for another, and then angry.

"She doesn't have suitors yet, does she?"

"Rennick!" she exclaimed, laughing outright. "Are you remembering your own youthful pursuits?"

"Yes. And at that age, they're not pursuits, they're obsessions. She needs to know how to protect herself from the predatory little bastards."

He scowled at the seat beside her and Julia grinned, thinking that he indeed seemed to have changed since she'd last seen him. The Rennick St. James of old wouldn't have condemned a fellow rake for anything short of criminal behavior. "And Christopher?" she asked. "Is he still a boy in your mind?"

He gave her a chagrined smile and shook his head. "No, I've always been acutely aware of how old your son is getting to be. Sixteen, right? And looking more like Giles with every passing day?"

"I think he's going to be taller than Giles was. He's already broader across the shoulders. And his feet . . . Lord, keeping him in shoes has been a major expense the last year. I swear he needs a larger pair every month."

"A boy that age needs a firm hand, Julia. Who's been guiding him since Giles passed?"

"My brother."

She couldn't tell whether Rennick groaned or snorted. The sound seemed to be a bit of both.

"James is a fop. What does he know that a normal, hot-blooded boy of sixteen needs or wants to know?"

"Apparently not much," she had to admit. "I'm afraid that Christopher's taken to running at the sight of James's carriage coming up the drive."

"Your son has always had uncommon good sense. What does he think of ol' Lawrence as a potential stepfather?"

Christopher thought Lawrence had all the charm of a stick and Lawrence always called him Christian. "I think that it might be for the best if we didn't talk about Lawrence."

"Why?" Rennick pressed, his smile quirking. "As a presence in your life, he's a bit difficult to ignore, you know."

"True," she granted. "But you're not at all likely to cast him in anything approaching a positive light and he's not here to defend himself or counter your assertions. It's hardly fair."

"I'm not interested in fair."

"My point, precisely."

He tilted his head to consider her and then asked, "Why did you choose him?"

It appeared that his sense of persistence hadn't changed one whit. "I'm not discussing it with you, Rennick. Ask another question. Something that has nothing whatsoever to do with Sir Lawrence Morris."

He sighed, then leaned forward to rest his elbows on his knees. His hands clasped, he met her gaze and quietly said, "I haven't yet expressed my condolences on Giles's passing. Very poor manners of me to have delayed in doing so."

"Yes, it was."

He nodded in acceptance, gave her a weak, apologetic smile, and then said, "I am sorry that he's gone, Julia. He was a good-hearted, decent, caring man."

"And a good husband and father."

Again he nodded. Looking down at his hands, he chuckled softly. "He was also one of the most tolerant and trusting men I've ever known. I never will forget the day he looked over his cards at me and told me that he was perfectly aware that I was lusting after his wife."

Her heart skipped several beats. "Dear God!"

"He was so incredibly affable about it," Rennick went on, apparently unconcerned with her horror. "No anger at all. Just a passing statement of fact. Which, in hindsight, I can see amused him greatly."

"I hope you had the good judgment to deny the assertion."

"Darling," he drawled, looking up at her, "Giles might have been old, but he wasn't blind or stupid. I could have denied until pigs fly, but it wouldn't have been believable." He straightened and sat back in his seat, shaking his head. "No, the only thing I could do under the circumstances was admit the obvious truth and pray like hell that he didn't call me out for it."

"Giles would never have done that," she said. "It wasn't in his character."

"And he knew that it wasn't in yours to accept my advances. Which is why he found my hopeful persistence so entertaining." He leaned his head back in the squabs, closed his eyes and grinned. "God, he even wished me the best of luck. And then laid down a flush. In hearts. I always thought there was an incredible irony in that."

Giles had never said one word to her. Not one. She'd always thought that she'd been successful at protecting him from the unpleasantness of it all. To learn now that she'd failed at that important task . . .

"I'm sorry that I wasn't here when you both needed me. When the children needed me," Rennick said quietly, his voice tight. "I hope his passing was swift and peaceful. He deserved it."

In a way he had been there, Julia remembered. Late at

night, when she'd been alone and facing the uncertainty that lay ahead, she'd pretended that he was, crying and confessing her fears and her regrets. And in the darkness and solitude, she'd been able to imagine what he'd say and found comfort in it.

Julia swallowed down the lump in her throat and found a reassuring smile for him. "Giles gently faded over the course of a single month and then, one night in his sleep, silently slipped away. There was no pain until the very end and the opium tinctures freed him from the worst of it."

Clearing his throat quietly, he asked, "Were Christopher and Emma devastated?"

"They were saddened, of course," she supplied. "But we all knew the end was rapidly approaching. The good-byes had been said, the instructions given and the promises made. We laid Giles to rest according to his wishes and with no regrets."

"And then moved on with life," Rennick added, the tightness in his voice easing. "As should be done."

"Giles had insisted that we do so."

He opened his eyes and met her gaze. "He made you promise to marry again, didn't he?"

"Yes," she admitted, wondering how Rennick knew of that private conversation. Did he also know of how painfully difficult it had been? "He said I was much too young to be a widow for the rest of my life."

"And so," he drawled, "after you'd mourned him, you dutifully injected yourself into the London social whirl and saw it done."

"You make it sound like a bad thing."

He didn't shake his head. He didn't nod or shrug, either. He simply looked at her and said softly, "Giles was right. You are too young to be a widow."

"But?" she offered, tensing. "I should have waited for you?"

His smile was a weak effort. "Well, yes. That."

"And?"

He hesitated, considering her. And in that pause, the carriage rolled to a slow stop.

"Ah, we've arrived," he announced with what seemed to be a great deal of relief. "We'll have to finish this conversation some other time."

She wasn't sure that she wanted to. Something in Rennick's manner suggested that she wasn't going to like the direction he intended to go. She watched him vault out of the carriage, marveling at his fluid grace. That was a constant about him, she realized. Rennick never misstepped, never stumbled. He knew where he was going, what he was going to do, and always acted with unshakable commitment and confidence.

When he held out his hand, she accepted it without hesitation and let him assist her down the steps and onto the drive. She looked up at the sprawling, softly lit, ivy-covered mansion. "Is this Greenfield House?" she wondered aloud.

His grinned and looked at her askance as he guided her up the front steps. "I would definitely recall having brought you here previously. And I don't."

"Everyone knows about Greenfield House, Rennick," she laughingly countered. "It's renowned as your country pleasure palace. As opposed," she added as he opened the door for them, "to Warwick Place, your London pleasure palace."

Rennick paused, struck by an unpleasant realization. He'd brought countless numbers of women here in the past; he shouldn't have brought Julia. She was different from all the rest. "Would you prefer to take rooms at the local inn? I understand if you do."

"No, but thank you," she hastily replied. "This is considerably less public. The chances of emerging from the next few days with my reputation intact are far better here than they would be anywhere else." She smiled and shrugged a shawl-draped shoulder. "Except if I were in my own home, of course."

"Not if I were in residence with you there," he pointed out, resuming their course, deciding that if she agreed to marry him, he'd sell Greenfield. And Warwick, too.

"Would you really have bribed my footman into letting you in?" she asked as he closed the door behind them.

Rennick grinned, led her to the stairs and up. "His name is Paul. He's twenty-two and favors voluptuous blondes. He wouldn't have been so much bribed as incredibly distracted. For quite some time."

"You are a rogue to your marrow."

"Actually, I'm a reformed rogue."

"Since when?" she laughingly challenged as they reached the upstairs hallway.

Since he'd stared at her banns and realized that he'd come to the most important crossroads of his life. "I prefer to think of myself these days as a paragon of creativity and resourcefulness in the pursuit of true love."

She looked at him askance and rolled her eyes. "Creativity?"

"It's often the littlest of things, you know."

"For example?"

"Snuffing your porch light was a masterful move, even if I say so myself. If I hadn't, I would have had to openly challenge Sir Passionate for you."

Julia stopped dead in the center of the hall and stared at him, her pulse racing. "You wouldn't have."

"I would have won, too," he assured her, his grin wide and bright. "But," he added, sobering slightly, "you would have been furious with me for it, and slinging you over my shoulder and hauling you off kicking and screaming wasn't exactly the way I preferred to go about it all. We have a sufficient number of obstacles to overcome already."

She was still reeling when he stepped past her, opened a door, said, "This will be your room," and then disappeared inside.

Julia followed. Reformed? Not in the least. When it

came to the art of manipulation in the name of seduction, Rennick St. James was the best. He always had been and he always would be. And Lord knew why that fact amused and thrilled her; she didn't.

But she did know why she loved the room in which he was ensconcing her; it was beautiful, softly feminine, perfectly appointed and wondrously scented. Julia glanced around, taking in the whole of it, thinking that it had been created to frame the vase of dusky pink roses on the bureau. Roses, pinks, creams, and the tiniest sprigs of pale green. A fire burned cheerily in the hearth. Jars of creams, a spritzer of perfume, and a silver-backed brush and comb had been arranged on the dressing table. The tester bed had been turned down, the lace-edged pillows fluffed, the pale pink linen sheets smoothed. And at the foot of it, on the rosy silk-covered bench, sat a huge, neatly towering stack of white boxes, each tied with a gauzy opalescent ribbon.

"It's lovely, Rennick," she whispered, slipping her shawl from her shoulders. A realization stole over her and she laughed softly. "It's a garden of delights. A feast for the senses."

The mischievous sparkle in his eyes was an admission. He motioned to the second door in the room, saying, "On the other side is my chamber. The door's not locked."

Of course it wasn't. And for some inexplicable reason, she was incredibly tempted to walk over, open it, and see what lay on the other side. She exhaled and brought the impulse under control.

Even as she did, Rennick said softly, "The choice to open it is yours. I won't force you to make it, Julia."

"Thank you," she replied, knowing with absolute certainty that he meant it. She crossed to the foot of the bed and fingered one of the ribbons. "And what's all this?"

"Two weeks of concerted work by one modiste and her three assistants. I told you that you'd want for nothing. I had them start the day my father showed me your banns in the *Times*. They finished just yesterday."

She counted the boxes, noting their sizes. Clearly it was a complete wardrobe. "You must have paid them a fortune," she mused aloud.

"I didn't care what it cost."

"What if I had refused to be blackmailed?" she posed, turning to meet his gaze. "What if I had refused to come here with you?"

Standing beside the bed, his hands in his trousers pockets, he gave her a soft, deliciously roguish smile, winked, and said, "I appreciate the fact that you came along willingly."

Good God, he was handsome; tall and broad shouldered, his face so ruggedly chiseled, his hair so dark and inviting. And how very tempted she was to glide across the distance separating them and set about slowly, methodically discarding his well-tailored suit. But she knew Rennick and the power he had over her senses. To take a single step toward him would commit her to making love with him. And she wasn't at all certain that she could do that and walk away when the time came.

"Have you been planning these days for the last two weeks, Rennick?" she asked, looking back down at the ribbon she was rubbing between her fingers. "Since you returned from Ceylon?"

"Planning for these specific days, yes. But I've been hoping for this time together for thirteen years. Since the day I met you."

In her weakest moments, she'd hoped not only for these days but also that a golden forever would grow from them. And felt guilty for it all when she was stronger. After Giles had passed, her hopes had been tempered, not by guilt, but by the reality of Rennick's nature and the impossibility of her gilt-edged dreams.

"The sun will be up soon," he said, quietly intruding

on her thoughts. "Perhaps we should sleep while we can. Since you'd undoubtedly rest more comfortably in a night rail than you would your evening gown . . . And since I didn't think to blackmail your maid into accompanying you . . ."

"You'll undo my buttons and laces for me?" she concluded, thinking that it was indeed a most creative and resourceful tack to take. Not necessarily in the pursuit of true love, but most definitely in the quest for a casual seduction.

"And I'll behave myself while doing so," he promised, pulling his hands from his pockets to motion her to come toward him.

Julia went, her pulse skittering, and obediently turned, presenting him her back. Her breath caught as his fingers brushed the skin above the first button on her gown. She held it, savoring the sweet shudder that cascaded down the length of her spine, acutely aware of the warmth radiating through her as he smoothly worked his way down.

The gown began to slip from her shoulders and Julia crossed her arms over her midriff to hold it in place, to keep it from puddling around her ankles. And then, when he reached the last of the buttons, he eased aside the fabric of her gown, plucked loose the ribbon of her petticoat, and began to loosen the strings of her corset.

Julia tightened her arms as everything outside her chemise started to slip downward. If he brushed a kiss over her nape . . . If he reached around and cupped her breasts, nibbled at her ear . . . She wouldn't be able to fend him off. And, more alarmingly, she honestly wouldn't want to. Her knees trembling, Julia forced herself to swallow.

"Thank you," she murmured, stepping away and turning to face him while she still had the strength to do it.

"It was a pleasure."

The wicked light dancing in his eyes told her that he was perfectly aware that she'd enjoyed the small intimacy every bit as much as he had. Her heartbeat quickened and her blood warmed.

"You need to know, Rennick," she said softly, unable to draw a breath deep enough to make her voice firmer, "that I'm not going to call it off with Lawrence. You mustn't hope for something that isn't going to happen. I care for you too much to let you do that."

His brow inched up. As did one side of his smile. Slowly, ever so deliberately, he reached out and took her gently by the shoulders. Bending his head, he stepped closer and she closed her eyes, her heart racing, her hands clutching her clothing to her.

The brush of his lips over hers was feather-light, there for a second and then passing away even as she strained to meet it. Her sigh of regret was involuntary, the reward instant and ever so softly deliberate. She leaned into him, savoring the caress of his lips, reveling in the taste of him, in the sweet promise of surrendering to his mastery.

He nibbled at her lower lip, catching it gently between his teeth to leisurely trail the tip of his tongue along the sensitive inside curve. The sensation was as deliciously exquisite as it was powerful. A splendid heat arced through her, igniting desire and turning her will to ash. She slipped her arms around his neck and melted against the length of him, softly groaning in a wordless plea for deliverance.

And he obliged her, deepening his kiss, taking certain possession of her mouth as he wrapped her in his arms and leaned her back. The feel of cool linen bolted through her awareness and then was gone, swept away in the flood tide of magnificent sensation and a torrent of consuming desire. She couldn't breathe, couldn't remain still. Julia strained upward, hungering for more, wanting with a desperation that engulfed all that she was.

He moaned in response and then slowly drew his arms from around her, gently eased his kiss and ended it. Breathless, her senses still reeling, Julia opened her eyes and gazed up into his.

"That, my darling," he whispered, his breathing ragged, his smile knowing and satisfied, "is what a good-night kiss should be." He kissed the tip of her nose then pushed himself up and onto his feet. His smile turned devilish as he winked and softly added, "Sweet dreams."

Julia watched, stunned and disbelieving, as he walked to the door connecting their rooms, opened it and then closed himself away on the other side. Collapsing back into the softness of the bedding, she stared up at the ceiling, listening to the thunder of her heartbeat and the inner voice of certainty.

Rennick was a man of his word. He wouldn't force her to open that door and join him in his bed. He didn't have to. She was going to go willingly. The wantonness of surrendering to temptation didn't matter. Neither did the foolishness of it and the heartbreak that would come at the end. And the betrayal of Lawrence, of his trust and his hopes . . .

Julia sighed and sat up, then started as she caught her reflection in the dressing table mirror. Her dress and corset bunched around her waist, her budded nipples were clearly visible through the sheer lawn of her chemise. Her hair tumbled down over her left shoulder, the pins precariously dangling among the untidy curls that now framed the face of a woman who looked . . . Well and thoroughly kissed. Radiant and wantonly happy.

It wasn't right. It wasn't sane. But her heart couldn't bear being denied. Not any longer.

She'd confess her folly to Lawrence before it was too late. He would either forgive her or he wouldn't. Which didn't matter to her. Not when weighed against the pleasure of being in the arms of Rennick St. James.

Yes, she was going to go to Rennick's bed willingly and happily. Julia studied the door that led to his room and smiled. But not tonight. She was simply too tired to properly express thirteen years of waiting and wanting. Come tomorrow, though . . .

CHAPTER 4

Rennick leaned down and pressed a little kiss to the corner of her mouth, pleased that it instantly turned upward. Feathering one to the other corner elicited a contented murmur and a most tantalizing little wiggle of her hips. He drew back, smiling and watching her eyes flutter open. "And that's what a good-morning kiss should be," he said softly, brushing a golden strand off her forehead.

"Rennick," she whispered, her smile curving dreamily.

His loins tightened and in that moment he'd have sold his soul to have her draw him down into her bed. Before he could do something he'd regret, he straightened and turned away, saying "Breakfast is served," and retrieving the footed tray from the bureau.

Sitting up, her back propped against pillows and the silk-covered headboard, she considered the meal he placed in front of her with wide eyes. "My God. There's enough food here for a dozen people."

"And you're going to eat every bite of it yourself," he declared, filling the little china cup with coffee for her. "You're too thin, Julia. If nothing else, I'm going to spend the next three days putting some meat back on your bones."

With a nod, she picked up the napkin and spread it over her midriff. "Dining alone isn't good for the appetite. Even if I'm hungry," she added, picking up her fork, "I often find myself deciding that I'd rather not bother."

Lawrence didn't take the evening meals with her? She sat at her dining room table alone while he supped with friends and business associates? Rennick clenched his teeth in irritation and then deliberately forced himself to set it aside, reminding himself that Lawrence was the past and that Julia had eaten her last meal alone.

When he thought he could manage a tone approximating cheerful, he countered, "Well, I'm here to keep you company, darling. So eat heartily. We have much to do with the day and the morning's half gone already."

Julia forked up a bite of eggs and ham, watching him sort through the rubble she'd made of the modiste's box tower in her search for a night rail. "Have you eaten?" she asked, thinking that she couldn't consume all of the food he'd brought her. Not even if he gave her a week to do it.

"Hours ago," he said, carrying a dress to the armoire.

"I should have taken care of that last night," she apologized, absently stabbing a chunk of fried potato. "That I didn't implies that I'm unappreciative. Which isn't the case at all."

Hanging the dress in the cupboard, he grinned at her rakishly. "Or it might imply that you were too distracted to think of it."

"You are very distracting," she had to admit. "It never crossed my mind."

"Eat, Julia," he commanded, chuckling and heading back to the foot of her bed.

How did one go about seducing a man? she wondered, eating and watching him put away her things. With Giles, it had never been something she'd needed to consider. And for as long as she'd known Rennick, the question had been how to avoid being seduced *by* him. She hadn't let herself think of reversing their usual roles. Until now.

Simply asking outright if he'd like to make love with her seemed just a bit too businesslike. *Would you like your hedges trimmed, Viscount Parnell?* Another possible course was to push aside the covers, flutter her lashes, give

him an inviting smile, and hope he presumed to take matters from there. Which struck her as being not only too
passive, but also just a bit on the . . . well, tawdry side.

Sliding out of bed to stand in front of him while slipping out of her night rail would be much more direct. She
could well imagine Rennick's unholy grin if she did. It
would require a certain degree of panache and confidence,
though, and since she'd never in her life done anything
blatantly predatory, she wasn't at all convinced that she
could do it without a blush ruining the entire effect. And
it would be truly embarrassing to lose courage with only
half the buttons undone. What would she say then?

Still, leaving it all up to Rennick didn't seem right or
very fair. And, Lord, what she wouldn't give to be able to
rock him back on his confident, worldly heels. She really
should have given all of this some thought years ago. If
only, she amended, it had occurred to her years ago that
she might someday actually want to seduce a man.

She watched him lay a white gown and rose-colored
weskit across the foot of the bed and made another mental
amendment. She should have thought about what she was
going to do the day she surrendered good judgment and
wanted to seduce *Rennick.* It wasn't as though any other
man had ever ignited her desire the way he did. And it
certainly wasn't as though deep in her heart she hadn't
known that this day would eventually arrive.

But since she hadn't given any of that the least bit of
prior consideration, she didn't have any choice now other
than to muddle through and trust that both a perfect opportunity would present itself and that she'd instinctively
know what to do when it did.

"I gather that's what you intend for me to wear today?"
she said, laying aside her fork as he finished putting her
undergarments in the bureau drawers.

He nodded and came to the bed, a small wreath of dusty
pink roses in his hand. "It's May Day," he announced
brightly, placing it atop her head, "and we're going into

the village for the festival." Stepping back, he considered the effect and then cleared his throat to add, "Please don't put up your hair. You're perfect just like that."

A woman her age out in public with her hair down was scandalous. But if it pleased Rennick, then she'd pretend that she didn't hear the gasps and the whispers. Not, she admitted to herself with a soft smile, that there was any way to avoid the whispers. They rippled in the wake of any woman who ventured out into public on the arm of Rennick St. James. That they would attend her . . . It was a price she would happily pay for the pleasure of his company. She reached up and brushed her fingertips over the softness of the rose petals. "It smells heavenly."

He studied her, the gentle intensity of his appraisal and the desire in his eyes making her heart skitter and her pulse race. Would he mind too terribly much delaying their trip into the village? Would he think her horribly lacking in finesse if she simply asked him if he'd like to join her in her bed? Deciding that she'd never know unless she acted, Julia lifted the napkin from her lap, tucked it under the edge of her breakfast plate, and took a steadying breath.

Her movement seemed to start him out of his reverie. He blinked and, hastily stepping forward, grasped the tray handles in his massive hands, saying, "I'll take this down to the kitchen while you get dressed," and started to back away.

"What happened to your hand?" she asked, noticing for the first time the thin, jagged line running across the knuckles of his right one.

Shrugging with one shoulder, he smiled sheepishly and replied, "Roses have thorns. And I overlooked one while making your wreath."

He'd made it for her himself? She stared at him, her heart melting. "Thank you, Rennick," she whispered.

"For?"

"Everything."

He winked and then left her alone to consider what a

rare and incredible man he was. And to wonder how she'd managed to resist him for as long as she had.

Rennick got two paces into her room before his step faltered and his senses overfilled. Julia was standing in front of her dressing table, dressed in the loosely flowing gown and closely fitted weskit, her hair tumbling in golden cascades down her back, the circle of roses nestled among the curls on her crown. His beautiful, delightfully luscious May Queen.

Turning to him with a radiant smile, she held her arms out from her sides and asked, "What do you think?"

That he didn't want to go into the village. That he didn't want to spend the day sharing her with everyone within ten miles. That he wanted to close the bedroom door, strip that gown off her delectably curved body, lay her down on the bed and make love to her until he dropped dead from sheer, sated exhaustion.

Which, while completely honest, might well be a bit more honest than Julia was prepared to hear. Much less consider at this point in their contest. He moistened his lips and drawled, "That if I can get through the day without having to fight someone for you, I'll be damned lucky."

She laughed. And in the sound of it, in the sight of her unbridled happiness, the years they'd spent apart melted away. No other woman could brighten his life the way Julia did. No other could make him forget that a world existed beyond them. He loved her with all his heart.

"Could we send these before we go?" she asked, picking up two parchment packets from her dressing table and handing them to him.

He glanced down at the top one. "Anne Michaels?" he read aloud, surprised and confused. "Why are you writing to her?" he asked, lifting his gaze back to hers. He cocked a brow. "Surely you're not telling her where you are?"

Julia shrugged a slim shoulder and replied, "If something should happen to one of the children—God forbid—*someone* needs to know where I am."

He shuffled the missives to read the address on the other. It was to her staff. Knowing there was a better explanation than the one she'd given him so far, he asked, "And your butler or your housekeeper wouldn't do?"

As a smile played havoc with the corners of her mouth, she walked past him and out the bedroom door, saying ever so blithely, "Neither of them dared me to live boldly."

Oh, this was interesting. Rennick turned and went after her. "And Anne did?" he pressed, falling into step beside her as they made their way down the hall toward the stairs.

"She also dared me to court gossip."

"Well, bless her heart," he drawled, grinning. "I take back every horrible thing I've ever said about her."

Julia stopped at the top of the stairs and turned to face him. Her arms akimbo and laughter rippling through her voice, she demanded, "What has Anne ever done to you?"

"She fancies herself a matchmaker," he supplied, adoring Julia's spirit, reveling in the enticing challenge of her. "You have no idea how many women she's planted in my path over the years."

"And just what was it about that that you didn't like?"

Rennick leaned closer and softly countered, "She did it to keep me away from you."

"Oh," she said, sobering slightly. "I had no idea." Then she grinned, shrugged, and started down the stairs, saying, "Well, apparently she's had a significant change of heart."

He stared after her, his jaw sagging. Anne was now attempting to put them together? Had hell frozen? "She actually suggested that you court gossip with me?" he said doubtfully, bounding down the stairs after her. "She *actually* suggested that?"

Reaching the foyer, Julia stopped, turned back and waited for him. "You know Anne as well as I do," she answered, looking up at him, her blue eyes sparkling. "You know she never *suggests*. She says things plainly. And her recommendation was that I put you on your back as quickly and as efficiently as I could."

Jesus. The image playing in his mind was wicked. And so thoroughly inspirational that he either had to walk away or ask her if she'd be willing to lay him down right there in the foyer. Unfortunately, the latter wasn't a viable course since he could hear the jangle of his housekeeper's keys coming from the next room. He silently swore and opted to exercise common sense and far more restraint than was comfortable.

"I'm going to send Anne—that wonderful woman—a bottle of my best champagne," he declared, moving off toward the parlor doorway. Jesus, who would have thought Anne Michaels would suddenly decide to help him get Julia into his bed? And to think the church said that miracles didn't happen anymore.

"Anne doesn't drink."

Another inspiration flitted through his mind. "Then *we'll* drink the champagne and toast her incredible wisdom."

His housekeeper looked up from the task list she was making. "Please see that these are delivered before noon today," he instructed, placing Julia's messages on the buffet just inside the door. "And if you'd be so kind as to have a bottle of champagne chilled by mid-afternoon, I'd be most appreciative."

She nodded and he went back to Julia, slipping his arms around her waist. She wasn't wearing a corset, he realized, his heart leaping and the blood surging hot and hard into his loins. Sweet Jesus, she felt so good in his arms.

"You're not planning to make an entire day of the festival?" she asked, smiling up at him.

"If we do, we do," he supplied with a quick shrug, knowing even as he did that it wasn't likely. Not if he had any luck at all. "If we don't," he added, "it'll be because we've thought of other things we'd rather do. And the champagne will be chilled and waiting for us."

Chuckling softly and smoothing his coat lapels, she

said, "You are the most perpetually hopeful man I've ever met, Rennick St. James."

Well, yes. He knew from long experience that persistence, when combined with just the right amount of charm, usually won the game. He grinned. "I just don't want Anne to be disappointed with you. You've buoyed her spirits with that note, you know. I just can't imagine how you could, in good conscience, crush them."

Her smile said she knew what he was about. Her laugh said she was willing to play along. "So I should sacrifice myself for the sake of friendship?" she posed.

Not for Anne's. And not, he realized, for theirs, either. "For love would be better," he countered, trying, and largely failing, to sound cavalier about it all.

"Yes, it would."

She'd said it lightly and her smile was still in place, but the light in her eyes had changed. It was bright but somehow darker, too. His heart raced and he struggled against an intense temptation to lay *her* down on the foyer floor. And in that mental image he grasped the means of his salvation.

"So are you?" he asked, summoning a cocked brow and a rakish smile. "Going to put me on my back?"

Her eyes widened and her mouth formed the most delectable little O.

"Quickly's rather moot at this point," he went on, his pulse racing. "My idea of quick would have been in the Wellses' garden last night. But if you're considering efficiency, I'd be more than happy to show you a few useful techniques."

Julia saw the possibility and happily seized it. "That would, purely in the name of instruction, happen to put me on my back?"

The devil sparkled in his eyes as he countered, "I promise that I wouldn't take undue advantage of the situation."

"Then why," she asked, "would I be at all interested in letting you tumble me over?"

He blinked, tilted his head to consider her, and then slowly moistened his lower lip. "Darling," he drawled, "do you have any idea of how closely you're dancing to the edge?"

"Yes."

He blinked again and shifted his stance. "Do you care if you fall?"

"I'm rather hoping to, actually."

"Would your heart be broken if you didn't get into the village today?"

Julia shook her head. "Or tomorrow, either. Or the day after."

His smile slowly faded as he broadened his stance another degree. "Think before you leap, my love," he admonished quietly. "If you're not absolutely sure . . . This is your last chance to back away from it. I've wanted you for far too long to be a gentleman at the last moment."

There was no going back. From the day she'd met him, they'd been moving inexorably toward this moment. What lay beyond this time they had together didn't matter. She'd face it when she had to. For now her heart was singing and her soul was brimming with the delight of having finally reached the end of the struggle.

"I think thirteen years is quite long enough, Rennick," she murmured, slipping her arms around his neck and twining her fingers through the hair at his nape. "Please don't turn into a gentleman. I'm so very tired of being a lady."

His joy was boundless, his world on the verge of complete. Sweeping her up and cradling her in his arms, Rennick headed for the stairs. He'd love her tenderly, slowly, he promised himself. He'd control the desperate fire consuming him. He'd tease and kiss and take the time to banish any niggling doubts she might still possess.

Halfway up the stairs, she untied the stock at his neck and threw it away. Then stripped away his collar and tossed it away, as well. At the top of the stairs, the up-

permost button of his shirt parted with its hole, slamming
his heart hard against the wall of his chest and sending his
blood racing hot through his veins. And when she turned
her head and kissed the hollow at the base of his throat,
what he could remember of his good intentions was turned
to instant ash.

"Your room or mine?" he rasped, striding down the hall
as she opened another button on his shirtfront.

"Mine."

He grinned, remembering that he hadn't thought to
close the door behind himself when he'd raced off after
her. Fumbling about trying to open a door was such an
amateurish thing to do. And it took time, too. Time he
wasn't inclined to spend fondling a crystal doorknob. Not
when he had so many other delightful tactile possibilities.

He carried her across the threshold, paused just long
enough to kick the door closed, and then hauled his shirt-
unbuttoning temptress to the side of her still unmade bed.
Had they managed to discard more than a stock and a
collar along the way, he'd have dropped her into the rumpled linens and not wasted a single moment in rumpling
them even further.

Resolved to be about that pleasant pastime as soon as
he could, he set his darling Julia on her feet and turned
her to face him squarely. Whether he actually drew her to
him or she stepped into his arms of her own accord, he
didn't know and he certainly didn't care. She was there,
her fingers tangling in his hair, her body warm against his,
her kisses fervent and mind-reeling.

He kissed her in hard and deep prelude, then reluctantly
drew away, just far enough to look into the sapphire depths
of her eyes as he unbuttoned her weskit and slipped it off
her shoulders and down her arms. It fell to the floor at
their feet in the same heartbeat that the ribbon of the simple gathered neckline of her gown opened at his slight tug.
Just as he'd asked the modiste to insure that it would. And,
just as he'd planned to do from the moment he'd laid the

garment on the foot of her bed, he used the palms of his hands to deliberately smooth the cream-colored silk off her shoulders.

Rennick blinked as the sensation rippled up his arms to fully register in his desire-clouded brain. He looked down, his breath caught low and painfully in the center of his chest. There wasn't another layer under the dress. There were no chemise straps over her shoulders. No chemise. No corset.

In the deepest, farthest recesses of his brain he was aware that he'd stopped breathing. It didn't matter. Not like the satin-smooth creamy expanse of bare skin appearing as the gown slipped away. In the vaguest sort of way, he felt it fall from his fingertips. His heart thundering, he drank in the sight of her standing in front of him wearing only a pair of sheer silk stockings. Tied at mid-thigh with lacy, pink beribboned garters.

"Oh, God," he moaned, hardening another impossible degree. "Oh, my darling, wicked Julia."

Her smile was unholy, wanton, and supremely satisfied. He dragged a breath into his lungs and fumbled at the buttons of his shirt, desperate to be rid of his clothes, aching to hold her, to feel bare flesh against heated bare flesh. And the goddamned buttons wouldn't part!

Julia arched a brow and stepped forward to brush his hands aside and undertake the task herself. His breathing ragged, he slipped his hands to her waist to keep his knees from giving way, closed his eyes to better endure the long torture.

The tug was sudden and so deliberate and forceful that he rocked back on his heels. He gasped and opened his eyes just as he heard the buttons clattering over the floor. He looked down at his torn shirt in amazement. She gave him no time to collect his wits, to seize control of the seduction again. No, Julia slipped her hands to the front of his trousers, nimbly undid the buttons, pushed the fabric aside, and took the hardened length of him in her hands.

Rennick threw his head back, sucking a breath through his teeth. Her possession was certain, knowing, and provocative beyond his dreams.

And if he didn't stop the magnificent friction, he was going to finish way too soon. It required that desperation and every bit of his staggering concentration to take her wrists in hand and step out of her caress.

In the absence of immediate, compelling physical sensation, his vision cleared enough to recognize the amusement that danced with desire in her eyes. She knew that she'd rattled his composure to the core. And she was delighted by it. She was also, in his experienced opinion, far too in control of herself. But not for long, he silently vowed, releasing her hands and setting about stripping away what remained of his clothes.

She watched him, her eyes bright, her breasts rising as her breath caught, falling as she sighed. And when he was finally naked and she reached for him again, he caught her hands and placed them on his hips, saying softly, "My turn to touch. Don't move."

Her eyes widened and a brilliant spark flashed to life in them as he brushed his fingertips over the dark crests of her breasts. They instantly hardened and it was everything he could do not to moan at the exquisite sensation. He cupped her breasts in the palm of his hands and, with his thumb teasing their pebbled crests, bent down to lay a trail of branding kisses from the corners of her mouth to the tip of her chin and then down the long, slender column of her throat. Her fingers wound through the hair at his nape. She made a tiny strangled sound and arched upward, pressing herself against his lips, against his hand, fanning the flames of his desire.

She felt the intensity of his heartbeat, the strength in the corded muscles and heated flesh beneath her palms. Her heart matched the cadence of his as an unrelenting desire swept through her body, through her senses, and consumed her very soul. She gasped before the power of the undeniable need, moaned in a wordless plea for swift deliverance.

He wanted more, and patience and finesse be damned. She'd asked him not to be a gentleman, said that she didn't want to be a lady. He'd have to take her at her word. If she hadn't meant it, he'd apologize later. Much later.

His tongue boldly claiming her mouth, he slipped his hands down and cupped the perfectly shaped mounds of her bottom. She moaned in wordless sanction and silent demand as she closed the distance between them, as he drew her hips firmly against the heat and hardness of his desire, and arched her back to lay her gently down on the bed.

Julia softly whimpered with pleasure as he laid a trail of searing, nipping kisses along the length of her throat and downward. Her eyes shut, her breathing ragged, she held his head to her breast, straining to endure the spiraling, desperate need for release. Teasing her nipples with his tongue, his teeth, his masterful fingers, he rewarded her pleas and sent bolt after breathtaking bolt of heat through her body and into the molten core of her womb.

Her fingers tangled in his dark hair, and holding him close, she cried out as a sudden current rippled intensely, exquisitely through her senses. Hunger, primitive and fierce, swept her past patience and endurance.

"Rennick," she gasped, drawing his head gently up from her breast. "Please, Rennick."

She moved against him, her hips pressing urgently, and he couldn't deny her, couldn't deny himself. He kissed her in acceptance, in deep promise, his hands quickly lifting her hips and drawing her to the very edge of the mattress as he fitted himself between her parted thighs.

His pulse thundered as he skimmed his palms over the edges of her gartered stockings, up the soft satin of her inner thighs to brush his fingers over her dampened curls. She moaned and arched up to stroke them along the length of his manhood.

Need and desire became one, burning bright and consuming every fiber of his being. Closing his eyes, he surrendered to the exquisite prelude, to the power she had over his heart and soul. And then, as though she knew he couldn't bear any more, she slowly eased back and looked up at him, her eyes dark and yearning.

He couldn't deny her, couldn't endure the depth of his wanting any longer. His gaze holding hers, he joined them, deliberately and fully, savoring the wonder of her readiness, the fluttering tightness of her welcome.

Julia gasped in sweet triumph and closed her eyes, surrendering all that she was to the heady potency and heated perfection of their union. Only Rennick. Only with him. She tightened about him as he drew back; whispered in assent when he filled her again. Her legs wrapped around him, she moved to the rhythm of the ancient dance, arching up to meet him, the unbearable need deepening and intensifying with every beat of her heart.

Agitated, desperate for release, Julia mindlessly cast herself into the swelling storm. The rhythm of their dance quickened, hardened, and she rode the growing waves of ecstasy, crying out in gratitude as they bore her ever up, as her body trembled and quaked and she was cast over and into a universe of glittering light and bone-melting satisfaction.

Rennick drew a sharp breath as the intensity of her culmination invoked his own. Surrendering himself to the irresistible wave, he pulled her hips closer and higher and with a triumphant moan filled her with every measure of his heart and his soul and his seed.

She was fading away with the fading stars, gently easing back to earth. Sated. So incredibly, deliciously, luxuriously sated. Julia sighed, lazily moistened her lips, and opened her eyes to meet Rennick's smoldering gaze. His breathing as quick and winded as her own, he skimmed his hands up her hips, over her waist, and then slowly moved them inward to caress her breasts. She drew a shuddering breath as the new pleasure arced into the lingering embers of desire and rekindled the fire.

"I love you, Julia," he whispered, his pulse hammering in the deep hollow at the base of his throat. "With all my heart."

"As I love you. As I always have," she replied, wrapping her arms around his neck and moving her hips to hold him close, to keep him within her.

"Julia," he murmured, smiling as he hardened again. He planted his hands in the bedding on either side of her head and leaned down to kiss her tenderly, thoroughly.

He released her lips slowly and she whimpered in protest as she tightened her arms around his neck and frowned up at him. Grinning, he shifted his position and deepened their union. Her eyes widened as her lips curved upward and parted with a soundless gasp of pleasure.

He moved down, taking a taunting nipple into his mouth, suckling until she moved against him and moaned his name. Releasing his prize, he gazed down into her brilliant blue eyes. "Let's try it more slowly this time," he murmured.

"Let's try you on your back," she countered, her grin lusciously wicked.

With a knowing smile, Rennick eased down beside her, rolled her atop him and took her hips back in his hands. God, he was the happiest man who had ever lived, he realized as she settled astride him. The waiting was done. And the prize was worth all the years it had taken to earn it. Julia was his. All that was left was to hand Lawrence Morris a handkerchief.

CHAPTER 5

Julia sat in the window seat of Rennick's room and watched him survey the damaged gardens at the rear of the house. The afternoon had turned to night as the storm had settled over the countryside, but they'd passed it in his room, cocooned in his bed and each other's arms, and let it rage on without them. A time or two, in sated lulls, they'd been aware of the howling wind and the heavy rain, the lightning and the thunder. But most of the time it had been a part of the world beyond their lovemaking, beyond their laughter. They'd heard the limb from the oak tree explode, though. And in the next flash of lightning they'd peered from the window to see the garden wall—and much of the garden itself—lying crushed beneath it.

When the storm had finally rolled on, Rennick had dressed, kissed her, and promised not to be overly long at his duties as master of his realm, as the comforter of his elderly gardener. And then he'd left her alone in his bed with only her thoughts for diversion.

Julia glanced at the sun and sighed. Their time together had come to its end. Part of her wished that she could simply pen a brief thank-you note, place it on his pillow, and then slip away while he dealt with the damage from the storm. It would be easier that way. She smiled wryly, knowing that "easier" wouldn't last one second longer than the time it took for him to find and read the note. After that it would be a matter of which of them could move faster and how well and how long she could hide from him. Which wouldn't be long at all since, thanks to the publishing of her banns, he knew that he could find her at the altar of the Westland Mews Chapel at eleven o'clock tomorrow morning. The certainty of facing Rennick's anger and disappointment in the center aisle and in front of a hundred gaping, wide-eyed guests . . .

No, it was far better to deal with their reality now and privately. She sighed again and smoothed the skirt of the day dress he'd had made for her. The color matched her eyes and if she continued to eat as much as he'd been feeding her the last three days, it would soon fit perfectly. And shortly after that, she added with a tiny smile, she'd be bursting the seams.

A movement at the edge of her vision called her from her musing and she looked out the window to see Rennick striding toward the rear of the house. Cold dread filled her, turning her stomach to lead and her hands to ice. She turned on the seat and squarely faced the bedroom door, knowing that the hour of bittersweet reckoning had come and that there was no way to escape it.

Rennick stripped off his jacket as he made his way down the upstairs hall, thinking that having to step outside the house for a while had been something of a godsend. He'd looked past his mangled garden and his gardener's distress and noticed, seemingly for the first time, the lake and the island that rose up in the center of it. And that had jogged a memory; that just the month before he'd had to flee the country, he'd ordered the construction of a cozy little hideaway deep in the shadows of its trees.

Assuming that it had been completed and furnished in his absence, and that the dinghy would just happen to slip free and float away, it would be the perfect place to ensconce Julia for the next twenty-four hours or so. Not that he thought he really needed to take such drastic measures, but Julia did tend to have a strident conscience and where that was concerned it was better to be safe than sorry.

"I have an idea," he announced happily as he strode into his room. He stopped dead in his tracks, his heart lurching at the set of her shoulders, the resolute angle of her chin. "Let's take the boat out on the lake," he went on, desperately hoping he was wrong, "and watch the sun set from the island."

"I think I should be home by sunset," she said quietly, slowly rising to her feet, confirming his fear. "Lawrence is due back this evening and it wouldn't do to not be there should he come by the house."

His stomach knotted and his blood ran cold. "Julia . . ." he began, tossing his jacket down on the bed as he moved toward her.

"I told you before we began this that I wasn't going to call off the wedding."

Well, at least her voice was quavering. It suggested that the line wasn't drawn as firmly and finally as she wanted him to believe. He still had time and the room to maneuver her. "Julia," he said, reaching for her, intending to wrap her in his arms. "I love you."

"And I love you," she admitted, her smile tremulous as she deliberately stepped away from his touch.

Pride kept him from pursuing her and forcing himself on her. Love made his heart ache with desperation. But it was a burgeoning frustration that prompted him to cock a brow and ask, "Then why the hell are you bent on marrying Lawrence Morris? Do you love him more?"

"No," she supplied readily, shaking her head and absently making little pleats in her skirt.

"Do you love him at all?"

She looked away and sighed softly. "I definitely recall that we agreed not to talk about Lawrence."

Frustration melded into anger. "I agreed for the sake of placating you," he countered, his blood mercifully warming. "And in the hope that by today he'd be nothing more than a man who had to be told he'd lost his bride. But since he's not, then, by God, I'm not going to pretend that he doesn't exist. Answer the question, Julia. Do you love him at all?"

"I've grown fond of him," she said with a little shrug, still refusing to meet his gaze. "He's . . . he's . . ."

"Dead from the neck down," Rennick supplied sardonically.

Her gaze snapped to his, her chin came up, and her hands went to her hips. "As opposed to you," she countered firmly, "who's dead from the waist up."

"What do you mean by that?" he demanded, wishing she could feel the sharp pain twisting in the center of his chest.

She closed her eyes and sighed. After a long moment, her shoulders sagged and her hands slipped down to her sides. "Rennick," she said softly, her eyes still closed, "I have known you for a little less than half of my life. And throughout that time I have watched you blithely seduce an untold number of women. For you, it's sport."

It had been. He'd admit that freely. But the instant that he'd learned she was free—

"The greater the risks, the more irresistible you find the challenge." She sighed again and opened her eyes. "You've been gone the last three years because you couldn't resist seducing the wife of a man renowned for his jealousy and quick temper. You're incredibly lucky that he missed you and you only wounded him."

"I didn't seduce Giles's wife, did I?" he asked, struggling to contain the panic beginning to claw at his chest. "Have you ever wondered why?" He didn't give her a chance to answer. "Because I've always wanted to marry you, Julia. From the moment I first looked into your eyes that winter day thirteen years ago. And as low and despicable as it may be, I knew that someday Giles would be gone, that you'd be free, and that if I were patient, I could have you."

"And your fantasy has come to pass," she said quietly, attempting to smile. "You've had me. Now it's time for you to move on to another."

God, what mistake had he made in the last three days? What hadn't he done that he should have? How could this be going so terribly, nightmarishly wrong? How could she be so utterly determined to throw away their love and happiness?

"I don't want another," he assured her, pouring his heart into his words. "All the women who passed through my bed between the day I met you and the day I read your banns were nothing more than distractions. Very necessary distractions, Julia. I won't tell you that they were completely meaningless because they weren't. When I closed my eyes, they became you. If I hadn't had them, I'd have destroyed your marriage."

"In other words, you were being gallant in bedding half of England's females."

The reality sank slowly, painfully, into his brain; he was damned any way he went. "Julia, don't do this to us," he pleaded, raking his fingers through his hair. "We're so very good together. You can't honestly tell me that you haven't been happy the last three days."

"Happier than I've ever been in my life," Julia admitted freely, her heart breaking.

"Then why do you want to leave me?" he asked, the pain shimmering in his eyes. "Why are you still committed to marrying Morris?"

Her courage ebbed away. She couldn't bring herself to be honest with him, couldn't add to the hurt she'd already caused. It had been a terrible mistake to come away with him. "He's a good, honest man, Rennick," she offered, desperately searching for a way out that allowed her to protect his heart. "Giles put the management of the estate in his hands until Christopher comes of age."

"Did Giles hand you over with the ledgers?"

There was an edge of anger in his voice and she found a small measure of comfort in it. "No. Of course not."

"Then why him, Julia?"

"He's very active with social causes and various charities."

"So am I," he countered. "Would you like to compare our lists and the size of our annual contributions?"

She shook her head and swallowed down her tears. He wasn't going to give up. He was going to keep pressing until she had no choice but to tell him the truth.

"Perhaps you'd like to compare our bank accounts. I'll guarantee you that mine has more in it than his does. And when it comes to titles, I'll remind you that an earl trumps a knight of the realm in any game."

"It's not about money or titles or—"

"Then what is it about? Give me an honest answer, dammit! You owe me that much."

Yes, she did. Her knees shaking, her heart in her throat, she faced him, squarely meeting his angry gaze. "Because I'll never love him the way I do you," she confessed. "And because he isn't you, Rennick. He'll never even notice that another woman exists and he'll certainly never have an affair or leave me for another. He'll never break my heart."

"And you think that I will?" he asked, clearly stunned.

"I know you will," she said as gently as she could. "Not out of malice, but simply because you won't be able to resist the temptation of a challenge. And I'd rather choose the time and place and the depth of my heartache than leave the choosing to you. It's been hard enough to watch other women go into your arms over the years and wishing—God forgive me—that it could be me. Watching them as your wife would be infinitely more painful. I couldn't endure it."

She saw him swallow, saw pain and confusion and desperation flicker across his features. And she saw him make a decision in the half-second before he turned on his heel and strode to the bedside table. He took something from the drawer and then turned and came toward her, his jaw set, the light in his eyes dark and resolved.

He held out his hand, palm up, saying crisply, "Take this."

"Rennick!" she gasped, taking a half-step back as she stared in horror at the little pistol.

Refusing to allow her to retreat, he snatched her right hand, pulled it up between them and slapped the weapon into it. She tried to pull back, to drop it, but he wrapped her hand in both of his and pulled it hard against the center of his chest.

"I swear to you, Julia," he said, the muzzle of the gun pressed to his heart. "If you ever think that I'm having an affair, you can hold it right here and pull the trigger. I'll let you without a fight."

"No," she whispered, tears welling in her eyes. "I could never do it. I love you too much."

Gently, calmly, he replied, "Then marry me, Julia. Please."

"I need to go home," she declared, choking back a sob and pulling her hand free from his grasp. Stepping around him, she dragged a breath into her burning lungs, summoned what she could of her dignity and poise, and moved toward the door connecting their rooms while saying, "Emma is due in on the train this afternoon. Christopher will be down from Eton by nightfall."

"Is Morris the stepfather they want?" he asked from the far side of the room.

She stopped in the doorway, knowing that she didn't have the strength to look back at him but also knowing that she couldn't walk away and leave him with unanswered questions. "No, you are. They've both made themselves very clear on that."

"Then marry me if for no other reason than the sake of your children's happiness," he posed, nearer this time. "We can grow a true marriage from that seed. It'll be enough."

For how long, Rennick? If only she believed it would be for ever. "My son is largely gone from home already and my daughter will follow him off into her own life in a few short years. And I won't have them looking back, seeing my heartache and regret, and feeling guilty for the choice I made in their behalf."

"Then think of poor Morris," he countered, nearer still. "How do you think he's going to feel when he realizes that he's married to a woman who's in love with another man? How can you be so cruel to him?"

He'd reached the end of his hope if he was using Lawrence's feelings as a ploy. Julia smiled in weak relief. "The only thing Lawrence loves is his work," she admitted. "Loving a *person* isn't a consideration of marriage for him. He'll never notice that my heart isn't his."

"Your life is going to be empty, Julia," he said softly, standing behind her. "Cold and lonely and empty. Why are you choosing that over the happiness we can have?"

It was the hardest thing she'd ever done in her life, but she turned around to look at him, to face the horrible pain she'd caused, to add, in the name of honesty, her own to that he already bore. "Because I can't imagine any loneliness deeper, colder, and darker than that which comes when true love ends."

He swallowed, opened his mouth to reply, and then closed it to swallow again. Finally, he cleared his throat to ask, "Is there anything I can do to convince you that I'll be a faithful husband?"

Her heart tearing in two, she reached up to trail the backs of her fingers over the hard angle of his cheek and whisper, "I love you for who you are, Rennick. Not for the man I wish you could be."

His chest shuddered as he drew a breath and then he turned his head and stepped back. "I'll have the livery colors removed from the horses and carriage," he said, staring at the wall. "No one will know it's mine that delivers you to your doorstep."

It was done. There was no sense of accomplishment or

joy in reaching the end of the course she'd chosen. Feeling as though she were numbly adrift in a vast sea, she nodded and replied, "Thank you, Rennick. That's very considerate of you."

"I'll be there for the ceremony tomorrow," he added, still staring off, his voice sounding hollow and distant to her ears. "People would think it odd if I weren't. They'd speculate as to why I wasn't and . . ." He sighed. "You don't need the scandal."

She almost wished he'd deliberately create one, that he'd stop being so calm and accepting and strike out at her in anger and hurt and vengeance. She wouldn't blame him at all.

"And in case you're worrying about it . . ." He lifted his gaze to hers. There was no smile, no pretense of happiness. The dim flicker of exhausted resolve was the only light in his eyes. "I won't offer an objection when the parson calls for them, Julia. I promise I won't create a scene and humiliate you."

She nodded, the tears crawling up her throat and making speech impossible.

"But if you decide that you can't go through with it, my arms will be open for you. I'll bear the scandal and never for a single second regret it."

After all the condemnation, all the pain she'd put him through? He'd still take her?

Rennick watched the tears well along her lower lashes. Before they could spill over and crush the quaking dam holding back his own, he turned on his heel and walked away. *One foot in front of the other*, he repeated to himself as he went. *Just get through it for now.* Tomorrow would be another day. The dense fog in his brain would lift by then; he'd think of something. Something other than how deeply and forever his heart ached.

Julia paused outside her front door to take a steadying breath and to press her fingertips to her eyes. The lights burning in every window of the house told her that both her children were home and the last thing in the world she wanted to do was greet them with tear-swollen eyes. They'd be relentless in their pursuit of an explanation and she couldn't give them one. Not without dissolving into yet another sobbing puddle. It had taken every last measure of her will to get them stemmed as the carriage had rolled out of Rennick's drive. She didn't have the strength to fight that battle again.

Satisfied that she might have a chance of passing their scrutiny, she took another fortifying breath, pushed the door open, and stepped into the brilliantly lit foyer.

They both vaulted up from their perches on the bottom stair, exclaiming in unison, "Mother!" and racing toward her.

"My darlings!" she cried, opening her arms and sweeping them both into her embrace. "How I've missed you both." She hugged them tight and long, and then set them back to look at them both with her mother's eyes. "Christopher, you've grown again," she said on a sigh, thinking that he was almost as tall as Rennick. "And Emma," she went on, turning her attention to a younger mirror image of herself, "you look positively glowing. I like what you've done with your hair."

"Mother," Chris blurted, calling her attention back to him. "Rennick St. James is back in London. George Holcomb told me the news at the station."

Emma nodded. "And Elizabeth Johnson's older sister actually saw him at a ball four nights ago."

"What wonderful news," she managed to say, her heart hammering and the tears threatening again. She turned away to strip off her gloves and stare at the stack of mail that had come during her absence. "I know that you've missed him terribly," she went on, laying her gloves on the foyer table and reaching up to pull out her hatpins. "Perhaps he'll be at the wedding. If he is, I'll see that the place cards are set so that you share the same table at the reception." Placing her hat beside her gloves, she picked up the mail, shuffled through it and asked, "Is there any message from Lawrence?"

"No," both declared with obvious relief.

"We can only hope that he's dropped dead."

She looked over her shoulder at her son. "That's unkind, Christopher."

"It's also honest," he pointed out, ramming his hands into his trouser pockets. "I'm not about to pretend that I like him."

Her heart jolted. Lord, he sounded so much like Rennick.

"And if he calls me Emmaline one more time, I'll scream," Emma announced hotly. "I swear I will."

She'd get through this; she had to. Putting the mail aside, she stepped between her children and linked her arms through theirs, saying, "Let's go see what Cook's prepared for dinner. I'm starving." With a bright smile she took the reins of conversation in hand. "And I simply can't wait to hear all about your recent adventures and triumphs. Every single detail."

Julia sat before her dressing-table mirror, staring at her reflection. The bride was back. The old, bone-weary, and dull-eyed bride. She looked down at the three-word note that had arrived during dinner.

I have returned.

Her heart twisted and in that moment she knew that she didn't have any choice but to tell Lawrence the truth about Rennick St. James.

CHAPTER 6

Rennick leaned his head back in the squabs and closed his eyes, unwilling to see the chapel drawing ever nearer. He wasn't at all sure that he could do this. Not without exercising more self-restraint than he'd ever in his life possessed. But he'd promised Julia that he'd be there, that he wouldn't create a spectacle. And maybe, just maybe, the weak voice of Hope suggested, if she saw him honoring that promise she might be willing to believe all the other promises he'd offered her.

And if she didn't . . . If she said her vows and walked out of the chapel as Lady Morris . . . He didn't know what he was going to do. Crying stood as a distinct possibility, though. The tears had been clawing at his chest and throat since he'd handed Julia into the carriage yesterday afternoon. Drinking himself into numbed oblivion also stood as another probable course. In all likelihood, he'd probably do both. And when he eventually sobered up . . .

The carriage drew to a halt. Rennick sat where he was, staring at the opposite wall, his gaze fixed on the future. He could ask Anne Michaels to toss a suitable woman into a wedding gown so that he could get on with the responsibilities of being the next Earl of Parnell. His father would be thrilled. Eventually, the title would be passed to yet another generation. It was what he should do, what St. James men before him had frequently done, what countless numbers of his own peers had done in the name of family and prestige and wealth.

But he wouldn't, he knew. He couldn't. He'd stood on a ballroom floor years ago and promised Julia that he'd wait for her as long as he had to. He'd meant it then. He still meant it. If he couldn't marry her, he wouldn't marry at all. But, by God, he wasn't going to let her walk up the aisle without giving her one last chance to save them both from a life of abiding regret.

Resolved, Rennick shot his cuffs, expelled a hard breath, lifted his chin and resolutely set it. Only then did he let himself out of his carriage. He'd barely closed the door behind himself when a tall, young version of Giles Hamilton dashed up to him, his hand extended.

"Viscount Parnell!" he said, his voice considerably deeper and harder than when Rennick had last heard it. "Thank God you're here!"

"When you're almost tall enough to look a man in the eyes," Rennick replied, pleased with the firmness of the boy's grip, "you can call him by his given name. It's good to see you again. How are you, Christopher?"

"At the moment, I'm fit to be tied," he confessed, freeing his hand to wave it in the direction of the little church. "You've got to do something. You can't let her marry him. You're the only one who can stop her."

Rennick weighed his own hopes against the desperation of Julia's son. There was a considerable difference, he knew, in being hopeful at thirty-five and being hopeful at sixteen. His own hopes were tempered by experience, by the inevitable failures and disappointments of life. Christopher's were the boundless ones of youth and the boy was going to hurt like hell if a miracle didn't happen.

"No one has the right to stop her," Rennick said, determined to do what he could to prepare the boy for the very real possibility of disillusionment. "The choice is hers."

Christopher glanced at the doorway of the chapel, then

rammed his fingers through his dark hair, saying, "Dammit, Rennick. It's no secret. I have eyes. It's *you* she loves."

"Sometimes love isn't enough," Rennick supplied quietly. "It's a tough lesson to learn and an even harder reality to endure, but it's the truth, Chris. Wishing and hoping and dreaming won't change it."

"Well, I'm not going to let her do something so obviously and incredibly stupid," he declared. "I promised Father I'd take care of her and—"

"No," Rennick interrupted, laying his hand on the boy's shoulder. "It's not your place to interfere in her decisions. Don't you dare stand up and object when the time comes. You'd mortally embarrass her."

Chris sighed and stared down at the ground between their feet for a long moment. Finally, he lifted his gaze to meet Rennick's and asked, "Have you tried pleading? Have you gotten down on your knees and begged her not to do this?"

Rennick withdrew his hand and managed a smile of sorts. "I've tried everything I can think of, everything I know. When your mother settles her mind on a course, it's settled."

"Don't you love her?"

"With all my heart," Rennick admitted, looking at the doorway and willing Julia to walk out of it. "I always have, Chris. I always will."

"Then how the hell can you calmly stand there and let her marry someone else?"

He wasn't calm. And he wasn't "letting" her. She hadn't given him a choice. And deep in his heart, he understood why. If there was any good to come of his mistakes, it lay in passing the too late learned wisdom to someone for whom it could make a difference.

"A quick life lesson for you, Chris," he said, watching the door, his heart heavy. "There are consequences for everything you do. Some of them are immediate and some of them take a while to come back at you. Most of them are fleeting things you can brush aside and forget. But some of them can stand between your past and your future like the stoutest, thickest of walls."

"What did you do that Mother won't forgive?" he demanded, obviously thinking that he could present the logic of it all and make his mother see the world through his eyes.

"It's not a matter of forgiveness," Rennick explained. "It's forgetting that she can't do." He expelled a long breath and then squared up to Julia's son. "Chris, I was a rakehell. Unabashedly, unapologetically, ruthlessly. I could walk into that chapel and point out at least a half-dozen women I've bedded at one time or another."

"So?" the boy asked on a disparaging snort. "If you love my mother, none of them matter."

"You're thinking like a man," Rennick countered, shaking his head. "Women see things differently. Especially when it comes to protecting their hearts. I can't blame your mother for wanting to keep hers safe. I've spent my entire adult life proving myself to be a bad matrimonial bet. And the consequence of that is your mother's inability to believe that I can be faithful to her for the rest of it."

"But—"

"She's perfectly entitled to think that way," he cut in, firm in his defense of Julia's perspective. "I've earned the doubt, Chris. Every time I bedded a woman and walked away from her, I put a brick in the wall between us."

"You were supposed to be a monk?" Chris asked angrily.

"You're thinking like a man again," he pointed out. Smiling tightly, he added, "The incredible irony in all this is that I know how women think. All rakes do. That's how we get what we want from them. But never once in all the time that I was bedding women did it occur to me to think of how your mother was seeing it. I should have. It would have made all the difference in the world. I'd have stopped building that wall."

With a long sigh, Chris ran his fingers through his hair again. His gaze was back on the chapel doorway when he asked, "Have you bedded my mother?"

Rennick's anger instantly flared. He tamped it down just as quickly, reminding himself that at sixteen the mouth oftentimes ran faster than the brain did. "That's none of your business," he replied, his tone deliberately even and measured. "And if I ever hear that you've asked your mother that question, you'll be picking your teeth up off the ground."

"Christ, Rennick. I'm desperate," he exclaimed, throwing his hands in the air. "The thought of her in his arms makes my skin crawl. Doesn't she know what she's giving up?"

Yes, she knew. And he had no one but himself to blame for her fear. "It's not our choice, Chris."

"I don't want that bean-counting stick for a stepfather," the boy growled, glaring at the chapel doors. "The son of a bitch can't even remember my name. He calls me Christian."

"Well, it's close. If he ever gets around to shortening it, you'll—"

"It should be you, Rennick," Christopher declared, turning to face him squarely. "You should be my stepfather. Emma feels the same way."

And if who Julia married was decided by a democracy, they'd all live happily ever after. "Well," he drawled, certain of at least one course in his future, "I'm likely to give you both more fatherly advice and help in the coming years than you'll like. I won't ever again be far away, Chris."

"Until you marry," the boy grumbled. "And have children of your own."

"I've decided that the title's going to die with me. I

can't give up your mother any more than I can quit breathing. It would be cruel to ask another woman to live with that reality."

"How can you live like that?"

Not well, he knew. Not in any fashion approaching happily.

Chris brightened and his eyes—Julia's beautiful blue eyes—went wide. "Let's kidnap her. She'll thank us eventually."

He'd tried a version of that already. That's how he knew just how much the blindness of his past was costing him. Rennick shook his head. "It won't work, Christopher. I've offered her the moon and the stars and all that I am. The only thing left to do is hope that when push comes to shove, she'll choose love."

"God."

"Another life lesson, Chris," he said gently, draping his arm around his shoulders and turning him to face the doors. "Sometimes you have to suck it in and smile while you walk through hell. It's time to go inside, sit down, and pretend we're happy for her."

"I can't do that."

"Yes you can," Rennick assured him, resolutely starting them forward. "Very few men are really brave. Mostly we're just good actors." And in showing Christopher how it was done, he might actually have the strength to survive it himself.

Julia paced the little dressing room, her bouquet in hand, as she listened to the desk clock tick away the seconds. It was so like Lawrence to be late for his own wedding. No doubt he'd become involved in some sort of business puzzle and had lost all track of time. With any luck, one of his household staff would remember that he had somewhere to be and get him on his way. This would all go so much more smoothly if—

The door opened and her heart lurched, stopped, and then raced at the sight of Anne Michaels's frown.

"It is with sincere and deep regret," her friend said from the doorway, "that I inform you of the blasted groom's arrival."

Julia sagged in relief, glad that matters could finally get under way. "Thank you."

Anne considered her and Julia braced herself, knowing precisely what was coming. "It's not too late to change your mind. If you want to run, I'm perfectly willing to throw myself in front of his carriage wheels so he can't come after you."

Yes, it was exactly what she'd thought Anne would say. "Such sacrifice," she observed, chuckling dryly. "You're a true friend."

"Rennick is here, as well," Anne countered, her brow arched. "Christopher and Emma are sitting with him in the chapel."

Of course, she thought. Rennick was a man of his word. And her children weren't above committing emotional blackmail. They'd learned a great deal from Rennick over the course of their childhoods.

"Julia—"

"Don't even begin, Anne," she said, holding up her hand and shaking her head. "I've had quite enough of my children's harping and pleading. There's absolutely no need to add to it."

Her friend sighed. "I could just shake you."

"Actually, you did a very good job of that at Lady Wells's party," Julia admitted, smiling, remembering, and grateful for what had come of it. "Thank you. Now go, take your seat, and say a prayer for me."

Anne cast one more beseeching look at her before turning and walking away. And leaving the door open behind her. Julia smiled, knowing that she had intended it as a subtle hint, an aid in the hoped-for quick departure. Unfortunately, running away wasn't a possibility.

No, she'd merrily danced and now it was time to pay the piper. Hopefully, it wouldn't be too ugly, too painful. Julia shifted the bouquet in her hands, squared her shoulders, crossed the room, and then resolutely stepped across the hall.

At her knock, he wrenched open the door, saying, "I'm perfectly aware that I'm late, Julia. I was going over Denham's ledgers and simply lost track of the time."

She took a deep breath. "Lawrence, there's something I must confess."

Rennick knitted his brows and watched the parson lean down and whisper in the organist's ear. The musician shrugged his shoulders, closed his sheet music, and stood up.

It took every bit of his self-control to keep himself from leaping to his feet and punching his fists skyward with a triumphant cry. She'd done it! His darling, sweet, passionate Julia had come to her senses!

"Something's gone wrong," the boy beside him whispered.

"Not wrong, Chris," he corrected, his heart singing, his pulse racing. "It's all about to come perfectly right."

The proof of his assertion came in the next instant when the door at the side of the chapel opened and Julia glided through it, her chin high, her bouquet in one hand, her skirts firmly grasped in the other. She was moving purposefully toward the front of the whispering assemblage when Christopher started up out of the pew.

Rennick threw his arm across the boy's chest and pinned him back, saying quietly, firmly, "Sit right where you are and don't move. Don't make a sound. Either one of you. Let her do this her way. If she wants our help, she'll let us know."

She stopped and turned, her gaze arrowing to his. The

light danced in her eyes and her slow smile said, "Yes, Rennick, you've won."

Julia watched him grin and settle back against the pew. Delight and certainty washed over her as he silently mouthed, "Thank you, darling."

Her world centered, her course clear, Julia tore her gaze from his, drew another deep breath and faced her second great challenge of the day. "I'd like to thank everyone for attending," she said, sweeping her gaze over the wide-eyed guests. "I sincerely regret that your time has been wasted this morning."

The murmurs were instant and full. Those who weren't exchanging comments with their pewmates were staring at her, their jaws slack and their mouths gaping. Christopher and Emma and Anne all grinned. Rennick's smile was soft and adoring.

"As you might have surmised," she went on when the murmurs had died down a bit, "I've had second thoughts and decided that it would be unfair and horribly unkind to tie Lawrence to a woman of such shallow and wavering commitment. The fault lies entirely within my own character and I hope that each of you will make a point to express your sympathies to Lawrence when next you see him."

Rennick listened to the wave of startled comment sweeping through the crowd, his mind clicking. It was so typical of Julia to accept the full burden of the scandal. Typical, but unacceptable. She wasn't in it alone. He'd done his part to create it and he'd take his share of the social outrage.

"The reception luncheon will still be served, of course. I hope you stay to partake and enjoy it," Julia went on brightly, watching Rennick gain his feet and step into the aisle. He started toward her, his arms open and his smile wondrously wide.

There was a collective gasp and then absolute, stunned

silence. "And that you'll forgive me for not sharing it with you. I have a journey to make," she said happily, moving to meet him halfway.

He caught her in his arms and lifted her clear off the floor to spin her around and grin up at her. "You'll never regret this. I promise."

"And I believe you as deeply and forever as I love you." He set her gently onto her feet and drew her close. Her bouquet resting on his shoulder, her fingers twined in his hair, she looked up into his loving eyes and whispered, "I'm so sorry for what I did to us yes—"

His kiss was slow and deep and knee-meltingly thorough. She sighed and leaned into him, her heart and soul grateful for the gift of his undying love, her body heating in the fire of the passion he so easily kindled.

Breaking their kiss, he drew back, the sparkling light of certainty in his eyes, an utterly wicked smile on his face. In the next instant he swept her up into the cradle of his arms. With a quick, reassuring wink, he looked past her and at her children. "We'll need witnesses," he said. "Kindly get yourselves up and out to my carriage."

She laughed at their delight, at their stumbling scramble to obey.

"Oh, Julia, I'm so proud of you!" Anne cried from behind her. "What a delicious scandal this is going to be."

Julia peered over Rennick's shoulder to grin at her friend. "Won't it, though?" she called as the great love of her life carried her past the stunned and appalled guests. "We're off to Gretna Green. And you can tell anyone who wants to know that Julia St. James doesn't care what they think."